Jake Bernstein is a little baffled when he's called upon in his position as an FBI analyst to assist Britain's MI5 with an investigation. Turns out they suspect an American woman of having been a Nazi spy in WWII Great Britain — one who potentially cost many people their lives. It so happens the old woman and her granddaughter are taking a two-week tour of Great Britain, and they've secured Jake a place on that tour. So it's off to the UK he goes!

Meg Larsen thought it would be a great idea to take her aging grandmother on a trip to Great Britain, to revisit places she hasn't seen in many years, including her ancestral Irish home. What Meg hadn't counted on was being so instantly attracted to a fellow member of their tour. Jake Bernstein is certainly easy on the eyes, and she feels comfortable with him. As if she's known him forever. But when he starts asking some very strange questions, she begins to wonder what his real motives for being there are.

Jake's growing feelings for Meg are quite the complication. Can he objectively carry on his assignment, knowing he is trying to expose Meg's beloved grandmother as a Nazi criminal? Or will he be tempted to cross a line he very well knows he shouldn't cross? And for what? After sixty years, can the sins of the past ever be forgotten or forgiven . . . and should they be?

Undercover Lies
Copyright © 2023 Donna Del Oro
ISBN: 978-1-4874-3883-8
Cover art by Martine Jardin

Published by eXtasy Books Inc

Look for us online at:
www.eXtasybooks.com

UNDERCOVER LIES

BY

DONNA DEL ORO

DEDICATION

As always, I dedicate this book to my family, whose encouragement and support inspires me to do what I love doing, no matter the time or cost.

PROLOGUE

June, 1940

The four-decker ferry tossed about in the Irish Sea. Clare Eberhard, keeping her sea legs, stood and peeked through the curtains of stateroom number five. In the darkness, rain lashed the window with unleashed fury. She glanced at her watch. It was time.

Her stomach tightened into a hard ball. An attack of nausea threatened but she schooled it down. The extensive training she'd received from the Intelligence Bureau of the SS calmed her. Clare willed her mind and heart against any sentimentality. This was wartime, a time for drastic measures and sacrifice. Every loyal German was a soldier.

A pounding at the door.

"I'll get it," Clare said to the girl sitting on the bunk. The pretty blonde Irish girl looked up from her book of poetry and smiled.

"'Tis the cabin steward with the tea I ordered. Please join me, Miss O'Donnell."

They'd met each other an hour before boarding, had teased each other about their similar looks — their height and figure, hair and skin color, facial features — they could have been sisters. The Irish girl, Mary McCoy, wondered aloud why they'd never met, considering they were both about the same age and educated in Dublin. They'd discussed their plans for jobs in London, hit it off famously, and decided to share the cost of a stateroom. After all, it seemed prudent for two single women traveling alone to do this. They'd become friends in a matter of minutes.

Clare opened the door a crack, recognized the man and stood back so he could burst into the small room, then slammed it behind him. The Irish girl opened her mouth to scream, but Horst was quick. He clamped a big hand over her mouth and hit the side of her head with the butt of his pistol. Clare handed him a towel, which he used to cover Mary's head. As an unconscious Mary sprawled on the bunk, he crouched over her and hit her again and again, smashing her skull. Clare watched, fascinated by the brutal attack, though she flinched every time she heard the crunch of bone. By the time Horst was finished, the white towel had turned completely red. Not looking at Clare, he panted as he washed his hands in the stateroom basin and dried them with another towel. He took a deep breath, then exhaled.

"If her body's found, it will appear that her head was crushed in the explosion," he said in fluent English, his Irish accent still in place.

Horst looked satisfied with himself. He'd executed a clean kill and the girl hadn't suffered. After all, he was a skilled assassin.

Clare turned aside and began gathering into Mary's satchel various items the girl had laid on the bedside table. A small purse with her lipstick and comb, passport, letters, Irish driver's license, and ferry ticket. She picked up from the floor the book of Irish poetry — part of her cover. Clare stuffed it into the satchel.

"Hurry now — *schnell,*" Horst whispered, switching to German as he undressed the Irish girl's body. No blood stained her clothes, the towel having absorbed it all.

Already in her slip, Clare pulled on Mary's wool skirt, sweater, and coat. She grabbed the scarf hanging on the side of the bunk and wrapped it around her neck. Then came the

2

long strap of Mary's satchel. *Mustn't lose this.* The passport, Mary's papers, letters with her signature, the book of poetry that she'd been seen poring over at the ferry terminal — all were vital. In their short time together, she'd studied the Irish girl's mannerisms, her soft voice, the slight burr in her English. Still, Clare wished there'd been more time . . .

"Leave your fake documents on the table in case the boat doesn't sink," barked Horst. Clearly rattled by what he had to do next and its greater risk, he added, "Give me ten minutes. And don't forget. The first explosion — you go outside. Find the lifeboats and the crew members in charge of them. Stay with them."

As though they hadn't rehearsed this a hundred times, Clare nodded dutifully. Their eyes locked together for a moment but they didn't kiss. No time. Horst squeezed her arm.

"You shall be fine, Clare. You're a born mimic. A superb actress. That's why we recruited you. You have my name and address in Waterford. Write to me once you've settled in London. If I move before then, I shall contact you."

She nodded, her mouth trembling a little.

"Until we meet again, *mein schatz*," she said in German.

Then he was gone. Gone into the bowels of the ferry.

Clare stared at the closed door for minutes, refusing to glance at Mary's body. What was one life to many? It had to be this way. After tonight's horrors, Clare would go to the War Office in London and save lives. German lives.

She was no longer Clare Eberhard. No longer the Wehrmacht trainee, code-named Hummingbird. She was no longer Katy O'Donnell with her fake documents.

She was now Mary McCoy of Killarney, Ireland.

Ten minutes later — right on schedule — the first explosion rumbled through. The boat lurched violently to the side.

Now!

CHAPTER ONE

2005
FBI Headquarters, the Hoover Building
Washington, D.C.

Jake Bernstein plopped down at his desk, having wolfed down his lunch in ten minutes. The tuna sandwich and Coke bunched like a hard knot in the pit of his stomach. With his fist, he pounded his sternum and gulped down the last of the Coke.

Well, too friggin' bad. Anger simmered just beneath his calm exterior. Every night he fought an urge to run the dark streets until he dropped. Usually his limit was five miles, but lately that wasn't enough. His life was out of balance again, but his ol' damned work ethic kept him at the ol' damned grindstone.

All work and no play made for a repressed libido. His pal Eric's mantra.

Libido? It was there all right, pacing like a caged animal, making him tense and restless. When was the last time he'd slept with a woman? A quick mental check — ah yes, two months and three Saturdays ago. After a couple of calls, the woman — what was her name? Nicole — had given up on him. A pang of guilt added to his queasy stomach. Wasn't so cool to have sex with a woman then dump her. Though he didn't really dump her. You had to have a relationship with a woman to call it dumping. One date was not a relationship.

Jake pondered his predicament. What was more

4

reprehensible? Ditching a woman you just slept with, or stringing one along just for the sex? There'd been no chemistry, no spark there, and he'd made one excuse after another to avoid seeing her again. Leading a woman on just for sex always came back to bite you in the ass.

But damn, he needed a change or he was going to go nuts. The old stirrings of cabin fever, the need to escape the office confines and just explore the world . . .explore women . . .were pulling him apart.

He'd even lost interest in having loveless sex . . .

Damn strange, but there it was.

Eric, a bachelor like himself, thought he was bonkers to turn down free sex.

Not so free, Jake thought. The guilt, sense of obligation — all that discouraged him from putting on a front. Ironic, since putting on a front — or cover — was what he was sometimes paid to do.

His inter-office phone rang. He flushed his mind of thoughts of women and sex. His boss, Terry Thompson, was old-school, and preferred to use the phone over office email.

"Yeah, Terry?" Jake sat up in surprise as he listened to his supervisor. The Assistant Deputy Director of Investigations was giving him a heads-up.

MI5 would be contacting Jake today. As his boss, Terry had already given British Intelligence the okay on an ongoing investigation of theirs. A naturalized American woman was their target. She was suspected of World War II espionage and possibly a truckload of other war crimes.

"So I recommended you, Jake. You've got the qualifications for this job. It's undercover field work. You need a break from the paper mill. Clear the cobwebs, see the world. Shouldn't take more than a week or two. Check your email."

Jake was digesting this as Thompson rang off abruptly.

"Okay . . ." he said aloud, turning to his computer. While

it was typical to receive communications from other intelligence services, domestic and abroad, an urgent request directly from MI5 was rare. Usually the legate at the American Embassy in London was their liaison. The encrypted message was directed to him personally: *Special Agent Jacob Bernstein, Intelligence Division, FBI Headquarters.* Followed by a name and phone number in London. Steeped with curiosity, his heart pounding, Jake punched in the number on an outside secure line. Several clicks later, a deep baritone voice answered.

"MI5, History section. Major Phillip Temple, Case officer."

The stilted British accent made Jake smile. He introduced himself and added, "How can I help you, Agent Temple?"

"Call me Major, Agent Bernstein. I'm retired army, but the moniker has stuck." The man then spoke for over five continuous minutes while Jake took copious notes on a legal yellow pad. At the first prolonged lull in Temple's narrative, Jake jumped in.

"Major Temple, let's see if I'm getting this. An old Irish guy, a veteran WWII sailor, has been writing and calling your office for the past ten years . . .claiming his cousin" —Jake consulted his notes—"this Mary McCoy vanished around 1940 . . .and he suspects foul play. He thinks someone killed her and assumed her identity in order to gain access to Churchill's War Department. That whoever did this might've been an old Third Reich spy. Is this correct?" To Temple's affirmative, he added, "Does this WWII sailor have any concrete evidence? Other than conjecture?"

"A smattering of inconsistencies, mainly. Relative to my own investigation, there was only one Mary McCoy, a Dublin College graduate with a gift for foreign languages, fluent in French and German, who worked for the War Office from mid-1940 to early 1945. Ten years ago this Mike McCoy tracked down and met this woman, thinking she was the cousin he'd grown up with. She turned out to be living in Texas, the widow of an American Air Force officer. According to this old veteran, biographical details matched, but this tenacious old chap was convinced after meeting this woman that she couldn't possibly be his long-lost cousin."

"Oh yeah? What convinced him?"

"Her eyes. They were a different color of blue than he recalled. His cousin's eyes were an unusual shade of turquoise. The Texas widow had dark blue eyes. Also he claimed his cousin, this Mary McCoy from Killarney, Ireland, was fluent in French but knew no German. The Mary McCoy in the War Office was a transcriber of radio messages, which required fluency in both French and German. She handled secret communiques from our undercover agents abroad, many of whom were French and German citizens working for the Resistance."

"So maybe he was mistaken about her eyes and about her speaking German. Y'know, old people and their faulty memories. After all, this Mike McCoy must be in his eighties or older—"

"Seventy-three at the time of his death nine years ago. I inherited his file this year. Nearly seventy pages worth. Replete with his inquiries, details about his cousin, and some of his own personal investigations. He was the stubborn pitbull sort, kept calling every week until his death. After this World War II veteran died, his son took over—a Mike McCoy, Junior. My predecessor, unfortunately, didn't take the man or his son seriously. I do. I did some checking, rang up a few old-timers in Killarney who recalled the young Irish beauty . . .the one with the bright turquoise eyes . . .who went off to Dublin then London after her parents died. Managed to survive a terrible ferry disaster just before reporting to the London War Office. Close to sixty souls went down with the ship."

Jake wrote furiously on his yellow pad. "Okay, Major, so

the old man got the eyes right. Eye color doesn't change, but maybe this woman in Texas was wearing colored contacts and the old guy didn't know it. Maybe his cousin learned enough German at the university to become a translator. Something the old man wasn't aware of."

"It's possible, Agent Bernstein. In any event, if this Irish girl were killed and her identity stolen by a German spy, so help me, it's incumbent upon me, even after all this time, to set things right."

"Sixty years, sir?" Jake was incredulous, but he knew Mossad and the JDL weren't the only ones still hunting Nazi war criminals. The Brits hated the thought they'd been duped by a clever Nazi. Just like Americans hated being duped by Islamic terrorists.

"It's fallen upon my shoulders to discover the truth. I believe President Truman said in 1945 that Nazi war criminals would be hunted to the ends of the earth. We believe in doing just that."

"I understand, Major Temple. Assuming the old man was correct—and that's a big assumption—you want me to investigate this American grandmother... this Mary McCoy Snider. To confirm her innocence or guilt."

"That sums it up bloody well."

"I'm not a regular field agent, Major, although I've been trained for field work and the Bureau occasionally farms me out on undercover assignments for various task force teams. Mainly, I analyze data."

"Agent Bernstein, I'm familiar with your employment file and your special qualifications for this assignment. I've already cleared your participation with your supervisor, Assistant Deputy Director Thompson, and he agrees. He also assured me that...uh, considering your background, you'd take this assignment to heart."

His background...

Jake immediately understood what the MI5 officer was re-ferring to. His grandfather, Nathan Bernstein, was a Munich-born Jew who had immigrated to the U.S. in 1934 following the summary firing of all Jews working in the German film industry. His grandfather, an award-winning film editor in Berlin, was one of the lucky ones, however. As it turned out for the few lucky ones back then and the rest of Jake's family still living today in Southern California, Grandpa Nate and other displaced German Jews received help. Famous German-Jewish emigrants, like Billy Wilder and Marlene Dietrich, pro-vided food, shelter, and jobs for the ones who'd followed them into the Hollywood film industry in the 1930s.

The biggest break of Grandpa Nate's life.

"I see. Any other reason I was requested for this assign-ment, Major?"

"You speak German. And, according to your file, you've traveled extensively in Germany. You're familiar with the various dialects. If this woman, Mary Snider, was a Nazi spy, as soon as you get her to speak German you'll be able to tell if she's a native speaker. Or someone who learned it whilst in Dublin."

"I get your point," muttered Jake. Despite his own fluency in German, as soon as he opened his mouth the average man on the street in Stuttgart or Hamburg could tell he was Amer-ican.

The Brit cleared his throat. "Another consideration, not un-important. You're single and . . .from your file photo, rather good looking. We need an agent who can . . . uh, charm the ladies."

Jake cringed. Whenever the Bureau needed an undercover agent to schmooze a woman to get information—Grandpa Nate had called it *schmoodling*—they sent for him. Seduction was his dubious claim to fame at Headquarters. A kind of typecasting that he was beginning to resent. Annoyed, he blew air out of his cheeks.

"Major, if all this is true—this old Irish guy's suspicions that the real Mary McCoy's identity was stolen by a very clever Nazi mole—how much damage do you figure this spy actually did?"

Over the line, Jake heard the man snort with disdain.

"Incalculable. British counter-espionage was able to round up and hang or turn into double agents most of these Nazi spies. Nevertheless, we think a few may have slipped through the cracks. It was wartime, and with the chaos created by the Luftwaffe's Blitz over London—well, it's conceivable that a Nazi agent undetected in the War Office might have been responsible for the deaths of thousands, maybe tens of thousands. At the very least, she would've been in a position to expose the identities of Resistance members and deep-cover agents all over Europe."

Jeez.

"Resistance fighters didn't just blow up railway tracks and sabotage German supply lines, old chap. They often hid Jewish families and smuggled many people to safe havens. They also saved Allied soldiers and helped them cross enemy lines. Exposing these Resistance fighters would have been the same as putting bullets through their heads. And condemning hundreds, maybe thousands, of others to certain execution or the SS death camps."

The man sounded committed to seeing this thing through. Fury, barely controlled, seeped through the man's tense voice. His words vibrated with outrage.

To an older generation of Brits—and Americans—the horrors and hardships of WWII still lingered. In their collective consciousness, the Nazis and Hitler's Gestapo were still the boogeymen. The embodiment of everything evil in mankind.

"Agent Bernstein, if we can prove this Mary McCoy Snider was a spy for the Third Reich, we'll seek extradition and put her on trial. Charge her with a multitude of war crimes and hang her sorry ass, as you Yanks like to say. The media shall have a field day, and some bleeding-heart American senators may object, but rest assured, we'll see justice done. Even sixty years after the fact."

"An eighty-something year-old grandmother?" Jake shook his head slowly from side to side. Going after this woman seemed pointless after all this time.

Nevertheless he could sense his grandfather, dead now these past two years, nodding his approval. His entire family had been slaughtered in the death camps. If nothing else, Jake owed it to his Jewish heritage to give MI5 a thorough, objective investigation. He could hear his grandfather's voice, his English thick with a German accent. "You go get'em, Yaakov. Go get dose sons-a-bitches."

"Okay, Major, I'll get on it right away although I've got a desk full—"

"You don't understand, Agent Bernstein. This assignment begins tomorrow morning, London time. Just as soon as you can catch the red-eye flight to London—"

"London? Tonight?"

"—your ticket's waiting at the United counter at Dulles."

Jake's blood thundered in his ears. He nearly dropped the phone. No, not possible. His workaholic mind was crowded with the details of several ongoing investigations. Why would ADD Thompson clear Jake's desk so abruptly . . .unless this MI5 investigation had special priority.

A sixty year-old espionage case? Priority? Somebody higher up the bureaucratic food chain must have given this mission the green light.

Hmmm . . .not for him to question why. He was a foot soldier, not a general.

"Tonight?" he repeated. Then the man's words registered fully. His pounding pulse was interfering with his usually sharp, analytical mind. "You want me in London, but this woman, Mrs. Snider, lives in Texas. Near Dallas, you said."

"Sorry, old man, I see your confusion. It so happens that our computers picked up her hotel registration two days ago at the Kensington Hilton. She's in London as we speak. With her granddaughter, a Meghan Larsen, a high school foreign-language teacher. Close to your age . . ."

Temple's pause was pointed, implicit with meaning. Jake scowled.

"They've booked a two-week tour of Britain and Ireland. Retracing her origins, perhaps? Or revisiting the scenes of her crimes? At any rate, we've persuaded an American gentleman to take another tour — at our expense, naturally — and so you're taking his place. There's no better way to gather evidence, is there, than an on-the-spot investigation. This Mary Snider should trust an American over a Brit, no doubt. The American legate here in London has been informed and he approves. Our PM also approves. You'll report to me directly, and I'll keep them in the loop. It's all set up."

Jake looked around his small office, scanned the stack of files next to his computer. Field work . . . on such short notice? Well, why the hell not? The change would do him good. More than good. He was going stir-crazy. Anyway, he had no choice. His boss had already given the go-ahead.

"All right, Major, looks like I'm your man."

"Jolly good. We knew you'd cooperate. You know, Agent Bernstein, it's never too late to see justice served."

He wasn't so sure about that. Sixty years was a long time, even for wartime justice. Yet Nazi war criminals were being prosecuted even into the twenty-first century. He recalled the recent case of a former SS death camp guard, uncovered in New Jersey living on a pensioner's salary. He'd been extradited to Germany and tried and was now serving a life sentence in a Berlin prison.

Lady Justice, though blind, had a long memory.

"Well, we'll see, Major Temple. Let's put the facts before the theory, see where the facts lead us, okay?" After all, that was all the Irishman had—this Mike McCoy—a theory supported by a few memories and maybe a few coincidences.

"Yes, of course. I'll meet you at Heathrow, seven AM London time. Don't laugh, but I'll be the fuddy-duddy in a tan trench coat and plaid sporting cap."

"Shouldn't be hard to miss."

Jake punched off, smiling. *London. I'll be damned . . .*

He unlocked his lower right desk drawer. From it, he retrieved the Bureau-issued credit card, his official badge, passport, and his pistol—one of the FBI's new Smith & Wesson 10-mm semi-automatics. The weapon lay secure in its plastic-and-foam case for traveling. He grabbed his shoulder holster, along with two fully loaded magazines, and stuffed it all into his gym bag. In four hours, he'd call it a day, go home and pack.

In undercover work, you never knew what you might encounter. He had no doubt MI5 would clear his piece. The excitement and unpredictability of being out in the field energized him—recharged his instincts and honed his judgment. Forced him to apply his critical thinking skills and old Navy Seal training to real-life situations. Kicked his adrenaline up a notch. His heart was already beating like a rocker's drums.

Finally, a much needed adventure.

But an eighty-something year-old grandmother and her high-school-teacher granddaughter? What could be dangerous about them? A week schmoozing them, and he'd be bored out of his skull. But he'd be conscientious and do his job to the best of his ability.

By-the-book Bernstein.

On an impulse, he took out his wallet. Inside the billfold section was an old photo he carried with him always. His grounding. Taken a year before his grandfather died, Grandpa Nate, then eighty-six, stood next to the rest of Jake's family — his father, mother, Jake's two younger brothers, David and Isaac, and himself. Absent were all the German-Jewish uncles, aunts, and cousins who'd been rounded up and killed by the Nazis. By 1939, they were gone. All of them. Just five years after his grandfather had left Germany.

All of them murdered in cold blood.

They hovered in the photo like invisible phantoms.

Clamoring for justice.

Even for him, a member of the X generation whose recollections of WWII were the old *World at War* DVD's that his father sometimes watched and an occasional Hollywood movie, the Nazis struck fear in everyone's hearts. For Jake, evil was a black-uniformed Gestapo officer with SS-lightning strikes on his collar, restraining an enraged German shepherd while herding Jews into a death camp. The red flag with the black swastika in the white bulls-eye still had the visceral power of a kick in the stomach, evoking palpable fear and hatred.

He knew that was the main reason he was chosen for this assignment.

Well, Grandpa Nate, we'll see what we can do to find justice in our little corner of the world.

Chapter Two

London

M ajor Temple was, in Jake's opinion, the stereotypical
Englishman. Of average height and pale complexion,
his graying blond hair was indeed covered by a plaid cap and
his tan trench coat hung loosely about his lanky frame. Jake
was certain he'd seen the same outfit on a BBC production's
main character — a police constable named Inspector some-
thing-or-other. When this man spoke, his crooked yellow
teeth clenched an unlit pipe, grinding the wood like a dog
gnawing his bone.

The major filled Jake in about the assignment as he wended
his way through London commuter traffic like a teenaged
stock-car driver. Adrenaline pumped through Jake's brain
and his synapses fired in rapid succession, his hands white-
knuckled and clutching the dashboard in front of him, Jake
reveled in the ride. On the wrong side of the road. Like
bumper cars without the bumping fun. His first adventure.
He would've enjoyed it more if it weren't for the dull ache in
the back of his skull.

Unfortunately the thrill ride was over too soon. When they
reached a *Best Western* hotel in the Leicester Square area, Jake
was disappointed. To match his cover as an insurance analyst — a job that Major Temple assured him no one would ask
him about, as dull as it sounded to most people — Jake could
not be seen as overly affluent.

"Maybe I've got family money. Or I hit the jackpot at Vegas

and decided to splurge on this vacation," Jake countered, chiding the man from the fatigue of a sleepless night.

They were standing in the small lobby of the Best Western, waiting for the Global Adventures motorcoach to arrive and pick him up. A large suitcase on rollers, topped by a leather carryon, leaned against Jake's leg, about as irritating as the Major's choice for his cover. He knew nothing about insurance but a lot about real estate and investments. His best buddy, Eric White, often regaled him over drinks about his career in the investment brokerage industry, his harangue enough to cross Jake's eyes. Still, Jake had listened and learned. And had a healthy stock portfolio to show for it.

So screw the Major's cover. He knew how to play this.

The Englishman smiled, glanced around at the cheap furnishings and dismal decor. "Sorry, old man, this will have to do. So as not to break cover, take care with what you say to the granddaughter."

"I've done this before, Major, with far more dangerous unsubs. I know how to maintain cover, thank you. I read most of the encrypted file you sent to my computer on the plane. It appears that Mary McCoy transcribed a lot of the coded communiques from the French Resistance regarding Operation Overlord."

"Yes. Sadly so, if Mary McCoy was indeed the mole," Major Temple gritted out. Shaking his head, he lowered his voice. "British Intelligence took extra precautions keeping the Wehrmacht off base regarding the Allied invasion's location — what we called Operation Overlord. The French Resistance was helping us determine what the Germans knew and what they were simply guessing at. One thing they knew for certain, those Krauts, was that the Allied Forces would invade in the summer of '44. They didn't know the exact date or location for the beachhead. The entire northern coast of France was considered, of course. Some, including Hitler himself, were convinced the most logical place would be Pas de Calais, that being the shortest point across the English Channel. Elaborate measures were taken to convince them of this, including a facade of fake airbases."

Jake nodded. "Yeah, I've heard of that. So you think Operation Overlord's true landing sites were compromised by one of these Nazi moles?"

"Certainly possible and more than a little likely. Some of the German High Command believed this intel, so they kept army divisions along the Normandy coast."

Another reason why the Brits were so desperate to catch such a spy. D-Day, as the Allied invasion of France was called, was the most crucial day of WWII. Tens of thousands of Allied soldiers were killed in the Normandy invasion.

"But Major, you have no proof it was Mary McCoy that may have passed on the actual date or location plans, do you?"

"No. But one of our Double-Cross agents—a turned Nazi spy the Brits had captured—spilled the beans, so to speak, and offered up two possible female moles in England at that time. He gave up their code names, but sadly not their English covers, which he claimed he didn't know. He said one of these two women may have worked for the war department in some capacity."

"And these two females knew the true location of the Allied invasion?"

"Supposedly, according to this Double-cross agent."

It was Jake's turn to harrumph.

"So, no one in the Abwehr—the German army—knew the English covers of these two Nazi moles?"

"The German military defense was so paranoid that only a direct handler knew the true identity of a secret agent under his control. In the files, only a code name was used. We know this from the captured war records in Berlin at the end of the war. Mary McCoy could have been one of the two females on that list."

The chill on this early June morning ran through Jake, making him shiver. He zipped up his brown bomber-style leather jacket and frowned. MI5 sounded convinced of Mary McCoy's guilt already. So much for their objective investigation, Jake groused to himself. Was he here just to validate *their* conclusions?

"Maybe this Mary McCoy was neither of the two. Let's suspend trying and lynching this American grandmother before we gather the evidence, okay?" He sighed heavily and massaged his forehead. The mild throbbing pain had moved from the back of his head and now stung right behind his eyes. "What were the code names of these two female moles?"

"One was Hummingbird. We think that referred to the Nazi Party's Night of the Long Knives, also called Operation Hummingbird, when Hitler ordered a purge of a rival group within the Nazi Party. The SS and Gestapo carried out the killings."

Hummingbird. "Okay, and the other?"

"Black Widow. We have no idea what that referred to."

Black Widow. "I'll read that part of the file later. When I've gotten a good night's sleep," Jake added pointedly.

A large white motorcoach pulled into the curved driveway in front of the hotel. The tour guide, a dark-haired man in his forties, dressed in a white bulky sweater and brown cords, hopped down, a clipboard in his hand. Glancing about, he looked a little harried and peeved that another stop had to be made to pick up the one American tourist who hadn't stayed at the Kensington Hilton like all the others on the tour. Major Temple nudged Jake.

"Your carriage awaits, Bernstein. I shall take my leave now. Don't forget to report in every evening at ten." The major handed Jake a secure mobile phone, which he tucked into his jacket's inside pocket. Acknowledging the older man's military background and bearing, Jake gave a quick half-salute, biting back the sarcastic retort that sprang to mind. *I'm thirty-two, Major, not thirteen.*

"Will do, Major." He grabbed the handle of his suitcase. "Where the hell is this coach going, anyway? Besides the Republic of Ireland?" Major Temple's gray eyebrows arched. "No, didn't have a chance to read the itinerary. Too busy with the files."

Temple chomped on his pipe, one side of his mouth upturned in the closest thing to a smile Jake thought he'd see from the man.

"Oh, southwest England, Wales, Republic of Ireland, a bit of Scotland. Two weeks' worth."

"Two weeks? And if I conclude this investigation in less time . . ."

"Then we debrief and back home you go. We'll handle the filing of charges and arrest warrant. Or extradition, if necessary. Well then, good luck, old man."

Jake nodded and took his leave. He hailed the guide, a friendly, outgoing sort who introduced himself as Robert Morse. The man quickly and efficiently turned over the suitcase to the driver who stowed it in the storage bin at the side of the motorcoach. As soon as Robert checked him in and indicated that he could take his carry-on on board, Jake moved to the front door of the coach. He suddenly stepped aside as a young blonde woman climbed down, spun around, and helped an elderly woman to descend.

"Sorry, Robert, my grandmother has to make a trip to the restroom."

The blonde glanced over at Jake. She smiled in greeting, then took her grandmother's arm and followed the direction of Robert's sweeping arm. The two women entered the glass-fronted hotel lobby and walked slowly around the corner of the registration counter. Jake's gaze clung to them.

So there they were. Mary McCoy Snider and her grand-daughter, Meghan Larsen.

"Quite a looker, that one," Robert murmured to him, his eyes following their progress as well.

An understatement, Jake thought as he nodded to the man in agreement. The granddaughter was lovely. She had the face and figure of a Hollywood starlet. Despite her lack of makeup, she had a wholesome but sexy look about her. Her navy-blue pea jacket and black jeans concealed much of her curves, but the overall effect of a beautiful, symmetrical face, a tanned complexion, long blonde waves partly covered with a large, black beret, and graceful motion was powerful. Like a slap of warm sunshine in this cold, damp country. Schmoozing that girl was going to be a perk, not a chore.

Already he was warming to this assignment.

The grandmother, bulky in a long wooly coat, looked attractive despite her purported eighty-one years of age. The elderly woman was well preserved, he decided, and must have been quite a beauty in her youth. Like her granddaughter, she would've turned men's heads when she walked by, carried her power over them like a regal princess.

"Would you care to board, Mr. Bernstein?" Robert, the tour guide, interrupted his reverie.

"Call me Jake. I'll wait until the women return."

To which the tour guide tossed him a knowing smirk.

A few minutes later, Jake was helping the elderly woman up to the steep first step. Mary McCoy Snider paused on the steps, holding onto the railing on the coach door. She looked back at Jake, her dark blue eyes sharp with intelligence.

"Thank you, young man. What's your name?" A slight Texas drawl softened her naturally strong, clear voice.

"Jake. Jake Bernstein from Virginia." He smiled up at the elderly grandmother, who then nodded and moved up into the coach. He slid his gaze down to the granddaughter, who'd paused at the door. The top of her head came to his jawline.

"Thanks for helping . . .Jake," the beautiful blonde muttered, blinking up at him before climbing the steps herself. Her long honey-blonde hair brushed his shoulder when she moved past him. There was a self-conscious shyness in her manner which Jake found odd for such a beautiful woman. His pulse revved up.

Watch yourself, Bernstein. You're on duty.

Wasn't that why they chose him? So he could schmooze the women in question?

Sure but don't forget why you're really here, dude.

He proceeded up after Megan Larsen, appreciating the view from the rear. Too bad, he thought, when the two women took seats near the front of the packed coach. He nodded a friendly greeting to the mostly couples as he passed them on his way to the vacant seat at the back. Another single man, an older guy in his fifties, sat at the halfway point in the coach, two single women of about the same age — maybe early forties — behind him. They perked up as he walked by, shot him wide smiles beaming with anticipation.

He knew *that* look.

After stowing his carry-on underneath the empty seat next to him, Jake sat down and leaned over. He could see the blonde's wavy locks falling about her shoulders from his vantage point. She was sitting on the opposite side of the coach in the aisle seat, her grandmother in the window seat. Damn, he'd have to find a way of sitting closer to them. Maybe their seats on the coach weren't fixed . . .or he could feign motion sickness and ask Robert to place him farther forward.

At that very moment when he was plotting a way to chat up Mary Snider and her granddaughter while they tooled around the city and countryside in their leviathan on wheels, the blonde swiveled her upper body and looked down the aisle. Their eyes locked together briefly and she smiled. Despite a night without sleep and being heavy with jet lag and a burgeoning headache, his pulse kicked up. Something lurched in his chest. His groin clenched.

Jake returned the smile.

Good, she noticed me. Contact made.

CHAPTER THREE

M eg's skull tingled. Someone was staring at her . . . she could tell, but she ignored the sensation. Something else held her attention for the moment. Inside Westminster Abbey, she'd been looking up at the clerestory windows. Long shafts of light filtered in, falling among the huge columns like ethereal angels. If subatomic-sized spirits were floating in the dust particles of that light, then those beams were heaven-sent. Maybe even the spirit of Grandpa Snider was floating up there, watching over them, approving this visit to the old country.

A fanciful notion, she realized, but the idea pleased her.

They're always here among us. All the ones we've loved and lost. They're never far away.

The tingling sensation persisted. She was accustomed to being stared at, especially by men, so she usually ignored whoever was staring. Not this time. She sensed his presence very near.

Whipping around suddenly, she practically bumped into *him*.

The new guy who'd joined the coach tour.

Jake Bernstein. From Virginia.

"Sorry." He backed up a step, "I was standing too close. I'm trying to hear our guide—sorry I got too close."

Meg gazed at his face. The face of a magazine model. Fine-boned with high cheekbones, a strong jaw, dimpled chin, and chiseled mouth. Gorgeous. Simply gorgeous. But that was his problem. He was *too* handsome, *too* tall and muscular, *too* self-confident. He was a babe magnet. Wary, she looked away. Heat flushed her cheeks and her heart banged against her ribs.

Fool, she berated herself. *What happened to the last good- looking man you fell for?* Derek. A Brad Pitt lookalike. They'd become engaged after three months of dating, moved in together, and two months later she discovered the truth about him. He was a closet player. Trolling for women while engaged to Meg. As if someone she knew in the Dallas area wouldn't someday come across his deception and report back to her. When she'd confronted him about it, he'd shrugged and confessed. Too many women, too little time, he'd said without an ounce of remorse.

A lesson she'd learned. Men that good-looking felt as though nature had bestowed them with such gifts for a reason. To lavish those gifts on just one woman was a waste. They were owed.

Too many women, too little time.

"No problem . . . Jake," she muttered, turning her back on him.

"You know *my* name. What's yours?" he asked, bending over her left shoulder.

She put a forefinger up against her lips to shush him up. Their guide, Robert Morse, was explaining something about the Poets' Corner, but she hadn't been paying much attention. Now it was too late to learn what he'd said.

When the group moved on, following Robert slowly along the right side of the nave, Meg hung back. Wouldn't hurt to be friendly to the new guy, after all. After what she'd experienced with Derek, she was immured to exceptionally handsome men, so keeping him at arm's length shouldn't be difficult. She watched her grandmother shuffle alongside a middle-aged woman. A French Canadian, Meg thought. The two women were speaking softly in French. Well, *good*. Gran was making friends too.

"Meg Larsen. And you're from Virginia, right?" She raised her eyes to meet his. Deep-set under dark brown brows, his were the color of dark malachite, a dark green, tinged with gray. His face was clean-shaven but showed a day's dark stubble. His dark-brown wavy hair sported a medium cut and was combed straight back from the widow's peak on his forehead. He looked weary. She gauged him to be in his early to mid-thirties.

"Good memory," he remarked quietly. "I flew all night to make this tour. Kinda last minute. But I got a call from the travel agency. They had a cancellation, so here I am."

They began to follow in the wake of their tour group. Meg liked his strong deep baritone voice, but she didn't like the way her body was responding to his attentions. Still, they were the youngest people in this tour group. It was natural they'd gravitate toward each other. She lowered her own voice because of the abbey acoustics, for fear the sound would carry to other visitors.

"Breathtaking, isn't it?" She indicated the expanse and quiet beauty of the abbey. These Gothic heights were meant for music. Almost on cue, somewhere from the mid-chancel area, an organ began to play. "Oh my, that's lovely."

They stopped to listen.

"Beethoven's Requiem," Jake said. His face lifted to the same clerestory windows and shafts of light beams that had entranced her just a minute ago.

"Really? How do you know?"

"I like classical music—what little I know. This song was played at my grandfather's funeral. He loved Beethoven." He frowned as if slightly embarrassed, then indicated they should catch up to the group.

"Forgive me, but are you a model?"

The hunk shot her an embarrassed look. "No, investment

banker. Although I admit I modeled during college. Helped pay the bills. Don't hold it against me. People think it's such nothing work. Which I suppose it is." He rubbed the dark stubble on his chin. "What about you? What do you do? And the old lady you're with. She's your grandmother, isn't she? I thought I heard you say . . ."

"Yes, she's my grandmother. I'm taking her to see her hometown of Killarney. That's on this tour, y'know. And Dublin, where Gran studied at Trinity College. What do I do? I coach tennis and cross-country. I also teach high school French and Spanish. Is this your first trip to England and Ireland?"

"England, no. Ireland, yes. A country I've always wanted to see."

"Grandma's Irish born. McCoy's her maiden name. Can't get any more Irish than that."

"No, I guess not. Funny, I overheard your grandmother and that woman over there speaking French."

Meg glanced over at the two women, their heads huddled together over a guidebook. "Gran's a whiz at languages. Fluent in several. That lady's French Canadian, so Grandma's having a ball practicing her French. Doesn't get much of a chance at home."

The hunk smiled at her. His teeth were even and white. When he blinked, she noticed his long, dark eyelashes. He ran a hand through his wavy dark hair. His bangs curled a little. *Oh lord . . .*

"You teach French and Spanish, so it must run in the family. That linguistic talent."

Feeling extremely self-conscious, Meg shrugged and clammed up. It was common for strangers to ask these sorts of questions, dance around the facts of each other's lives with stilted questions and replies. It wasn't that so much as the way he looked at her, as though something was troubling him. Ha, maybe guilt, she decided.

She glanced at his left hand ring finger. No ring. No indentation or pale skin to show where a ring normally sat. But that meant nothing. Derek the jerk had been lying about his single status for months. One of the women he'd tried to pick up was one of her single colleagues. She'd shown Meg the guy's card, reported what he'd said to her. How careless of him. Engaged and still passing for single.

Too many conniving scoundrels out there, preying on naïve, lonely women. Meg was lonely, maybe, but not naïve. Not any longer, anyway. She'd learned to be friendly to men without encouraging them, but her distrust ran deep. Distrust of them but also of herself and her own weakness.

Lifting her chin, she joined the rear stragglers of their group. Whatever Robert was now telling her fellow visitors, however, Meg couldn't focus on. She couldn't put her finger on what, but there was something different about Jake Bernstein. A gravity or seriousness that seemed to temper what he said. As if he were there but didn't really want to be.

How foolish was that?

Even more foolish was her body's reaction to him.

Hadn't she learned anything in the past few years? For most men, seducing women was a form of recreation, like Saturday tag football. A sporting pastime. Some of them collected trophies of their conquests or wins. A girl's panties or bra. Derek had kept one of her lacey black bras, refused to give it back—the creep. Meg wouldn't be surprised if he'd tacked it on his wall.

The hunk was standing by one of the Gothic columns, gazing up at the ribbed stone arches overhead. This one, Meg sensed, had deep waters despite his gorgeous GQ looks. Then again, she could be wrong. Maybe she knew diddly squat about men, even at twenty-six. Maybe she knew diddly about life, too, except that when you were wounded, you found a way to heal. And then you kept on going.

Surviving . . . broken-hearted or not. That was what it was all about.

One day at a time, keeping faith in yourself. Doing your life's work.

As though sensing her, Jake's eyes dropped to the stone floor. Then he looked at her and smiled . . . a thoughtful smile. Not the least bit seductive or predatory.

A smile that made her heart flip over.

Oh you stupid girl.

"Let's just sit for a while, Grandma," she suggested. "Robert's in his element in that gift shop. I think he gets a cut of every souvenir his tourists buy. This may take a bit. I told him we'd wait here."

Westminster Abbey, the two houses of Parliament, and then back to the entrance to the Abbey. What a whirlwind morning.

After a fast-paced stroll around the House of Commons and the House of Lords, followed by the Abbey gift shop, Meg urged her grandmother to rest on the bench outside the entrance. Pangs of guilt stabbed at her.

She was painfully aware that the elderly woman was suffering from shortness of breath and chronic rheumatoid arthritis, even though she was physically active for her age. The past two or three years, however, Meg had noticed her grandmother's decline in energy and good spirits. Her high blood pressure and atherosclerosis exacerbated her general age-related problems.

This wasn't the first time Meg regretted taking this trip, especially since the idea had been hers to begin with. Returning to her grandmother's origins was meant to lift her spirits, not dampen them or make her suffer.

Mary Snider took a small bottle of Tylenol from her purse and shook out two into her palm. Her hands were gloved, as much to keep the cold out as to conceal her gnarled, arthritic fingers.

"Meggie, give me the water bottle, sweetheart."

Out of her big hobo bag, Meg produced the water. She unscrewed the cap and handed it to her grandmother.

"Gran, maybe we shouldn't have come. I feel like I'm dragging you around. You don't seem to be enjoying it very much."

After a long drink, Mary Snider handed back the bottled water and smiled weakly. Although sunny, the breeze skittering along the sidewalk and forecourt was cool, causing the woman to gather her coat more closely about her.

"It's the cold, Meggie. Dallas is so warm in June, these ol' bones aren't used to it anymore. It's been a long time ... I barely recognize any of it anymore." Mary looked about her, glanced up at the Gothic facade of the eight-hundred year-old Abbey. "A very long time since I was here. It's all changed."

"Maybe it's turning out to be too much for you. I thought you'd enjoy visiting your old stomping grounds. Now I'm thinking we waited too long."

Mary made an impatient noise. "Nonsense. Your grandfather kept wanting to bring me back, but I put him off for years. Too busy, other places to see—there were always excuses. Your Uncle John wanted me to come back. The truth is, sugar, I never really had any desire to come back. Only with you now, it seems like the right time. One last look at, uh, everything . . ." She smiled at her granddaughter and sighed with fatigue. "Being with you, spending all this time together . . .that's all I really wanted."

She patted Meg's knee and shrank back against the bench.

Again, Meg felt more than a little guilt. They should never have come. This was her fault for insisting, for pushing the idea on her grandmother. But in all truth, she'd had no clue that her grandmother's gradual decline would take such a sharp downturn.

A shadow loomed above them. Meg looked up. She shaded her eyes and recognized, with a sudden lurch of her stomach, the tall, handsome banker from Virginia.

"Jake Bernstein . . .from Virginia," her grandmother remarked drily. She appeared perturbed by the interloper.

Not Meg. Her pulse quickened. Her grandmother had physical ailments, but there was no problem with her memory. Neither one had forgotten the handsome hunk's name. Smiling up at him in greeting, she let her eyes devour him from bottom to top. Again.

As her eyes traveled upward, she noted with a quiet inner pleasure the muscular length of his legs, the slim hips emphasized by the lower hem of a leather bomber-style jacket that sat at his waist. Her gaze raked over the width of chest and square shoulders, the lanky span of arms. His handsome face, whose beautiful green eyes seemed to penetrate her like laser beams, had just enough ruggedness to avoid being pretty. His skin was lightly tanned, as though he spent time outside every day. She liked the fact that he had whiskers on his cheeks—kept his face from being perfect. But who *was* this man? He'd given her sidelong looks all morning.

"Don't blame you for taking a break. We've been going nonstop for hours. Time for tea and crumpets?"

"I think Robert's a coffee man. We've been stopping at Starbucks every morning." She smiled. "Have a seat," Meg invited casually, tethering her leaping heart. She was determined to be friendly to this total stranger but maintain her distance. "You've met my grandmother, Mary Snider. We're from Frisco, Texas." At his puzzled look, she added, "Near Dallas."

"Mr. Bernstein, what do you do in Virginia?" Her grandmother moved over to give them all more room as the man took a seat next to Meg on the far side of the bench.

"Call me Jake, ma'am." The hunk leaned forward,

maintaining eye contact with both women. "I'm an investment analyst for The Bank of Virginia. Regional director for investments. My home's in Alexandria."

"We'll have to ask him about your portfolio, Gran. How is Wall Street doing these days?" Meg asked him.

"Okay, if your portfolio is diversified. Not okay if you're overweighted in financials at the moment."

"Was this a bad time for you to leave work?"

"My assistant and his summer interns are on top of things. This was now or never. So when a vacant spot opened up, I grabbed it. I've been to Europe many times but never Wales or Ireland."

"You arrived late," Mary Snider reminded him. "What a shame you missed yesterday's tour of Buckingham Palace and . . .uh, where else . . .oh yes, Hampton Court."

"Also Churchill's underground War Rooms," Meg added. "My grandmother showed us all where she worked during the war. The very room . . .it was exciting."

"Where all the translators had their desks. Horrible, cold, stuffy rooms." Mary Snider threw him a wry smile. "The claustrophobic ones didn't last long. The concrete above our heads, they claimed, was several feet thick. When the bombs landed nearby, dust from the ceilings would sprinkle down on our heads. We started wearing scarves to keep our hair clean. The men wore hats. It was like a rabbit warren down there . . .just horrible, squalid little rooms."

Meg stared at her grandmother. Strange, the day before Gran hadn't wanted to share much with the tour group and their guide. Perhaps it had taken a full day for the war memories to begin drifting back so she could speak about them so dispassionately.

"Hmm, I must see them sometime . . .maybe my next trip," Jake remarked casually. He glanced Meg's way. "So Meg, what did you think of Churchill's War Rooms?"

Hearing him say her name sent a fluttery sensation to the pit of her stomach. She hid the feeling. Her hand flew up to tuck behind her ear a stray lock tossed across her face by the stubborn breeze. Attention from the handsome Jake Bernstein was making her a little nervous. His nearness reminded her that . . . all right, admit it. *I'm lonely. And horny as all get out.*

"Like Gran said, the rooms were small, austere, cold. A real underground bunker. Churchill had a tiny bedroom down there."

"Amazing, really, that Churchill and his advisers conducted war strategy under those conditions."

Meg nodded in agreement. "Successfully, too, since the Allies won the war."

Mary Snider snorted softly and waved her hand dismissively.

"Not all the time, Meggie. The British made many mistakes—"

They were interrupted by the sudden clamorous noise from their motorcoach group. Robert Morse emerged from the knot of people, gesticulating in one direction then another. Everyone seemed to be talking at once.

"Our fearless leader," her grandmother said before sighing.

Meg assumed that Robert Morse, their democratically-minded tour guide, was doing his usual thing—trying to include everyone's opinions about the restaurant choice for lunch. When the collective decision-making turned chaotic, Morse imposed unilateral rule. Their guide's quirkiness amused her, an observation she shared with their new travel companion.

Jake laughed in appreciation.

"You'll have to give me more tips over lunch." He offered her grandmother his arm as they stood to join the others. "The pound doesn't buy very much, does it? Rate of exchange sucks. And, Mrs. Snider, I'd like to hear more about your experiences during the war. World War II is kind of a hobby of mine."

"Is it?" her grandmother muttered, taking measured steps after heaving to her feet with Jake's assistance.

Meg took the other flank, her forearm grasped by her grandmother's gloved hand. Mary Snider was so vain that she refused to use a cane or show her arthritic fingers, something Meg sympathized with. Her grandmother used to be a beauty, even when Meg went to live with her at the age of two.

Back then, when they were in their late fifties, Mary and John Snider were always the handsomest couple Meg knew. Seeing one's beauty erode must be difficult. She empathized with her grandmother's wishes to conceal whatever ugliness she could. In Meg's view, that wasn't all vanity — rather, fear that everything Mary had once taken pride in was now slipping away. At twenty-six, Meg understood that fear intellectually but not emotionally. Not when the best part of her life lay before her, not behind her.

She hoped, anyway.

Jake caught her eye. "Meg, what other languages do you speak? You said you teach French and Spanish?" Their gaze met over her grandmother's head. My, he was nice and tall — maybe six-foot-two or-three.

"Yes, but I'm studying German now."

"Wow."

"The German teacher at my school is retiring next June and he wants me to take over his classes. So I began taking German this year. There's no shortage of Spanish teachers in our area, and German's still popular in Texas. There's a number of German-immigrant communities near us."

Jake shot her that sexy, gleaming smile of his. "You're in luck, Meg. I speak German, although my American accent is

thick they tell me. Feel free to practice German with me anytime during this tour."

Oh boy, that's not all I'd like to practice with you . . .

Meg squashed that thought as quickly as it sprang into her
horny little head. "Hmm, maybe. If you promise not to laugh
at my two-year-old vocabulary. I only know the present tense.
Are you fluent in German?"

"Pretty much. High school, college . . . My grandfather
taught me the Munchener and Berliner dialects. He was born
and raised in Bavaria, studied and worked for a time in Berlin
as a film editor. Until 1934, anyway. As a German Jew, he saw
the writing on the wall. Got out when he could. He was one
of the lucky ones."

"Oh, I see." Meg's tone softened. "Good thing he left."

Her grandmother looked up and threw her a sharp glance,
then dropped her hand from Jake's arm. She shook off his
help rather rudely, Meg thought, surprised at Gran's behavior.

"I can manage with my granddaughter," Mary said abruptly as they rejoined their group.

Meg shook her head slightly, in a kind of tacit apology, relieved when Jake smiled and lifted one shoulder in a small
shrug. As if broadcasting to the world, Robert Morse announced the pub's name and location—just four blocks away
off Victoria and Chadwick Streets. Meg stepped back a pace
and leaned over to catch Jake's attention. Their arms brushed
together lightly.

"I'd like to hear more about your family. And whatever
else you know about wartime London. My grandmother
doesn't seem to want to talk about it much."

Jake nodded, his eyes turning dark.

"Over lunch. That is, if your grandmother doesn't mind—"

After that, their tour guide's loud instructions and directions—for those who couldn't keep up with the bulk of the

group—drowned out Meg's reassuring reply.

As she and her grandmother fell behind the group, trailing an older couple from New York, Jake strode abreast of an older man, traveling alone like himself. Another Canadian, Meg thought. Soon enough, the only other two single women on their motorcoach—two sisters—scurried to take their places on the sidewalk directly in front of the two men. The four, forming a loose knot, chatted together.

Disappointment weighed heavy on her chest. The foursome's laughter drifted back to Meg and crushed her spirits. Silly, but she wanted to get to know Jake Bernstein. There was no one else on the motorcoach who was closer to her in age. Thanks to her grandmother's abrupt coldness, she doubted he'd speak to her again.

What had gotten into her? Only two days into their travels, and her grandmother was behaving like a witch. Testy and bitchy. Meg blamed this mood swing on her grandmother's aches and pains and general exhaustion from trying to keep up with the rest of the group, most of whom were twenty or thirty years younger. Still, there was something else about Mary's behavior that was different. Out of character.

Whatever it was, Meg could not put her finger on it.

Gran harrumphed beside her. "Meggie, you and good-looking, worthless men—you're like magnets."

Meg dismissed her grandmother's cynicism with a short laugh.

"Maybe this one's not worthless."

Another deep-throated harrumph.

"Oh Gran, don't worry. I've learned my lesson. My heart's turned to stone."

With a sinking feeling in her stomach, Meg watched Jake's profile as he bent over and said something to one of the sisters. The auburn-haired woman smiled up at him and tucked her hand into the crook of his arm. Meg's disappointment morphed swiftly into anger at herself. Her face flushed hotly. *Well, shoot!*

CHAPTER FOUR

Jake smiled and waved her over. He'd saved two seats for Meg and her grandmother at the table with the single Canadian man and the two sisters from New Jersey. Walking more slowly than the rest, Meg and Mary Snider had brought up the rear when they entered the large private dining room in the Ol' Draught Horse Pub. He noted Meg's broad smile as she and the elderly woman approached their table.

Pulling out their heavy, cumbersome chairs, he also noted the pointed look Mary Snider cast his way—a look-but-don't-touch kind of warning to him on behalf of her granddaughter.

Well, too friggin' bad, lady. I'm just doing my job. And not a bad job it was, he thought, fixing his eyes on the smokin' hot Meg. Besides, the young woman appeared to enjoy his presence. For his part, he'd never dug an undercover assignment as much as this one. He found himself really liking this high school teacher, Meg Larsen. If they'd met in D.C., he'd be asking her out on a date. Any time, any place.

Grandpa Nate would say he was a little smitten. Smitten over the kitten.

Jake called it lust at first sight.

The acoustics in the dining room were bad, unmitigated by the dark wood-paneled walls, the hobnail floor, and the heavy drapery. The place was noisy and the food very English-pubby. Bangers and mash with a side of mushy peas and onions. Okay if you'd been camping in the wild for weeks. Not okay if you lived within five miles of some of America's best restaurants. Damned glad he wasn't eating on his own dime.

Guinness on draft—two pints' worth—gave him a mild buzz and brought down the raucous noise to a dull roar. Meg drank a small glass of light beer along with her grandmother, who ate very little. The topic at their table—their upcoming afternoon tour of Knightsbridge, Harrod's, and Hyde Park—consumed Hank, the Canadian, and the two sisters, Judy and Jeannie. The tours were all glimpses of the sights, enough to whet your appetite for more. Enough to make your head spin.

Jake kept wondering how he was going to get the old lady to speak German.

"Tell me about your grandfather," Meg coaxed him during a lull in the conversation. "He sounds like he's led an interesting life."

Good, just the opening I need. And a first. A beautiful young woman wanting to know about Grandpa Nate. The old guy'd be tickled.

He chose his words carefully, glancing back and forth between Meg and the old woman beside her.

"As I said, he was German-born. He was working in the film industry in Berlin when the Nazis came to power. He'd already won several awards for film editing. Well, by 1934 he and all other Jews were banned from this and other industries. Laws were passed which took away the German Jews' citizenship and other civil rights. Less competition in the job market, you see, and these were depression times. Few Germans protested. As the Reichstag's laws became more and more oppressive and exclusive, my grandfather began planning to emigrate. When he got help from some of his former colleagues—those who'd left and found jobs in Hollywood—he left Germany with his wife and young son . . .my father. He begged his parents, his two brothers and two sisters, their spouses and children, to join him."

"What happened?" Meg set down her glass of beer.

"His family wouldn't leave. They had businesses, properties, bank accounts—"

"Fools, all of them," Mary Snider cut in harshly. "One should never get too attached to things in this world."

"Grandma! Please." Meg's face blanched at the older woman's callous tone of voice.

"She's right, Meg. Mrs. Snider, you're so right. Ultimately, Grandpa Nate's family lost everything, anyway. And were slaughtered like cattle four or five years later. All their things did them no good. If they'd come to America, they would've done well."

Meg grew quiet as did the rest of the table, but her eyes teared up. She looked away while Mary Snider took a swig from her glass and sneered.

"They all should've left. Stupid to stay where they weren't wanted."

Meg's head whipped around. She gawked at her grandmother, her lovely mouth dropping open. Shock and shame froze and tightened her features. Jake covered her hand with his in commiseration, as if to say it didn't matter. He'd heard worse from jihadist groups tracked by the FBI. Yet he never let an argument on this topic slide by.

"1934 to 1945. Six to eight million Jews in all of Europe. Where do you suggest they should've gone, Mrs. Snider?" Jake asked mildly. "Even the U.S. couldn't absorb those numbers. There was no Israel then. Some got away. Emigrated elsewhere."

The elder woman retreated with a smug grin and a heavy shrug of both shoulders. The gesture made Jake want to slap her silly with one of her uneaten bangers.

Meg said nothing for a long time. Jake dropped the topic and spent the remainder of his meal chatting about British food and beer. Finally, as lunch was concluding, she grabbed his arm as he stood to stretch.

"I'm sorry, Jake," she whispered. Her warm breath fanned his neck, making his cheeks flush warmly from her close contact. "My grandmother—she hasn't been herself lately. No excuse, I know, but I think this trip's been very difficult on her."

Jake bent his head, fighting the urge to brush his fingers over Meg's lovely face. Her full rose-colored lips, freshened with lipstick, almost seemed to beckon him. Her dark-blue eyes dropped to his mouth too. They both froze in this tableau of mutual attraction. Just briefly.

His beer-buzz had lowered his inhibitions, a dangerous dropping of the shield in undercover work. He'd been there before so he knew how to handle this, knew how far he could let the pretense slip. Being his natural self made him all the more believable when it came time to dissemble.

He smiled. "Was coming here—to England and Ireland—her idea or yours?"

"Actually, mine. But then she got excited about it. Or so I thought. This motorcoach tour sounded like the easiest way of seeing everything. Especially Ireland, her birthplace."

Their hands touched as they stood together. A ripple of lust surged through him, his libido raging out of its cage. He had an impulse to grab her, gather her in his arms, and crush those rosy lips of hers.

"Meg, do you like to jog?"

"Yes. I do five miles a day when I'm coaching cross-country." Her slow, hopeful smile sent his blood racing. "What do you have in mind?"

Seizing the excuse to help her on with her jacket, Jake let his hands rest on her shoulders. Just a light, harmless caress.

Yeah, they belong there. All over her.

"When we get to the hotel tonight, somewhere in Bath I think, let's go out and get some exercise. Just you and me. Game?"

"Sure, sounds fun," she said softly. Her eyes rested a moment on his chest and shoulders, then moved up to lock with his own.

A definite connection there, Jake confirmed, much to his pleasure. Their chemistry was undeniable. Meg Larsen liked what she saw and wanted to pursue whatever he had to offer. Despite the bigoted old lady and all that stood between them, Meg was telegraphing her message—*I'm available.*

Still, there was a hesitancy about her. As though she was afraid to trust him. A pang of guilt shot through him. She wouldn't be far wrong on that score. She shouldn't trust him. He might end up having to destroy her grandmother. Maybe her whole family.

An instant later, Meg was helping the old woman to her feet.

"C'mon, Grandma, back to the coach. No more walking today, I promise. You can take it easy and sleep on our way to Bath."

"Thank God," grumbled a surly Mary Snider.

Jake let them pass in front of him. Well, he thought, now there was one female who remained a total mystery. Who *was* this old woman? Somehow he couldn't wrap his mind around the possibility that this crotchety but harmless old lady was once a murderous Nazi spy.

Not possible.

If she wasn't, then who were "Hummingbird" and "Black Widow"? After all this time, would they ever find out?

In all truth, did he even care?

CHAPTER FIVE

In their double room at the modern but stylish Bath Inn, Meg pulled on a black, spaghetti-strap cami, then topped it with a zip-up sweatshirt that matched her gray sweatpants.

"Going out, Meghan?" Her grandmother's gnarled fingers fumbled with the buttons on her flannel pajama top.

Meg slipped on her sneakers. "Yes, I am, Grandma. Going jogging with Jake." With alacrity, she went over to help, fastening the buttons and assisting her grandmother into bed, despite the elderly woman's weak protests.

"I'm not a child, Meggie. I just have problems with . . .my buttons. And climbing stairs."

"And dressing, combing hair . . .being nice to people. Getting old's a bitch, Gran. I realize that and I sympathize. I really do. But it doesn't take much to extend just a little common courtesy to Jake, does it?" Meg hoped she wasn't sounding too harsh. Her grandmother's growing helplessness tugged at her heartstrings. Which, of course, made the old woman even more irascible.

She turned the TV on so Mary could fall asleep. A long habit of hers, her grandmother couldn't relax her mind enough unless the TV's light was flickering and there was ambient noise in the room.

"The way you talked to him today, about his Jewish family — you sounded anti-Semitic, Grandma. That doesn't make sense. Ruth Weisman is your best friend in Frisco. We went to her grandson's Bar Mitzvah, for crying out loud. So why did you say those awful things to Jake today?"

There was no reply from her grandmother's bed. Finally a crooked, arthritic hand jutted out from beneath the covers.

"Turn down the telly, Meg, just a trifle. There, jolly good . . .Thank you."

Meg did just that, musing over her grandmother's penchant for adopting the slang of the area, in this case British idioms. Her grandmother had a chameleon's talent, at least linguistically. A born mimic. In a short period of time, she could speak like the natives and adopt their slang and mannerisms. Grandpa Snider often said that his Irish bride took to Texas like a June bug on bluebonnets.

Meg flicked off all the lights in the room except the one bedside lamp, which she turned low. After she swept her long hair into a high ponytail and fastened it with a large, wide barrette, she was ready. She pocketed her room key.

"You like this boy, Meggie? This Jake Bernstein?"

"Yes, I do. He's nice to talk to . . ." She emitted a soft, low giggle. " . . .and look at. He's gorgeous, for sure, but there's something else, Gran. I can sense his . . . strength of mind. Strength of character."

Mary Snider snorted disdainfully. "Strength of character, ha! You're talking to your grandmother, not some old senile fool. What you young people call eye-candy is all you sense. Well, you can have a sample, or a taste. But that doesn't mean you have to buy the whole box."

Meg sputtered with surprise and spun around.

"C'mon, Grandma I'm not so independent that I can't be a little lonely."

"Look at the last good-looking man you went with. That Derek fellow. He was unworthy of you, Meggie—a real scoundrel."

"Oh Gran, let's not talk about *him*. You'll make me gag. Speaking of young men, you've talked about all the gorgeous men who chased after you during the war. Even the married ones in the War department. And the Royal Air Force pilots—"

"Flyboys, they were called."

"Besides, Gran, Jake lives in Virginia. A thousand miles away. How can I date a man who lives a thousand miles away?" She shrugged and frowned. Her grandmother nodded wisely and said nothing. "No, Gran, some people are meant to be just friends. " She sighed volubly. "So, did you have a favorite . . . before you met Grandpa Snider?"

From what Meg had learned, Captain John Snider of the U.S. Army Air Corps had won her heart from the moment they'd met at a USO benefit for victims of the Blitz.

"There was one Raffie, a Scotsman, who had bright red hair. He made me laugh, made me forget my loneliness. He was a talker, couldn't keep a secret if he tried. He used to tell me what cities they were going to bomb the next night. What places were off-limits. He was full of stories too."

Meg frowned. "Did you have to report him, Grandma? Y'know, that wartime warning. *Loose lips sink ships.* That saying on the poster in those underground war rooms, showing a pretty blonde—*Keep mum; she's not so dumb.* So, Gran, what happened to him? Did they censure him or put him in prison for blabbing war secrets?"

"In the brig? No, heavens no. I never reported him. I had top security clearance. He knew he could trust me. Heavens, they all trusted me."

Meg noted the pride in her grandmother's voice. Finally, some good memories were coming through.

"What happened to him?" she repeated. "Why didn't you marry him?"

"Germans got him one night. During a bombing run over Berlin." Her grandmother's countenance was impassive, her tone of voice flat. "Germans found out the Raffies were flying over that night and had their big anti-aircraft guns ready. Lots of planes never came back that night."

The room grew quiet, then, as Meg stared at Mary's still form. It was remarkable how her grandmother's mind worked. She could recall details from the distant past—especially the war years in London—and yet forget to buy one of two items on her grocery list.

"A lot of flyboys died," Mary added matter-of-factly. "The death rate was, I think, sixty percent. Glad your grandfather survived. He saved my life. And gave me two children and a comfortable home. What more could I ask after what I saw during the war?"

Meg had heard the story before. How despondent Mary McCoy had grown toward the end of 1944, when it was apparent the war was winding down and the Allies were winning. She'd seen too many good people killed, too many beautiful cities destroyed and—Meg suspected—was heartsick at having lost a few loved ones. How she was considering suicide—she'd been given a small caliber pistol for self-protection, considering her vital role for British Intelligence. How falling in love with Captain John Snider, leaving the SIS—Intelligence Service—and receiving a visa to emigrate—all of this changed her life. Gave her hope for a new future. A new start.

"I'm glad, too, Gran. Grandpa was the best."

John Snider had died five years earlier on the operating table while undergoing his second cardiac bypass. Meg felt her grandmother hadn't been the same since—deflated and defeated. Highly distractible and forgetful.

"Love and time can heal many wounds," her grandmother said. "It's a cliché but so true. Now I have just you, Meggie."

A wave of compassion coursed through Meg. She crossed the room to sit on her grandmother's bed, give her a tight hug.

"Not true. Jack and I both love you. Uncle John loves you, too. So do my cousins. Everyone's just so busy with their own lives. You know how it is."

She kissed her grandmother's forehead and settled the blankets under the woman's chin and around her shoulders. Their roles had reversed, Meg now the nurturing mother and Mary now the dependent child.

In all truth, Meg could understand her grandmother's feelings of neglect and loss. Meg's half-brother, Jack — the product of her mother's second marriage — was now clerking for a federal appellate court judge in San Francisco and called once a week, if that often.

Her mother, four-times divorced, was now living with husband number five in Sedona, Arizona. They were both writers and *life coaches* – a joke, as far as Meg was concerned. Their life philosophy could be distilled into one sentence — *Do what pleases you, no matter who you hurt.* A law student at the time, Fiona had abandoned two-year-old Meg and turned custody over to Mary and John Snider so she could pursue *her studies and men* – as Grandma later would describe her daughter's choice. Three years later she did the same with Jack, so it was no surprise when the Sniders disinherited her and assumed full custody of their grandchildren even though they were in their fifties.

Meg's biological father, Kurt Larsen, a corporate executive based in Seattle, had vanished from her life long ago after he remarried. Jack frequently saw his father, a San Francisco businessman. She was happy for him that he had that connection.

Overall their fragmented, dysfunctional family came together for a day or so at Christmas. And even then they were like uneasy, guarded strangers, sharing little but their genetic material. She supposed that was the reason why Meg and her grandmother were so close and relied so much on each other. Gran was her only close relative besides her half-brother, Jack, with whom she kept in phone contact.

"You have me, Grandma," Meg sighed. "You're my real mother. You've always been there for me, you and Grandpa. Always encouraging me, never judging me. You've always been my number one cheerleader. You don't know what that has meant to me."

Mary stared back into Meg's face a long moment, a wide smile creasing her wrinkled face. Genuine love radiated from her countenance.

"You're the woman I could've been, Meggie. You're good and strong. No matter what happens in your life, you must promise me you'll stay that way. You won't turn hard and mean . . .like me. Life can change people. The ugliness of war can change people."

Meg patted the woman's shoulders. All this talk of war bummed her out.

"Well, the war's long over, Grandma. I know coming back has made you remember a lot of the bad things that happened. If they bother you that much, try to put it out of your mind. Just think about the good that's happened to these countries in the past sixty years. The prosperity of England and Germany. All of Europe has flourished, hasn't it? Enjoy the people, too, their courage and good humor."

A flicker of emotions passed over her grandmother's face, most of which Meg couldn't decipher. Had she said the wrong thing?

"Meggie, you know your grandfather and I have done fairly well with our investments. When I go, it's all going to you and Jack. And John Junior's two sons. Just the grandchildren. But the house in Texas is yours. To do with as you like."

Meg shivered with dread. Even hinting at her grandmother's possible death made her ill. No, she couldn't bear to think about that. She hastily gave her grandmother another hug and stood up.

"Gran, don't even talk about stuff like that. It freaks me out.

Eighty is the new seventy, they say. So you've got lots of time left." Meg smiled brightly. "Now, there's a very nice guy I'd like to spend some time with and get to know. So off I go." She kissed Mary's crepey, tissue-soft cheek. "Is there anything I can get you before I leave?"

"Bring a glass of water, Meghan, and my bottle of Tylenol. On second thought, the bottle of sleeping pills. Just in case the pain keeps me awake. I need a good night's sleep."

"Okay, but only take one. You know what the doctor said."

Minutes later, after running down the hallway and catching the downward elevator—lift, Meg reminded herself, in Brit-speak—she met up with Jake in the lobby. His beaming smile made her almost dizzy with pleasure.

Seven o'clock—still light enough to squeeze in a couple of miles.

"Tuck in Granny?" he teased.

Meg grinned. "Listen, Jake, Grandma's the one person in this world who loves me unconditionally. She raised me from the age of two. So mind your manners . . .and please, don't mind her. No matter what she says, she doesn't mean it. Not really."

She cast him a sideways glance to see if his face registered annoyance at her gentle scolding. It didn't.

"Okay, just for you, I'll cut Granny some slack." He opened the hotel door for her and followed her out.

She smiled as she breezed past him.

Meg breathed in the dusk air, redolent with moisture and the scent of flowers. The city of Bath awaited them.

Jake showered and dried his hair with a hand towel, his body with a large bath towel. Then he sat on his bed, wearing only a black T-shirt and black briefs. An amalgam of pleasurable feelings permeated his entire being as he recalled their conversation during their four-mile jog around the city. They'd stopped at a Roman ruin in the downtown area and marveled at the ingenuity of Roman plumbing. Even in cold England, Roman engineers had found a way to keep the caldariums hot and the tepidariums warm.

It was there at the Roman ruin, circling the upper floor and gazing down into the lower, excavated pool area, that the fine dark hair on the back of Jake's neck stood up. With Meg at his side, staring into the huge, open-air bath, he played it cool. They walked around, murmuring to each other. Every few seconds or so, Jake canvassed the area. He spotted a middle-aged couple in rubber galoshes. They certainly weren't tourists. Once in a while, the man would hold the woman back as if he were reminding her not to close in on their mark. Another man in a fedora appeared to be the spotter.

By the time he and Meg stepped into the adjacent gift shop to check out the Roman coins, Jake was certain about the tail. They were an incompetent surveillance team. The couple had screwed up, appeared too tentative. Jake, of course, said nothing to Meg while he watched her buy a couple of coins for her brother and uncle. She said she wanted to remember the charm of old Bath, so she bought a coin-medallion to wear on her gold chain.

Jake liked the fact that Meg was a sentimental girl and wasn't embarrassed to show her broad streak of kindness and good humor. The sophisticated D.C. career women he'd dated were all trying so hard to be like men—cold and unfeeling. He didn't know why, but it seemed to be a trend. One that put him off.

Forgetting his assignment was easy when he was with Meg. As though he was two men—one an unattached banker attracted to a pretty woman who, without even seeming to try, was finding a way into his heart. The other, a ruthlessly objective secret agent who was gathering information . . .

albeit slowly so far . . .that might cause this pretty woman a great deal of pain.

Not a pleasant quandary he found himself in.

And now someone was on his tail.

He huffed out a breath and made the call to Major Temple.

A couple of clicks told him the call was being transferred and encrypted, also recorded in a secure room at MI5's headquarters in Thames House. Temple's clipped British speech announced him.

"Major Temple, History section."

"Agent Bernstein here." He didn't feel like being very friendly tonight but he forced himself to keep his voice light. "So how's the weather in London? Foggy and wet? It's beautiful and clear here in Bath. Great town. Fun pubs, too."

He and Meg had stopped at a pub on the last leg of their jog and enjoyed two drafts in a quiet little corner.

"So . . . ?"

Was he lucky or what, getting the only Englishman in the country without a sense of humor. Jake frowned.

"So nothing else to report. Contact's been made. Mary Snider doesn't care for Jews. Not exactly grounds for prosecution. If so, you'd have to hang half the planet. Oh, and who's the dick in the fedora?"

"I'm not amused, Agent Bernstein. We're keeping the motorcoach under surveillance in the event you need help."

So it *was* MI5's surveillance team. Jake had thought as much. Didn't they think he could remain impartial? Get close to the girl and her grandmother and still probe the old American lady for evidence? Or was the major just being overly cautious? Did they know something he didn't? This third alternative disturbed him the most.

"What, in case Granny tries to kick-box me in the balls? Don't you trust me to get the job done? You don't think I'd turn in a fellow American even if I found out she *was* a Nazi spy and killed thousands of people?"

The major was silent.

Well, fuck you!

With a sudden rise of temper, he snarled, "Tell your people I spotted them. Next time, lose the rubber boots and fedora. Is there something I should know, Major, that you haven't told me?"

A long pause, then, "No, not really."

I'll bet.

Jake didn't believe him for an instant. The major was holding something back. Tamping down his resentment, he said, "Goodnight, Major!" and hung up.

Something else was going on . . . and he suspected he wasn't going to like it one damned bit.

CHAPTER SIX

Jake rolled over and glanced at his watch to check the local time. Six AM, his digital, glow-in-the-dark watch told him. He groaned loudly. His body was wide-awake, especially his groin. Too bad his mind was slogging behind.

Breakfast in the hotel dining room was at seven. Next stop Cardiff, the capital of Wales, then their ferry over to Ireland. He'd finally looked over the itinerary. The motorcoach would be leaving late that afternoon, after a tour and lunch in Bath. A quick perusal of the day's agenda showed him they had the afternoon free to wander around Bath and do some shopping. Maybe he could invite Meg and her grandmother to spend some time with him.

Still drowsy with sleep, he glanced over at the pillow next to his. Visualizing Meg lying there, her lush hair with all its variegated blonde hues fanned out, stirred him. The erection he'd awakened with grew harder. Not surprising, he thought, considering his celibacy of late. Strictly his choice, despite the offers tossed his way.

The opportunities had been there and he'd ignored them, stubborn as he was. Even late last night, when the two New Jersey sisters called and invited him to a private party in Hank's room. He'd declined tactfully.

At thirty-two, he found himself holding out for more.

Stupid fool, he scolded himself. Or, as the Brits would say, sodding wanker. Or something to that effect. He should learn to take it when it was offered to him on a platter, free of charge. All he had to do was be nice to a girl for a few hours, promise to call her, and then . . .

Ah, but as Grandpa Nate would say, "*nussing is free in dis vorld*".

Dreams of Meg had plagued him—rather entertained him—all night. Even now, recalling how her small, plump breasts bounced up and down while she ran alongside of him, how her long ponytail swung back and forth, filled him with unbridled lust. The one time they'd stopped—at the Roman ruins—they'd let their arms brush together. Neither pulled away. Just a light touch had flooded his insides with longing. She appeared to feel the same. She'd flushed to the roots of her hair. And after that, she'd touched him in some small way every chance she got. Each touch was electric, sizzling.

What he liked about her was her total lack of coyness or flirtatiousness. Meg was straightforward, without guile—she wasn't playing games. He could read the honesty in her face when she told him about her breakup with the ex-fiancé and her distrust of men and their empty promises and vows. All lies, she'd mused with just a hint of bitterness. She'd finally come to accept the reality of men.

Or some men, she'd amended, adding a quick apology, as if she had offended him. *No*, he'd said. *I agree with you. Most men lie through their teeth. It's a guy thing.*

That admission had elicited a small, rueful laugh from both of them. And she'd let her arm brush his again, as if to assure him. He was different, she was saying.

No, I'm not, he wanted to say.

I'm a liar, an impostor. And you're going to hate me when this is all over.

Another time, as they stopped at a Starbucks for coffee, they'd circled around the same theme.

"Why do people lie?" Meg asked.

"I suppose they lie when they want something and they know the truth isn't going to get it for them."

"Hmm. I think people need one person in this world they

can count on to always tell them the truth." She smiled. "Like my grandmother. She's brutally honest, always has been."

He said nothing for a long moment. "You're right about that. Finding that one person is . . . well, I sometimes wonder if it's possible."

The bald-faced truth, Jake now realized, even though he still puzzled over it. He was wildly drawn to Meghan Larsen, more so than he'd ever been to any woman before—so much, he almost couldn't believe it. Normally, as suspicious as he'd grown of women since his marriage to Barbara had crashed and burned four years before, he took a while to warm up to women, to trust them.

Now he felt as if he carried a bubble of air inside his chest. His nerve endings felt crackly with synaptic firings.

Rationally, there was nothing Jake could base this feeling on except her beauty, her pleasing personality, and his own instincts about her basic decency and integrity. More than that, he'd sensed in her a deep capacity to love. And a deep desire to *be* loved. Truly and honestly. Beyond that, he'd felt a deep kinship, an intense connection, a sense that he could trust her with his life. There was a basic decency there, a desire to help people and give purpose to her life. She didn't just want a man, she wanted a purposeful life. A meaningful life.

Jake could understand that. That was why he'd chosen law enforcement as a career. Why he was a patriot.

From their conversation, Meg was still a little gun-shy with men. This came after breaking off her engagement to a lying, cheating jerk the year before. As a result, she distrusted men, liars in particular.

Which, of course, didn't bode well for Jake. Deception, after all, was the basis of their budding friendship.

Which made him face the fact he'd have to give her up before he could have her.

The pain was sharp, like a dagger to the gut. Pangs of guilt stabbed through him. Remorse for having to deceive her. But what could he do? That was his job.

He switched off his circular thinking. No point to it, after all. What was the time difference between England and California? Seven hours? Eight?

His personal international four-band cell phone took but a moment before he heard the phone ring. Then a gruff male voice. Annoyed at the interruption.

"Pop, it's Jake. I'm calling from . . ." *Where the hell was he?* " . . .Bath, England."

"Bath? You're taking a bath?"

His father was hard-of-hearing. He took off his hearing aids late at night while reading in bed. A rustle over the line and then Jake tried again.

"Oh, Bath, as in England?" his father said, apparently after popping them in. "On assignment, you say? Wish the *machers* at the university would send me to Europe. I'm lucky to write off my annual American Chemical Society conference. So, Jacob, you called to *kvetch*?"

Jake's father was a Reform Jew but still liked to throw in some Yiddish every now and then. He'd observed once that America had diluted the Bernsteins' devotion to their religion, but he'd said this without rancor. He also said half-jokingly that God was a scientist. A generation later, Jake had come to regard himself and his father as secular humanists by temperament, Jews by heritage. Which suited him fine.

"Just called to shoot the breeze, Pop How's the family? Mom, David, Isaac? Oma?"

Within a minute, he'd gotten his father's thumbnail update. His mother had grown tired of portraits and was now doing seascapes. David was promoted to bank manager and his wife was expecting her second child any day now. Isaac was finishing law school and wanted Jake to come out to California for his graduation party. His grandmother, Grandpa

Nate's widow—whom they called Oma—was doing well after her cataract surgery.

Then he got down to the real point of his call.

"Pop, you said you fell in love with Mom at first sight, right?"

Jake knew his father would gleefully relate the familiar family story. He supposed hearing it again might confirm the possibility of such an unlikely miracle.

"True, Jacob. I was a T.A. for Chem 10. Bonehead chemistry for non-science majors, the bane of all graduate students. I was quizzing the prof's students for a midterm exam. Your mother sat in the front row. I knew her name but I had never spoken to her. Of course I wanted to. She dazzled me. Absolutely dazzled me. So I called on her, asked her what element B on the periodic table represented. Without blinking or hesitating, she said Bernsteinium. The class laughed. So did I. After class, I called her up to the front and asked her out. I was just the T.A. at the time, so it was allowed. Anyway, she said yes, and the rest, as they say, is history."

"So you believe in love at first sight? Or love right away?"

"Oh yes. You just know deep inside, this person is The One. This person is . . .good for you. Or right for you." A pause. "You meet someone, Jacob?"

"Yeah, but it's unbelievably complicated. If it goes the way I think . . .or hope it goes . . . things might work out. If it doesn't, well . . . she may end up despising me."

"As your Grandpa Nate would say, Yakov . . .*mitzvah*, be brave. Go after her. Love's not for the faint of heart. So *mazel tov*, son."

Jake smiled at hearing Grandpa Nate's German accent rendered so perfectly by his father. The dear old man came alive for a moment. After listening to more family gossip, he rang off.

When he checked his watch, it was thirty minutes before

the scheduled group tour breakfast. He took the printouts of the decrypted, declassified MI5 material that had been sent to Jake's FBI computer. Declassified didn't mean open to public scrutiny, of course, so Jake kept the files in a locked, hidden compartment of the aluminum suitcase he sometimes brought along on undercover assignments. He'd transferred the files, which he'd perused on his transatlantic flight, into the carry-on but locked them away once he'd landed at Heathrow.

For the moment he decided to forego a second reading of the transcripts of Mike McCoy's interviews and notes from the man's investigation of his cousin. He'd review them again once they arrived in Ireland, since that was where Mike McCoy's investigation had taken place. Everything might make more sense once he hit the ground himself. Sensing that one of the keys to unlocking the mystery of Mary McCoy Snider rested with Mary's life during the war, Jake decided to concentrate on the Brits' War Department files. How and where she lived, her professional life as an SIS translator-transcriber . . . which to Jake amounted to the same thing.

Fluent in German and Hebrew — thanks to Grandpa Nate's insistence on Hebrew school — Jake was often used as the Bureau's liaison to Mossad bureaucrats and agents-in-place. The State Department often assigned him in delicate dealings with Israel's Knesset. Sometimes he'd act as an oral translator, helping to facilitate high-level discussions or briefing sessions. Other times he'd be asked to translate classified documents in Hebrew from the Mossad. For him, translating documents was easier than on-the-spot oral translating, which required a native's up-to-date knowledge of idioms. Although he often read Israel's weekly news magazine, he'd have to spend a month in Israel every year to stay up-to-date on idioms and slang. Language was fluid, constantly changing. Still, by American standards, he was considered fluent.

Which was why if he ever heard Mary Snider speak German, he'd know right away by her accent and her use of idioms whether she was a native speaker or not. Whether she was current in the language or whether her knowledge of idioms and slang was dated — as in World War II dated. Getting her to speak German — how was he going to manage that?

It appeared, looking over the old SIS dossiers that had been scanned into MI5's databank, that their clerical support staff received periodic reviews and evaluations. Mary McCoy was no exception. Pulling out a personnel review dated July 15, 1942, Jake read closely. Evidently the staff was kept under spotty surveillance — randomly checked or followed, their patterns of behavior and transit dutifully recorded. Using a map of London, Jake could picture a very correct Englishman in a homburg and walking cane trailing a young, pretty Mary McCoy as she emerges from Churchill's subterranean offices near Clive Steps and crosses the street to St. James Park. Or maybe he'd follow her up Whitehall past Charing Cross to her ladies boarding house on Henrietta Street near Covent Garden. Then waiting around to witness and record any gentlemen friends who came to visit her in the evenings.

Yes, he could picture it all. Or the tail might've been a young chap in dungarees cycling behind her through St. James Park on her days off, duly noting any persons of interest Mary might have stopped to speak with. Surely the young Mary McCoy would've been forewarned to expect such scrutiny. That came with the job. If innocent of spying, she would've shrugged off such surveillance but would've been discreet in her associations with strangers. By training, however, a Nazi mole would've taken great care to avoid contact with known Nazi sympathizers. The Brits had complete records of this Fifth Column, as these quislings were called.

That didn't preclude that favorite tactic of all spies the world over — the dead drop. Wearing a certain colored scarf or hat through the park or into a certain pub on a prearranged day could've signaled that a dead drop was to be made at the signal site. A secret note or communication could be hidden in a discarded sandwich bag or fish 'n chips wrapper, thrown into a refuse container, to be fished out later. Even expert surveillance could reveal only so much. A cautious, clever spy would know when they were being followed. If the spy didn't have that sixth sense, that special instinct of caution and survival, he or she wouldn't last long.

The fact that these two women — Hummingbird and Black Widow — had never been caught testified to their extraordinary survival instincts.

These two women were master spies. And very, very lucky.

Like many Nazi spies, she — whoever Hummingbird or Black Widow were — may have had a wireless radio. According to this 1942 report, Mary McCoy and another SIS translator lived at the same boarding house on Henrietta Street. Mary lived on the top floor, the fourth, in a room by herself, the other woman on the same floor but in a room across the hall. Mary liked to play records in the evening and was partial to American jazz, swing, and big-band dance music. Jake knew that wireless radios during the Second World War had better reception closer to the rooftops.

German Heinkels — the Luftwaffe's heavy bombers — regularly flew overhead and were able to receive at certain secret military frequencies. According to Major Temple's files, radio operators in Hamburg had transceivers that were powerful enough to send and receive coded messages up to five hundred miles away. A prearranged day and time would have been set. Say, on Sunday evenings at nine PM. A spy couldn't risk detection, so she'd limit her radio time to five or ten minutes. Messages would be sent in code. The music she listened to in the evening would have masked the transmission sounds from her wireless radio.

The Brits, like the Germans, had radio intercept monitors that could detect enemy shortwave frequencies, so Hummingbird and Black Widow would have had to keep their coded transmissions very short and to the point. Staying on an enemy frequency longer than necessary was a surefire way to get caught, which meant a quick trip to the gallows. During wartime, justice was swift and cruel.

Jake looked up, his mind wandering. Imagine old lady Mary Snider swinging from a hangman's noose somewhere in a dungeon in today's London. No, impossible. Meg and her family would hire a slew of lawyers to keep that from happening. They'd fight extradition for years—the ensuing scandal no doubt harming American-Anglo relations in the process. No wonder MI5 and the FBI chose him, a stickler for thorough intel analysis. He wouldn't jump to conclusions right off the bat.

Helluva lot at stake here. That very fact sent a shiver down the back of Jake's skull. This assignment could be a career maker or breaker.

Jake sucked in a mouthful of air.

Back to the MI5 dossier. In all fairness, Mary McCoy was a prodigious reader and knitter, loaned out books to the other single women in the house and knit wool sweaters for everyone, including the boarding house's owner, a war widow. She had few close friends but was cordial with all the women in the house.

Jake made a small harrumph. Mary Snider, cordial? Well, why not? Sixty years could change a person's character and personality. Couldn't it?

On her free days, Mary liked to cycle through the various London parks and along the Strand, although St. James appeared to be her favorite park. She never once in her four years in London returned home to Killarney, Ireland. When asked why, Mary explained that her parents' death in April of 1940—a bizarre drowning on the lake in Killarney's Ross Park—was too recent—going home was too painful.

The boarding house owner, a Mrs. Watson, had confirmed Mary's quiet, respectful ways. The few gentlemen callers Mary received were entertained in the downstairs parlor. Entertaining in the girls' rooms was, of course, forbidden considering the era. There was one Scotsman, a Royal Air Force captain—a Captain Ferguson—who pursued her, took her out to dinner and dancing at the various clubs and ballrooms in the city. He was killed in '44 during a bombing run over Germany, a month after D-Day—the Allied invasion of Europe.

Mary McCoy's life in London during the war must've been a very lonely existence for a pretty young Irish girl, Jake imagined. He wondered how deep her relationship with this Captain Ferguson had been. There were few other men. Several young women in the house confirmed Mary's correspondence with the Killarney parish priest, Father Dillon, and a male cousin named Thomas McCoy. Or a man Mrs. Watson—who noted all the mail going out and coming in—assumed was her male cousin. They shared the same last name.

Jake paused. Thomas McCoy?

Not Mike McCoy, the old man who'd visited Mary Snider in her Dallas suburb home . . .when? Ten years ago, according to the first page of Mike McCoy's compilation of notes—an impressive eighty-four pages long. Tenacious old coot.

From the surveillance officer's five reports, dated 1940, 1941, 1942 and updated again in 1943 and then for the last time in 1944, those were the only two people Mary McCoy corresponded with during those war years. Father Dillon and Thomas McCoy. The letters from both men were postmarked from Ireland, began in mid-1940. Father Dillon's correspondence continued through the end of 1944.

Jake double-checked the date on the abrupt end of Thomas

McCoy's letters. One letter dated from Ireland in July, 1944. That was the last one.

Evidently Mrs. Watson had been asked to keep diligent track of Mary McCoy and the other SIS translator, and her notes were included in the dossier. This was a common practice in Great Britain at the time. Every British subject was asked to report any suspicious activity or any strangers in town to the local constable, whose duty it was to investigate. Many spies and Nazi sympathizers and "unfriendly aliens" were rooted out in that manner. A kind of nationwide Neighbors' Watch program. Highly successful, too, considering the large percentage of Third Reich spies found in the British Isles who were either turned into double agents or hanged.

So who was this Thomas McCoy? An asterisk added in pen by Major Temple, and explained in the footnote, confirmed that Mary McCoy had no cousin by that name. So could this man have been an acquaintance of Mary's from her school days, have the same last name but be no relation to her? That was possible, Jake thought. He wondered if Major Temple had checked out Mary McCoy's neighbors in Killarney or the roster of her school chums in both Killarney and Dublin.

Jake made a note on a separate yellow pad to ask Major Temple about this. It might be important that Mary didn't write to her cousin, Mike, but did write to Thomas, no relation to her. 'Course, Jake had a few cousins from his mother's side that he wouldn't correspond with, either. Not if his life depended on it.

The surveillance report was signed by the tracking officer and also by Mary's evaluator and supervisor at SIS/MI5, Herbert Arthur. In his views, her work habits were faultless—always punctual, modest, and discreet in her demeanor. Worked overtime without complaint, spoke and wrote flawless French. And although she spoke passable German with a heavy Irish-English accent, her transcription skills in German were better. Her knowledge of idiomatic German was rudimentary at best. That of a third or fourth year student of German. Which could only mean that Mary studied German while at Trinity College in Dublin.

Jake added that tidbit of information to his notes and underscored it. A Nazi mole would be fluent in German and have no accent if she were German-born herself. Of course, a mole might want to hide that fluency too. Part of her cover — the pretense of being an Irish girl with no previous visits to Germany? And just a book knowledge of the language?

His head began to swim. His stomach growled. Damn, he was hungry. Ten minutes to go before breakfast was served.

Back to the report. Mary McCoy was a fastidious worker. There was no hint of a security breach or even criticism of her linguistic skills, except that her German was limited. That didn't appear to be a problem or concern for her supervisor as other translators — English subjects who'd studied or worked in Germany for years — were available. Those staff translators in German had the task of monitoring German radio intercepts, writing them down in a kind of shorthand before transcribing them verbatim into English.

Elsewhere, such as Bletchley Park — the famous code-cracking campus in the countryside — code breakers applied their skills to the transcripts. Since German military ciphers were changed all the time, this presented an ongoing challenge.

Mary McCoy did the same — monitored radio intercepts — but only in French, and in this her work was considered remarkable. It sounded, if Jake was correct in reading between the lines, like Herbert Arthur was half in love with the young lovely Irish miss. Perhaps the married man's crush had colored his evaluation reports, even though the reports appeared thorough. Of course, Jake was trained to be skeptical of everything. Suspend belief until the evidence proved otherwise.

So far the evidence indicated no suspicious activity on

Mary McCoy's part. She did her job for the SIS well enough and led a quiet, discreet personal life while in London. Her social life consisted of dates with British airmen and the occasional American soldier. By January of 1945, she was exclusively dating Army Air Corps Lieutenant John Snider.

Jake's mantra was *follow the evidence.*

His discomfort suddenly spiked as his thoughts circled back upon themselves. Would someone later make the same observation about *his* investigation of Mary McCoy Snider? That his lust for her pretty granddaughter made him look the other way and ignore the plain facts of the case? The possibility made his stomach churn with bile.

That won't happen.

He checked his watch. Time for breakfast.

About time . . .

CHAPTER SEVEN

The hotel dining room, noisy with motorcoach travelers and other tourists, was warm with bodies and hot food. The party-size coffee urns beckoned him like an oasis in the desert. His stomach-grumblings slowly subsided as the aromas drifted over him. On his way to the coffee table, he nodded to the Canadian, Hank Philemon, once again sitting with the two sisters from New Jersey. The man had been vague about what he did — some kind of freelance writer for sports magazines. The sisters were both nurses on holiday. Swinging sisters. Bet Hank was having fun.

They motioned him over but he just smiled and continued on.

He poured himself a cup of black coffee, hoping all the while it was brewed thick and strong, the way he liked it. Yeah, good, it was. The rich aroma gave him a heady pleasure . . .

Out of the corner of his eye he saw Meg approach. Schooling himself to keep his cool around her, keep it friendly and keep his pulse rate under control, Jake turned to face her.

Her broad smile warmed his heart. Sent his pulse skipping.

"Good morning, Jake. Come and join us over there. We're sitting with the French-Canadian couple from Montreal." Her eyes sparkled, her dimples showed.

Boy, was she a charmer. She knew he was hooked, Jake mused. That should've worried him, but it didn't. To her, a beautiful young woman, he was just another male conquest. Another guy to add to her male fan club.

Which suited his cover just fine. That would explain why he was spending so much time with Mary Snider and her granddaughter. Nodding his assent, he followed her to their table set for five.

Meg was wearing her hair in a lengthy pony-tail, revealing a long, lean neck. He found himself staring at the back of her neck, the nape where a few short blonde tendrils curled. His stare continued downward, taking in her tight jeans and cropped sweater top. Her body was perfect, Jake decided. Curvy in the right places, lean in others. He had the crazy urge to wrap his arms around her waist—

His attention snapped to the friendly older couple who greeted him in French-accented English. Even Mary Snider smiled in greeting, although the smile never reached her eyes. Apparently finished with her breakfast, Meg moved over to make room for him. He set down his coffee, pulled up a chair next to Meg's, then went back to forage at the buffet tables.

Ten minutes later, Jake was halfway finished with his breakfast, a typically large English breakfast, enough to make your abs bulge. Blood sausage, bangers made from God-knew-what, scrambled eggs, poached tomatoes, fried potatoes, and damn . . . even pork 'n beans. Another day of this calorie-laden food and he'd have to add a couple of miles to his daily run.

He'd been idly listening to the French Canadians speaking rapid-fire French with Meg and her grandmother, noting Mary Snider's total lack of an accent. In fact, he'd swear her French pronunciation—though he didn't speak French, he'd heard the various accents all over France—was Parisian, with the clipped inflection and nasal tonality of the Parisians. Naturally, Meg the French teacher was fluent.

Strange, Jake thought, for Mary, a woman who supposedly had never been outside Ireland and Britain before the war. He caught himself. Her French teacher at the university in Dublin

might've been a Parisian. You tended to learn the pronunciation of your foreign language teacher, he knew. And, of
course, the older woman could've visited Paris after the war.
Even Meg spoke French without a trace of an English accent.
Of course she spoke it every day at the high school, but it was
apparent she'd spent some time in France. Probably with her
grandmother.

He washed down a forkful of eggs with a long sip of strong,
Italian roast coffee and sighed with pleasure.

"You and your grandmother speak French with no accent,"
he observed to Meg. "It's a remarkable gift, to have such an
ear for languages. I'm fluent, but I speak German and Hebrew
with a heavy American accent. As soon as I open my mouth,
they can tell I'm a Yank."

"Jake, we're mimics. Parrots, Grandma says, but with understanding. We can hear a foreign phrase spoken and repeat
it with perfect pitch and tone. That's why I became a foreign-
language teacher. I can teach my students as if I were a native-
born Spaniard or Frenchman. It's my only talent, I'm afraid,"
she added ruefully.

Jake doubted that but didn't say what immediately sprang
to mind.

"It sounds like you and your grandmother have been to
France."

Meg smiled. "Oh yes, many times. I'm sorry, it's rude to
leave you out of the conversation. Please, *pas de francais
maintenant.*" No more French.

She smiled a half-pleading, half-apologetic smile at the
French Canadian couple. When her dimples creased, who
could refuse her? Jake caught himself staring at her beauty.
The only makeup she wore was a little rose-red lipstick, and
maybe a smidgen of mascara. God was good to her—she
didn't need anything else to enhance her natural beauty.

"But of course," exclaimed the husband. "We apologize. It

is just so nice to hear our mother language. And Mary and Meg's French is *formidable.*"

Jake held up a hand, palm outward. "No need to apologize." He smiled at Meg in gratitude. Here was his opening—might as well blunder ahead.

"You're learning German, you told me. Does your grandmother speak German, too?"

"Yes, I heard her speak German when we were in France and met some German tourists. What about it, Grandma? How's your German?"

Mary Snider paused in mid-chew. She glanced over at him and then smiled at her granddaughter. The elderly woman drank from her glass of orange juice, all the while fixing Jake with a cool look.

"You're right, Meggie, we're forgetting our manners. Mr. Bernstein, you've met Pierre and Madeleine Le Blanc, haven't you?"

Jake noted that the elderly woman had completely ignored his question. He nodded at both French Canadians. The couple was oddly matched, he thought. She was tall, pretty, and dark-complected to his short, pale and homely baldness. Both looked to be in their sixties and appeared well-heeled by their clothes and jewelry. Pierre's Rolex watch sported three rows of multi-colored diamonds while Marguerite wore a sporty belted jacket of sable mink. Retired and rich. What a way to go.

"To answer your question, Mr. Bernstein, yes," Mary Snider offered proudly, "I speak German fluently—*Hochdeutsch*—the way it should be spoken. I was a French and German translator during the war."

Had Mary Snider just admitted that her German was fluent? Or was she exaggerating—preening and boasting—to impress the wealthy French-Canadian couple? Jake needed to test her.

"Oh, yes. You worked for British intelligence, right?" He switched immediately into the Bavarian German he'd learned initially from his grandfather, but for this occasion, haltingly and with a third grader's vocabulary. "Please, Frau Snider, ask our friends here to pardon us while we speak a little German. To give me practice. And give Meg, too, a chance to practice."

Mary Snider did so in French. When the couple nodded and Meg leaned his way, obviously captivated by the opportunity to speak her fledgling German, Jake continued.

"*Sehr gut*, I need the practice. Meg, jump in whenever you like." He looked over at Mary. "I speak a Münchener dialect, which my grandfather taught me. He often said we should never forget the country and heritage of our forefathers. That included the language as well. He was proud of being German-born."

Mary's chin lifted a little. "*Naturlich, Herr* Bernstein. We must always be proud of our heritage." Jake listened intently as the elderly woman expounded upon the merits of maintaining pride in one's country no matter what mistakes the government makes. The people continued on, and the struggle to keep one's country pure and homogenous must continue as well. It was a shame how England was losing the purity of its race, how diluted it was becoming with immigrants from all over the Third World . . .

Jake sat there, listening intently. Inside his heartbeat revved up. He could barely contain his excitement. He finally had something noteworthy to report to Major Temple.

For the next minute, Mary Snider spoke in unaccented, perfect German about a few topics, most of which sounded uncomfortably like the speaking points of a certain right-wing political group. She'd chosen her words carefully. They were highly educated terms for eugenics, racial purity, homogeneous populations, and economic protectionism. She definitely abhorred globalization. All of these no doubt meant to swamp Jake's comprehension level and leave him drowning linguistically.

Her accent, he noted also, was northern Germany but he couldn't place exactly where. Hamburg . . .Hannover . . . Maybe somewhere in Lower Saxony? Her accent was Niedersachsen, he thought, but he couldn't be sure.

When he had an opening, he spoke of the inevitability of globalization. Again he spoke with a child's language, hoping that his limited vocabulary would encourage her to let down her guard. His idea seemed to be working. Meanwhile his head was buzzing with the significance of what he was hearing — and he was barely through his second cup of coffee.

Jake was stunned. Mary Snider was either German-born or she'd learned fluent German from a northern German. What would've been her motive, then, for lying to the SIS? Pretending that her German was limited? Why, during wartime, did she pretend to speak passable German with a heavy English accent? What had she been afraid of? Afraid that no one would believe she could be so fluent, an Irish girl who'd never been to Germany?

Jake waited for a sign from Mary that conveyed something . . .some emotion. There was nothing, no effect at all. No passion. As if she were reciting from a right-wing propaganda handbook. Interrupting her grandmother, Meg spoke up in English. Apparently her grandmother's monologue had left her confused.

"I think I understood one-fourth of what you said, Grandma. You too, Jake. You're both too good for me to follow. And here I thought you were joking or exaggerating, Jake. Your German sounds great."

He basked for a moment under her warm, affectionate gaze. Her attraction to him seemed genuine. Again, unbidden, he visualized her lying next to him in his bed. Damn but she belonged there.

If only that were possible . . .

"I generally say what I mean, Meg. And mean what I say." Well, that wasn't entirely true—certainly not when he was undercover. Still, he smiled back at Meg, basking under her open look of admiration. He struggled to conceal his longing for her as a surge of sudden heat deepened within him. What this was he wasn't sure, but it was more than lust. With difficulty, he pried himself loose. Switched gears and looked at Mary Snider.

"Mrs. Snider, where did you learn to speak such fluent German?"

Mary hesitated but a brief moment. "In Dublin. I had an excellent German teacher."

"Grandma, didn't you have a German boyfriend in Dublin? A student who had to return to serve his country when the war with Germany broke out?"

"Yes," Mary said quietly. Jake thought he saw her wince slightly at the mention of this young man.

"You see, I told you, Jake." Meg smiled proudly. "Grandma and I are both parrots. Born mimics. You learned your German from your grandfather? The film editor?"

"Partly. I studied it in high school and college. Spent some time in Germany during my Navy days."

"Really?" Mary Snider queried, one whitish-blonde eyebrow cocked. "The U.S. Navy's in Germany? I'm not aware of any Navy bases there."

"Pentagon liaison work with Mannheim Air Force Base. Strictly administrative stuff. Nothing exciting, I'm afraid." Turning his full attention on Meg, he smiled. "So, Meg, anytime you care to practice with me. Y'know, use it or lose it."

"We'll speak German while we jog in the evening, okay? That'll be fun, Jake."

He nodded and returned Meg's stare. The sparks between

him and Meg got a rise out of her grandmother. Her face like a stone mask, Mary Snider let flow a stream of rapid German.

"My granddaughter is quite taken with you, young man, and her feelings are important to me. She must not be hurt again. You're too good-looking, too smooth, too glib. I think you have a wife and family in Virginia, and she is just . . .a plaything to you."

Jake coughed in surprise. "No, there's no wife," Jake said in German. "No kids. I'm divorced, been single for four years. I just want to be Meg's friend."

The elderly woman pondered his admission — a lie, actually, since he wanted so much more from the woman's granddaughter — while Meg looked as though she'd understood only a little of what he'd said. She was now blushing at her grandmother's effrontery. Being spoken about in your presence like a child was not very flattering.

"I don't want you to seduce her . . . or even try to," Mary Snider went on, her gaze on his face unswerving. "Your type will break her heart." She seized her butter knife with the point of the blade facing upward. "I will make you very sorry if you hurt her. If you try to intrude into our lives."

Jake was bowled over by the woman's hostility. "Frau Snider, are you threatening me? For making friends with your granddaughter?"

"*Jawohl, mein Herr.* Don't intrude, Herr Bernstein. Stay out of our lives. She's happy enough without you. I see to that."

A small gasp from Meg let him know that she'd understood some of the last exchange. Yet she was obviously confused by her grandmother's words. Easy to miss, for Mary Snider's tone hadn't betrayed her, her voice and expression remaining pleasant. They could've been discussing the variety of food on the buffet tables.

Though Jake's blood was turning cold, he kept a small, ironic smile in place, trained on the elderly woman. Mary

Snider was old, but she was cagey and gutsy. And her antenna was up. She didn't miss a thing. He noticed for the first time her hands, covered by dark blue leather gloves. Even while she ate. An odd affectation, he thought, even for an eccentric old bat.

"Well, Frau Snider, your warning is duly noted," he went on in German. "I understand your position. Now understand mine. I'm not a womanizer. I respect women. The failure of my marriage still weighs on me. Now I'm married to my work. I have no intention of seducing your granddaughter. Just want to hang out with her on this tour."

Mary's posture cracked. A nasty laugh broke through.

"You're a liar, *meine junge Herr*. You intend far more. I've known handsome men like you. They're selfish and they're trouble."

To that accusation Jake halted, their argument winding down to a stalemate. Mary Snider was right.

He *was* a liar. This whole situation was based on *his* deception. And yes, possibly Mary Snider's. True, men like Jake were selfish. His ex-wife had often told him so. He'd cared more about his work than he'd ever cared for her. That was the whole fucking truth in a relationship rife with deceit. Had she not tricked him — telling him she was pregnant and her Navy career was in jeopardy as a result — Jake would never have married her. Her supposed miscarriage was the catalyst to a marriage already doomed by mistrust.

Jake grabbed his cup and lurched to his feet. He excused himself and made a return visit to the coffee urn. Choked with guilt and anger because he'd allowed Mary Snider to get to him, he poured himself another cup while waiting for his heartbeat to slow, his hands shaking as he brought the cup to his mouth.

Dammit! He'd let the old lady rattle his cage.

Just then Robert Morse, the tour guide, appeared in the

doorway of the dining room. He looked unbearably frisky as he rubbed his hands together.

"Morning, all you chipper mates. Looks like you enjoyed your breakfast. No dodgy meals with Global Adventures, are there? Time to board the bus for a city tour of Bath. Hop to, hop to! Then off to South Wales we go after a marvelous lunch of shepherd's pie and a tad of ale! We're bloody excited now, are we not?"

Jake itched to say *Hell no, I want my friggin' coffee!*

People stirred, got up, and left. Jake made no move.

As he sipped from his third caffeine infusion, Meg sidled up to him. Embarrassed at the mix of emotions he was wrestling with, he kept his posture rigid and guarded.

"Whatever Grandma said, Jake, that upset you, I'm so sorry—" Meg broke off, seemingly at a loss. Jake said nothing. He couldn't look at her.

Mary was waiting by the doorway, leaning on the door-jamb for support. She looked very helpless at the moment. Meg sputtered in her frustration then left to join her grandmother. Jake made no attempt to stop her or call her back.

Yeah, he was trouble. Trouble for both women. If they only knew . . .

Finally the realization hit him . . .like a punch in the gut. Mary Snider had been testing him. Not only the extent of his German, but all her right-wing rhetoric and insolence was meant to drive him away. She knew he'd be offended by her personal assault on his character. But he was more upset at himself than the old witch.

Objectively the brief exchange he'd had with Mary Snider had been productive. He'd learned three things. First, Mary McCoy had lied to Churchill's War Office. She *was* fluent in German, spoke with a northern German accent in fact—as far as he could tell, anyway.

Unless she became fluent . . . after the war. Like during a

posting at one of the American air force bases in Europe. Where were the Sniders stationed after the war? Colonel John Snider retired from the U.S. Air Force in the late 1970's.

He'd make a call to Headquarters and find out.

Why Mary McCoy lied about her fluency in German back in 1940 — if she indeed was fluent then — he didn't know. Maybe a German boyfriend in Dublin whom she later learned was a spy and was just using her to gain secret information? Was she afraid of being accused of treason by her association with the guy?

Was her German boyfriend this Thomas McCoy who she corresponded with during the war until 1944? Was she spying for him?

Second, Mary Snider and her granddaughter were natural mimics. They had the talent for learning a foreign language in record time and speaking it without an accent. He'd known people like that, especially students at the Military Foreign Language Institute. A couple of Navy Seals and Army Rangers he knew were chosen for espionage training because of that very facility. So Mary's fluent, accentless German didn't necessarily mean anything.

Third, Mary Snider was exceptionally perceptive. Jake had to be extra cautious around her not to tip his hand. Or scare her into clamming up. The old lady had sharp instincts. Always on the alert for danger. Like a mother bear, always protective of her granddaughter.

She was also clever and cagey.

Not to mention, one cold, harsh bitch.

CHAPTER EIGHT

L unch with Harry Philemon and the two New Jersey sisters, Judy and Jeannie, passed uneventfully. Thank God, Jake mused. He needed a break from Mary Snider's dramatics and hostility even though he risked losing Meg's goodwill.

That thought made his chest tighten with pain.

Somehow Jake knew he had to win the old lady's trust to let him get close to them. Mary Snider was keeping him at bay in her attempts to protect her granddaughter. Maybe something else was going on — a kind of sixth sense or intuition that Jake wasn't who he said he was. That kind of intuition would have helped a Nazi mole survive in wartime London. Would have prevented her from letting down her guard and getting caught. Survival instincts had to be super keen. An intelligence operative's antenna.

Absolutely necessary for survival.

Jake's skepticism over Mary Snider's motives weighed on his mind all during their lunch of deep fried cod, French fries, and salad — or fish 'n chips. His gut was telling him one thing, his mind another.

Bantering with Harry and flirting with the girls lightened his mood a little, helped him forget why he was really there. Comparing the Roman ruins in Bath to Roman ruins elsewhere in Europe occupied the four of them, like a game of Jeopardy. The sisters wondered if the gay baths in San Francisco were anything like the ones in ancient Rome — places for men to meet and engage in sex.

He did his best to ignore Meg and her grandmother,

although he did note who their table companions were—the wealthy French-Canadian couple again. He did his best to ignore the hollow ache in the middle of his solar plexus as well.

After lunch he made a call to Headquarters in D.C. and asked for Colonel John Snider's stationings from 1945 to the time of his military retirement. The analyst in the office next door, his longtime pal Len, said he'd have the info in two hours and to expect a call back. No need to encrypt, as the information wasn't classified.

Four hours later, after crossing the River Severn and arriving in the Welsh capital of Cardiff, they endured another forgettable, high caloric meal at their hotel, the ultramodern St. David's Hotel. By then Jake was ready to bolt. He declined the two sisters' invitation to join them and Harry for drinks in the hotel bar lounge and went up to his room to change clothes. A good run was what he needed, despite the overcast sky and dark rainclouds sweeping in from the Irish Sea nearby.

He played back Len's call. Colonel John Snider had spent his military career as a logistics and air materiel manager. His postings included Kadena Air Base, Okinawa, and other bases in the Philippines, Taiwan, South Korea, California, Alaska, and other states west of the Mississippi. He finished as Commander of McClellan, the Sacramento Air Materiel base, home of the F-series of fighter jets. He never returned to Europe after WWII.

Which meant that the colonel's wife, Mary McCoy Snider, could only have mastered accentless German if she'd taken frequent trips abroad to Germany. Or if she had studied German in a special immersion program. He'd have to find out. Eliminate all logical possibilities before drawing a conclusion.

As he slipped a sweatshirt over his tee and shook off his tan Dockers, a knock sounded at his door. He strode over to it, clad only in black briefs, navy sweatshirt, and athletic socks. Opened it a crack.

Meg. His heart did a somersault. Ready for a run in a tank top, running shorts, and sneakers. And wearing a wry smile.

"Mind? Or do you hate me, too?"

Her hopeful manner melted the icy pain he'd harbored all day. He opened the door wide and let her in. A perverse need to show her a little of his body—or just plain male arrogance—drove him. He stood before her in little more than his skivvies.

Like *look what you can have if you ignore your granny's paranoia.* Which—come to think of it—Meg was doing.

"Come in, I was just changing to go running." He ignored her wide-eyed stare at his bare legs . . .and clingy cotton, ass-molding underwear. "I don't hate you, Meg, or your grandmother. She makes me angry, but I can deal with that. She's old . . ." Stumped for words, he ended up simply shrugging. The diplomatic way out.

Facing her, he shrugged on his dark navy-blue sweatpants, did the waist tie. Then went to get his Nikes. Meg was watching intently. If he was not mistaken, almost hungrily.

Damn, her look made his cock harden.

"Not to excuse her, but she's taken care of me since I was a baby. She's been more of a mother to me than my own—anyway, it's not your problem, her overprotectiveness. Whatever she said to offend you, I apologize on her behalf. Truly."

Her words worked its magic on him and melted the rest of his resolve away. He approached her, stood close, daring her to move away. She didn't.

"I don't blame you for your grandmother's . . .well, crotchety behavior. I couldn't. In fact, I'm struggling to keep from liking you too much."

One of her graceful hands raised and settled on his arm. Her face angled downward, she looked at him from beneath black lashes, her dark blue eyes enthralling him.

"I'm struggling, too. Is that a bad thing?"

He grinned like a schoolboy. "Well, for one thing, you live over a thousand miles from D.C. You've probably got a dozen guys hovering around you. Your grandmother hates me. Let's see, what else?"

"Certainly not a dozen," she teased. "I *do* like you, Jake, even if Grandma doesn't. I'm not my grandmother, y'know. Maybe I see in you something she can't see." Her face lifted and her gaze met his. "I'm glad we're spending time to-gether . . .alone. Away from the others."

He wondered if he should kiss her then and there. They stared at each other. If he kissed her, would he be able to stop? Would he be able to shove out of his mind what his real pur-pose there was? Her beautiful eyes seemed to question him.

Then the moment passed and Meg stepped back. She stared at the Navy insignia on one hip of his sweatpants and the big white letters that ran down one leg.

"You said you were in the Navy."

"Yeah. Served six years after UCLA. I was a Navy Seal for four of those years, then di . . .uh, administrative work."

"Why did you leave the Seals, Jake?"

"One of the ops we did in the Middle East. I can't tell you any more than that. It's still classified." Would he ever tell an-yone other than his Navy pals how badly that operation was botched? He doubted it. That was a black ops, in part success-ful—that's how it was written up for the top brass. He knew better, but he'd stuck to the Seals' code of silence. People were killed. Good men who shouldn't have been, cut down in the prime of their lives. Who had walked into a trap, Jake felt. Bad intel and a poorly conceived op, one that had no hope of suc-cess. He left the Seals right after that, disillusioned to his very bone marrow.

"Grandma said you're divorced." Her attempt to sound in-different fell flat. She sounded embarrassed, as though she shouldn't be interested but couldn't help herself.

He stood up and pocketed his room card-key.

"We were both Navy officers. When I decided to return to civilian life, we both agreed to call it quits. I moved to Virginia, found my current job. End of story. No children, no pets, no alimony. As I told Granny, I'm married to my work." He closed the door behind them. "Don't currently have a girlfriend, don't smoke. I drink socially. My only hobby is working out at the gym. Oh yeah, and reading. And I do all the maintenance on my townhouse in Alexandria. Dull life, dull guy."

At least, that much was truthful. Meg smiled and swung her long, blonde ponytail as she spun around in the hallway.

"Oh, I think you're anything but dull, Jake Bernstein. By the way, did you ever meet my uncle, John Snider, Jr. while you were in the Navy? He's up for promotion to Commander of the aircraft carrier the USS Constellation. Stationed in San Diego."

Jake stopped in the hallway. Of course. He hadn't made the connection before. That was why this assignment was given top priority, rushed up the chain of command at FBI Headquarters. Top Navy brass were behind this discreet investigation. The Navy didn't want the potential media scandal, so they made sure MI5 and the FBI chose an ex-Navy man with military intelligence experience. Maybe someone who'd go out of his way to clear MI5's main suspect.

Mary Snider.

A vice admiral in command of one of the Navy's newest carriers, the one-hundred-thousand-ton Constellation—with a fugitive Nazi spy for a mother? John Snider, Jr.—jeez, why hadn't he connected the dots?

Why didn't his supervisor tell him? Was he testing Jake's impartiality? Naturally an ex-Navy man might want to side in favor of a vice admiral's mother. Or was Jake meant to keep MI5 honest?

"Is something wrong? Did you forget something?"

He shook his head and turned on his charm.

"Thought I did, but no." One of his big hands automatically slid up her arm and gave her shoulder a light squeeze. "No, never met your uncle, but heard of him. Vice Admiral Snider? Impressive record. A good man, from what I hear. You up for a jog to Cardiff Castle? Maybe the bay?"

His groin clenched when Meg patted his chest with both hands, letting them linger there for a moment.

"Sure, let's go. You lead the way. I kinda half-dozed on the way in, missed Robert's lecture. I don't know anything about the area except that we're in South Wales. And this is the capital. And their flag is strange. A red dragon on a white-and-green field. What's with that?"

"You're right there, damn strange. Robert said it had to do with their Celtic history. The ancient Celts believed in the power and magic of dragons. Have to find a book about that." She removed her hands.

"Don't worry, Meg, I'll slow my pace down. I want you next to me, so we can talk." That produced an even bigger smile out of her.

A disquieting feeling twisted his guts.

Damn. He liked this girl too much. Maybe he was half-falling for her. A stupid thing to do, he rationalized. Even though getting close to her and the old lady was his job, getting involved emotionally wasn't. But there wasn't a damn thing he could do about it.

He suspected he'd already lost that fight.

CHAPTER NINE

A run down through the town to Cardiff Bay and its long dock took a half hour. Then back up Westgate Street past the Millennium Stadium to Castle Street — another half hour. They slowed down to an easy, measured jog the last half-mile as they pulled up to the entrance of Cardiff Castle. The two thousand year-old Roman site held a renovated castle bearing medieval, Norman, and Tudor architectural features. This was part of the town's ancient, proud heritage.

They caught their breaths while Jake paid their entrance fee. His chest expanded with pleasure at the sight of Meg's flushed cheeks and happy smile. He wished they were traveling by themselves, without a care in the world. Just two lovers enjoying the sightseeing and each other.

Meg was wearing a thong, the outline of which he'd already noticed and approved. Beyond that, he'd observed her more relaxed state. She seemed confident of their mutual attraction, and that it was as much returned as given. He'd done the right thing by admitting to her how much he liked her, as she was feeling the same toward him and now she didn't have to hide it. Despite his misgivings about the intensity of his feelings, Jake also felt . . .well, happy. Like something good and warm was growing deep inside him. A great feeling. The kind of joy he only felt around his family in Southern California. Like going home and finding yourself surprised but pleased to know how much you belonged there.

Still, his mind was on duty and there were pertinent questions he needed answered.

"When we—your grandmother and I—were speaking in German, you seemed to understand a lot. That's amazing after only a year of studying, Meg. You do pick up languages fast."

"Six months of German, actually." Five miles already covered in their run, they were both still panting a little.

"Amazing, this talent of yours. You must be a terrific teacher. How do you cope with all that teenage angst?"

She laughed. "Sometimes they make me feel old, they're so bustling with energy and hormones. Not that my hormones are dead or anything . . ." Meg grinned at her own gaffe. "Anyway, at times I feel almost their contemporary. I love teenage humor. It's always so full of hyperbole. Like, *I'm going to simply die if he doesn't call me!*" She looked at him squarely. "Your cheeks are so rosy, are you blushing?"

Jake felt the side of his face with the back of his hand. "No, just the Scots blood—my mother's side. She's a MacDonald."

"So the Bernstein men marry outside the Jewish faith?"

He smiled. "Any woman they happen to fall in love with, yes. We're secular. And strong-minded in our choices. My brother David has a *shiksa* wife."

"*Shiksa?*"

"Non-Jewish girl. So how is your grandmother so fluent in German? Has she ever lived in Germany?"

"No, not that I know of. We've been to Europe several times, but mostly to France, Spain, and Italy."

"Did you know she speaks German with a northern German accent?" Jake gazed at the Norman keep with its crenellated ramparts and pointed. "Want to climb up and see the view?"

Her frown morphed quickly into a smile. "If you can, so can I." He took her hand and led her across the grassy courtyard to the medieval tower. "I think Gran might've learned it from her German boyfriend. In Dublin before the war broke out. She never said where he came from, just that he was German. Maybe he was from northern Germany. I told you we're mimics."

Jake nodded then turned his attention to the stone steps. They climbed the spiral staircase to the top of the open-aired tower and gazed out at the view of the city. Jake pointed out the distinctive roofline of their modern hotel, the lines of the massive Cardiff Bridge, and the barges along the Taff River. Meg was breathing softly, her mouth parted. She tried to tell him with gestures that she was worn out. After the climb up the keep steps she hit the wall. Jake waited patiently and scanned the sky. He clasped her bare shoulder and rubbed her cold skin.

"It's getting dark. Rain clouds coming in, too. Maybe we should head back. First let's walk a bit around the castle, give you a chance to catch your second wind."

Meg gasped, "Yes," and nodded. "Let's check out the dungeon."

A group of tourists were leaving the dungeon, headed toward the gift shop. Jake breathed with relief. He wanted to be alone with her. When he took her hand for the descent, he felt like they'd been dating for months — his comfort level was so high with this woman. The relaxed bonhomie was mutual, if he read her expression correctly.

Still, questions nagged him.

"So your grandmother's never been to Germany?"

"Not that I know of. Why do you ask, Jake?"

"No big deal. I was just curious. So they raised you and your brother — the Sniders? What happened to your parents?"

A cloud passed over Meg's lovely face. "My father and Jack's father were no longer married to Mom, who was traveling around the country with her fourth husband by then. Jack and I are half-siblings, you see. My father dropped out of the picture when he remarried and started a new family.

Jack's father stayed in touch, thank goodness for Jack. Anyway, by husband number four, my mother was in her own Return-to-the-Earth world and lived on a commune that really was a cult. They grew marijuana. The cult leader was a scary guy, so Grandma and Grandpa Snider got custody of us and disowned hippie Mom."

She sounded a little bitter, but when she looked over at him, a genuine smile lit her face. "I bet you've had a more traditional family upbringing."

"Oh yeah. Grandparents lived nearby. Grandpa Nate had college funds set up for us—my two brothers and me—by the time we were five years old. When Grandpa died, Oma moved in to help my mother and because she was lonely. Gives Mom more time to paint and teach art classes."

"I envy you, Jake. That kind of close family sounds wonderful. If it weren't for Grandma and Grandpa Snider, I don't know what would have happened to Jack and me. We would have ended up in foster care. Or we would have been at the mercy of that crazy, hippie-cult leader." Meg sighed and shrugged. "Grandma and Grandpa Snider gave us opportunities, stability, affection—all the things kids need to grow and succeed."

She looked up at the sky then suddenly whipped her head around. Jake was intrigued with the way her long ponytail swung around to come to a rest on her shoulder.

"I just remembered something Grandma told me. About how she learned German."

"Oh?" He tried to appear indifferent, and he hated to trick her, but Meg's information was key.

"This German boyfriend in Dublin while she was at Trinity College. A foreign student, I think. He taught her German and she helped him in English. I think his name was Helmut . . .or Heinrich. Or Horst. Something like that. Her first big love. Sounded like they were very serious."

"What happened to him when the war started?"

"She said he went home. Said he had to leave. She guessed he joined the military. What's it called in German?"

"*Die Abwehr*. Also, *die Wehrmacht*."

"Yes, *Abwehr*. *Wehrmacht*. Anyway, she never heard from him again. She thinks he was killed in the war."

Jake wondered if this Helmut or Heinrich or Horst might've remained in England, gone underground. Or gone home and come back as a spy himself.

An idea struck him.

Could this Thomas McCoy, who corresponded with the young, single Mary McCoy while she worked for the War Office, actually have been her German lover? Did he encourage her to apply for the job, knowing her level of French and German made her employable? Or maybe he blackmailed Mary into helping him. Would she have passed on vital information to the enemy? In this case, a German spy who she once loved as a university student?

Was all this just nonsense? His theory sounded farfetched but hell, anything was possible. Especially if Mary McCoy Snider sympathized with the man's politics but worked for the War Office. Churchill's England had plenty of Nazi sympathizers to deal with from within Great Britain. Ireland was a neutral country during the war and a lot of Irish hated the English. But a lot of Irish joined the Allied war effort, too.

If Mary McCoy aided a Nazi spy during the war, any way you cut it, that would still be treason.

Minutes passed and Jake said nothing. Their hands still clasped, they took the stone steps down to the windowless dungeon. Though dark, dreary, and rat-infested hundreds of years ago, it was now well enough lit for safety but dim enough to maintain the mood of malevolence and horror.

Cold and damp, too. Meg began to shiver in her tank top

and shorts. While they studied the recreated torture chamber, with its rack, iron maiden, and manacles attached to walls and floor, Jake whipped off his sweatshirt. She protested but he insisted. She leaned into him as he helped her shrug it on. When his hand accidentally brushed her breast, his groin tightened in automatic response. His head fogged up with lust and longing.

Silently, they took in the torture apparatuses, each one more gruesome than its neighbor. The iron maiden, especially, its sharp spikes aimed inward to tear the flesh of any hapless soul forced to stand inside.

"You're very quiet," she said. The sky had darkened from overcast light gray to ink-blue. No moon or stars were visible in the cloudy sky, casting the dungeon into more gloom despite the electric lights. Definitely moody. Like an Edgar Allan Poe story.

"Terrible to think how cruel man can be to his fellow man," he remarked, his hands on her shoulder. He went to stand close behind her to soak up her warmth, to ward off the deepening cold outside. She moved back into him, letting her rump touch his groin. In spite of his best self-control, his crotch sprang stubbornly to life again.

"You should know from your Navy Seal experience."

"Yeah." He dropped his jaw to the crown of her head, let it rest there. "Saw first-hand a lot of shit. There's no animal on earth as cruel or cunning as man. It makes you wonder . . ."

"Wonder what, Jake?" She let her head roll back onto his chest. Instinctively his arms encircled her waist. Her hands rested comfortably on his arms. Long nails trailed along his forearms—his hair arm bristled and his skin prickled. Desire electrified his nerve endings.

"Sometimes I wonder if there's any good in the world. Grandpa Nate used to say after a few glasses of schnapps that mankind would one day get his just desserts. It used to make us sad to hear him talk like that. Then he'd look at us and his whole expression would change. Like he was reminding himself how lucky he was, how things had turned out for him and Oma. I think he had a lot of survivor guilt . . ."

Jake felt something inside him break, his eyes fill up with unshed tears, a sorrow he'd never shared with anyone, not even his brothers. He grew still. Strange he'd never told anyone about his grandfather's demons and how they'd affected him.

Some surface control broke between them. In one fluid and sudden motion, they were facing each other, clinging to each other, crushing each other's mouths open, their tongues hotly searching. Passion erupted like a geyser, flowing through him, igniting his loins. His senses tunneled as the blood roared through his head, coursed up and down the length of his overheated body.

Meg moaned his name. Her name caught in the back of his throat and came out as a hushed groan. He reveled in the feel of her . . . the plump breasts, the flat stomach, and sinewy thighs. The whole length of her fired up his imagination. What he could do with such a body, such a woman—

Then voices intruded. Visitors wending their way down the stone steps to the dungeon. They were no longer alone.

They pulled apart, initial embarrassment dissolving into awkward humor as Meg covered her mouth and smiled and then grabbed his hand and pulled him to the steps. Outside, they threw furtive glances at each other, grinning like teenagers caught breaking curfew.

"Not a good place to make love was it?" he joked.

Nothing more was said, but a line had been crossed and they both knew it. There was no going back, Jake realized. He was too far gone.

They held hands in companionable silence as they walked back across town in the direction of their hotel. Jake wondered if she'd come back to his room so they could finish what they'd started. From the look on Meg's face, she appeared to be contemplating the same thing.

His heart felt like a helium balloon about to take off. Why then was there a queasiness settling heavy in his stomach? He knew why.

He was about to cross a line he shouldn't.

CHAPTER TEN

"Meg, do you cook? Grandpa Nate used to say that's the first question I should ask any woman I meet and like." Jake shot her a mischievous smile.

Surprised by his question, Meg temporized. They'd known each other a mere four days and she was drawn to him like no other man she'd ever met. Nothing he said could ever bother her. Surprise her, yeah.

They were strolling, hands locked securely together, passing blocks of specialty stores, pubs, and restaurants, reluctant to end their time together. Meg had to smile in return. Why would he ask such a domestic question unless passing aromas made him think of food?

"A practical man, your grandfather. Funny you ask. It's my hobby, in a way. After my breakup, I moved back in with Grandma—I know how that looks but she has an enormous home and a beautifully stocked kitchen. I get to try out my recipes on a very appreciative fan and Grandma has me to look after her. We were both lonely, too . . .so it works out well for us."

"Ah, the perfect woman—she can cook!" He gave a short laugh. "Hey, I'd like to be one of your culinary guinea pigs . . .uh, you know what I mean."

She punched his arm playfully.

"Ow. I can't tell you how sick and tired I am of my grocery store's deli. Peas and bacon, potato salad and meatloaf are their standbys. Or macaroni salad and roast chicken."

"What about restaurants?"

"We have some of the best in the D.C. area. I eat out with my friend Eric once or twice a week. Or a couple of pals from work. Like me, they don't like to eat alone. The guys, we shoot the bull about our jobs, sports, cars. With women, you have to be on your guard, talk about what they want to talk about, pretend to be interested. Guess I just haven't found many women I'd rather eat with and talk to . . ." He looked at her. "Wish you lived in Alexandria."

"Wish you lived in Dallas," she countered, feeling him squeeze her hand. "I'm very selective, y'know. I don't feed just anyone. But you, I'd have you over a lot . . .to test my new recipes on." They smiled at each other, both knowing she wasn't just referring to culinary delights.

Jake pointed to the nearest pub, all alight and welcoming with noise and people. "Care for a nightcap away from the prying eyes at our hotel?"

"Oh yes." Avoiding their hotel bar, where several members of their motorcoach group were holding court, met with her hardy approval. For her part, she was happy to have him all to herself for another hour or two, away from the fun-loving but raucous New Jersey sisters. Who obviously adored him to High Heaven. It was time to learn a good deal more about Jake Bernstein.

And so she did over the next hour. Over two pints of draft Guinness, they shared biographical facts, exchanged anecdotes about their best pals, places they'd visited, places to avoid. Two topics they steered clear of in detail were his failed marriage — or, as he called it, his failure to make the right choice — and her failed engagement.

"I think luck plays some role in making good choices, don't you think, Jake? Finding the right person at the right time."

He downed the last of his beer. "Or maybe finding the right person but at the wrong time can still work out."

They were sitting side by side in a padded booth, their

91

upper arms and thighs occasionally brushing. Every casual touch sent hot currents through her. The pleasure was so intense, she let it happen often. She could imagine what lying next to him, or on top of him, completely naked would be like. That was going to happen someday, she'd decided, but now was too soon.

"If it's the right person, how can it be the wrong time?" she asked. Jake was six years her senior. Maybe he had more insight into relationships than she had.

He shrugged. "Oh, maybe there are complications beyond their control."

"Like being involved with someone else. Is that what you are, Jake? Are you involved with someone else? If you are, you must tell me . . .now."

"No, I'm not. I swear " —he held up the gold Star of David he wore around his neck—"on the faith of my fathers and all the way back to Abraham."

Although he smiled, she knew he was serious. She sensed his faith wasn't something he'd joke about.

Meg smiled with relief. "You had me scared. I'm so hoping you're not like the other men I've known."

"Timing, Meg, is important. I was too young at twenty-four. Wasn't ready for marriage, for that kind of commitment. Couldn't even commit to the Navy more than six years. It took me until now at thirty-two to figure out what I wanted with the rest of my life."

The waitress appeared. When Jake raised his glass and shot her a questioning look, followed by her nod, he ordered two more of the same.

"What *do* you want, Jake?" she asked him.

His dark eyes slid away and he seemed to tense up a bit. Maybe she was probing too much and overstepping her boundaries. Like most people, Jake appeared to relish his privacy. Tonight, though, was different. He was opening up to her. Mostly, he was serious, thoughtful, and considerate. Underneath, she detected a warm sense of humor and playfulness that he was keeping in check. With her, anyway, not with the New Jersey sisters. Why, Meg had no idea. Maybe he was worried they'd carry things too far too quickly.

Meg felt no urge to hold back. If he didn't like her personality or character, too bad. A bitter lesson she'd learned over the years. Her looks always attracted men, but she'd learned to never pretend to be something she wasn't. She'd never walk on eggshells around any man. Her motto was *Never hide your true self, like it or not.* Or, as Shakespeare put it, *To thine own self be true.* No matter what.

She nudged his arm. "C'mon, 'fess up. What *do* you want?"

Jake repeated her frank question then gave a short laugh, his eyes glinting over her playfully.

"From you? From myself? From life? Ah, Meg me darlin', you don't beat around the bush, do you?"

She joined him with a soft giggle at his attempts to sound Irish and waited for his reply as the pub's waitress returned with another round of Guinness.

"Well, to try and answer your question. Sure, I want to be proud of my work . . .humble though it is . . ." His eyes averted from hers, then returned to her face. " . . .and I'm ready to make a good choice this time. Fall in love, get married, have a family. Have a grand adventure with someone special. Isn't that what life is all about, having a grand adventure with people you love and who love you?"

Meg held up her glass and clicked it against his. "Here's to good choices, then. And grand adventures." A wicked little urge overcame her and she decided to have some fun with him. Jake was so serious right now and her heart was fluttering too wildly. Time to poke him a little, test him.

"Y'know, Jake, Grandma told me I should sample you but not buy the whole box. She says you're eye candy. What d'ya think?"

Startled, he sat back and straightened in his seat. He blinked a couple of times. For the first time in the four days she'd known him, he sputtered and appeared tongue-tied. Nearly dropped his glass, which he set down carefully on the table. Slowly a troubled frown formed on his handsome face. His cheeks flushed red.

"Your grandmother said that?"

"Yes, she called you eye candy. I think she was something of a femme fatale in her younger days. From what she's said, and Grandpa, too. She had lots of beaus, as she called them. So, what d'ya think? Should I use you for sex then dump you when I'm done with you?"

He gave out a short, cynical snort. "The first part, yeah. Not the second part. That hurts."

"Why not? Don't men do that to women all the time?"

He appeared to consider that for a moment, then frowned and took a long draw from his beer. By now, Meg was feeling no pain. Her natural inhibitions gone, she was enjoying this little game. She glanced up to find Jake's dark green eyes drilling into her.

"Is this revenge for what that slimeball, your ex, did to you? If so, leave me out—" He must've detected the slight twitch of her mouth, for he did a sudden about-face. "Okay, well, on second thought, use me, abuse me. By the end of these two weeks, you'll be begging for more. I guarantee it."

They both broke out in chuckles at the same exact moment then sat back, bumped each other's shoulders, and let the laughter roll out. Finally, her head swimming, Meg held up her glass for another toast. Had to strain to focus her eyes on the glass to keep from spilling it.

"Here's to good ol' Texas leg-pulling."

"You little witch! You really had me going there—" His big hand disappeared under the table and rested on her upper thigh. Then his big fingers curled under the cuff of her shorts till they grazed the silky edge of her thong. She held her breath. "I like your idea. Use me all you want."

His touch inflamed her cheeks. She had to resist the urge to fan her face. Or grab his muscular thigh . . .and maybe the nice package tucked between his legs. Her heart was pounding. Her pulse throbbed in her throat.

Good God, they were moving too fast. What about her vows of two days ago? Shot to hell, that was what. No, maybe not fast enough. Oh hell, she hoped they could wait . . .get to know each other a little more before . . . .She suddenly realized what was happening. A seed had been planted and had already sprouted. Something was taking root in her heart . . . and she intuitively sensed the same was happening to him.

But lord, if she was wrong again . . .what a fool she'd be . . .

He was watching her, her inner struggle no doubt visible on her face. Suddenly a woman's scream pierced the air. Jake's head whipped around. His hand was gone in a flash.

At a table in the far corner of the pub, a man dressed in a black hoodie and blue jeans lurched over the table's occupants. Pulled back, lurched again and again. Shouting ensued. The woman at the table screamed again.

Mesmerized, Jake was already on his feet.

"Stay here, Meg. He's got a knife."

"What?"

As the yelling escalated between the couple at the table and the man in the hood, their side of the pub grew tensely silent. Fear froze the other patrons, as if they didn't know what to do—intervene or not.

Jake reached the bar. He slipped past men on their stools who were bending back to watch the altercation. But this was more than that, Meg realized. This was an attack. The guy in the black hood slashed out with his right arm, connected with the man at the table. Another scream. More shouting. The bartender appeared to be paralyzed for a second. Then he sprang to the wall phone and placed a call.

Another slash. Blood spurted. The woman was on the floor, her companion tussling with the man in the hoodie on top of the table, trying to defend himself. Other women began to scream. The tables near the attack cleared out fast. One overturned and crashed to the floor.

Meg rose to her feet. She watched Jake skirt the bar and the booths flanking the opposite wall. Her hand rose to her mouth. She stifled a scream as she tried to cry out after Jake. Instead, her shock produced a whispered cry "My God, Jake!"

What happened next left her stunned.

Jake sprinted across the remaining distance. He grabbed the attacker's right arm and wrested it behind the man's back, all in one fluid motion. Seconds later, he'd brought the man to the floor. He heeled the man's hand with one big sneaker, meanwhile digging his left knee into the small of the guy's back. His muscular arms held the assailant's neck in a two-armed headlock. Abruptly he let go to flatten the man's head on the wooden floor, pinning him. Only when the attacker dropped the knife and someone kicked it away did Jake relinquish the guy's hand and drop his second knee to the guy's back.

"Get a rope or something!" Jake commanded the bartender, who'd just hung up the phone. "Something to tie up this punk. Also a towel for this guy's arm!" He indicated the man at the table, whose girlfriend was now at his side, trying to tend to him.

The bartender sprang into action, aided by another man. Like the other customers in the pub, once the danger had passed, Meg clustered around the scene. Jake still straddled the attacker like a pro wrestler over his defeated opponent. A man handed him a length of cord. Jake wound that around the attacker's wrists in a complicated figure-eight then secured it with a bowline knot. Meg recognized that because her Uncle John had taught her and Jack various kinds of nautical knots.

Only once did Jake look up and acknowledge her presence. Sweat dripped from his face and neck. His dark brown hair was shiny and plastered to his forehead and temples. With one hand, he raked fingers through his hair from forehead to crown, then stood. Jake looked calm and composed. He wasn't even breathing heavily. Strange. As if his exertion had been all physical, not mental at all. Meg felt herself exhale a deep breath once Jake seemed out of danger.

"Jake, are you all right?" Meg managed to gasp out.

"Fine. I'm fine, Meg." He smiled at her, then inched backward from the center of the crowd.

The onlookers moved back while a few men came forward to help calm the couple and wrap the man's arm. His arm bled profusely from two gashes. People stared at both the bloodied victim and the attacker. Although bound, he still thrashed his legs.

"Bloody hell!" The victim with the slashed arm exclaimed before he fainted and dropped to the floor. The girl beside him was still shrieking and weeping. She dropped to the floor too and continued to weep over the unconscious man. Jake issued orders to two men standing close by. One began to wrap the unconscious man's arm, stanching the blood. The other one helped the woman up. Jake yelled at the bartender to call the medics.

He's so cool-headed, Meg thought, her heart tripping wildly. Must be his Seal training. He was commanding the entire situation.

The attacker continued to thrash about until Jake stepped back and applied a big sneaker to the nape of the man's neck. He bent down and muttered something Meg couldn't hear. Eventually the attacker's half-crazed tirade subsided into low, guttural growls. Three other men came forward and helped to contain the attacker by sitting on him.

"Druggie, angry at his ex-girlfriend's new guy," Jake explained matter-of-factly to the bartender, who'd finally come over to assist.

"Coppers are on their way," the bartender assured the crowd. "Medics, too, miss." The girlfriend looked up, her weeping quieting a little. She attempted a small smile, then murmured, "Thank you" to Jake.

Jake just nodded. As though he disarmed crazed, knife-wielding dope fiends every day of his life. While on his lunch break. With one arm tied behind his back.

Realization fully registered on Meg. Although wet with perspiration, Jake was as calm as if he'd just finished a workout at the gym. No big deal . . .

"The constable's coming," the bartender said. "Thanks, mate. You American?"

"Yeah." Jake withdrew his foot from the attacker's neck. "Look, we're taking off. You don't need me to give an eyewitness report. The dozen witnesses here'll substantiate your story."

The bartender looked dubious. "The constable—he'll want to talk to you. Least give me your name, where you're staying. In case he needs it."

Meg's mind was all aswirl, a delayed reaction to the violence. She was relieved when Jake pulled her toward the door.

"Sorry, we're outa here," Jake called back. "Can't get involved. I did my job, you do yours."

The splattering of raindrops hit them in the face. They began to run the last few blocks to their hotel. Two police cars screeched to a stop in front of the pub just as Meg and Jake turned the corner. They slowed to a walk along one cobbled street that led to the hotel entrance. The large green-and-white awning with the red dragon—the symbol of Wales—

was a welcome sight.

Meg held him back. Questions crowded her mind. He looked at her quizzically—his face wet, his thick, dark hair plastered Roman-style over his forehead, his black eyelashes glistening with raindrops. He appeared to understand that she needed to talk.

"My room?"

She nodded vigorously. Who the heck was he, this Jake Bernstein? Super-hero, super-stud . . . or something in-between?

They walked at a clipped rate past the bar lounge and stepped into the elevator. As soon as Jake's hotel door was closed behind her, she lobbed her questions.

"How did you do that? Does the average banker know how to take down someone like that? Are you some kind of martial arts expert? Weren't you the least bit afraid? Do you know you could've been seriously hurt? I can't believe you did that! You acted like it was a walk in the park!"

They were cold and drenched. While Meg ignored her soggy state, still heated by her adrenaline rush, Jake plucked disgustedly at his sodden tee shirt.

"Okay, I'll explain. Just let me go to the bathroom."

He disappeared into the bathroom and she heard a toilet flush seconds later. Jake emerged a minute after in a terry-cloth bathrobe, halfway through toweling his hair with one hand. In the other, he carried a large towel for her.

As he approached, she nearly forgot her confusion at the sight of the confident smile on his handsome face. The collar of the bathrobe was open, revealing a triangle of dark chest hair, further distracting her. With one corner of her towel, and without hesitation, Jake patted her face and neck then handed over the towel to let her continue.

"You need to take a hot shower. Wanna share mine?"

Her eyes flared as his big hands rested on her shoulders.

Their eyes met. Dear God, he was stronger than his slim, muscular build appeared to be. He'd taken down that young, husky guy hyped up on some mania-inducing drug in just seconds. Without blinking an eye.

"Jake," she began again. "How . . . why . . . what happened back there?"

His hands remained on her shoulders yet she felt no fear. Meg knew — against all common sense or reason — that Jake would never harm her.

"Meg." Jake grew serious. "I told you, I was trained as a Navy Seal. What do you think Seals do? Scuba-dive all day and photograph marine life? We're trained to locate and disarm underwater mines. Like all special force units, we're trained in close-quarters combat, martial arts, munitions. Rough-water entries and exits, extractions, black ops . . . If we couldn't take a man down in under ten seconds, we were booted."

"But then you became a banker? How . . . why . . . after all that specialized military training?"

His dark eyes flickered over her hair as he took the towel that hung limply in her hand and applied it to the end of her dripping ponytail.

"Got tired of the violence. Oh, it was fun at first. Exciting . . . adrenaline-pumping. Why did I leave for that dull desk work? I told you. One of our assignments was compromised. Poor intel, and we lost a couple of good men. Mission failure, in my book. I learned then how vital good intelligence was. Anyway I left the Seals, eventually left the Navy. The training's always there, right below the surface. I guess you can leave the Seals but the Seals never leave you."

"You could've been hurt," she choked out. The thought of that possibility greatly affected her.

"I'm glad you care—"

Without further thought, Meg slipped her arms around his

neck. His hair felt damp to her fingers but his neck was dry and warm. She watched his eyes widen in surprise as she raised up on tiptoes and kissed his mouth. Warm, soft, pliable. Inviting. Tempting. Not the crazy, head-dizzying crush of lips inside the dungeon. This time there was something else in their kiss.

This was what she'd wanted to do for days.

He angled back his head. "Meg—"

"I don't want you hurt," she rasped. He tried to speak so she kissed him again, shutting him up. Then she heard him growl softly, deep in his throat. The gentle kiss Jake returned made her shiver all over . . .and not from the wet clothes still clinging to her body. Their warm tongues met, the tender contact drawing moans of pleasure from each other.

They thrust their bodies together hard. She could feel his chiseled torso, his muscular arms like iron bands around her back, his stiff erection through the cloth of the bathrobe. Big, strong hands slid underneath her sweatpants and cupped her behind. Their warmth on her chilled bare flesh startled her for a second. Liquid heat pooled in her belly. A deep urge inside her screamed to be satisfied. For a long moment, Meg thought she might stay with him. Make love for hours . . .ah, heavenly thought.

But no, she couldn't.

Her grandmother was upstairs . . .

Jake would think her an easy lay . . .a slut.

It was too soon. Didn't men like the chase?

Slowly, painfully, Meg strained against his fast hold. Loosened his embrace and stepped back but couldn't look him in the face. She berated herself for starting something she couldn't finish. And for feeling so conflicted.

"I—I'm so sorry. It's too soon."

Jake just nodded, didn't put up an argument. Her heart sank. In fact, Jake looked almost relieved. That bothered her even more.

Talk me out of it . . .please.

Silently, stoically, he led her to the door and said goodnight with a simple, quick kiss on her lips.

Her emotions clogged her throat, so much so she couldn't even say goodnight before she turned away and left.

CHAPTER ELEVEN

Jake went back to the bathroom, let the bathrobe drop to the floor. In a kind of daze of lust and longing, he showered and shook the chill off his body. His very blood and bones, though, felt on fire. The lingering aftermath of their kiss.

Not just the kiss. The way she kissed him. And what she'd said before they kissed. *I don't want you hurt.* Meg actually cared about him. Was maybe even falling in love with him.

He turned off the hot water and stood under a cold spray for as long as he could stand it. Slowly, his swollen, throbbing cock shrank back to normal.

Damn, he thought in wonder, once his head began to work again. Astonishment and pleasure flooded his insides. Of all times for this to happen. It wasn't supposed to happen like this — not when he was working. Not in the middle of a case.

Oh yeah, who says?

Human nature makes its own rules, Grandpa Nate would say. Fate and chance only mock us. Which means there are no rules. *Yakov, mitzvah, you're finally learning.* Jake shook his head in wonder.

Sonuvabitch, it jacks things all to hell.

You knew it would, Bernstein. Yet you let it happen.

Switching trains of thought, he pulled a yellow pad out of his suitcase, sat down at the small table by the window and pulled out the secure cell phone the Major had given him. While he waited for the series of clicks indicating the encryption was kicking in, Jake schooled himself and wrote down a few notes. He had to keep his mind on the task at hand. Later he'd indulge himself and let his sexual fantasies about Meg Larsen play themselves out.

"Temple. That you Agent Bernstein?"

"Just your friendly Yank, Major."

"It's past eleven, Agent Bernstein. Been painting the bloody town red with your new girlfriend? Apprehending villains in local pubs?"

"You have us under surveillance, you should know." Jake inhaled deeply. Mustn't let a proper British chiding make him lose his temper. "Listen, what I learned today. Mary McCoy Snider is fluent in German, as far as I can tell. Speaks German with no English accent. Claimed — to her granddaughter — she learned it from a fellow student in Dublin. A young German whose first name might be Helmut, Heinrich, or Horst. Supposedly her first big love affair. Check with Passport Control or Immigration to see if a German student entered England or Ireland in the mid-to-late thirties. If he stayed after the war broke out, he may've gone underground."

"No English accent, you say?"

"Yep. Like her granddaughter, Mary Snider's a mimic. Not surprising she can learn a foreign language and speak it like a native. You should hear her French. You'd think she was a Parisian."

Major Temple cleared his throat. "You may not be aware of this, Agent Bernstein. MI5 — we were known as the SIS then — ran a thorough check on all foreigners when war broke out in Europe. This was 1939. That's how most of the German spies were found. When there was no record of their leaving Britain, they were rounded up and broken. Many flipped sides, turned into double agents. The rest were hanged."

"Yeah, I know. But he could've left and sneaked back in. Lots of bays and isolated coves here in South Wales and Ireland. Isn't Ireland known for its sea smugglers ?"

"True. Despite their neutrality during the war, you may've

heard Ireland wasn't above welcoming U-boat crews into their coastal towns and tipping a pint of ale with those Kraut buggers."

"Major, I saw an old photo of just that in the pub tonight. Surprised the hell outa me. What about those U-boats off the coast of Ireland? This was commonplace?"

"Some months it was a regular flotilla, especially in the Irish Sea. We knew, of course, that spies were brought in by U-boats then sent ashore in rubber dinghies. British shores were heavily guarded by Civil Defense volunteers who took their tasks very seriously, as you can imagine. Most of these spies were picked up near coastal towns in England and Scotland. Bloody fools to think they'd escape the CD. Regular bloodhounds, the CD blokes were. But, of course, Ireland was a different story altogether."

Jake could hear the click of the man's teeth against his pipe stem as the major chuckled. The guy got a kick out of his wartime stories, so Jake let him go on until he wound down.

"One unlucky chap broke his leg parachuting in. Crawled to the nearest pub and gave himself up. Saved his life and worked for us the remainder of the war. He became one of our best double-agents. So, what are you thinking, Agent Bernstein? Some of the Irish along the coast were paid off and let a Nazi spy back in?"

Jake sighed heavily and massaged his temple. "I'm thinking just that. Follow my logic here, Major. If this Helmut or Horst guy left and came back, he might've been smuggled in by a German U-boat somewhere along the Irish coast. He would've been fluent in English, maybe the Irish dialect. Able to blend in. Maybe pass himself off as someone's kin. Perhaps the cousin of a Nazi sympathizer. Then he did some scouting for an Irish miss he could manipulate. Or maybe he knew her from before, from his time in Dublin. Didn't some of the Irish think that if England got its ass kicked by the Germans they'd stop interfering with Ireland? Well, maybe this German found the right mark and turned her into a spy."

"This German lover taught her German and persuaded Mary McCoy to become a spy for the Third Reich? That doesn't sound like the Mary McCoy in Mike McCoy's notes. This girl hated the Germans and told Mike she wanted to serve in the war effort."

"I know. I read MI5's summary of Mike McCoy's notes. It's just a theory. Because Mary Snider is a linguistic marvel and picks up foreign languages with incredible speed and skill, she could've learned German from this guy. Maybe he was a northern German and maybe he convinced her to take the job in London. Maybe he picked her for her trusting nature and vulnerability—"

Mary Snider, sweet and vulnerable? Well, maybe when she was young. People change, don't they, as they grow older?

Jake shook off those intrusive thoughts and continued.

"—or maybe he blackmailed her into helping him spy. Maybe tried to force her into applying for the War Office. When she refused, he killed her parents . . ."

Wouldn't be the first time someone had been duped into committing a crime to keep a lover happy—or to survive. Look at those German spies who turned coat and ended up working for the Brits to avoid the gallows. To Jake's mind, this theory was beginning to make sense. But it was just a theory. No evidence, no proof.

Not yet.

On the line, the Major harrumphed. Jake couldn't tell if the man was agreeing or disagreeing. Or if he thought Jake's theory was just so much bullshit.

"I'm thinking, Major, this Thomas McCoy that Mary corresponded with during the war—he could be this German. He might've been in Ireland somewhere, posing as an Irishman. Kept Mary on a tight leash, maybe threatened her. Arranged for dead-drops or face-to-face meetings. Their letters were probably coded. He'd convey intel back to his U-Boat contacts offshore. One possible scenario, anyway."

"Quite possible, Bernstein. I dare say there were many Thomas McCoys in Dublin and all over Ireland and England during the thirties and forties. There still are, I'll wager. One would choose that identity for its very ubiquity. I'll get on it right away and try and locate immigration records on this Heinrich or Helmut."

"Or Horst."

"Good work, Agent Bernstein. They told me you were incorruptible and fair-minded. Good at exploring all the angles. This is certainly a new approach."

"Or, Major, this could be just a bunch of bull. Just a theory, no proof." A slight pause. "Or Thomas McCoy could be just someone Mary met along the way and kept writing to because she liked him. I'll get around to asking about him in the next day or so. Also, following this same thread, Mary could be innocent and her cousin, Mike McCoy, could've been totally wrong about her at their meeting in Dallas. Could've gotten the eyes wrong, could've mistaken her reasons for avoiding him during the war and not acknowledging him afterward. Don't you have cousins, Major, that you avoid at all costs? I sure do, on my mother's side. Real dumbasses."

"Hmmm," was what Jake heard from the major.

On a roll, he continued. "Maybe there was another German mole in the War Office. Another woman. What about the clerk who shared the top floor of the boarding house where Mary McCoy lived? Have you run a thorough check on her?"

"We did. Historical records are quite complete. Catherine Collier was her name. She disappeared in early 1944. Strange but her body was never found. Her room was searched. No radio, cypher pads, or codebooks turned up. The fact that she disappeared, of course, is highly suspicious. There's nothing more to go on." A manly snort came through the line. "So, Jake, how is that extracurricular sporting with the comely granddaughter progressing? Is she proving to be helpful in this investigation?"

Jake said nothing. How could he admit that he'd just broken the cardinal rule of undercover work? Never fall for one of your marks.

"Meg's devoted to her grandmother. The woman raised her, is like a mother to her. I'm convinced she has no clue about any of this." He frowned as something else occurred to him. "Another thing, Major. Mary McCoy's correspondence with Thomas McCoy ended in 1944, didn't it? I'm stretching here, but maybe there's a correlation between Catherine Collier disappearing and the end of Mary's connection with Thomas. Meg said her grandmother told her that this German boyfriend went back to Germany and, for all she knows, was killed in the war."

"I'll check Passport Control—that dusty old basement where they keep the war records. It may take a while if they haven't been transferred to any of our databases. There's a slim chance there just might be a link between the two. Could be a coincidence, however."

"I don't believe in coincidences. Do you?"

"Not really. So, that's it, Jake?"

"That's it for now, yep."

"We'll check out this German student in Dublin—this Helmut or Heinrich or Horst. He may've been a foreign student at Trinity College or one of the private language institutes in the city. My own father attended Trinity in the early thirties. One of his best friends was the grandson of a Russian countess. It was and still is quite a cosmopolitan university."

With nothing more to add, Jake was about to punch off.

"By the by, Jake, our surveillance is for the safety of everyone concerned. No need to take offense. I'm afraid we do have cause for concern, old sport."

"Whaddya mean, Major?"

"The old adage the fruit doesn't fall far from the tree seems to apply here. Mike McCoy, Mary's tenacious cousin, has struck again."

"How's that possible? Didn't you say he died years ago?"

"The old man, yes, but his son, a middle-aged man who's been on mental disability for the past eight years—we've learned he's been on your tail for the past four days. We think he followed me to Heathrow that day I picked you up, trailed us to the hotel and observed the motorcoach and its occupants. He's discovered through an obliging travel agent that Mary McCoy Snider is on your tour. We believe he harbors the foolish notion of confronting Mrs. Snider. Apparently he has the same fixation on this woman that his father had, though I suspect there's something else he wants. The one time I met with him, not quite a year ago, he kept asking about a deed that Mary was given when her parents died. What he hopes that will accomplish, I have no idea. You should be on the alert, however."

"What does he look like? Is he armed?"

"He's in his fifties. Six-foot, stocky of build, half bald with a monk's fringe. Gray hair, blue eyes. Has a deep voice, heavy Irish accent. Various personality disorders make him unemployable and his wife left him six years ago. Sad case all around. Dotty old chap. Whether he's armed, we have no way of knowing. He has no permit for a gun. Not with his history of mental afflictions."

"Great," Jake said sarcastically.

He mused over this additional complication but was satisfied that Major Temple had informed him. And now he understood the reason for the surveillance team Temple had ordered. He just didn't understand why the major hadn't let him know from the beginning. Maybe the man was embarrassed they'd let this crazy guy slip through their fingers.

"So you heard about the pub disturbance tonight?" Jake asked Temple. He could hear the man grind his teeth against his pipe stem. Was the major extra nervous tonight?

"Our surveillance team was in the pub. Impressive, the speed with which you disarmed the young wanker. Good work, Jake. Although you could've blown your cover, as you well know."

"Not a problem, Major. Meg knows I'm ex-Navy Seal. Undercover works best if you mix in some truth with the lies."

They rang off cordially.

Halfway to the bed, what he'd just said struck him. That had been an accurate statement about undercover work — mixing some truth with the lies — but he wondered if Meg, a civilian, would ever understand or accept what he was doing. Would she hate him when the time came to reveal everything?

Most likely. His stomach dropped, his guts twisted.

Another thing struck him. He'd forgotten to ask Meg about Thomas McCoy, although it was very likely she knew nothing about him. If, according to Meg, her grandmother was a *femme fatale* when she was young, she would've played men like a violin. This Thomas McCoy could've been an admirer.

That didn't mean, of course, she couldn't have been played herself by some conniving German student-turned-Nazi spy. The guy could've been her handler — this so-called Thomas McCoy, whom Jake was now convinced was a cover name. He should've asked Meg about him. How to do that without raising suspicion, though, he wasn't quite sure.

That had been an oversight, Jake admitted. Never would have happened if he'd kept a clear head about him whenever Meg was near.

So the other salient question. How was he going to keep his

feelings for Meg from compromising this investigation?
He had no answer for that one.

Jake turned off the bedside lamp. He lay back against the pillows, stacked his hands behind his head and closed his eyes. The scent of her wet hair and warm flesh lingered in his mind. As did the press of her mouth, the sweet taste of her tongue, and the feel of her hard-and-soft rump in his hands.

Well, damn . . .

CHAPTER TWELVE

"Another lovely, two-thousand-calorie English breakfast. Good lord, they're making me fat! I could barely zip up my pants this morning!"

Judy, the youngest of the two New Jersey sisters, stood up and gathered her purse. Her sister Jeannie followed suit.

"I know what you mean," Hank Philemon concurred. The three agreed that between the long motorcoach drives and the fattening meals, each of them would return home with at least ten extra pounds to shed. Jake was tempted to suggest a long jog in the evenings instead of sitting and drinking in the bar but decided to stay quiet.

"Aren't you coming, Jake? People are boarding." Jeannie shot Jake one of her brightest smiles. The prettier of the two sisters, she seemed determined to win his attention.

Meg and her grandmother hadn't come down for breakfast, a cause for concern. He put down his cup of coffee and stood. What was their room number? Meg had told him. Like a household detergent, one he used.

"No, go on ahead. Tell Robert I'll be there. Going to check on Meg and her grandmother. They're usually among the first down to breakfast. Haven't seen them yet."

Jeannie looked disappointed but covered it smoothly and tossed back her dark hair with a flippant, "Will do!"

The three filed out of the dining room while Jake headed for the elevators. Detergent . . .he used it in his kitchen and bath . . .yes. 409.

Jake punched the 4 button, the carry-on strap cutting into

112

his left shoulder. Unmindful of the discomfort, he wondered about Meg and Mary Snider. Uneasiness weighed on his mind.

He knocked on their door. Meg flung it open, relief swamping her face as soon as she saw him.

"Thank God, Jake! I need your help."

He followed her into the room. Mary Snider sat on the edge of her bed, dressed in a brown pantsuit, sweater, and loafers. Her hands were exposed and, for the first time, Jake saw them gloveless. He now understood why she covered them up. The fingers were brown-spotted, horribly gnarled and twisted. Like deformed crab legs.

"She's having problems putting on her gloves and she won't let me help her." Frustration heated Meg's tone of voice. "Grandma, please let me—"

"I can do it myself!" After another futile try, the elderly woman gave up. She threw Jake a hard, hostile look. "What are *you* doing here? No one asked you—"

"Grandma, I asked him in. He can help—"

"No he can't. He can't be trusted." Mary Snider gazed up at Jake standing over them. She squinted and her mouth curled downward.

"I'll get your carry-on," he began, seeing it open on the dresser. A ziplock baggie held at least ten containers of pills in a variety of shapes, sizes, and colors. Meg now held one of those containers—a plastic, rectangular dispenser divided into seven compartments, one for each day of the week.

"No! Leave that alone!" barked the old woman at Jake, followed by a snarl, "Meg told me what happened in that pub you took her to. You're a cop, and I don't trust cops."

Meg sighed. "Grandma, don't get paranoid on me. Jake's not a cop. Like I told you, he used to be a Navy Seal. You've got to stop this nonsense. Here, take the glass of water. I'll dole out the pills. Today's Tuesday, so . . ."

The old woman, her narrow, flinty stare never leaving Jake's face, opened her mouth. She let Meg place one pill after another on her tongue, following each one with a sip from the water glass. Meg glanced over at him and managed a smile.

"Grandma takes pills for high blood pressure, painkillers and anti-inflammatories for her rheumatoid arthritis, heart medication, anti-depressants. You name it, she takes it. Last night she took one too many sleeping pills. It was the devil trying to get her up this morning."

Jake marveled at Meg's patience with the old lady. He thought about Oma and how his own mother and father handled her cranky days. It was tough getting old, he knew. He couldn't help but wonder if he'd be called upon someday to help his own parents deal with their aging problems. He was the elder son, after all. He'd be expected to take charge.

"I don't want to take that ferry. Ferries are dangerous. I should know." Mary Snider's dark blue eyes tracked him as he retrieved her coat and Meg's jacket from the other bed. "I almost drowned because of a ferry. The Irish Sea is a dangerous place. Not like the Mediterranean. It's cold and foggy and stormy. If we *have* to go to Ireland, Meggie, we should fly there."

Meg snapped shut the lid to the weekly pill dispenser, then bent down to tug on her grandmother's brown, calfskin gloves.

"Grandma, we've talked about this before. You said it would be okay, now you're changing your mind. Well, it's too late. We're getting on that ferry and I'll stay by you. Nothing bad's going to happen. I promise."

Jake gnawed impatiently on his lower lip then shifted the coat and jacket to one arm before he picked up the carry-on Meg had just zipped closed.

"Mrs. Snider, the ferries nowadays are larger, faster. They don't capsize. This one takes cars, trucks, the motorcoach—

speaking of which, everyone's getting on it right now."

Meg helped her grandmother to stand. "Jake, Grandma's got a history with ferries. She nearly drowned when she was—what, twenty years old, Gran? She was crossing over from Ireland to Wales, on her way to England for her job with the War Office. What year was this, Gran?"

"Um, 1940," grumbled Mary Snider. She looked a bit befuddled and groggy. "Where's my coat? My purse?"

"Jake's got your coat, I've got our purses. Okay, let's get out of here before they leave us behind. You know how punctual Robert is. Likes to leave on the dot."

Wielding both carry-ons, one on each shoulder, his right arm loaded with Meg's jacket and Mary Snider's coat, Jake paused to scan the room. Meg did too. When their eyes met, she smiled again in appreciation. Their brief look transmitted volumes. He held the door open while Mary leaned on her granddaughter's arm.

"Mrs. Snider, you'll have to tell me what happened on that ferry," commented Jake, walking slowly abreast with them down the corridor. It'd be interesting to hear it from Mary's perspective, sixty-something years later. Would her recollections be as sharp and as accurate as the eyewitness accounts in MI5's file, taken within twenty-four hours of the catastrophe?

"Too horrible to talk about," clipped the old woman.

"There was a fire. An explosion," Meg filled in. "From what Grandma told us, people jumped into the water. Couldn't wait for the lifeboats, so many of them drowned. The ferry capsized eventually, and even the skipper went down with his ship. Bodies were found later, floating by the shore at Fishguard, the place where they were supposed to dock. Some of the passengers and crew on the manifest were never found. Swept out to sea. Grandma made it to a lifeboat, thank heavens, with just her purse and coat. Some people believed it was an attack by a German U-boat. Grandma kept the news clippings and showed them to us."

Part of the account jived with MI5's report, Jake noted, but not the cause. Evidence from the salvaged ferry showed that the explosions and resulting fire originated from within the engine room. Sabotage had caused the ferry disaster. Not a German U-boat's torpedo.

Major Temple believed either the impostor Mary McCoy or her accomplice—or someone entirely different—arranged the explosion. Perhaps to cover up the murder and disappearance of the real Mary McCoy? Even Jake thought that was over-kill—a lot of trouble and risk to go through to make one young woman disappear. Simpler methods would have sufficed.

"Amazing to live through such a thing, Mrs. Snider," Jake said. "But like Meg assured you, there's no need to worry. Today's ferries are very safe. They have modern, computerized ballasts. Faster, too. Our crossing will take only three-and-a-half hours. Your crossing back in what, 1940, took—how long?"

"Don't remember," Mary Snider mumbled. "Much longer. It was an overnight crossing and I had my own stateroom. I remember it. Stateroom 5-C."

Jake again mused at the old woman's selective recall. She remembered the number of her stateroom but blocked out other details. Unless she was lying, of course.

"Grandma, you told us you shared the stateroom with a girl who drowned. You said they never found her body." Meg patted her grandmother's arm. "You were lucky then and you'll be lucky now. Besides, we're crossing in broad daylight."

Jake gazed at the old woman as they rode the elevator down to the lobby. If Mary Snider was one of the saboteurs that caused the deaths of fifty-six people on that ferry, she was one cool customer. Even after sixty-five years, he expected to see the woman exhibit some emotion. According to the file he'd read about the incident, over two-hundred passengers and a crew of fifteen were on that ferry that fateful night. One quarter of them wouldn't live to see the dawn.

"Good thing the ferry was close to shore," he remarked casually. "In the middle of the Irish Sea, at night — with few fishing boats around — everyone would have drowned."

The old lady's head whipped around. Dark blue eyes drilled into him. "How did you know we were close to the Welsh coast when it happened?"

Shit! Had Meg mentioned that? Didn't she say that bodies washed up near Fishgard? The town along the Welsh coast?

"I just assumed," he covered, shrugging. "Since bodies were found near Fishguard. Wouldn't more people have drowned if the ferry had capsized in the middle of the Irish Sea?"

The old woman nodded.

"So good thing it happened close to shore," he repeated.

"It was planned that way," Mary Snider muttered, her eyes unfocused for a second, then refocusing quickly to meet his gaze again. "The newspapers said the U-boat planned the attack that way. So more people wouldn't die."

What had Mary Snider just said? Jake tried to maintain his composure. Inside, his mind was swirling.

"Why would a German U-boat attack a passenger ferry? I mean, Ireland was neutral during the war. Why would the Germans attack a neutral country's ferry? Wouldn't that risk turning the Irish against them? Make them side with the British?"

Mary made a small snorting sound. "The news didn't say why. U-boats were all around the Irish coast. One surfaced one morning near Dungarvon Bay. Everyone was talking about it."

Jake started at the mention of Dungarvon Bay. He'd read the name in the major's file. It was true about the news stories' coverage at that time of the ferry sinking. There had been a lot of speculation about the incident, including the local belief that the Nazis discovered a cache of money meant for the English war effort was on board and that perhaps was one reason why the ferry was sabotaged.

Would this bogus Thomas McCoy—maybe passing as a dockworker—have been instrumental in learning this vital bit of information? Would he have seen this ferry crossing as the opportunity to kill two birds, so to speak, with one stone? Eliminate two problems with one explosion? Cover up Mary McCoy's murder *and* destroy or steal the cache of money earmarked for the English war effort?

Something stabbed Jake's finger. He frowned and looked down at Mary's coat and flipped aside the lapel. A large, glittery pin attached to the lapel had become unfastened and had stuck his knuckle. He shifted the weight to his other arm and sucked on his knuckle for a second to stanch the blood. Meg's attention was drawn.

"Oh, Grandma, your pin came undone. Jake, do you need a band-aid? I carry a nurse's first-aid kit in that carry-on."

"No, it's nothing."

With her free hand, Meg took the pin off the coat lapel.

"Don't want to lose this, do you, Grandma? Your hummingbird pin. I told you not to bring it. It's too costly to replace if it gets lost."

He wasn't sure he'd heard correctly. A hummingbird pin? Jake looked over, studied it.

A jeweled bird, its plump, sapphire-filled body flanked by ruby- and emerald-encrusted wings, nestled in Meg's palm. Its long beak held a series of small diamonds. It was a beautiful, intricately designed pin. Glittered like a starburst. Looked valuable. And old, maybe WWII vintage.

Hummingbird.

Code name for one of the Wehrmacht's female spies.
Hummingbird and Black Widow. Two Nazi moles never
caught by the Allies. Two clever, diabolical women who'd
managed deep-undercover lives all during the war. Jake swallowed. His breakfast began to rise up. He willed the bile
down, studied the pin again.

"Some jewelry, Mrs. Snider. Did your husband give this to
you?"

The old woman stared ahead at the elevator door as it
opened. She stepped out with Meg, ahead of Jake.

"Don't remember," she mumbled. Meg turned around and
smiled at him. Her grandmother pulled on her arm, urging
her in the direction of the motorcoach.

"Grandma does too remember. She told me a friend of hers
gave it to her during the war. In exchange for a big favor. It's
beautiful, isn't it? And unusual."

"Some friend." He arched his eyebrows at Meg. Her expression was innocent. She didn't have a clue about its significance, he was certain of that.

"One of her beaus," Meg leaned back and whispered then
winked at him. Jake tried to smile.

Mary Snider let go of her granddaughter's arm. Took the
proffered hand of Robert Morse, whose cheerful, escort fa-
çade was close to cracking.

"Hush now, Meggie, that's personal. We're the last ones,
by gosh. Why, thank you, young man." Mary turned a tight,
specious smile up to Robert, hooked her arm around his and
added, "I don't like ferries. Will there be beer on board? To
help me relax?"

"Naturally, dear lady. You can drink yourself into a stu-
por." He leaned down conspiratorially. "Maybe half the
group will do just that. Then we'll have a pleasant, quiet
crossing. We'll be in Ireland before you know it."

The man blathered on about the other amenities on
board—the lounges, cafes, cinema, child's playground corner,

119

etc. Jake tuned him out. He watched Meg safeguard the valuable hummingbird pin inside her purse. Then she turned to hoist the carry-on with its portable pharmacy off Jake's shoulder. Her hand lingered on his arm.

"Thanks, Jake. You're almost too good to be true."

"Yep, that I am," he gibed. He heard the touch of irony in his voice and felt a stab of guilt. A part of him sighed with sorrow for Meg. She was oblivious. She trusted him as a child might trust a smiling stranger.

More and more, the mounting evidence pointed to Mary Snider. He could almost hear the bewigged English barristers in court as they listed her war crimes. Espionage, sabotage, conspiracy to commit treason, cold-blooded murder of civilians. Still, he needed proof. A jeweled pin in the form of a hummingbird was *not* proof. Mary's lawyers would tear that case apart.

If Mary Snider *was* the Hummingbird spy, Meg would have to learn the truth someday about her grandmother. Jake would have to reveal his role in exposing her. His stomach churned at the thought. Bile rose again and burned his throat.

What exactly was this truth, anyway? Hell if he knew. All he'd managed so far was to piece together a couple of suspicious facts and circumstances into an amorphous, blurred picture. Still, the picture was emerging.

A theory supported by circumstantial evidence. Nothing more.

One thing was sure. He still didn't believe in coincidences.

CHAPTER THIRTEEN

On board the fourteen-deck, diesel-powered ferry, Jake upheld his promise to assist Meg. He carried their gear as they climbed from deck five, the vehicle-storage deck, where their motorcoach was safely parked with all the other trucks and cars.

In front of them was the entire motorcoach group, trudging up the five flights of stairs.

The going was especially slow for Meg and her grandmother. By the time they emerged onto the vast lounge area on deck ten, the old lady was huffing and puffing. He found Meg and her grandmother a comfortable place along a curved, upholstered bench that ran the width of the lounge. Tables and chairs crowded the area, all facing a huge screen on which CNN flashed the latest news with a ticker of superscript.

Behind them on the fore side of the ship, two large cafeterias lured the passengers who couldn't go four hours without eating or drinking something. Beer and alcoholic drinks were available at a small bar along one side. Already, as Jake surveyed the scene, truck drivers who'd left their vehicles below on deck five were lining up to tip a pint. Probably figuring they'd clear their system by pissing it all out before they docked in Ireland.

"Can I get you ladies some hot tea? Coffee?" he asked Meg and Mary Snider as he laid down their carry-on. He'd left his on the locked coach.

Meg smiled. "Tea sounds great. Thanks, Jake. I'll treat you

to drinks tonight at one of the pubs in Killarney."

Her grandmother looked at them both and frowned, then gazed out the enormous side glass, her mouth pursed in a taut scowl of disapproval. In her own way, Jake realized, the old lady was tolerating a situation she apparently disapproved of but had no control over. The younger generation was not to be thwarted and all that.

Jake wondered what she was thinking. Was she plotting a scheme in her mind to break up his and Meg's fledgling relationship? Or were her memories taking her back to that fateful night on the Irish Sea? What really happened on that ferry? Or rather, since Major Temple had included the specifics — an explosion in the engine room, followed by a fire and more explosions at various locations — the more germane question was *who was the saboteur?*

He or she had never been caught. The bodies of the one engineer and his apprentice were never found, along with those of a dozen passengers. Forty-two other passengers drowned, their bodies found floating near Fishguard, the nearest dock in Wales. All the rest of the crew and thirty-nine passengers were rescued from two lifeboats and four rubber dinghies. The ferry itself went down. Not until a week later was the British Navy able to salvage what was left. By then the gold bullion meant for the Allied war effort was gone, the drowned bodies of the guards found, also.

Jake had reread the news clippings that Major Temple had included in the file about the ferry disaster. Civil Defense volunteers had spotted the antenna of a German U-boat in the vicinity just days before. The wrecked ship and the stolen gold bullion — well, it didn't take a Cambridge degree for the Brits to draw their own sober conclusions. The public was outraged over the fifty-two people killed in the ferry's sinking but the War Office had more pressing matters, the Blitz being one. The United States hadn't yet entered the war and precious supply ships sent from the U.S. faced attacks by those same damned U-boats.

With the historical facts in mind, Jake paused at the condiments counter. His back to the lounge, he turned on the digital recorder in his jacket pocket and affixed the American flag pin to the lapel. The wireless mike would pick up anything within a radius of twenty feet.

A few minutes later, Jake returned to the women with two paper cups of hot tea and one cup of the strongest coffee he could squeeze out of a large, impersonal urn. As they all sipped and watched the Welsh shore recede from view, Jake, tired of dancing around the issue, decided on a frontal assault. One that bordered on rude but he figured he had no choice.

"So, Mrs. Snider, what big favor did you do for that beau of yours during the war that earned you such a valuable pin? The one with all the jewels?"

Meg turned to her grandmother and nudged her. "C'mon, Gran, tell us. I've never heard the whole story either."

Mary frowned, kept her eyes on the glass wall. "I don't remember."

"Gran, did you sleep with the man? Is that how you got the pin?" Meg settled mischievous eyes on the elderly woman and patted her arm. "You can tell us. It's been so long ago, who cares, anyway? Was it like an engagement present?"

Slowly turning her head, Mary glanced first at Jake then her granddaughter. A shrewd smile formed on her mouth.

"Yes, an engagement present. The pin was more important to me than a ring. I didn't want people to know I was engaged."

"Why not, Gran? Surely, the War Office wouldn't care if you were engaged, would they?"

"They would if he were a German soldier . . .and the enemy." The old woman shrugged, as though the mere mention of such a long-ago occurrence was barely worth mentioning.

"Of course, we were all soldiers during the war. There were no civilians. Every man, woman, child — all soldiers defending their country."

Meg appeared shocked. "Grandma, you never told me you were engaged to a German soldier during the war. Was it that Helmut guy you met in Dublin?"

"Horst . . .his name was Horst." Old weary eyes swiveled on Jake. "Horst Eberhard," she added quietly. "He was a man of great courage, strength of mind and character. And loyal. You could always depend on him to get things done."

Meg's voice gentled. "Was he the student who had to return to Germany? The one who died in the war?"

Her grandmother assumed an air of sorrow, as though a small part of her still grieved. Shoulders slumped, the old lady's mouth quivered when she nodded.

"Oh, Gran, how sad."

Jake witnessed Meg's tenderheartedness as the girl draped an arm around her grandmother. He, on the other hand, fixated on the old woman's words.

"What do you mean, Mrs. Snider? He always got things done?" Jake asked after taking a slow sip of coffee. This conversation was so vital, he half expected his hand to tremble a little. But no, it was as steady as a rock. Yet he kept his voice casual. As if he were just killing time and going along with Meg's inquiries.

Mary Snider looked up at him, her eyes growing hard. Her mouth had stopped quivering and was now set in a thin, stubborn line. What an actress, he marveled. Yet Meg saw none of this subterfuge.

"Done? I meant, he was a good soldier. He carried out the Third Reich's orders. They gave him medals. Then he made the ultimate sacrifice and died in the war. November 1944. They gave him the Iron Cross, the Abwehr did. The least they could've done."

"What do you mean, Grandma?" Meg looked confused. "How do you know they gave your fiancé the Iron Cross?"

Jake said nothing for a whole second, reluctant to tip his hand prematurely. Again the elderly woman just shrugged off her question.

"I learned about this in a communiqué the War Office intercepted. After Horst was killed, they gave him the Iron Cross of the Third Reich. The highest honor a soldier could earn." Pride filled her voice.

"The Abwehr was the Third Reich's Defense department, or military," Jake explained for Meg's benefit. "They controlled spies and informants all over the globe. I recall reading about an Abwehr agent who'd infiltrated a U.S. Naval shipyard in Evansville, Indiana. *She* escaped, was never caught."

Meg's mouth gaped open. "German spies in Indiana during WWII? And a woman? How is that possible?"

"From what I've read, women spies were often the most effective. You know, the old stereotype of female roles back then. Dumb and helpless. Damsels in distress."

"German spies and sympathizers were all over Britain." Mary Snider's eyes flicked over as if to gauge Jake's reaction. "And British spies were all over Europe too. This was before spy satellites, Meg, so that was how military information was gathered. Horst was a spy, but all spies were soldiers for the Third Reich."

Jake held his breath. His heart began to hammer in his chest. Did he hear correctly? Mary Snider was exposing her relationship with a bonafide Third Reich spy?

"My God, Grandma!" Meg looked stricken. She was starting to connect the dots. Jake nodded at the old woman, as if agreeing with her statement. If he could get her to talk, what a wealth of information she'd be—former Nazi spy or not.

"So your German fiancé was an Abwehr spy? Wasn't Admiral Canaris in charge of the Abwehr then? I remember reading about him in one of my history books on World War II. The Gestapo and the SS hated him, distrusted him, and eventually executed him. Because of the false information he passed on to Hitler, Switzerland was never invaded. Which would have been a fool's errand, anyway, given the narrow mountain passes." His gaze fell on Mary Snider. "Do you agree?"

The old woman shrugged again. "Perhaps."

Jake smiled benignly. "Of course, working for the War Office, Mrs. Snider, you would have learned all this. You would have known about Admiral Canaris and his attempts to undermine the Nazi cause from within."

They'd wandered a little off-topic, and Jake knew he had to maneuver the conversation back to Horst Eberhard. His pulse was racing with excitement. Finally they had a definitive name . . .unless Mary was lying, of course.

"So your German fiancé, this Horst Eberhard, gave you the valuable pin then returned to Germany," Jake went on. "And you learned about his death in an intercepted radio message?"

"Yes. I was manning the French and Italian desks, keeping track of the Americans' march up the boot. Horst was killed in Italy. A secret cell of the Italian resistance sent the message as the German division retreated. I remember it like it happened yesterday."

"How terrible that must have been for you." He tried to infuse his tone with sympathy. Meg silently clasped her grandmother's hand.

Mary Snider narrowed her eyes at him. "Yes. It was."

"Grandma." Meg gave her grandmother's shoulder a slight squeeze with her other hand. "I'm so sorry you lost your fiancé. But then you met Grandpa later that year, didn't you? So things worked out."

Sweet Meg, Jake thought, smiling at her. Always

concerned about the other person's feelings. Always finding the silver lining. His heart warmed at her kindness, her empathetic smile and warm gestures. Then he frowned. Back to business.

"Was that why you couldn't reveal your engagement to Horst Eberhard, Mrs. Snider? Because he was a German soldier and if the War Office had found out, you would have been suspected of harboring Nazi sympathies?"

Her dark-blue eyes steady on his face, the elderly woman merely nodded. "Exactly."

Jake sat back and crossed his legs. He kept a poker face and schooled his voice to remain neutral.

"Good thing you kept that secret, Mrs. Snider. Don't think the War Office would have understood that relationship. Did he — your German fiancé — ever conduct espionage activities inside England or Ireland? That you know of?"

Again Mary nodded.

Jake's mouth dropped open. "And you didn't report him?"

Mary's eyes flickered down to her lap, her gloved hands clasped together in a tense knot. She shook her head, then lifted it in a gesture of defiance.

"I couldn't betray him. He was the man I loved. And now it's water over the dam. So what?"

He looked over at Meg, who appeared to be processing all she'd just heard. She was frowning, knowing that what her grandmother did — by not exposing her fiancé as a spy operating within Britain during the war — in essence had betrayed the country she lived in and worked for. Although Ireland was still neutral, in essence she'd been working for the Allied cause. In the British War Office, no less. Mary Snider had betrayed the war effort by not reporting her fiancé.

Good. Relief flooded him. At least Meg was beginning to hear it from her grandmother, not him. Later, that might be easier . . .

The truth was gradually leaking out . . .like a dammed-up river that strains to break free. He suspected Mary Snider's burden of shameful secrets was wearing away at her defensive wall of silence.

But was her revelation the entire truth?

"Did he ever ask you to spy for him? For the Third Reich?" There, he'd finally asked the all-important question. Meg shot him a look of panic — as if to say please don't go there. He had to ask . . . and he had to know.

"Yes." The old woman raised her chin and smiled, a granite-hard, all-knowing smile. "But I refused. He never asked again. We both knew our boundaries, young man. We had jobs to do. We were both soldiers and we knew what we had to do. I worked for England and he worked for Germany."

Jake felt as though a pinball machine was clanging around inside his head. He wasn't sure he could believe the old lady. She sounded sincere just then, but she was also one good actress.

"Why are you so interested?" Mary suddenly asked him. Her brows were arched stiffly, her wrinkled mouth now screwed up in a moue of distaste.

The old gal was cagey. She'd given up something she knew was important. Now it was his turn. Jake knew he could easily confess the truth of his identity right then and there. He should warn them about MI5's investigation. But he couldn't.

"It's fascinating history. Like I said, World War II is a hobby of mine, partly because of my grandfather's personal history. I've got the whole collection of the *World at War* DVDs. When I was a teenager, I watched them with my father and grandfather. Every year for four or five years. In the lull between football and baseball season." He added the last with a wry grin. That was all true, time well spent with the two most important men in his life.

Mary Snider said nothing, but her look said it all. She

didn't believe him. Her antenna was up.

Jake stood up. "Excuse me, I need to walk around. Get some fresh sea air. Meg, wanna come?"

Still obviously bewildered and distressed, Meg glanced up at him and shook her head. She looked upset, although Mary Snider appeared unruffled.

What a pair.

One an innocent. The other, God only knew what.

He needed to walk. And process it all himself.

CHAPTER FOURTEEN

After thirty minutes of pacing the upper, outside deck—Deck 14—and getting windblown, Jake raked fingers through his thick, dark hair. The cold air had cleared his head. Mary Snider's words had just supported his theory that the German spy had somehow influenced her. What he hadn't expected was her admission that Horst had tried to recruit her but she'd declined. There was probably no proof that she had declined, no proof that she hadn't.

The hummingbird pin meant nothing. That was just a pricey gift. Perhaps originally meant for a spy code-named Hummingbird that Horst Eberhard ultimately couldn't deliver. And so he targeted an Irish lass who fell for him but refused to spy for him.

So much for this investigation. Should he conclude it? Report to MI5 that their suspicions were groundless, pack up and go home?

The thought was tempting. But then he might never see Meg again. No, he'd find a way to keep the friendship going. But once she discovered his true identity, learn that he'd used her to get to her grandmother, she'd probably never speak to him again.

Not a happy thought.

He ambled down to the lounge area. Noises greeted him almost immediately. People were staring in the direction of the bench and tables area where he'd left Meg and her grandmother.

He halted. A gray-haired man with a bald head and

tonsure cut, dressed in a rumpled, dark green jacket, was bending over them, his hands gripping Mary Snider's arms. Meg jumped to her feet and pulled at the man's hands, trying to yank her grandmother free. She was hollering for him to go away. The huskily built man reached over and pushed her down to the bench. When Meg sprang to her feet again, the man slapped her. Meg's head jerked back from the blow. Mary screamed.

Jake instantly identified the man as the mentally unbalanced Mike McCoy, son of Mary McCoy's cousin — the old man who'd started the whole investigation. Rage purged Jake's mind of further hesitation as he took off at a sprint.

In seconds, he sprang upon the intruder. Seizing the man in a headlock, Jake wrenched him around and away from the women. With the momentum, they both tumbled headfirst onto the carpeted floor. Jake's shoulder caught the edge of a table. A stab of pain shot up through his arm and down his back. He applied more pressure to the man's neck, causing him to gag and cough. Not enough to snap his windpipe, though. The guy was middle-aged and mentally ill. Jake eased off on his strangle-hold. A mistake, as it turned out.

The older guy was feisty, though, and strong. The bastard kept jabbing Jake in the ribs with his elbows. They rolled over each other. When Jake found himself underneath, the guy took advantage of the position and punched downward. Jake caught one on the chin before rolling away.

McCoy was up and ready, his right foot swinging upward towards Jake's groin. Seizing the man's collar in both hands, he turned to the side just in time. The vicious kick caught Jake's thigh instead. He yelled in pain and released his hold just enough so that McCoy lurched out of Jake's arms. Clambering away, the man regained his balance and took off. His mind automatically switching into FBI-training mode, Jake rose to one knee and reached for the pistol in its shoulder holster.

Dammit! The gun was still in his suitcase. His leg hurt like hell. He rubbed it as he used a nearby table to help himself up. Upper teeth biting into his lower lip, he kept himself from swearing out loud.

Meg grabbed his arm. When he turned to look at her, he almost gave in and swore anyway. One side of her face bore the reddish mark of the man's slap. Other than that, she appeared unharmed, though greatly rattled and frightened. She was fighting back tears.

"Are you okay?" she asked breathlessly.

Jake was panting so hard, he had to force the words out. "Fine, just roughed up a bit. Tend to your grandmother. I'm going after the sonuvabitch."

Two men in jeans and workers' jackets and caps approached him and offered their help. One pointed in the direction of the fleeing assailant.

"Want some help?"

He nodded gratefully.

"One of you stay here. In case he comes back."

Jake and the younger of the two men—a blond-haired guy in a plaid wool shirt—ran toward the central stairway. Jake hesitated. Did he go up to the open-air deck or down?

"I saw him go down."

They took two steps at a time leaping down the staircase. Jake ignored the pain in his leg as the adrenaline raced through his system. They burst through the door at each deck and scanned the area. No sign of the gray-haired lunatic. Jake didn't have the breath to ask whether he was part of the major's surveillance team or not.

They repeated the process at four more decks. By deck five, the vehicle storage bay, they both slowed down. Jake sensed the man had come this way, seeking the cover and safety of his car.

"Take that side, I'll go here," he commanded the blond worker. A heartbeat later. "You Temple's team?"

"You got it, sport," the kid called out. "Sorry we were late to the fracas. We were in line at the coffee bar. Then we saw the bloke go for the ladies."

One by one they looked inside each car, climbed up to the cab of each truck and checked it out. Jake took extra time with two vans, their privacy windows making it impossible to see inside. Their doors were locked. Otherwise, he would have looked inside — at the risk of eating a boot or facing down the barrel of a gun. *Don't be a fool, man,* he kept scolding himself. *Don't corner a lunatic. You're unarmed.*

His thoughts sprang to Meg. *There's too much to live for.*

Standing outside the white van, he noted the license. Republic of Ireland plates. So were half of the vehicles on this deck. He peered through the front tinted windshield. Couldn't see much except a map of London, lying flat on the dashboard. *Could be our man.* He pounded on the van's door with his fist.

"Come out, you asshole! You're such a coward you like to hit women?"

Nothing. No sound within.

A half hour later, after checking each and every vehicle, they reconnoitered back by the metal, deck-exit door. The man had disappeared into thin air.

"No sign."

"Sorry, Agent Bernstein. The major warned us about this McCoy character. Quite batty, I've heard."

"Yeah, looney-tunes. Will you be staying undercover?"

The blond nodded. "Yes, Major's orders."

"Fine with me. Just good to know you guys are around." He hated to admit it, but that was the truth. This assignment was proving to have a dangerous wrinkle or two.

By the time Jake limped back into the lounge, Meg appeared to have composed herself. The other man on Temple's surveillance team excused himself and rejoined his friend. They kept a visual on the little group while pretending to be distracted by an island the ferry was passing.

"How's your leg, Jake? Did he hurt you?" Meg asked. He suspected the bruises had turned purplish. She jumped up. "I'll get you some ice for that." She pointed to his jaw.

His attention turned away from his pain. Jake grabbed Meg's arm as she started to stand and studied her face. Her bruise was now darkening, like his.

"Your face needs some, too." Distracted by Meg, he'd forgotten to look at Mary Snider. The elderly woman was leaning back on the bench, her head lolling forward on her chest. Drool trickled out of one side of her slackened mouth. What the heck?

"What happened?"

"I had to give her a trank, she was so upset. Crying, nearly hysterical, Jake. She was shaking so hard, I thought she was going to have a stroke or . . . or a heart attack. I gave her just one tranquilizer pill and that put her to sleep. I didn't know what else to do. That man really frightened her. Frightened me, too. He acted so crazy. God, my heart's still pounding."

He hated that Meg was caught in the middle of this mess — this tangled web of lies and deception. Every ounce of his being felt sympathy for her. Anger boiled up inside him, against Mary Snider for causing it all. Why hadn't Mary resolved whatever her cousin's beef was?

Why couldn't the late Mike McCoy have let sleeping dogs lie? Jake blamed himself for letting this case get out of control.

Stroking her upper arms, Jake examined Meg's face. They'd both have dark, angry bruises. Letting the crazy bastard get away bruised his ego even more. Resentment coursed through him. He longed to get the man in another headlock. This time, he wouldn't be so easy on him.

"What did he want? What did he say?" He enfolded Meg

within a close embrace. He soothed her until she could collect her wits.

"I don't really know. He kept calling her Mary McCoy. Kept saying *It's mine, that property's mine. You have no right to it.*" She was breathing deeply, calming herself as she relived the experience. "Grandma kept saying she didn't know anything about this property. That someone named Dillon had all her parents' papers. Ever since they died—"

"Father Dillon, the Killarney priest...?" Jake instantly caught himself.

Meg leaned back, searched his face in total confusion. "Father Dillon? Jake, how do you know about him? He was her priest since childhood. The only one in her hometown she said she wrote to during the war. Grandma said he was a good man. He praised her for what she was doing for the war effort."

When Jake said nothing, their eyes locked, his dark and troubled, hers now full of alarm. Damn, how much could he tell her without blowing his cover and the entire case?

"Jake, what's going on?" she persisted. "All those questions about the war, the spies, her German fiancé? I need to know what's going on. If you care at all about me, you'll tell me on the truth. Who is this man who attacked us? Do you know about him too?"

He slowly blew air out his cheeks and let go of her arms. He stood up, looked over at the old woman slouched over on the bench, and actually felt a pang of pity for her. Meg's outraged expression, however, was what drew his full compassion. Her face was flushed and she was panting a little.

His chest felt as though it was going to explode, the weight of his deception so heavy upon his mind and heart. Never before in all his undercover work had he felt this burden. The dilemma of both wanting to break cover and maintain it. Meg adored this old woman and *he* had to be the one to tell her that her beloved grandmother was suspected of having committed war crimes . That it was his job to gather evidence against her.

"Meg . . ."

God help him, he couldn't.

" . . .I can't tell you. I'm sorry, I just can't."

To her credit, rather than erupt in fury, she exhaled like a child — half sob, half sigh. He wanted to take her in his arms again but didn't.

"Is it true? Are you a cop? Does this have something to do with Grandma's work during the war?"

Jake couldn't even nod. The way she said *cop* – as though it was an obscene word — made him choke up. Was Meg's mind as poisoned as her grandmother's against the authorities? He could understand Mary Snider's fear . . .but Meg's?

Did Meg know more than she was letting on? Or did she just suspect something was out of whack with her grandmother?

Jake had no choice but to maintain his cover, flimsy though it now was. Once his cover was compromised, he'd be removed from the case. That had never happened to Jake before and it wasn't going to happen to him now. Such a stigma would follow him all his career — -the guy who blew his cover because he'd gotten too close and let down his guard. He'd never be assigned field work again.

He didn't want Major Temple to lose faith in him or the FBI. After all, dammit, he was a professional. If there was a way, he'd deal with it somehow . . . some way.

He remained silent. Meg's eyes filled with unshed tears which abruptly spilled over. After a swipe at her cheeks, she appeared to find the steel within her. She blinked twice and looked away. Her upper lip thinned as she bit it hard.

"I'll get some ice," she said coldly. She brushed past him without another glance.

CHAPTER FIFTEEN

There were murmurings in the motorcoach all during their long ride from Waterford to Cork for a brief stopover at the Blarney Castle for lunch. The word had dispersed, like sneeze spray in an elevator, about the assault on Meg, her grandmother, and even Jake, who'd intervened to help them. So while her grandmother dozed, Meg and Jake fielded all the questions. They thanked everyone for their concern. Afterward Meg refused to talk to Jake or join him for lunch.

At a pub within fifty yards of the Blarney Castle, Jake settled in a booth with Hank and the two New Jersey sisters. Hearing about his and another man's chase after the attacker, Judy and Jeannie bombarded him with questions, openly turned on by his bold chase of the attacker around the ferry.

The youngest, Judy, fluttered her dark eyelashes while he tasted his shepherd's pie. Hot and flavorful, he decided, while fending off her flirtations. Outside the cozy pub, rain lashed the windows and the wind howled. Their first Irish rainstorm, and only a few hardy souls willing to take the trek up the hill to the castle with Robert and his umbrella.

Judy declared, "Who wants to kiss a disgusting stone that hundreds of thousands of people have left their saliva on? Not me!"

Jeannie smiled slyly. "Yeah, I know something else you'd like to kiss instead." Both girls giggled as Jake exchanged a rolling-eye with Hank.

"Seriously, Jake, join us tonight for drinks. Unless you enjoy running in the rain. I wouldn't if I were you, especially with lightning about."

Jake made a noncommittal, diplomatic gesture that was somewhere between a shrug and a nod. Again conversation drifted to the attacker on the ferry and Jake explained for the fifth time that day that neither Meg nor her grandmother knew the crazy man. Which was true. Mary McCoy would never have met her cousin Mike's son, who was close to thirty years her junior. She'd already emigrated to the States long before he was born.

The other three at the table chalked it up to a random case of being at the wrong place at the wrong time. On the coach drive from Waterford to Blarney, Robert Morse had reassured the group that he and the driver would keep a vigilant eye out for the "the bloody ol' wanker".

That, of course, hadn't stopped everyone from checking their carry-ons for anything that could double as self-defense weapons—in case they were the next targets. One middle-aged lady had held up her nail files, another her Swiss Army knife—scissors, screwdriver and all, which she'd transferred from her suitcase to her purse.

Jake had considered his 9mm pistol for all of two seconds then decided it would be like bringing a cannon to a turkey shoot and left it in his suitcase. Carrying it in his shoulder holster would frighten everyone, destroy his cover, and end up alarming MI5 as well as Global Adventures. They'd call him a Wild West cowboy and yank him out of his assignment faster than he could say Operation Hummingbird. Before his plane touched down, the news would have traveled all the way back to D.C. and that'd be the ignominious end to all further undercover cases. He would be consigned to desk duty for the rest of his career.

After their lunch stop in Blarney, due to Robert's silly daily game of musical chairs, Jake had moved up clockwise in the coach. He was now sitting across the aisle from Meg and her grandmother, who'd moved a couple of seats toward the back. What would have pleased him five days ago, and played into his plans at getting acquainted, now seemed to mock him. Meg sat, her arms folded across her chest, and stared out the window at the passing scenery, shunning him completely.

She was angry at him, and he couldn't blame her. If he'd been in her place, he'd have been furious. His cover as a banker who just happened to be extra curious about the war and who just happened to be adept at martial arts and hand-to-hand combat was now shot to hell.

Feeling deceived must hurt too. She wasn't dumb. She'd been insightful enough to ask him just one question while applying the ice pack to his face. "Was this all an act? Coming on to me to get to my grandmother?"

He made the mistake of confessing the truth. "At first, yeah. Not after Bath. Certainly not after Cardiff—"

She'd turned away then and had refused to hear any more explanations. Even to his ears he sounded so pathetic he had to cringe inside.

Good grief, man, you couldn't come up with anything better than that . . .

Still, the truth hurt.

Four hours later the coach and its sleepy passengers pulled into the driveway in front of their Marriott motor inn in Killarney. Jake's whole body ached from sitting so long. Most of all, his thigh and shoulder felt as if they were on fire. He planned to take a long, hot bath after a quick run around the town of Killarney.

He had to learn the layout of the place, where important landmarks were, familiarize himself with Mary McCoy's hometown. Certainly the Catholic cathedral had played a part in her upbringing. Father Dillon had been a pastor there. According to the major's files, the house where Mary grew up in a fairly affluent family was nearby. By Irish standards, the

McCoys had been upper-middle-class Catholics. Her father had owned a pub, store, and gas station downtown. He had to check out those properties as well. The property Mike Junior had railed about on the ferry was probably one of those four pieces of real estate.

When Robert mentioned the location of the motor inn, on Muckross Road, south of town, Jake sat up. If he recalled correctly, that was close to the very street on which Mary McCoy and her parents had lived just before the outbreak of the war. He looked over at Meg's grandmother, who'd begun stirring from her nap. She didn't appear to recognize Muckross Road or its name, for she said nothing to Meg. Of course, Mary's hearing wasn't perfect and memories could fade.

He needed to ask them if Mary had kept any pre-war photos of her parents or the town of Killarney. A person would think she would have taken some with her to London, especially after her parents' deaths.

"Meg," he tried, leaning over the aisle. "Wanna go for a run after dinner? Scope out the town?"

She appeared to hesitate as she glanced at the window. The rain had stopped and small patches of blue sky were visible. From all appearances, the weather was clearing up. When she finally cast doleful eyes his way, he knew what her answer would be.

"No, I don't think so, Jake—or whatever your real name is."

"Wanna see my driver's license?" Not appreciating her stubbornness, he dug into his pocket and fished out his wallet. Showed it to her. She studied it.

"Is this fake, too?" Her dark blue eyes drilled into him, challenged him. Her lovely mouth was turned down in a slight sneer. She wasn't about to believe him, no matter what he said.

"'Course," he said drily. "I always carry fake IDs with me."

"Now *that* I believe." Blonde locks twirled in front of his face as she turned away.

Women.

He angrily stood up with the others and grabbed his carry-on case. His trouser fly and butt were at her eye level as he waited his turn to disembark. In the corner of his eye, he saw her stare at his body despite her determination to hold him in contempt.

"Suit yourself," he said. "Thought I'd get to know your grandmother's hometown before it got dark." The hint at his ongoing investigation of the old lady got Meg's attention. Her eyes flared but she said nothing.

This time, he didn't help the two women with their carry-ons. Instead he left the coach and went directly to his room. No longer feeling hungry—in fact, feeling downright depressed—he skipped dinner, changed into his running sweats, T-shirt and sneakers and went to scout the area. After a few minutes, his stiff muscles warmed up and he was able to ignore the soreness in his shoulder and leg. Moving his body felt good.

Compared to American towns its size—no more than 100,000 population—it was smaller, more compact, easy to get around and size up. Roughly shaped in a square, with major roads running in and out of town on all four sides, the downtown area centered around the cathedral on Port Road, the Garda—or local Irish police station—on New Road, the shops along High Street, New Street, and Main Street, and the Franciscan Friary, now apparently the Killarney Youth Centre.

He was alert for any tails. Mike McCoy's crazy son was out there somewhere, but as far as Jake could discern, the man wasn't following him on his run around the town. Neither were any of the major's men.

His breathing shallow and steady, he fell into a rhythm that relaxed him. His body ran like a well-oiled machine while his mind's pistons pumped. His senses took in everything. The damp, earthy smells, the occasional sweet exhalations of an Irish summer, the grainy aromas of the downtown pubs. The cool, bracing air suffused him with extra energy and vigilance.

He ran past sports fields by St. Anne's Road, just north of the downtown area, apparently used for Gaelic Games and Pitch and Putt—whatever that was—according to the posted signs. The buildings in town were a mixture of old and very old. Some dated back to the seventeenth century, he guessed.

Most of the neo-Gothic ones, however, including the cathedral, were built during the reign of Queen Victoria, the mid 1800s. The ornate sign in front of St. Mary's Cathedral dated the edifice back to 1856. Constructed of gray fieldstone and black granite, its Neo-Gothic style reminded Jake of St. Paul's in London. Another St. Mary's was a smaller Anglican church closer to the downtown area.

There was a large national park west of the town, but he decided not to explore it by himself. With that lunatic around somewhere, that would be foolish. It would be dusk in about thirty minutes. He suspected the lake—Lough Leane, where Mary McCoy's parents drowned—was located in that park. Tomorrow in full daylight, he'd check it out.

Making the loop back to Muckross Road, he noticed a side street. Countess Road. The stateliest homes and mansions were located along this street and Muckross Road, according to the hotel brochure. This was the neighborhood where Mary McCoy spent her childhood and where their hotel was located. Mary Snider should recognize Countess Road—if Major Temple's notes were accurate, nothing much had changed. The stately homes and mansions appeared the same as the historical photo in the major's file, the one supplied by Mary's cousin, Mike McCoy Sr. He must have taken the photo in the early 1940s.

By nine PM he'd returned, soaked some of the aches away in a hot bath, and was settling down to write some notes. What had he learned that day as a result of his conversation with Mary Snider on the ferry? A lot, he recalled. Also what about the attack? Why weren't Major Temple's men more alert and on top of things? Maybe they could've prevented McCoy's assault on the two women, maybe not. Where was the crazy old coot now?

An hour later he made his nightly call to Major Temple and cut to the chase.

"Here's the lowdown. Mary Snider—and I believe her—admitted to her granddaughter and me that she was once engaged to a German spy. His name was Horst Eberhard. I got the impression he worked for Admiral Canaris, the head of the Abwehr during the war. She seemed to disapprove of Canaris' execution later in the war by Himmler's SS. The Abwehr was dissolved after that and, as you know, intel was taken over by the Schutzstaffel, or SS. Which effectively deprived the Wehrmacht and the anti-Nazis within the German army of an intelligence service of its own. After that, Himmler's control of the military was total. Canaris essentially did his best to contain the Nazis' lunacy. Due to Canaris' doctored intel, he prevented the German invasion of Switzerland, among other things."

"Hmm, yes," was all he heard on the major's end. Jake's little history lesson was falling on deaf ears—or was he preaching to the choir? The major certainly knew all this.

"Anyway, Mrs. Snider said she kept the engagement a secret for obvious reasons, said her fiancé asked her to spy for him but she refused. He was killed in 1944. She thinks Italy, during the German retreat."

"Did she say this Horst Eberhard was the Thomas McCoy she wrote to during her time with the War Office?"

"No and I didn't ask, but I bet he was. That would have been an easy way to stay in touch . . .and he was most likely using the Irish name as a cover. Which means he was fluent in English, maybe even Gaelic—or as they call it here in Ireland, the Irish tongue. My guess, this Horst Eberhard was deep undercover, probably in Ireland for years before the outbreak of the war. Doing surveillance, contacting Nazi sympathizers, setting up radio posts. Oh yeah, he gave Mary a pin. Covered with precious stones in the design of a hummingbird—"

"*What?*"

"A hummingbird. Yeah, I know. The Abwehr's code name for one of their top female spies."

"Could Eberhard have recruited her, despite her declarations to the contrary? He could very well have been her control officer," Major Temple added. Jake could hear the tension in the man's voice.

"Possibly." He hoped for Mary Snider's sake she'd told the truth.

"Well, it won't take long to find out if this Horst Eberhard was an Abwehr spy or if he worked for Himmler's SS. You have to give it to the Germans. They kept excellent records of all their activities during the war. As though they were making templates for future militant Aryan generations to follow, God forbid."

"I suppose he could have recruited her," Jake said resignedly. His stomach churned with acid at the thought. "Maybe she was lying about refusing to help him, I don't know. Why would he give her a pin in the shape of a hummingbird? It looked custom-made and expensive. Not mass market jewelry."

"The hummingbird spy, according to one of the double-cross agents, worked for the SS. Hardcore Nazis were in the SS. Most of them murderous thugs."

Both Jake and Temple were silent for a long moment, then the major cleared his throat.

"Good work. I've got enough to bring her in for questioning."

Jake swore silently to himself. His pulse began to race as he thought of Meg. He doubled over as acid pain shot up his chest. The blood rushed to his ears and his head throbbed. Gone was the physical euphoria from his run.

"Look, Major, all you have is a pin in the shape of a hummingbird."

"Not quite, Agent Bernstein. We have her admission about Horst Eberhard."

"Can you hold off a bit? I think what I was getting today were bits of truth mixed in with some lies but I don't know which is which. Give me a little more time, okay? We're in Killarney, her hometown. If she can prove to me she knows the place, if she can recognize childhood landmarks, then I think we have to assume she really *is* Mary McCoy. And maybe she's telling the truth about Eberhard. That she didn't spy for him, that they were just romantically involved. He tried to recruit her but she turned him down. Then he went back to Europe and got killed." Jake paused and rubbed his chin. You couldn't help who you fell in love with. Love just happened. For a second, his thoughts turned to Meg.

"Don't you think it's possible? That wartime enemies could fall for each other? That two people can connect on a real basic level?"

"Oh sure. And I also believe in wee leprechauns."

"Major, give me a little more time."

"Why do you think Mary Snider gave up all that information? To you and her granddaughter?"

Jake considered the reasons. "I'm not a psychologist, Major, and this'll sound like so much psychobabble nonsense." He sighed. Might as well give it a try. "I'd have to say her age and infirmities are catching up with her. Her wall of lies is cracking. Maybe the stress of carrying this burden — -guilt, remorse, fear, whatever — is getting to be too much for her. Too much for a woman her age."

He gasped as the acid reflux worsened. Now his throat ached with shooting spurts. In desperation, he reached for the bottle of antacid tablets, popped a couple and grimaced at the chalky taste.

"Are you ill?" Major Temple inquired.

Chewing away, Jake took a deep breath and closed his eyes. Immediately, the pain lessened.

"No, just skipped dinner tonight. Shouldn't have. I get heartburn when I do that."

Jake instantly recalled the way Mary Snider locked eyes with him as she revealed the identity of her German lover. As though she was challenging, even daring, him to uncover the truth. The woman was old and tired.

"Maybe she sees me as someone who can help relieve her burden. I don't know."

Major Temple harrumphed loudly. "Or she's using you to help her cover up her crimes. This eleventh-hour catharsis of hers sounds bogus to me. When she worked for the War Office, she took a loyalty oath. Meaningless, of course, if she were a German spy. I believe she's trying to avoid a not-so-comfy prison cell for the remainder of her life."

That statement sank Jake's mood into the depths. He could picture Meg's reaction to that. She would blame *him*. She would despise *him*.

Not to mention the reaction of Navy Commander Snider — his elderly mother in a British prison cell. The scandal in D.C.

And if the old lady were indeed telling the truth, she wouldn't deserve to end her life that way. Sure, betraying her oath to England's war effort was unconscionable, but wasn't protecting her fiancé an extenuating circumstance that could be forgiven after all this time?

"Give me more time, Major. And while I continue working on this, keep that psycho away from us. He scared the shit out of the women—the whole motorcoach group, in fact. He's here in Killarney somewhere. I'd bet my ass on that. The hair on my arms is telling me he's close by and he's not giving up. I've half a mind to start packing."

"Packing to leave?"

"No, packing my weapon."

"Yes, sorry about that. The team should've been there. After the tongue-lashing I gave them, they will be from here on. By the by, that psycho, as you call him, runs the Muckross Stag, the pub in town that he inherited from his father, old Mike McCoy. Runs it successfully, by all accounts."

"Well, sonuva—"

"Killarney's his hometown too. And by weapon, if you're referring to that FBI pistol of yours, I dare say there's no need. My boys will run interference, as you Yanks like to say. No need to upset the Irish. Remember, we're operating on *their* soil now. The Republic of Ireland is not part of the United Kingdom."

"No shit," Jake grumbled. "So, will you let me continue carrying the ball?"

"All right, old chap," Temple said. "But take care with the Irish. Even Sigmund Freud said they were the only nation on earth immune to psychoanalysis. Even the most sane are a bit dodgy."

Jake had to grin. "The way you Brits see it, you'd have to lump Americans in there too."

"Oh we have. At any rate, we know where to find young McCoy *and* Mary Snider. And you. Never far from the comely maiden, I suspect."

"Meg just found out today about her grandmother's past, I assure you. The surprise on her face was genuine." Thanks to

Mike McCoy's assault, and his own slip-up, her suspicions were now on high alert. He doubted he'd get any more help from her.

Seconds later he ended the call, tossed the cell phone into his carry-on next to his laptop. So much for paralysis by analysis. So far he'd analyzed this case to death. Now that they were in Mary McCoy's hometown, he sensed things were going to heat up.

Jake threw down his bath towel and slipped on a pair of clean briefs. Then popped another two antacid tablets. Groaning aloud, he huffed out a breath of air as he lifted the laptop and plugged in the wireless connector. Punched in his encrypted password. Then two more passwords to get past the FBI firewalls. Time to write that updated report to the legate in London and copy Terry at Headquarters.

Fuck it. This wasn't going to be pretty.

CHAPTER SIXTEEN

Meg gave her grandmother the last of her evening pills then crossed to the mirror above the low dresser to brush her hair. She began her nightly ritual, necessary to keep her long, thick locks from tangling into a nest for mice, as her grandmother would say. Her eyes met Gran's in the mirror.

Something wasn't right. She felt a kind of fraying in the strong bond that linked the two of them.

"You feeling okay, Grandma?" She tried to put a note of cheer in her voice. Difficult to carry off. She'd been moping all evening and was so subdued over dinner she'd barely spoken a word to her table companions. Her grandmother must've noticed her mood but probably didn't realize the real reason.

"It's been a stressful day," Mary Snider said, getting settled in bed, smoothing down the sheet and blankets about her. The wrinkle between her eyes creased into a deep furrow. "The ferry — it seemed to take forever. Then all those questions that Bernstein fellow asked. Then that horrible man . . ."

"You're right, Granny, it's been a bad day. A very bad day. I was thinking of the German word, *weltschmerz*. You know it, of course. Doesn't it mean world weariness? Or weary of the world? That's the way my German teacher explained it. That's what I think you have, Gran. I think you're weary of the world."

Her grandmother's deep blue eyes seemed to darken and sink within their eye-sockets. One edge of her thin, creased mouth curled up into a brittle smile.

"*Weltschmerz*. I haven't heard that word in a long time."

The elderly woman's eyes focused on Meg. "Don't worry about me, Meggie. *Weltschmerz* comes with old age. You'll feel it too one day. One day when all the promise and hope in your life is suddenly behind you. You look back and, if you're cursed with my kind of memory, you see the past too clearly. Then you wish you had it to do all over again. So cliché but true, what they say. You wish you could live your life all over again. Make other choices."

Meg frowned at her grandmother. The woman's intellect sometimes frightened her, certainly continued to awe her. Along with her abiding admiration the young woman felt an unwavering obligation. And the need to protect her.

"Gran, if it weren't for you and Grandpa Snider, Jack and I—well, God knows what would have happened to us. You saved our lives, don't ever forget that. Whatever else happened in your life that you regret, just think of that. You saved a few lives. Maybe more than a few, with your War Office work."

"Hmmm, yes. I think you're right. What is that saying, about history books being written by the victors?" Mary closed her eyes, sank more deeply in her pillow. She sighed. "Imagine if the Germans had won. I'd have come home to a victory parade."

Her grandmother's voice had faded with the last sentence, so much so that Meg wasn't sure she heard correctly. A chill ran up her spine to the base of her skull and sent a shiver rippling up to the crown of her head. Meg put down her hairbrush and stared at her grandmother, her drowsiness quickly subsiding into another early night of sedated sleep.

"Gran, what did you just say?"

Her grandmother mumbled something, her words incoherent. Meg frowned and sat down on her bed.

"You were right about Jake. I think he's a private detective and I think he's investigating you. It might have something to do with your work during the war. Because you were engaged to that German spy. They—whoever hired him—must think you spied for the Germans, too."

Meg looked at her grandmother's gloves, which she insisted on peeling off herself every night. The process was tedious and painful, but her grandmother refused to let anyone help her—her one remaining display of dogged independence, she'd explained once. Saying nothing now, Mary Snider turned her head to the wall. She looked so shrunken and thin in her double bed as Meg stared across the little divide from her own bed. In about five or ten minutes, Meg knew, the sleeping pill would put her into a deep sleep.

"Gran, tell me. Did you spy for the Germans?"

The elderly woman rallied her energy one more time but kept her head turned away. "G'night, Meggie. Don't worry . . .no one can prove a thing." A long pause . . . then "I love you, child."

"Night, Gran. I love ya too."

Meg covered her face with her hands and inhaled a long, shuddering breath. *Oh God, I should never have brought her here.*

She sat quietly, listening for her grandmother's soft, even breathing as the pill took effect.

An addiction, those sleeping pills. Her grandmother's physician had prescribed the sedatives as a way of dealing with the woman's anxiety and wakefulness at night. For years now, her grandmother had suffered from insomnia, anxiety attacks, and dangerously high blood pressure. Stroking was always an omnipresent risk. Her blood pressure pills helped but, of course, were no guarantee against a stroke.

The insomnia was another problem. Her grandmother would pace at night, muttering at shadows, turning on every lamp in the house as she moved from room to room. As if haunted or consumed with fear. A paranoia that Meg used to think was just an old person's affliction. Now she wasn't so sure.

No one can prove a thing.

Those words explained a lot, Meg realized. The trauma of war had saddled her grandmother with something like PTSD. Was her deep-seated anxiety based on the fear the British would accuse her of treason, just because of her German fiancé during the war?

How could someone love the enemy of one's country, Meg wondered. How could she, someone who'd never known war, even begin to understand what propelled people to do what they did in wartime? What drove them together? How could she judge her grandmother for something that happened so many years ago?

Meg thought of their shared house in a safe, upper-class neighborhood outside of Dallas, as secure as one of the downtown city banks. Motion sensor detectors had been installed on the windows and doors. Lights surrounding the two-story contemporary were on sensors, too. Deadbolts and multi-locks on every door. A locked, wrought-iron gate at the end of their short driveway. That was the most thorough internal security system Meg had ever seen.

And her grandmother had insisted that Meg learn how to use a gun. They kept two pistols and one pump-action shotgun in the house at all times. Always loaded and ready to fire.

As though Grandma was expecting the Gestapo to burst in and take them both away to death camps. Meg had watched such scenes in the movies — wrenched from your home in the middle of the night. Marched out in the street with just the clothes on your back. Forced onto cattle cars for the terrible journey to Auschwitz, synapses of hope still sparking in your brain. While clutching your loved ones tightly to your side.

Her grandmother's even breathing reassured Meg. She stood up and went back to the dresser. The reflection in the mirror stopped her. From old photos of Gran shortly after she'd married Grandpa Snider, Meg knew she resembled her. The pretty features, the dark blue eyes and blond hair. What she saw was an Irish miss, eager to help the war effort. Lend her mind and talents to the Allied cause.

Mary McCoy, the young, idealistic Irish woman, worked for the Allies. She hadn't spied for the Germans. She'd told her and Jake that very day. She'd turned down Horst, her German fiancé. Refused to spy for him. Meg believed her grandmother. Why shouldn't she?

Maybe Jake believed her too. And he'd conclude his investigation or whatever it was he was doing and pronounce her grandmother—-what, innocent of any wrongdoing?

A pounding on the hotel door interrupted Meg's thoughts. Half-naked in a short nightie with spaghetti straps, she wasn't about to open the door to anyone. She held it open a crack.

"Who is it?" she asked quietly. No one answered. Another loud pounding sounded on the door next to hers. More poundings, then strident calls from a male voice. That crazy man was back! But how did he know where they were?

Meg opened the door and peered down the hallway to her left. The same gray-haired man with the monk's haircut was running down the hall, pounding on each door, yelling out, "Mary McCoy, I know you're here somewhere on this floor. We need to talk! You have something that belongs to me!"

Her heart instantly leaped into overdrive. His back to her, Meg quickly closed the door, made sure it clicked shut. Her thoughts aswirl, she rushed to the phone on the desk beside the dresser. Automatically punched in Jake's room number.

"Jake, that crazy man's back! He's in the hallway—"

"I know, I heard him, too. Stay inside your room, Meg. I'll be right there!"

She exhaled the breath she'd been holding then contacted the front desk. The line was busy. Everybody on the floor—all of the motorcoach passengers—must be calling in panic.

Seconds later she heard heavy thuds down the hallway — as if the man were hitting the walls in a burst of fury. More shouting followed by a mixture of male voices. A woman screamed, then another. She heard what sounded like running. More shouting. More male voices raised in anger. Curiosity spiking, Meg couldn't stand the suspense any longer. She opened the door just as Jake sprinted up.

He wedged himself in as Meg stepped back, her eyes wide. "People are having a shit-fit out there but it's taken care of. Hotel security's taking — what?"

Her eyes bulged, her mouth hanging open. Jake was bare-chested and barefoot, wearing tight jeans that hung low, waistband unsnapped, showing the tops of his white briefs. She'd never before seen him entirely bare-chested. His shoulders broad, his pecs defined, the muscles in his upper arms rippled from tension. His wet hair clung to his head like a swimmer's dark cap. Lord, he was gorgeous — all six-foot-plus of him. At the very sight of him, all her pent-up anger vanished. Lust replaced the fear that caused her pulse to race.

In his right hand, he gripped the stock of a large black pistol. She stared.

"Nothing. I'm just . . .shocked the guy came back," she covered, stepping back a foot. Now he was the one to stare.

His gaze took her all in as well, and she could just imagine the way she appeared to him. Her bare shoulders and cleavage, the way her plump breasts spilled over the snug, Grecian-styled bodice of her short nightie. Her bare thighs, legs, and feet. Her long hair flowed down her back but several long locks curled about one shoulder.

"Hotel security caught him. The Garda — local Irish cops — just arrived." Jake glanced down at the pistol in his hand. "Guess I overreacted. Thought he might be armed this time. Your grandmother . . .is she okay?"

"Yes, she's asleep. Didn't hear all the ruckus, thank God.

She takes a sleeping pill every night."

"She takes a lot of pills, doesn't she?"

Meg sighed and nodded. "She suffers from insomnia . . .and a whole slew of health problems."

Jake peeked around the corner of the small foyer, seemed satisfied at the sight of the sleeping figure of the old woman, then moved back to the door. He stroked Meg's bruised cheek with a forefinger, gave it a peck then straightened up to leave.

"Well, glad you don't hate me at least. Call me anytime. Believe it or not, I'm here to help."

She frowned. "How can you help? You're prying into my grandmother's life. You think she was a Nazi spy, don't you?"

"I'm hoping she wasn't." His eyes ran over her from top to bottom. He cleared his throat and glanced to the door. "Excitement's over. I'll get back—"

No, don't leave! In one swift, fluid motion, Meg flung her arms around his neck and thrust her body against his. Her hands clung to his nape as though she were hanging off a cliff and he was her only fingerhold. Her hips nestled against his, her mound crushed against his groin. She pressed her lips against the side of his bruised jaw, trailed down to his neck. God help her but it was hopeless. She shouldn't be doing this. But with every inch of her body she telegraphed her desire.

A fragment of a thought. Jake was her own personal bodyguard and she was crazy about him. What more was there to this equation?

"Let's finish what we started last night," she whispered. She pulled her head back to gauge his reaction.

Jake blinked twice and swallowed. His strong arms enfolded her and squeezed hard. He kissed her and then relaxed his hold. Finally he let her go. The expression on his face bordered on frantic.

"My room. Ten minutes."

Then he was gone.

Her heart flipped over. Twice. Thrice. She smudged on some lip gloss, grabbed her card key then sat down to wait. Jumped up to slip on her lightweight bathrobe. Not that she'd be wearing it for long but she had a length of hallway to traverse.

Ten minutes. Time enough to think and chicken out. Maybe change her mind. *No.* No more thinking. *Just feel.*

Time for action. And tons of pleasure.

CHAPTER SEVENTEEN

Jake signed off, having cut short his report by a page or two. Amazing how succinct he could be when he was pressed for time. He closed his laptop, slipped it into the carry-on then noticed his FBI-issue pistol lying on top of his suitcase. Putting it safely away in its blue-plastic case took a mere 30 seconds. Locking up his suitcase took another minute or so when he misplaced his keys and couldn't find them. Finally he tossed them on top of the suitcase, sprang up to turn off all the lights except the one in the bathroom and the bedside lamp. Mood lighting. Good.

Blood pounded in his ears. His cock was wood hard.

A quiet knock. Despite his eagerness, he greeted Meg with a diffident smile and open arms. She walked readily into his embrace. Even then he felt it necessary to give her a chance to change her mind. All the while wishing, of course, she wouldn't.

"Are you sure you want to do this?" he murmured into her hair.

Her reply was to slip out of her bathrobe. She hesitated for a second before shedding her nightie top. There she stood like a blonde goddess in all her naked beauty except for a small strip of black pantie. They came together—kissing, touching, clutching each other like playful tigers. Aggressive but with claws sheathed. He shucked his jeans before lifting her and carrying her to the bed. Meg cried out in surprise at the small pile of condom wrappers her bottom rubbed against.

Damn. In his haste to get out a couple of condoms, Jake had

yanked a ziplock bag out of his suitcase pocket. The bag had violently opened and let fly a supply of condoms, bottles of antacids, Advil, vitamins, deodorant tubes, and other grooming needs onto the bed. His ready-to-travel pharmacy. He'd swept them all back into the bag except the dozen or so square-shaped wrappers.

She started to laugh. "You're very optimistic, Jake."

His humor intact, he smiled at her barb. With one arm, he swept them all onto the carpet at the foot of the bed except for one. Yanked off his briefs and gently slid on top of her.

They kissed, threaded their hands through each other's hair then began to explore each other's bodies. His lips trailed wetly down her neck, kissed the hollow of her throat. He cupped her breasts and artfully used his tongue to circle her nipples. Then he laved them as if they were the luscious tops of ice cream cones. They even had a slightly vanilla flavor, he decided. When she moaned, Jake came undone. His gentle sucking turned to nips along her waist and belly.

He mentally turned off all thoughts, worries, concerns—surrendered to tasting her delicious body, feeling its texture, the dips and hollows, the fleshy curves and mounds. He felt her shift her legs, inviting him in. Felt her fingers close around his sheathed cock, pulling tenderly, urging him to consummate. When he finally slid inside her, his entire being was shouting *Yes! Yes! Yes!*

This was right, this was good . . . this was where he belonged. Elation—a feeling he'd never before felt with a woman—overtook him. Strangest damned thing . . .

He was swamped with sensations of pleasure, ecstasy, release as they spasmed in syncopation. They nuzzled awhile and whispered sweet nothings to each other. Her voice, sounding happy and content, lulled him. So relaxed he dozed off.

Much later he half-awoke to find her facing him, staring at

him with wonderment. They were snuggled together, their arms and legs tangled, rubbing together. Under the covers, warm and drowsy, he reached down to cup her bottom with one hand. She stirred, brushed her hair back, draped one long leg over his hip, claiming him.

"Jake, I need a wakeup call for six. I've got to be back in my room by then. Before . . .y'know . . ."

He understood and set his watch-alarm to buzz softly. She relaxed again and let him scoop her up and roll her on top of him. Tacitly, Meg understood what he wanted. She scooted down his body until her lips and tongue had left a wet, enticing track down his torso. When she demonstrated what else her tongue and mouth could do, Jake groaned with pleasure, succumbed to the total mindless trip Meg was taking his body on.

When at last she impaled herself upon his penis, his pelvis, hips, and legs responded instinctively, let the ride of pleasure spiral them up and outward. Only once during their night of mindless sex did Jake utter the words he dreaded using. They implied such permanence. Women liked to hear them but he'd rarely spoken them in his thirty-two years.

"Meg, whatever happens . . .just know I'm crazy about you. I know how that sounds, after just five or six days . . ."

She hushed him with a deep, wet kiss. "I know . . .it's insane." Her hug was strong, then she seemed to dissolve against his body. Within seconds she was dozing off, her mouth slightly open, her breathing slackened and shallow. Again the little girl in Meg was sleeping, needing protection.

A profound sense of well-being overcame him, relaxing him into a deep sleep.

Meg awoke to a small, buzzing sound. For a couple of seconds she wondered where she was. Then memory flooded back and she felt his warm body next to her, his face turned aside. She could hear his soft, rhythmic breathing. But before she could press the alarm button on his watch he stirred, grunted once, and mechanically turned it off without fully waking. Until he sank back to sleep, Meg lay quietly, listening to the sounds he made as he moved, stretched, got comfortable.

When he was finally still, she rose from the bed and tiptoed to the bathroom. Taking one of the bath towels, she wet it and wiped herself then bent over the basin and splashed water in her face. Her image in the mirror caught her attention. No, she wasn't going to analyze what happened that night. What they'd done was too simple and too beautiful to tear apart. They'd fallen in lust and then made love. As starkly plain and simple as that.

Nevertheless, clawing at the edge of her mind was the question—why was he really there? Jake was no banker, that was for sure. He didn't carry around a 9mm semi-automatic pistol for nothing. Having grown up in Texas, most everyone Meg knew had guns. Pistols, revolvers, hunting rifles, shotguns. Her neighbor carried a small lady's derringer in her purse at all times, even when she went to the grocery store. But for Jake to carry a pistol of that size and quality on a motorcoach tour abroad meant only one thing. He was on duty. Either a cop, a private detective, government agent . . .

She dressed quietly in the bathroom in her nightie and bathrobe then went back to the bedroom. The unzipped carry-on was a dark, slim bulk on the desk, the corner of a laptop visible within. Prying inside, from the dimness provided by the bathroom light, Meg spied two cell phones next to the laptop. Various pockets appeared to hold computer paraphernalia.

No gun there. Her eyes went to the molded suitcase sitting on the low dresser. Its hasp appeared locked. A set of keys rested on top, carelessly tossed there the night before.

Wetting her lips, Meg's pulse began to pound. If Jake caught her searching his things . . .what then?

Too late. She was committed.

Unlocking the hasp, she slipped aside the heavy lock and lifted open the suitcase lid, braced it on the wall. With quick, deft hands, she rummaged through his clothes, paused her hands on the plastic case Meg knew was the gun case. Skipping over that—she'd already seen the pistol—she felt into the zippered pocket inside the lid. A leather pouch the size of a small clutch purse felt strangely lumpy. Meg pulled it out slowly and felt inside. The room was too dark to discern the different objects inside, but the shape of one metal object was obvious. Police cuffs. She rapidly dumped the contents on top of Jake's packed clothes.

A leather wallet opened to show a badge. Meg took it over to the bathroom door. A gold-metal FBI badge. She'd seen two before, when two agents from the Dallas field office came to question her and her grandmother about her Uncle John. They'd been performing a background security check.

Special Agent Jacob Bernstein was printed on the ID on the opposite side of the wallet.

Jake—an FBI agent.

Meg didn't stop to think but instead moved back to the suitcase. She didn't need to see any more. The only possible conclusion was Grandma was in very serious trouble.

Hurriedly she put everything back in place, closed the suitcase lid and relocked the hasp. Her hands trembled so badly that this effort took several attempts. Then she replaced the keys on top of the suitcase, took one long look at the sleeping figure on the bed and left the room.

Jake lay still, pretending to softly snore, his mouth open but face turned away. He could hear Meg padding about in her bare feet, first in the bathroom and then by the foot of the bed. Little noises told him what she was doing, even when she padded over to the bathroom, came back and then left his room. So now she knew. And he was glad. In fact, he was damned relieved.

Sweet Meg. Athletic Meg. Laughing, teasing Meg. Angry Meg. Wanton, sexy-as-hell Meg. And, like most females, curi-ous-as-a-thousand-cats Meg.

She had guts and spunk. Not for nothing Jake was falling in love with her.

Still, had she opened his gun case, with the loaded pistol inside, he would have sprung out of bed in a flash. Expelling a long-held breath, Jake was relieved she hadn't. He won-dered what she'd do now that she knew who he was. Get her grandmother on the first plane out of Ireland and back to their lawyers in Dallas? If he were her, that's exactly what he'd do. Go home and lawyer up.

For Meg's sake, he was hoping she'd do just that.

CHAPTER EIGHTEEN

Jake woke up famished, having been so depressed the night before he'd skipped dinner. He bolted upright in bed. Friggin' incredible the difference a night of hot, lovin' sex could do for a man's spirits. He was fired up and rarin' to go.

He showered and dressed in black jeans, black tee, and his well-worn but favorite leather bomber jacket. The sky was its usual — Overcast. But not his mood. His mood soared like a freed falcon climbing to the sun.

When he entered the hotel dining room, the usual breakfast smells assailed him. This time, instead of turning his stomach, hunger pangs drove him ahead. He bypassed the hot table, where the pork 'n beans, blood sausage, and over-fried eggs and bacon could be found, and headed toward the toast, cheese, and jam section. He'd no sooner poured himself a cup of steaming, strong coffee and concocted his own version of a breakfast sandwich, inserting a slice of prosciutto and Swiss cheese into a bread roll, than his attention homed in like a laser beam on Meg's table. She was sitting with her grandmother and the French-Canadian couple. His heart tumbled with joy at the sight of her.

As soon as their eyes met, Meg jumped up and joined him at the buffet. She looked troubled despite her warm smile.

"Morning, Jake." She touched his arm. It took all his restraint not to seize her in his arms and plant a smacker on her lovely lips.

"Hey, baby," he whispered, leaning over her. "I missed you this morning. My bed got cold without you."

"I know . . .I had a good time." Their eyes met and they exchanged a knowing smile. "Listen, Jake, I wish you could join us, but Grandma's in a tear. She woke up in the middle of the night, saw I was gone . . .and, well, this morning she ragged me to death. Called me names I've never heard her say before. I think she's cracking up, I really do." Meg was holding back unshed tears. She looked away and sniffed.

"Did she react the same way when you were engaged? Y'know, sleeping over with what's-his-name?"

Meg frowned. "No, but I wasn't living with her then. I had my own place . . .so it was never . . .y'know, in her face."

"Sweetheart, you're twenty-six, not sixteen. Wasn't she the one who told you to sample me like a box of candy? Why should she care what we do anyway? We're adults." They moved off to the side against the back wall of the room, out of the way of servers and busboys.

"I know, I know," grumbled Meg. "I don't know what's eating her. Maybe the stress of the tour, your presence, you and me getting together, all your . . .questions." The look she settled on him then was a mixture of anger, worry, sympathy, confusion—even a come-hither yearning. "Maybe we should . . .take a break from each other. Just for a day or so. Let her calm down."

His heart sank. Meg was already pulling away. Jake glanced over at Mary Snider. The old lady glowered at him, her mouth downturned like Scrooge's. He nodded.

"Okay, I'll respect your wishes. May not like them, but I'll respect them."

The way she averted her eyes made him realize she was afraid. Hell, who wouldn't be? Most people he met socially, as soon as they discovered his occupation, were taken aback. For a few, especially those whom he sensed had something to hide, finding out about what he did for a living was a conversation killer.

"Meg, you know about me. You know I'm just doing my job," he added in a whisper. "But I'm a man, too. And I'm crazy about you."

Her upturned face and big, luminous eyes trained on him was enough to calm his worries.

"What I did was sneaky but I had to find out," she admitted.

"Anything else you want to know?"

She glanced down at her feet. "Not right now."

From here on, Meg would shut him out and he didn't blame her.

Yeah, he'd blown his cover, but he wasn't about to reveal that to the MI5 team. They'd sweep in and haul both Mary Snider and her granddaughter back to England for questioning. He'd be damned if he'd allow that to happen.

"Can I trust you to keep it quiet . . .for now?"

She nodded solemnly. "Yeah. But you're wasting your time, Jake. My grandmother didn't do anything wrong."

"I hope not, for her sake. And yours."

She frowned then suddenly flashed him a hopeful grin. "The group's going on that jaunty car tour of the park and town. Killarney is Gran's hometown."

"Right," he said. "What time is that?"

"Eleven o'clock. It's supposed to last a couple of hours. Then we're on our own for lunch and the rest of the day."

Jake already had a plan. "I'll be back by then. Save me a seat in your horse cart."

"Where're you going?" she asked, her blue eyes fixed on his face.

"Jail," he said cryptically. He shot her his best lopsided smile.

The four officers at the Killarney Garda station were in their twenties and thirties, wore white shirts and khaki-green trousers, and sported gun holsters at their waists—Jake figured Beretta .45mm semiautomatics—and truncheons. Silver badges added sheen to their uniforms and swagger to their posture. Jake approached the baby-faced kid at the desk and introduced himself as an American tourist with the Global Adventures motorcoach group in town. They shook hands.

"Last night you brought in a man named Mike McCoy, is that right?" He laid on a thick southern drawl.

The kid folded his arms over his chest. With a yank of his head, he motioned the other three officers over.

"Yep, we did. Were you with that flock of tourists who were scared witless by that crazy loon? The hotel manager insisted we book the ol' curmudgeon and charge him with disorderly conduct."

One of the other officers, a stocky fellow with red hair, barged in. "We're not so sure we'll do that. He's been tame as a lamb all night. He's a local chap, don't ya know."

Jake nodded. "Slept off his drunk, huh? Well, then you probably won't mind if I have a word with the guy. Y'see, this Mike McCoy approached a friend of mine, an old woman who's with our group. He acted like he knew her. Like they were cousins. I didn't want her upset, so I came down to talk to him. Find out what he wanted with her."

"How do you know his name . . .Mister, uh . . ." The kid stood up and adjusted his holster and gun.

Jake smiled. The kid was trying to establish his authority here, posturing to show the other men how he could control the situation.

"Jake Bernstein. This Mike McCoy told us his name on the ferry coming over from Wales," explained Jake calmly. "He tried to talk to us, but the situation got out of hand. The old lady became frightened and emotional. So I was hoping to have a man-to-man with him. Find out what he wanted and see if I could help him in some way. Y'know . . . defuse the situation."

The kid glanced over at his three colleagues. They appeared bored and were wandering back to their desks, having realized the American stranger wasn't a threat. He opened the desk drawer, took out keycards held together on a metal cord, and clacked them together.

"Well, let's see if the old fart's wanting to see you."

"Fair enough."

A minute later, after following the kid down two hallways, past a modern security door, which he opened with one of the keycards, Jake stood in front of an old-fashioned jail with a grid of bars fronting eight five-by-ten cells. Only one other cell was occupied, and that occupant was snoring loudly on his top bunk.

Mike McCoy was sitting alone in his cell on the lower bunk. He hung his head in his hands, his bald crown gleaming in the cell's single, bright light. He looked downright pathetic, Jake decided.

"Chap to see you, Mr. McCoy," the kid announced. He stepped back, his hands on his belt, his legs apart.

The middle-aged man looked up, bleary-eyed and stubble-faced, his expression bewildered. He was slack-jawed from a hangover. Then instant recognition lit his face and he sprang to his feet and grabbed the bars.

"This man—he works for British intelligence. I saw him with that officer from MI5. He tried to kill me. I was just talking to them on the ferry and he attacked me."

Jake whirled around, feigned innocence, and shrugged for the cop's benefit. "Sorry, the man's delusional. I did no such thing."

The Irish cop frowned at Jake. "You work for the British?"

"Aw, hell no! I'm a banker from Virginia."

Appearing satisfied by the sound of Jake's accent, the kid

took a more belligerent stance with the old drunk.

"Just shut up and talk to the man, McCoy. He claims he's a friend of some old lady and he can help you. I'll be right on the other side of that door." The kid looked at Jake and pointed to a buzzer button by the security door. "Punch that if you need help . . ." He screwed up his face. "Don't think that'll be necessary. You look like you can handle yourself. Just keep away from the bars."

With the kid gone, Jake dropped the polite mask and the Southern accent. He sized up the middle-aged, mentally ill man inside the jail cell. And remembered how he'd grabbed Mary Snider, slapped Meg, and kicked him in the shin.

"Listen, you bastard, that chokehold I gave you yesterday is nothing compared to what I'll do when you get out. I want the truth from you—"

"You *are* with British intelligence, you asshole!" McCoy fumed.

A big, stocky man, he shook the bars until plaster dust from the ceiling rained down upon his bald head. Seemingly shocked at his own strength, he stopped and brushed dust off his head. And underwent a transformation, to Jake's amazement. The man before him now was almost calm, looked even like he'd shrunk in size. Certainly subdued and defeated. Was this guy bipolar? Manic one minute, depressed the next? Or worse—a schizophrenic off his meds? Temple hadn't said.

"I keep telling that MI5 officer, Major Temple, the pub's mine. That woman's not Mary McCoy. Me Da knew that. He knew the pub should've been mine." He swung his head like a puppet on a string. "Should've been all mine. It was in the will. Clear as day. The Muckross Stag's mine. The good priest showed me Da and me the will. Our cousins are all dead and that pub's legally mine."

"Look, Mike, your father might've been right about Mary McCoy, that American woman we know as Mary Snider.

Whatever you want from her you might get it, but only through me. Got that?"

Mike McCoy Jr. grew still but continued hanging onto the bars. Scruffy-faced, his clothes dirty and rumpled, he resembled a vagrant. Now, before Jake's very eyes, the man's stare grew more focused, his expression skeptical but patient. At least he was no longer acting like a hyper nutcase. Jake decided to proceed with caution, in case a careless word or tone of voice sent the man spiraling out of control again.

"I need to tape your testimony." Jake drew a miniature digital recorder the size of an iPod from his jacket pocket. When the man protested that he'd given it all already to MI5, Jake assured him he needed to hear it himself. "Tell me, Mike, what exactly was in this will and whose will was this?"

Huffing out a ragged sigh, McCoy slumped over the bars and began to tell his story. Five minutes later, Jake turned off the recorder.

"So Patrick and Elizabeth McCoy, the parents of Mary McCoy—your father's first cousin—left a will when they died. This will left their main heir, their daughter, all their property *except* the pub. This pub was left to two heirs—Mary and her cousin Mike. And this legal will, along with the deeds to these properties, were kept in the rectory's files by the parish priest, this Father Dillon." Jake knew from the MI5 file that after Mary's parents drowned—in the lake by Ross Island—the house on Countess Road and the gas station were sold by Mary McCoy shortly before setting off for London.

"Your father, Mike McCoy, Patrick's younger brother, kept the pub, this Muckross Stag—"

"On High Street," interjected a dispirited Mike McCoy Jr.

"—he kept this pub going after the war and was willing to split the profits between Mary and himself. But he didn't know where to find Mary McCoy after 1945. Your father thought she'd gone to America but he could never find her.

Rather he found a Mary McCoy Snider but she was not his cousin. So all these years, Mary's profits from this pub have been gathering interest in the local Bank of Ireland. You're saying if Mary's dead you should be sole owner of this pub and that account."

"I'll have you know that money's still there. I haven't touched a pence of it. Not a single Euro."

Since the Republic of Ireland had joined the European Union, its currency was now the Euro. Jake digested this information, wondering if the man was completely honest about the money. Not his concern anyway, but it was strange that Mary Snider, though legally entitled to her portion of the pub's profits over the years, had made no claim to them. Not that she appeared to need the money anyway. Her late husband seemed to have left her financially well off.

Mike's agitation was mounting. "Here's this American woman pretending to be my cousin, Mary McCoy, but me Da knew her for an impostor. Curse it all, I'm stuck in a legal . . ."

"Limbo," Jake supplied. "You can't buy out Mary's part and you can't inherit her half because she's not legally deceased." He wondered why Mary Snider hadn't cleared this up. Fine if she didn't want to admit a family relationship. But to dangle this man in some kind of legal quandary all these years made no sense. Why not just sign over to Mike McCoy the Irish version of a quitclaim deed?

Unless, of course, Mary Snider knew nothing about the will, nor where it'd been safeguarded. But hadn't she corresponded with Father Dillon during the war? Surely the priest safeguarding her parents' will and family legal records would have told her they were in his possession. Or maybe not . . .not if the priest suspected something was wrong.

Unless, of course, Mary McCoy knew about the pub but never expected to return to Ireland to claim half-ownership. Or didn't care. In London, Mary's life was so different. Was she no longer concerned with provincial life in County Kerry? Or any of the people she left behind?

Or Mike McCoy Senior was right and Mary Snider was an impostor. Her signature and handwriting would have been so different from the real Mary's. Anything could be forged but it took a great deal of skill to forge someone's handwriting. Was that why Mary McCoy, the War Office translator, sent typed letters to Father Dillon?

Mike McCoy Junior stared glumly at him from the other side of the bars, waiting for his reaction.

"There's an office supply store in town," offered Jake, to placate the man. "If I can get a — what we call in the States — a quit claim deed and get Mary Snider to sign her fifty percent portion of this pub, the Muckross Stag, over to you, will you be satisfied? Will you leave those women alone?"

"You bet, young fella. I just want what's mine." The tall man shrugged his big shoulders, pulled up his trousers and stood straighter. "If the American woman had my cousin killed and took her place — as me Da figgered — well, mebbe it's too late to do anything about that. Though that's not right neither. Least I can get what's rightfully mine."

Jake frowned and pocketed the recorder. "No, it's not right, Mr. McCoy. They're still rounding up war criminals from World War II. Some people want justice done, no matter how long it's been." For a moment, he thought of Grandpa Nate and the justice he'd longed to see for his own family.

"Tell me what you remember about your uncle's and aunt's deaths. From what your father told you?"

"Not much. Just that they drowned in the lake — Ross Bay, by the castle. You can see the castle ruins from shore."

"Anything else?"

"Just that old Father Dillon thought it was foul play that caused them to drown."

"Why foul play? You mean the priest thought someone

murdered them?"

Like this Thomas McCoy, alias Horst Eberhard? To force Mary McCoy to spy for him?

McCoy nodded soberly. He cast his reddened eyes to the bare, concrete floor.

"That's what Father Dillon thought. Me Da always said his brother was a damn fine swimmer. The best swimmer in Killarney 'tis what he said. A drinking buddy of Uncle Paddy's told the priest in confession that Paddy was taking a man out on the lake to fish."

"A man?"

"Told the priest—this buddy of Paddy's—he felt like he'd sinned that he didn't tell the Garda 'bout it right after it happened. But those were strange times. War had broken out, people were nervous, U-boats were all up and down the Irish coast. The man was a foreigner, Paddy told his buddy. Dutch, I think. Wanted to pay a good price for the gas station and Paddy was out to impress him with some local ale. Took a picnic basket 'n all. So the two of 'em, Uncle Paddy and Aunt Lizzie, went out on the lake with this foreigner. They ended up drowning and the foreigner disappeared."

Jake was astounded. None of this was in the MI5 files.

"Did you tell MI5 about your father's and the priest's suspicions? All these details about the McCoys' drownings?"

McCoy nodded. "It was all there in me Da's notebook. What he called his investigation. Took him over seven years to put it all together."

Most likely someone on the MI5 staff had distilled all 140 pages of Mike McCoy Senior's notebook into the ten pages Jake had perused. These details had been omitted in their summary. MI5 had discounted, apparently, the hearsay testimony of one man. Perhaps no one else had corroborated the man's testimony.

"Where was Mary, the daughter, when her parents drowned?"

"In Dublin. Me Da said she came home for the funeral. Da was there, too. Shipped out the next week. The priest thought Mary was going to do away with herself, she was so frantic with grief. After she sold the house and gas station—me Da said 'bout a month or two later—Mary left Killarney for good. Went to London to do her part for the war effort. Anyways that's what she told me Da. She wanted to do her part for the war effort."

"Even though Ireland was neutral?" Jake probed.

"Me Da said Mary hated the Nazis. Called them all hell-bound and evil. Satan lovers." McCoy hawked and spat behind him in the cell. "That's why she said she wanted to help in the hospitals. Donated half the money she got from the sale of the house and gas station to the Irish Catholic relief agencies. The rest she was going to donate to the hospitals in London. Because of all the wounded during the Blitz over there. A lot of her friends at Trinity College were English, you see."

Jake's head shivered. The picture that McCoy painted of Mary, his cousin, was a far different one than he personally knew. Mary McCoy Snider hating the Nazis?

"So Mary was a devout Catholic? Did she ever mention to your father that she'd met a German student in Dublin?"

The man shook his head. "No, don't reckon he mentioned that. But devout she was. When in town, she was at the cathedral every morning for mass. A good girl she was."

"And she didn't speak German, according to your father? Not even a little?"

The man made a small sign-of-the-cross over his heart. "If me Da was right, sweet cousin Mary hated the Germans. Wouldn't speak German if her life depended on it."

Interesting choice of words, Jake noted. *Maybe poor Mary's life did depend on it.*

CHAPTER NINETEEN

"So, Mike, can anyone verify any of this? I mean, the priest or anyone else in town?" Jake had just recalled that Father Dillon, according to the MI5 files, was already dead. "Good friends of the McCoys? Neighbors?"

McCoy scratched his chin then his forehead while Jake waited patiently. He could almost see the wheels and gears turning in the man's head. That's what self-medicating will get ya, dude, he thought. A sluggish brain.

"Oh yeah," the man said slowly. "The secretary at the rectory. Millie O'Loughlin. She took over the job when Father Dillon's secretary quit and moved away. Millie was with the good priest for over twenty years she was. She knew Mary McCoy. 'Tis true she was there at her parents' funeral. Still lives in Killarney too. I was over there yesterday at the cathedral, soon as I got here. Just to say hello. But Millie already went home."

Jake considered making a visit to the cathedral rectory and having a chat with Millie O'Loughlin. His watch told him he had sixty minutes to spare before the jaunty car ride, something he definitely did not want to miss.

"Okay, Mike, thanks. By the way, speaking of yesterday — the ferry. Where did you run to after our . . .little scuffle? Were you in the ferry's car bay? The white van or the black one?"

The man looked up, surprised. "The white van's mine. But I didn't go down there. I went up to the bridge. The skipper's a buddy of mine and he let me in. He didn't know I went

174

down to talk to that old American lady. 'Tween you and me, fella, she's no lady. She's a killer."

Jake raised his chin and narrowed his eyes at the man. Mike McCoy believed everything he was saying. He'd bought his old man's theory about Mary Snider, probably grew up brainwashed with the old pitbull's idea that his cousin and her parents were murdered. But being convinced of a theory didn't make him delusional.

"Look, Mike, I'll do what I can to get Mary Snider to sign over the pub to you. Or sell you her part. I promise you that." Jake moved to the security door. "I'll be in touch, man."

"Tell 'em out there I behaved, young fella!" McCoy shouted from behind the bars. His voice broke then and the next thing Jake heard from the man was soft sobbing. He shook his head and wondered if Mike McCoy wasn't as sane as the rest of them.

An emotional, alcoholic wreck, maybe, but sane.

He took his leave of the Garda police and was standing outside the station door before Mike McCoy's words finally hit him: *I went up to the bridge. The skipper's a buddy of mine.*

His memory of the chase on the ferry was crystal clear. The blond guy from MI5's surveillance team told Jake he'd seen McCoy run down the stairs. Not up the stairs to the bridge.

He'd sent Jake on a wild good chase.

But why?

Why didn't MI5 want the man caught and arrested? Especially after assaulting the two women on the ferry?

And why did Jake get the uneasy feeling he was more of a pawn in this game than he realized?

As soon as Jake stepped into the lobby of their hotel, he homed in on Meg standing in front of the concierge. A quick scan around the large room. Passengers were beginning to gather for the jaunty car ride—basically, a horse-driven cart that held up to eight passengers. Robert, the group's escort, was nowhere in sight. Neither was Meg's grandmother.

Then he spied the blond guy and his partner, MI5's new surveillance team, lounging on sofas, reading newspapers near the fireplace. The older man had a bulky briefcase by his feet.

The concierge was speaking to Meg. "I can reserve an American or Continental flight from Dublin to JFK then on to Dallas. Would an 8:30 am flight on Saturday, fit your schedule? Or would you prefer one later in the morning?"

Meg watched him approach, held a forefinger up to the man behind the concierge desk. "I'm not sure. I'll get back to you."

So she was running. Not that he blamed her. Jake smiled as if he hadn't heard her. He stepped up close to her, bent over and kissed her cheek. Whispered into her ear.

"Don't say another word. MI5's here and they've got a directional mike aimed your way. Come with me."

Blue eyes wide and alarmed, Meg let him steer her toward the bar, where they found a dark, private corner. Then she shook his hand loose and erupted.

"MI5? British intelligence? Like in James Bond? They're here? They're following us?"

"Yes, but not James Bond. That's MI6, the equivalent of our CIA. Meg, where's your grandmother?"

"In the back patio with the LeBlancs. MI5? Christ, Jake, what're you talking about? You're FBI, isn't that bad enough? Now MI5's involved. Did you call them and report my grandmother? You want to put my grandmother in prison, don't you?"

Placing his hands on her shoulders, he pressed her down on a chair by a bistro table, tried to calm her down. He scooted another chair over near her and propped a hip on the seat, leaned over her and touched her arm. With a hostile look, she shook his hand free.

"Don't you touch me! You're a heartless bastard. You used me!"

"Meg, keep your voice down. They'll follow us in here if they think we're arguing. You're upset, I know, but I'm trying to tell you MI5 brought *me* into this case. They've been investigating your grandmother for months. They're preparing an arrest warrant. They'll scare, shake, whatever they have to do to get the truth out of her. Under interrogation, she'll break like . . . like one of those Waterford goblets. She'll turn into a babbling idiot, confess to anything, and they'll have their case. Then she'll go to prison for war crimes."

That got her attention. Meg's lovely mouth gaped open. Her hands flew to her mouth.

"Oh God—"

"I shouldn't be telling you this—it'll probably get me fired—but I'm giving you fair warning. You and your grandmother should fly home as soon as you can. Get a good defense attorney for her. They'll be filing charges in another week most likely."

"My-my God, Jake. What do they think Grandma did?"

"Espionage, conspiracy to commit murder, the murder of fifty-four civilians in that ferry bombing. For starters . . ."

Meg's eyes filled with tears. She angrily swiped at her cheeks as the tears spilled over and streaked her face. Her pain weighed heavily on his chest, and Jake's own throat threatened to clog up. He cleared it noisily. This was no time for sentimentality.

"Look, Meg, baby . . ."

"Don't." She turned her tear-streaked face away. His heart hammered pain in his chest like a jackhammer drilling a hole. Sweat broke out on his forehead. Impatiently, he wiped it away. *Bernstein, what the fuck are you doing? If MI5 finds out, I've just shot my career all to hell.*

He took a deep breath and stepped over another imaginary line. A line he once swore he'd never cross.

"I'm stalling MI5, telling them I can get the truth out of Mary Snider the easy way. Cornering her with questions, pushing but not too hard, keeping the pressure up. I can keep them—MI5's team—at bay until Dublin. That's the day after tomorrow. I'll give them bits and pieces, enough to let them think she's on the verge of breaking down. Give you a chance to take off for home. I'll tell them I had no idea you were planning to sneak off."

"You'd do that? Risk losing your job for us?" Meg absorbed that, frowning at her tightly clasped hands on the table. "Jake, you're FBI. You don't owe us, not a thing. You don't owe . . .me."

"Maybe not . . .but I feel like I do." He smiled and glanced over at the bar entrance. So far, so good. The Brits were being patient and staying away, probably thinking the two lovers were having a little tête-à-tête. When he felt Meg's eyes bore down on him, he looked back at her.

"I didn't tell Grandma you were an FBI agent."

"Yes, I knew you wouldn't." He returned her a rueful smile.

"You're so certain?" Her eyes narrowed.

Jake shrugged. "No, just hoping you wouldn't. I think you're having doubts, too. So last night you were using *me* to find out . . .?"

"That would serve you right." She glanced away. "No, I didn't think about searching your stuff until later, until the next morning."

"What was last night about?" he asked quietly. "Us being stupid and weak? Or us . . .finding something special?"

Meg chuckled mirthlessly and whipped her head around to stare at him. Their eyes locked. There was fear and hurt in hers. "Yes, that's it. Us being stupid and weak." Her chin rose defiantly. "Look, I promise I won't tell anyone . . .if you'll let us leave when we get to Dublin. Gran's getting worse, anyway."

"I said I would, Meg. I'll keep my word." He paused. "Or . . ."

Her blue eyes searched his face in desperation. It pained him to see her so frantic and frightened.

" . . .or you can stay for the entire tour and let me get at the truth. Do you want to learn the truth about your grandmother?"

Meg slowly shook her head. "No, not if it means she'll be hurt." She looked away, apparently not so convinced, herself. "She's been mumbling a lot in her sleep. She's always been a very restless sleeper but . . .now it's so much worse. In her sleep, Jake, she's been mumbling things in German. What does that mean?"

He had an idea but he wasn't about to voice his fears to Meg. Not now, not yet. A shrug was the coward's way out.

Meg wasn't buying that. "You think she was a Nazi spy, don't you? MI5 thinks so too, doesn't it?" She shook her head vigorously. "How can that be? She was born here. She's Irish, for God's sake. You think she spied for her German lover, don't you? That's what this is all about. She told us she didn't and I've never known her to lie. In fact, she's always been so blunt-speaking. Overly truthful, if you ask me. You heard her, Jake. That Horst guy asked her to spy but she turned him down. And now MI5 and the FBI are trying to make her look guilty."

"Meg, hush. Keep it down. It's more involved than that. You don't know all the facts."

Sure enough, the younger, blond partner appeared in the doorway of the bar-lounge, crossed over to the bar and ordered a drink. He set the briefcase with him on the floor. One end faced their table.

"What do you mean, I don't know all the facts?"

"Meg, please quiet down," he urged her. Her eyes flicked over to the bar. Her mouth opened slightly but she hushed up.

So predictable, Jake thought disparagingly. Now that Major Temple had agreed to wait and see, his team was telegraphing their boss's distrust of Jake's strategy by recording and dissecting his every move.

Of course. They suspect you've crossed the line. And you have. They know you slept with Meg. You've compromised the investigation by carrying things too far.

"Let me paint a picture, Meg. " He leaned in closer and dropped his voice a register. "It's wartime. Your grandmother's job was to transcribe and translate radio messages sent from France, from the French Resistance. A message comes through, a Resistance fighter asking for help. He's harboring a family of Jewish refugees from . . .maybe Alsace-Lorraine. He needs them to be picked up and transported over the border to Switzerland. Or maybe picked up by Allied soldiers and given refuge. Instead the spy in the War Office transcribes it differently . . . or doesn't report it at all. But she marks down the coordinates. Then reports it to the SS on her secretly hidden transmitter. Black-uniformed SS officers sweep down and machine-gun the Resistance fighter, the Jewish family, and everyone else in the village—man, woman, child. Not before they torture the Resistance fighter into revealing the identities of the other patriots in the area." Jake frowned and took a deep breath. "Do you see the terrible damage such a spy would cause?"

Meg's eyes filled up again. "You think my grandmother could do such a thing?"

All of a sudden, Robert Morse's high-pitched voice could be heard from the lobby, gathering his flock. Then other excited voices.

"Come, mates! Time for an Irish jaunty-car ride!"

"Just observe, Meg," whispered Jake. He moved his chair closer to her, his back to the bar. "Observe what your grandmother does while we're on this little jaunt. See if she reacts to what should be familiar places to her. Remember, Mary McCoy spent the first seventeen years of her life here in Killarney and then three in Dublin. She should know this place like the back of her hand."

"Grandma's spoken very little about Killarney, or Ireland even. That's one reason why I wanted to come. I was curious."

"Meg, put that analytical, questioning mind of yours to work. Listen. Her parents drowned in Ross Bay." Jake opened up a local map for her and pointed out the spot. Then drew out a pen and circled the area of Ross Bay on the map. At least she was willing to listen to what he had to say though her posture was stiff and unyielding.

"We're going right by there today on this cart ride. From one of the drivers I just spoke to outside, we'll be heading through the park area back to the downtown center then over to St. Mary's Cathedral. The cathedral is where Mary McCoy attended mass every day of her life. She was a very devout Catholic. Father Dillon was assistant pastor there for many years. That is the priest Mary corresponded with during the war. He kept her parents' important papers in his files in the rectory office."

He was speaking fast, cramming as much in as he could. Meg appeared to be following all of this so he went on, making sure his back was to the bar, blocking the directional mike aimed their way.

"Downtown, on High Street, is where the McCoy pub is. It's called the Muckross Stag. Mike McCoy, the man on the ferry who assaulted you, is half owner of this pub. He's Mary McCoy's first cousin, once removed, and that's a substantiated fact, Meg. Mary McCoy inherited half ownership in that pub after her parents drowned. About here." Jake circled the place on the map. Meg nodded her understanding even though her brows knitted together. She was taking it all in.

"Another important landmark. The driver will be taking us down Countess Road. We'll be passing her childhood home." Jake circled both the cathedral and the approximate site of the home on Countess Road. "It's a three-story Victorian, now a B&B called Lough Leane House. Lough is Irish Gaelic for lake—like loch is in Scottish Gaelic. Anyway, that's the big lake in the park we'll be passing through today. Got all this?"

"Yes. I think so." She stared at the circles on the map. "Let me keep this."

He gave it to her. "Lough Leane House. I spoke to the owner. It used to be gray with white trim. Now it's gray with black trim but he claims it hasn't changed in the past fifty, sixty years. Except for the paint job, everything's the same. Same trees in front, same walkway. Your grandmother should recognize it." Jake pointed again to Countess Road on the map.

A small concession, perhaps, but Meg curtly folded the map in two and buried it in the pocket of her red blazer. He gave her an encouraging half-smile and leaned over to kiss her but she turned her face away from his hovering mouth.

Okay, still mad. Might be mad at me the rest of her life. What more can I do?

They slipped off their chairs and joined the others.

Mary Snider appeared in the lobby, holding onto the arms of both Pierre and Madeleine LeBlanc. Oversized sunglasses hid her eyes, and she wore her usual garb of coat, pantsuit, gloves and loafers. She coolly snubbed even Meg as she walked alongside the Le Blancs to one of the open-air horse carts. Jake followed closely behind, determined to be in the same jaunty car with Mary Snider and Meg.

Jake wondered if the old lady realized her big test was today. Would she pass or fail?

CHAPTER TWENTY

A huge, chestnut-colored, Irish draught horse stood snuffling in the cool air, looking more excited than the short, wiry old codger standing next to him. The driver that Jake had paid to take an extra detour down Countess Road was gap-toothed but wore a wry grin and a rakish sporting cap.

At a signal from Jake, the little man ushered the group Jake was with into the back of his cart. He introduced himself as Danny Boy. After he and Jake helped everyone into the back of the jaunty cart—four passengers on each side, facing each other—Danny Boy climbed up to his perch on the front bench. He took reins in hand, turned around to bestow his gap-toothed smile on everyone.

"Hello, me good folks. Someone once asked me, Danny Boy, how is tipplin' a pint of Guinness good for you? I says to him, I says, it makes you see double and feel single." He cackled and some of his passengers obliged him with laughter. Jake and Meg, sitting next to each other, went along with the old boy and smiled. "So if any of you pretty ladies want to sit up here with ol' Danny Boy, I'm feelin' downright single today."

One of the New Jersey sisters wedged between Hank and her sister agreed to do just that. She climbed over the back of the bench and plopped herself down beside the old rascal.

"So, are you married, Danny Boy?" She played along, the straight man to his comic routine.

"No, can't say I am, pretty lady. And why not, you might ask. Well, the women that were available weren't suitable.

The ones that were suitable weren't available."

And on the banter went, evoking appreciative chuckles and a few groans from the cartload of tourists. They took off, going north on Muckross Road. Jake knew where they were heading first, Danny Boy having already shown him the route.

He faced the Le Blancs and, beside them, Mary Snider — not that he could see much of her face in those Jackie Kennedy sunglasses. Maybe that was her plan. She'd occasionally throw a small smile the driver's way. Or a smug sneer at the Le Blancs, who seemed to regard this cart ride as a requisite form of lowbrow entertainment that had to be endured for the sake of group camaraderie.

Meg was next to him, facing her grandmother, who sat closest to the driver's bench. Jake noted that Meg took the map out as a reminder of the vital landmarks that should jog her grandmother's memory, though she kept it folded so her grandmother and the Le Blancs couldn't see the circled places. The cart jostled them a little as it wheeled down the road. He couldn't help but rub arms with Meg from time to time. The physical contact reminded him of their night of hot lovemaking and bolstered Jake's hope. Maybe, just maybe, he could win back her affections. In the next minute, when she leaned away, his hopes were dashed.

The leafy park grew cooler, the shadows deeper, the sounds and smells definitely earthy and woodsy. On one side going south loomed Ross Bay and the ruins of a medieval castle on a large island. White swans glided in the water among tall, spindly reeds. These were harvested for the local thatched roofs, they were told. The thick woods provided a lush green bower overhead as they veered off the asphalt road and took a smaller dirt path.

When Jake asked about the lake fish, he learned that various kinds of trout and salmon inhabited the lough. It made sense, then, that the McCoys would take a prospective foreign buyer out fishing on the lake.

Meanwhile, Danny Boy kept feeding a willing and not-so-gullible Jeannie a stream of pick-up lines.

"See that red deer over there" — everyone looked at the two does in a pasture they were passing — "that's a pretty gal, but I prefer the two-legged deer, meself."

"Are there any wolves in this park?" Jeannie asked coyly.

"Only one. 'Tis me, pretty colleen," a leering Danny remarked. "Ah, going through Monks Woods now. Know why they're named Monks Woods?"

"No, why?" the two sisters chimed in, enjoying the driver's repertoire of one-liners.

"Well, me darlin's, because the monks would but the nuns wouldn't." Groans. The old rake took a nip from his whiskey flask. "Savin' funeral costs. Embalming me body early."

Chuckles, followed by a titter of laughs from the women. Even Meg was enjoying herself. Her lighthearted laughter sounded pleasant to his ears. *Ah, Meg, if only things were different . . .*

Jake felt Meg elbow him. She was pointing to Ross Bay on the map. "Grandma, this is Ross Bay," Meg ventured.

"I know, that's what he" — Mary Snider yanked a thumb Danny's way — "told us. So? What about it?"

Meg shrugged. "Nothing. Just that Robert said something terrible happened here during the war."

"Nothing I know about. Did Robert talk about it, Madeleine? Pierre?"

The Le Blancs shook their heads. Meg frowned. Her prompt wasn't having any effect on her grandmother's memory bank.

"I might've misheard what he said but I thought he said someone drowned there." Another cue falling on deaf ears.

Danny Boy half turned in his seat. "I was just a tiny boy but

I recall, I do, a funeral for a family that drowned while fishing. Right on the bay by the point there. Don't remember their name but they used to own one of the pubs in town."

"Does that ring a bell, Grandma?" Meg asked.

"Nope. I must've been in London by then."

No expression, no emotion, Jake noted. Too bad he couldn't see the old lady's eyes. Clever old bat, trying to hide behind them. Or were her eyes just sore and strained from insomnia?

His arm draped around the back of Meg's seat, Jake leaned over her and whispered, "Not true. Mary McCoy was called home from Dublin for the funeral. After that, she sold the house on Countess Road and the gas station her parents owned. Then left for London."

Meg turned her head away, choosing to face the front of the cart.

Okay, Jake scolded himself, *take it easy. Let her arrive at the truth in her own time. It takes time for the heart to catch up to the brain. Meg's no different from anybody else.*

Danny Boy's horse turned west through a thicket of beech trees. Ferns grew wild here as did the prickly bushes that Danny Boy called gorse.

"I hear that there are no snakes in Ireland," Jeannie said.

"No, none atall. Just in the local pubs."

Traveling past another point in the bay, the horse cart veered north around a pasture of lowing cows with reddish-brown long-haired coats. A family of red deer scampered among the cows.

"See them cows? They're cousins to the Scottish Highlander cattle. They like the open range but we Irish like 'em in our stews and pasties, we do."

The two sisters made ee-yewing sounds of mock horror and Danny Boy cackled. Meg glanced up at Jake and smiled. As if to say it takes more than beef-eating talk to disgust a Texan. Heartened, Jake placed his left hand on her shoulder.

She shook it off.

Danny Boy led the horse to the right, heading back to town. The spires of St. Mary's Cathedral were visible in front of them, north of New Street Road, where they'd just turned onto after leaving the lush beauty of the park. Meg straightened in her seat and tensed up.

"St. Mary's Cathedral," explained Danny Boy. "Though I've never been inside. Against my religion, ye know."

Meg's neck craned as her eyes lingered on the neo-Gothic stone cathedral, then whipped back to her grandmother. No reaction from Mary Snider.

Clip-clopping on the asphalted road, Danny Boy's huge horse steered the jaunty car past the old church onto High Street, the main street of the town. Shops, pubs, restaurants, and offices lined both sides of the street. As they neared The Muckross Stag, Jake nudged Meg. She glanced down at the map, then up at her grandmother.

"Grandma, we'll have to come back tonight and eat at that pub. Doesn't it look charming? And the name, so quaint. The Muckross Stag." She emphasized the name loudly.

Mary Snider grimaced. "I'm not deaf, Meggie. Aren't you tired of these pubs? I am. I'll eat in the hotel tonight with Pierre and Madeleine. You go out." The elderly woman made a small gesture of irritation directed Jake's way then huddled down into her coat collar.

No sign of recognition. Not even the pub's name sparked a response. Meg's dark-blonde brows furrowed more deeply. As they passed the pub, Meg stared at it forlornly, as if it held the key to her grandmother's past. A past that was slipping away before her very eyes.

A fantasy that never was, not for Mary Snider, Jake thought. Part of her deep cover that she'd since forgotten.

They turned right to go south on High Street. St. Mary's Church loomed now on their left. Church of England, rebuilt in the 1870s, Jake had read. Danny Boy pointed out the stained glass windows and remarked wryly that he'd set foot in every pub in Killarney but was a stranger to the churches in town.

Meg again tried to evoke her grandmother's memories. "Grandma, isn't this the church you used to go to? You and your parents? It's St. Mary's."

Mary Snider looked around and nodded. "Yes, St. Mary's, that's it."

Jake posed innocently, "Weren't you raised a Catholic, Mrs. Snider?"

"Yes," the elderly woman said sharply. "Why would that concern you?"

"Oh, no concern," he replied. "Just that this church is Anglican, not Catholic."

He could hear Meg suck in a harsh breath. "Are you sure?"

Danny Boy had obviously overheard their exchange. "Sure, 'tis true enough, miss. This church, St. Mary's Church of Ireland, is Anglican. Has been ever since it was built oh, back over a hundred years. The cathedral, also named St. Mary's, is Catholic. Any more than that, 'tis certain I can't say, never having set foot in either one."

Jake could see the old lady frowning despite her huge sunglasses. He guessed she was hastening mentally to recover from her slip-up. After sixty-five years, the old spy had forgotten some of her cover story.

"That's what I meant, Meggie, the cathedral. The cathedral was where I went to church."

"So you're a Killarney native, missus?" Danny Boy inquired in his lilting accent.

"It's been over sixty years," Mary Snider remarked crisply. "I don't remember much. Everything's changed."

"I see," the driver said. "And what was your family name?"

"McCoy," Meg supplied, then added pointedly. "Maybe you knew the McCoys. They used to own The Muckross Stag."

Mary Snider appeared to visibly wince. Her bug-eyed glasses swiveling to Jake, she scowled- she'd figured it out. Only he could have told her granddaughter about the pub. Now, Jake realized with a mental flinch, the old lady would know for certain that he was investigating her.

What would she do about it? *Now that you're trumped, let's see your cards.*

"Ah, knew of them," Danny Boy said. "Though me pap didn't move in the same circles as Patrick McCoy and his wife. They was in the hoity-toity class. Proprietors, ye know." The wiry old guy slapped his leg. "Don't tell me this pretty lady here is the daughter that went off to London, is she?"

Mary Snider seemed to sink farther into her coat. Meg piped up. "Yes she is. Grandma's Mary McCoy, the daughter of Patrick McCoy. Aren't you, Gran?"

Jake knew Meg was hoping and praying her grandmother would prove herself. Somehow, some way.

All she got was Mary Snider's grunted reply. "It's been a long time." Then stony silence.

Danny Boy was relentless. "Well, then you lived on Countess Road. Where all the toffs lived from before the war. That's where we're heading next."

"Is that where you and your parents lived, Grandma? On Countess Road?" Meg played along, feigning ignorance.

Her grandmother shrugged, practically a turtle in her overcoat. "I don't remember."

Smart old fox, Jake decided. She was pleading old age memory loss. Maybe her legal team would use dementia in her defense.

Five minutes later, their jaunty car was lumbering up Countess Road, the draught horse slowing down and showing its disgruntled attitude at the change in route. Meaning it would take longer to get his reward of oats.

"Which house was yours, daughter of Patrick McCoy?" Danny Boy asked jovially, undaunted by the elderly woman's silent withdrawal.

Most of the mansions were either Victorian or Gothic in design, three- or four-storied with large, lush lawns in front. Well-maintained, too, Jake thought. Many had been converted to small hotels and B&Bs.

"Don't remember," Mary Snider mumbled.

Meg stared at the gray, black-trimmed mansion with an ornate sign bordering its long driveway. *Lough Leane House* was the kind of bed-and-breakfast inn that well-heeled Irish, Welsh, and English travelers might stay at while touring the Ring of Kerry or taking hikes in the surrounding County Kerry countryside.

"Gran, look at that place. Could that be your family's old home?"

Mary Snider glanced over at Lough Leane House. "Could be. It's been so long, Meggie."

Meg looked down at the map with an air of defeat. She crumpled it in her hand, then stuffed it in her jacket pocket. The shocked, devastated look on her pretty face was heartbreaking, causing Jake to look away.

The truth cut down to the bone. He knew and could understand how the truth could wound deeply. But Meg still had only suspicions. The woman who'd raised her like a daughter was feeding her lies. Treating her like a child. That much Jake knew Meg was feeling.

One thing was certain for him. Mary Snider was not Mary McCoy, the daughter of Patrick and Elizabeth McCoy of Killarney. Not before the ferry explosion on that fateful night in June of 1940. Only afterward. The real Mary McCoy ended her short life on that ferry and became fish food at the bottom of the Irish Sea.

A tragic end for a beautiful, young woman with so much potential. A tragic end for her parents too.

So who *was* this impostor wearing her name and nothing else?

CHAPTER TWENTY-ONE

Meg felt a hard knot in her belly as bile threatened to rise up. She swallowed it down hard. Her head was pounding with a rush of blood and her legs quivered. Climbing down from the jaunty car with Jake's help, she mumbled something to her grandmother about getting a cup of tea in the hotel's lounge to settle her stomach, the cart ride having made her a little sick.

"Fine," Mary Snider said crisply. "Just stay close by. I'll be in the dining room with Pierre and Madeleine. Then I'm going to my room for a nap. The Le Blancs will look after me, Meggie, if you want to go sightseeing."

Forcing herself to go through the motions, Meg bussed her grandmother's forehead. She felt nothing but a growing feeling of betrayal and a cold sense of fear. Smiling broadly for their benefit, nonetheless, Meg waved to her grandmother and their new Canadian friends as she turned away. At least Gran had people to spend time with. This tour was turning out to be the worst thing she could've planned.

A disaster.

MI5 agents hovering nearby. An FBI investigation underway. And yet, there was Jake.

Somehow she separated him from the FBI investigation, as if one was a man and the other just an idea. Wanted to, anyway. Thinking about him and their night of lovemaking made her pulsate with longing. Made her sick with guilt too. Oh God, what was she going to do?

No, that was easy, Meg decided. The solution was simple.

She was going to fly herself and her grandmother home the day after tomorrow. Nonstop, from Dublin to Dallas, as fast as their jetliner could carry them.

Ignoring Jake's presence behind her in the hotel lobby, Meg made a beeline for the lounge. Ordered a vodka-on-the-rocks instead of hot tea. The young bartender tried to make conversation but she discouraged him. Instead she hunched gloomily over the glass he placed in front of her.

A stiff, long swallow burned her throat but restored her sense of balance and perspective. Wait a minute. It didn't matter what or who Mary Snider was or had been sixty-five or seventy years ago. Gran was like a mother to her. She'd rescued her and her brother Jack from her mother's hippie commune and perverted cult leader, had given them a responsible family, a decent life, and a good education. Most of all, love. What more could she have asked for?

And now, to be persecuted by her own government — it wasn't fair. It wasn't right. Hadn't Mary Snider been a law-abiding citizen all these years? Did it really matter what she was or did during those crazy war years?

Gran — she couldn't have killed anyone. Maybe spied a little for that German fiancé of hers.

But then why didn't she recognize her own hometown? Why didn't she know the pub her family had once owned? The cathedral where she'd gone to mass?

Meg jumped, her nerves frazzled, when Jake took a seat at the bar beside her.

"Just don't say it," she warned icily. He sighed heavily.

"I'm so sorry. That's all I'm going to say."

She downed the rest of her vodka. "Sorry? Not good enough."

"Look, I know you're mad, you're hurt. Confused. Divided loyalties and all that."

"Another one," she told the bartender. Slowly she half-turned in her seat.

Jake had taken off his leather jacket and now showed rounded biceps under his knit polo shirt. His wavy dark hair was tousled from their horse-cart ride, his face slightly reddened from the cold air. But his eyes had a haunted look about them. She expected him to look smug and gloating but his expression appeared wounded, stricken, as though he were suffering as much as she was. No, she had to set him straight.

"Jake, there are no divided loyalties. You and I, we shared one night, that's all. Grandma and I, we've shared almost thirty years. Despite what may or may not be the truth, I love her. Always will." Without hesitation, she lifted the second drink and sipped it. "You, Jake, you've used me. You exploited me to get to my grandmother. How can I ever forgive that?"

She stared at his handsome face. She'd been blinded by his beauty, swept away by his attention and their enjoyment of each other's company. She'd felt such an immediate, strong connection with him that she thought he returned it one hundred percent. Things were different now. He'd deceived her. Played her like a harp.

So the blinders were off and she could now see beyond the good looks of this man and the emotions he inspired in her. Lies. Deception. The reality pierced her like little dagger stabs, made her bleed in a hundred places. Made her question everything he'd murmured to her last night . . . every look, every touch, every kiss.

Guilt and compassion suffused his sculpted features. Why should he feel anything for her? He'd done his job, it wasn't personal. He was a federal agent, doing what he was sent to do. The look he leveled on her now, though, was very personal. He cared for her, that was apparent, just not enough.

Dammit! When was she going to learn? Even now he could

move her, pluck those damned heartstrings of hers.

What a fool she was.

"Maybe you can't forgive me. I don't blame you if you never forgive me. I hope you can . . .someday." One big hand smoothed the side locks of her hair out of her face. His gesture was tender apologetic, but she was immured against it.

"Please don't touch me." She hated the pleading note in her tone. As though she were actually yearning for his touch.

"I can't stop," Jake rasped. "God help me, I can't shut off how I feel about you. I let this happen—"

"Please don't touch me," she repeated, this time with bite. "Or I'll tell your superiors how you tricked me. How you seduced me to get information out of me. Isn't there an FBI rule against doing that to a fellow American?"

Jake removed his hand, called the bartender over and ordered a Guinness. He warily turned back to her.

"With undercover assignments, there are few rules," he said evenly. "Survival's primary. Then you play it by ear and learn what you can. I'm doing my job, Meg. I just hadn't planned on falling for you in the process. You think I wanted this? I need this complication like a bullet hole."

Silence followed as they both downed their drinks. Though he sounded sincere, Meg decided she couldn't trust him. This could be another lie, another ruse to entice her to help him crucify her grandmother.

"Meg, come with me. I've got an appointment with a woman, a Millie O'Loughlin. She's retired but still works part-time at the cathedral rectory. She used to be Father Dillon's secretary. Y'know, the priest Mary McCoy corresponded with all during the war. Well, this woman's got a file of papers and photos you need to see. Maybe they'll exonerate your grandmother. Maybe not."

Meg looked at him and frowned. What now, she wondered. More ways to entrap her and her grandmother?

"No friggin' way. You can dig dirt on my grandma all by yourself."

Jake screwed up his mouth at Meg's angry outburst.

"Maybe we could get an early dinner afterward at The Muckross Stag," Jake added somberly, as if he were inviting her to a funeral. "You could speak to the son of Mary McCoy's first cousin, Mike McCoy. The old Irish guy you met in Texas about ten years ago. He came to your grandmother's house. Do you remember him?"

A memory sparked. Yes, she recalled that strange afternoon after she'd arrived home from school. The tall, skinny Irishman with the charming lilt to his voice. He'd been looking for his cousin, also named Mary McCoy. From Killarney.

Meg frowned and squirmed on her bar stool. She looked away as the memories of that strange afternoon crystallized in her mind.

She remembered feeling sorry for him. He'd traveled so far only to be disappointed. Her grandmother wasn't this Mary McCoy that the old man was looking for. He said the color of their eyes was different. His cousin had turquoise eyes—her grandmother's blue eyes were dark, like sapphires. Like hers. He'd studied her grandmother's face for a long time while he drank some iced tea. When he took his leave, Meg had walked him down the driveway and seen him off in his rental car.

She recalled how strange that had seemed at the time. Meg's brows pinched together and she nodded. "How do you know about that visit?"

"MI5. After that visit, the old man, Mike McCoy, went to British intelligence and reported your grandmother. He started a file, an investigation after that. Told them he suspected your grandmother of doing away with his cousin Mary and assuming her identity. All their biographical details fit, just not the eye color. He also said that his cousin wouldn't have hesitated to acknowledge him if they'd met up again.

That old Irishman kept bugging MI5 for years. Determined old guy. Well, that man's son, Mike McCoy Junior, was the man on the ferry."

"Meg, Mike Junior inherited his father's half of The Muckross Stag. Mary McCoy of Killarney inherited half ownership also. Her parents, the ones who drowned mysteriously in Ross Bay, left the pub to the older gentleman you met in Texas and their daughter, Mary McCoy. Did your grandmother ever tell you that she was part owner of The Muckross Stag? She would have known this before leaving for London."

At her surprised, open-mouthed stare, he gave her an ironic shrug. "Guess not. The real Mary McCoy would have known this."

Meg half-stumbled from her bar stool. Jake grabbed her and held her upright. The strength of his arms reminded her of how tightly he'd held her during their night of lovemaking. As if he'd been afraid of letting her go. Her thoughts swirled around in a stew.

The gist of Jake's remarks finally hit her in the face like a cold, wet gust of wind.

"My God. You think Grandma killed Mary McCoy and stole her identity? So that she could take her place at the War Office?"

"Yes, I do. So does MI5. Five days ago, I didn't think so. I'm sorry, Meg, but all the evidence points that way. I'm heading to the cathedral now. I need to see those papers."

He paused, his dark eyes drilling into her. Challenging her. "Are you coming?"

Meg angrily brushed off his hands and stood, balanced on her own two feet. Maybe she'd find something that would clear her grandmother of all suspicion.

"Lead the way," she snapped. She rocked a little from side to side.

His dark brows arched guardedly as he flicked her a small,

crooked grimace. "We'll take a cab."

St. Mary's Cathedral was situated on the corner of Port Road and New Street. Meg kept pace with Jake's long strides as they skirted the front and side of the enormous, neo-Gothic church in silence. The church was located on what appeared to be five acres of grassy grounds, bordered on all sides by a low stone wall.

Jake apparently had scouted out the location of this rectory office, so minutes later they were standing in the threshold of the hundred-and-fifty year old gray-stoned building. The interior—an antechamber and sitting room—was dim. A small fireplace in the corner threw off dancing firelight, dispelling the gathering chill in the air. Beyond those rooms, a short, middle-aged woman in a modern nun's uniform—black skirt, black wool sweater over white blouse, black hose, and clunky shoes—ushered them beyond the public rooms of the rectory into a large, well-lit office.

"Please wait here," the nun said quietly then left.

Odd, Meg thought. Her grandmother was raised Catholic, yet neither she nor Grandpa Snider had raised her and Jack as Catholics. In fact, they hadn't been raised in any faith. Perhaps their wartime experiences had destroyed their religious faith. God help her, but her curiosity was piqued.

Meg surveyed the square-shaped office. Every wall was covered by four-drawer file cabinets, most of them metal, but some of the wooden ones appeared to qualify as antiques. Evidently the office staff was clinging to old-school storage procedures, although Meg did spy one computer on top of a big, corner desk. An adjacent table held a printer. A moment later, Millie O'Laughlin appeared out of a side door.

"Good afternoon," she said cheerily. While Jake made introductions, Meg sized her up. The plump pensioner wore her dyed-brown hair in a short, frizzy hairdo and wore severe wool trousers and a loose sweater. Her cherubic plain face bore no makeup but held a kind, warm smile for her visitors.

Meg gave her a weak smile and shook her hand, wishing she'd worn something nicer than her cargo pants, bulky knit sweater, and sneakers. Nevertheless, she sensed that the woman could be trusted to tell them the truth, and that was the main point.

She sat in one of the wing chairs offered to her next to the receptionist's desk, apparently Millie's present-day part time job. Jake took the wingback chair next to Meg and they both declined the hot tea that Millie offered them. The clerk went behind her desk, plopped down and folded her hands on top of a thin cardboard box the size of an office-supply store's hanging folders box.

"When you called, Mr. Bernstein, I took the liberty of retrieving the McCoy file and made photocopies of everything in it, including the photos. You're the first visitors to this file since old Mike McCoy came here asking for it . . . oh now, nine or ten years ago."

"Thanks, that's kind of you," Jake said. Meg could tell by the earnestness in his voice that he intended to get down to business quickly. "Meg's grandmother is Patrick McCoy's daughter and she's now a naturalized American citizen, as I told you on the phone. Mary McCoy Snider is, as you can imagine, an elderly woman, and she's resting at our hotel. So it fell upon her granddaughter to collect all the information in that file. Of special importance is the deed to the pub, The Muckross Stag, a point of contention since Mary Snider is half-owner and might consider selling her portion to the other co-owner and present manager, Mike McCoy Junior."

"Yes, of course." Millie lifted the box and passed it over to Meg. "I know poor Young Mike, as we call him. His father, Old Mike, passed on a couple of years ago. Young Mike's always having a devil of a time with his bipolar disorder. When he goes off his medication, he gets a little . . .uh, squirrelly. Usually ends up in a stew of trouble. But then he gets back on the pills and rights himself. Father Donovan was a good friend to him. Tried to encourage him to keep his spirits up and not get depressed over his affliction."

"Yes, I spoke to Mike at length and he's looking forward to getting this pub deal squared away. He made a commotion at the hotel last night and he was arrested, but the Garda let him out today. We're going to see him as soon as we finish up here."

Millie's plump face split into a wide smile.

"Oh good. Young Mike's a decent sort of man when he's on his pills. Resolving that pub ownership problem has been his life's goal, it seems. His spirits will rise once that problem's taken care of." The woman looked over to Meg for confirmation. Meg nodded in assent. "Now, you said Mr. Bernstein, you had a few questions about Father Dillon's letters to Mary during the war. This is very curious, your interest. Old Mike was the only other one who wanted copies of those wartime letters. I remember Father Dillon telling me that one day. This was shortly before he died, almost five years ago. By the by, that's him on the wall over there."

They looked over at a large black-and-white framed photo of a pleasant-featured, dark-haired man in a priest's collar and black shirt and trousers. He was smiling at someone off-camera. Meg stared. So that was Father Dillon, the only man her grandmother had written to during the war. The only one Meg knew about, anyway. They must've been very close, the two of them. Yet her grandmother had made no mention of Father Dillon when he died. That would have been about four or five years after the old Irishman had come to visit them. That visit, too, with old Mike McCoy. Such an opportunity, yet her grandmother had never asked the old man from Killarney about the pub or anything about her favorite cleric.

That was bizarre.

But then, Meg reminded herself, they'd already established the fact that her grandmother was *not* the old Irishman's cousin. Meg had assumed there'd been another Mary McCoy he was looking for. Meg frowned, deeply perplexed.

"As I was saying, Father Dillon said that one day people would come looking for those letters. He'd kept them, though I can't be certain why, but he was a clever man, always one or two steps ahead of everyone else. He said to me those letters were a key. What he meant by that he didn't say and I didn't ask. But as you'd have it, before Father passed on, Old Mike came by and asked for them and everything else in that file. I gave him copies too, of course, since he was kin. What he did with them, I do not know."

Meg knew. Jake told her old Mike McCoy sent copies of everything to MI5. Now years later, they'd begun their own investigation.

Out of a separate stack, Millie handed a tied, small bundle of coarse yellowed-paper envelopes to Jake. Meg eyed them with concern. The priest had called them *a key*, but to what? She decided to open the box then and there and peruse the contents. The letters she'd look at later. Another possibility nagged her.

"My grandmother's birthdate is June twelfth, 1920. Was there no other Mary McCoy born in this parish that same year? Or even a year or two later?" she asked the woman. Her grandmother had always been a little vain. Maybe she'd fudged on her birth year.

"I looked at the cathedral's ledgers from 1915 to 1925" Millie glanced at Jake—"since Mr. Bernstein asked the same question when he called. There were a few other McCoy families in County Kerry at that time but no girls with that exact name were born or baptized here during that time period. The ledger for 1920 confirmed that a Mary Lewis McCoy was baptized in St. Mary's parish in August of that year. She was the two-month-old daughter of Patrick and Elizabeth McCoy of Killarney. June twelfth was the birth date given."

Okay, some things matched. Birth date for one, Meg thought. She exhaled a breath of relief, felt her pulse slow a bit.

For a few minutes, she and Jake pored over the different items in their laps. Meg rifled through birth certificates, a copy of the cathedral's banns for Patrick McCoy and his betrothed, Elizabeth Lewis, a marriage certificate. The coroner's report and death certificate of Patrick McCoy and his wife, listed as accidental drownings, the deed of purchase and the subsequent bill of sale to the house on Countess Road, the same for the *petrol store* or gas station that Patrick McCoy once owned, Mary McCoy's matriculation records.

After looking briefly at three black-and-white photographs of Patrick McCoy, his wife, and young daughter, and one very old, tattered, sepia-toned snapshot of Patrick and his tall, younger brother Mike, Meg came upon the graduation portrait photo of the daughter, Mary.

Meg gasped.

Jake looked up. Millie half-stood.

"That's the same photo the old Irishman, Old Mike, showed me that day in Texas," Meg cried. "I remember studying it closely and then telling him—" She stopped, her hand flying up to her mouth. *Shut up!*

Jake looked over at the photo, not realizing that ten years ago Meg had declared the photo was absolutely *not* that of her grandmother. Similar in some ways—the facial features and coloring, yes—but not the same person. To a casual observer, an elderly Mary Snider could indeed be the younger Mary McCoy. But not to someone who knew her as well as Meg did.

Meg leaned forward and speared Millie with an intense glare. "Are you sure that this is Mary Lewis McCoy, the daughter of Patrick and Elizabeth McCoy?"

"Quite sure, Miss. That was the photo Mary gave to Father Dillon upon her matriculation. He said he looked at the sweet girl's photo every time he wrote to her in London."

Meg's heart stopped. Her eyes unfocused. *Gran's not this woman. Not this Mary McCoy.*

Then who *was* her grandmother?

"What did you tell Old Mike McCoy about that photo, Meg?"

She pulled herself together rapidly. "I-I think I said something about it being like our high school senior poses."

Their eyes met for a split second. From Jake's expression, he could tell she was holding back something. She had to deflect his attention from the photo. All the while, she couldn't ignore the sinking, roiling feeling in her stomach.

Her mind was spinning. She felt sick but fought to maintain her composure.

"Those letters Grandma wrote to Father Dillon?" she asked shakily. "Anything?"

He nodded grimly. "Oh yes."

So there it was, their standoff. If she wasn't sharing, neither was he.

"Is Patrick McCoy's will in there, Meg?" Jake asked, his eyes hooded. "Concerning the heirs to the pub?"

Meg shuffled a few more papers in the box and found it. The hand-written Last Wills and Testaments of Patrick McCoy and his wife, Elizabeth Lewis McCoy. A thought struck her. Her grandmother never claimed to have a middle name, yet that seemed to be an Irish tradition.

She handed them to Jake. Then shuffled papers and looked back at the birth certificate of Patrick's and Mary's daughter. Mary Lewis McCoy. Her grandmother *did* have a middle name. Lewis, her mother's maiden name. Now, why would she—

No one ever forgot their middle name, did they? How could someone forget such a harmless thing as a middle name?

Except — as the photograph proved — her grandmother was *not* Mary McCoy. Not *the* Mary McCoy whose family history they were now poring over like voyeurs.

A sick despair overcame her. Her stomach revolted although she hadn't eaten all day. Willing it down couldn't keep the terrible truth from erupting out of her throat. Meg shot to her feet, spilling the contents of the box. She choked out what she hoped was an apology to Millie and ran out of the rectory office. She made it to the cobblestone pathway outside before vomiting into the nearest bush. Wave after wave of nausea swept up and out, purging her of her last shred of hope. Until all she had left were dry heaves.

And the terrible truth.

CHAPTER TWENTY-TWO

Weakly, she leaned against the cold stone outer wall of the rectory, closed her eyes and moaned. She had no idea how much time passed, but after a while, Jake was beside her. He pulled her to his side with one strong arm. She propped herself against him and whimpered. No tears spilled, just whimpers and moans.

"Meg, can you make it to the pub?" In his other arm, braced against his side, was the box of file copies. "Or shall we go back to the hotel? We'll have to walk a couple of blocks to the town center to find a cab."

She schooled herself to a kind of shaky but steady composure.

"You knew, didn't you?"

"Knew what?"

"Knew I'd find something. Some proof."

"I suspected. Just wasn't sure." He continued to support and guide her while they began walking. She saw nothing, was just walking blindly. His low voice was calming, soothing. "Guess the photo of a teenaged Mary cinched it? Only facial reconstruction would change features that much."

She steeled herself for more of the ugly truth. "The letters?"

"Incriminating. The letter that Mary McCoy mailed to Father Dillon *before* she boarded the ferry that June night in 1940 had a slightly different signature than the letters that came *after* the ferry catastrophe."

He let the significance of that revelation settle upon her before adding, "Those typed letters with a slightly different

signature came after whoever took the real Mary's place settled in London and began her work at the War Office. I'm positive the FBI Lab's handwriting specialists will find the signatures on those letters from London were forged. Even Father
Dillon noticed the difference."

"Whoever took Mary McCoy's place . . . that was my
grandmother?" The answer to which she already knew.

"Yes, I'm sorry to say."

"What happened to the real Mary?" She almost choked on
the question but she had to ask.

"We — MI5 and I — think she was murdered on the ferry before the killer set off the explosions. Her body's either at the
bottom of the Irish Sea or it was swept out to the Atlantic. It'll
never be found."

"Oh God!" Meg drew in a deep breath that caught deep in
her throat and escaped as a sob. "Grandma couldn't have
done that! I know her!" She dissolved into hot tears. "Must've
been that Horst Eberhard. He did it and forced Grandma to
go along afterward. Maybe he threatened to kill her."

"Possibly." Jake's tone was guarded. He tried to put his
arm around her but she fended him off. The FBI and MI5 were
ganging up against her grandmother because of Gran's association with that German spy.

Tears streamed down her cheeks until finally she composed herself. She inhaled and exhaled, trying to still the
quivering inside. Thoughts assailed her and she fought desperately to sort through them all. One caught the edge of her
mind, a sliver of hope.

She slowed her walking pace alongside Jake, maintaining
her distance. Jake made no further attempt to touch her.

"Did MI5 have a copy of that same letter? The one that was
sent to Father Dillon before the ferry sank?" she asked. If British Intelligence had it and didn't think the signatures in the
letters following the ferry explosion were forged, why would

the FBI arrive at such a conclusion?

"Good point. Thing is, they didn't. Millie just told me tonight, that particular letter — the only written document with the real Mary McCoy's handwriting — was in its original envelope and had gotten caught at the back of the cabinet. Millie just found it today as she was taking out the file to make copies. Talk about luck —" He halted in mid-sentence. "Sorry, Meg, poor choice of words. I know you're crushed. I'm sorry for that. If MI5 had seen that letter sent by Mary *before* the ferry sank, they would have indicted your grandmother long before now."

His hand went up to clasp her shoulder. The nausea having passed, Meg wrested herself out of his arm and took rapid steps by herself. "I'm sorry, Meg. I know how very hurt you must feel."

"I don't know what to think or what to feel," she expelled a shuddering breath. "It's a nightmare. I keep hoping I'll wake up."

Jake began taking longer strides down the street. "Meg, do you feel strong enough to walk a little faster?"

Jake kept looking back over his shoulder at the dark roadway of New Street. The town center was four long blocks away. The dark clouds that now sat like a lid over the town seemed to have sucked up most of the light.

It was still afternoon, only half past three, but looked like twilight. There were no streetlamps in this part of town, just the ambient lights from the cathedral and its parish buildings. The gathering, heavy mist cast everything in a shroud of opaque grayness.

The heavy mist fit her mood. She saw no way out for her grandmother.

She shook off another attempt by Jake to take her hand. New noises ruptured the silent street and she too followed Jake's glances. Beyond Jake, Meg now saw what was causing him to speed up. Faces hidden behind visors, two black-helmeted motorcyclists appeared to be tracking them. Stealthy and quiet at first, they were now riding abreast of each other about fifty yards behind — slowly enough to keep them in sight but hanging back.

"Who — ?" she cried.

"Don't know. They're not MI5. They're at the hotel, watching your grandmother. These two are tailing *us*."

Meg's pulse skittered with fear as she tried to keep pace with Jake's rapid strides. He stubbornly seized her hand and began to jog, pulling her along. Fear creased his handsome face, making her own fear bank even higher.

"Meg, stay with me."

CHAPTER TWENTY-THREE

Meg was now glad she wore sneakers as Jake suddenly broke into a sprint. She had no choice — he was dragging her with him. The motorcycles behind them gunned their engines, turned up their throttles. She tossed a look at the two bikers, no longer hanging back. Now they were flat-out pursuing. One of the bikers was pointing something at them. The asphalt by Jake's feet exploded.

"Shit!" Jake swore, almost losing his balance. He recovered just in time for another *pfft* and eruption of roadway.

Someone was firing at them? Normally there'd be the popping sound of a gunshot. A silencer?

She threw a glance at Jake. His face was pale in the darkness. With his left arm, his hand still clutching hers tightly, he indicated a zigzagging course down the road. They sped up their run. Meg let Jake's arm lead her as he yanked her left and right. In desperation, she stepped up her pace.

Ping! A third bullet landed behind them, sending asphalt chunks and gravel flying like darts of debris. One hit the back of Jake's leg. He stumbled but didn't stop.

"Damn!"

A fourth shot hit the pavement. Meg's calf was stung by a chunk of rock. She screeched out a cry.

"Meg, you hit?"

"No!" she screamed. From Jake's body language, she knew he was heading to the left. And speeding up. Her heart pounded as if it might burst in her chest. Good thing they'd been running every day, she thought. Otherwise she'd be flat on her face in the street. She felt sweat run down her back, her face, her neck. Gasping for breath, her mouth open, she began to pant heavily.

A long block ahead loomed the Killarney public library. On the corner of Rock Road and New Street, its arched windows were lighted and a small crowd lingered by the front entrance. Some kind of public event was taking place—people were taking a smoke break or leaving for the night. Meg saw Jake jerk his head in that direction.

They were little more than fifty yards away when the crowd heard the motorcyclists and saw the two in front running for their lives. Faces turned their way. Meg hazarded a look behind. The two bikers instantly banked off to the right, gunning their bikes for a fast race down High Street. They veered off the main downtown road just as Meg and Jake leaped to the sidewalk. Unable to check their momentum, they fell sprawling forward on the lawn in front of the library. They tumbled and rolled on the wet grass before both landed on their backs by the feet of a few townsfolk.

"Were those lads chasing you?" A man stared down at them.

"Bloody bikers! Someone should call the Garda!"

Jake stood and brushed himself off, then helped Meg up. The cardboard box and its spilled contents had scattered all over.

"We're fine," he assured them. His words came out in a gush of breath. He doubled over for a moment, clutching his thighs, then looked closely at Meg. "You okay?"

She nodded, breathless. Her knees and elbows hurt where they'd taken the brunt of her fall. Luckily they had no broken bones or sprained ankles. The soft grass had cushioned their fall, although now they were wet. Adrenaline still surged through her, warming her insides. She was still dripping with sweat.

"Someone call the police." she cried to the crowd. "Those men were shooting at us. They were trying to kill us."

A barrage of questions erupted, followed by Jake's silence as he picked up the file papers and stuffed them back into the box. Meg was confused by his subdued reaction but she remained the irate tourist attempting to answer their questions.

"They came out of nowhere. We just left the cathedral and there they were. We don't know who they are."

A woman in a Macintosh made a call on her mobile phone.

"The Garda, they'll be here soon. Just five blocks away they are." She pointed north.

"Shit," Jake swore under his breath but Meg heard him. She limped over to him, rubbing her knees, as he closed the lid on the box.

"Don't you want to report those bikers? I mean they fired at us, Jake!"

He gave her a blank look, then his eyes rolled up. Then he collapsed on the lawn. His face seemed bloodless, his eyes closed. Terrified, she sank to her knees beside him.

"Jake?" Her hand touched his right thigh, came away wet and bloody. His dark blue Dockers had concealed the blood but now she spied the hole in the pants leg. "God, you're hurt!"

His eyes fluttered open. "A ricochet. Help me up. The men's room . . ."

While he pressed one hand against his thigh, Meg and another man supported him. Jake leaned on the man and another one who offered aid. The three made their way inside the building. Her eyes fixed with worry on the front door, where Jake had disappeared with the two men, Meg still did her best to answer the questions shooting at her from the crowd.

"I don't know why. We just left the cathedral. All of a sudden those bikers came out of nowhere."

"American tourists are you not?" one elderly man asked, "Now why in bloody hell would those hooligans bother you?"

Meg heard murmurings in the Irish language that she didn't understand. From their collective expressions, now showing anger, she surmised they had an idea who the bikers were.

"Do you know who they are?" she asked. Five minutes had passed and still no Jake. Was he okay? Another minute and she was going inside that men's room.

"Thugs, 'twere sure."

"White supremacists," a woman supplied.

"Damn neo-Nazis," another one said. "They've come here before, they have. There's a camp of 'em nearby."

"A camp?" Meg sagged with relief when Jake reappeared with the same two men. He was limping but walking on his own. An overwhelming desire to rush up to him swept over her. Resenting her own weakness, she quashed the urge.

"A paramilitary camp," the same woman explained. "They target shoot, play war games." Her comments were followed by more Irish murmurings.

"I know," she explained for Meg's benefit. "My nephew joins them whenever they come around." She shook her head with emphasis. "They're thugs looking for a cause. They call themselves Celtic Wolves."

Jake and the two men drew up to the crowd. Meg went up to Jake and grasped his arm.

"Are you okay?" Her eyes searched his pale, drawn face, then his right leg.

"I'm fine. Just a piece of road rock. Went right through."

"We cleaned him up a bit, miss," offered one of the men. He jangled keys in his hand. "Look, the pub your friend said he wanted to go to is three blocks up High Street. I'll give you a lift. No point in trying to walk it. You'd be sitting ducks."

Jake looked over at the woman with the cell phone. "Tell the Garda we'll be at The Muckross Stag. Getting some liquid tranquilizers."

Several in the crowd patted his shoulders, the men claiming they'd do the same—head for the nearest pub—if they'd just had a narrow escape. They praised his spirit and joked that he must be half Irish.

Five minutes later, the man dropped them off with a repeated expression of outrage that tourists should be so abused by a bunch of hoodlums.

"Could be those skinheads. There's a bunch in Dublin causing mischief now and then. Sometimes they come down here, hold a camp in the hills. They think they're Irish militia but mostly it's an excuse to harass Jews and immigrants from the Middle East." Then he doffed his cap and added gentle admonishments to take a cab back to their hotel. They thanked him and took seats in the pub minutes before the Garda showed up in their white car with the green stripe.

The man's words didn't register until later. By then, they were gulping their first round of beer and fielding the Garda's questions.

"One of the women said they were Celtic Wolves," Meg said, "A gang of neo-Nazis. What would they want with *us*?"

The two young Garda officers exchanged glances. One took copious notes. Apparently Jake didn't want the local police involved in this matter anymore than necessary. Although he kept to his cover as a Virginia banker on tour, Jake gave his correct name. Meg had to conclude that Jake didn't want MI5's investigation exposed because the Irish probably wouldn't take too kindly to a foreign intelligence operation conducted on their soil without their consent or knowledge. At least that was what Meg assumed, that the Irish authorities were in the dark.

Prudently, she went along.

"They were firing at *me*, Meg, not you. Those bullets were warning shots. If they'd wanted, they could've drilled me in the back. They were good marksmen."

She could only stare in shock. "Why?"

"That's what I'd like to know." He leveled a sober look at the two local cops. For the next minute, she recounted for the Irish policemen the details of what happened even though it was difficult to concentrate. Her mind was churning. What could she do to protect her grandmother? Why were those thugs after Jake? Her head throbbed with pain. In desperation, she drank more beer.

Jake corroborated her story and one of the Garda policemen wrapped up his notetaking. The two cops shrugged in unison, said they'd go over in the morning to the Celtic Wolves camp nearby in the north hills. By the time they discovered anything, however, one of them reminded Jake and Meg, their motorcoach would be on their way out of County Kerry.

"'Tis boys taking sport with you," one of them said. It was clear where his loyalties lay.

"It's a goodnight to you, then," the second cop said as he clambered to his feet, tipping his duck-billed hat.

Jake grumbled a reply and restrained Meg as she bolted to her feet in outrage.

"That's *all*? We could've been killed!" He tugged on her arm until she frowned and sat down. She scrutinized Jake's face. "They act like it's no big deal. You look kinda pale. How's your leg?"

Jake smiled and winced. "I'll live. It's clear the Garda's going to whitewash this whole thing. One of them probably has a brother or friend at that camp. They knew, Meg. I kind of announced my presence when I went to see Young Mike at the jailhouse this morning. I used my real name, Bernstein."

Before Meg could react to his statement and its anti-Semitic implication, their attention was drawn to the bar. Jake's hand clamped down on hers.

"There's Young Mike. He's coming over to plead his case, Meg. Are you willing to listen with an open mind?"

The big man with a bald crown and gray fringe of hair, serving drinks at the bar, had stared at them the entire time they were sitting at their table. Meg was so freaked out by the shooting and their run to safety that she hadn't recognized the big man. When she did, she felt a jolt of fright. Her hand fluttered to her cheek.

"Yeah, that's the man who slapped you on the ferry. Young Mike McCoy. He co-owns this pub with Mary McCoy, his long-lost cousin. Legally that would be your grandmother. I think he's on his meds. 'Least he's acting normal tonight."

"Great," she muttered, forgetting her fear and letting her anger vent. "A perfect way to end this shitty day. Well, he better stay normal. If he raises a hand to me, so help me, I won't hesitate to use this." She held up the pepper spray canister on a key chain that she fished out of her pea coat pocket.

Jake widened his eyes. "Go for it, girl."

"Aren't *you* supposed to be armed?" she inquired archly, narrowing her eyes accusingly. "You're the big FBI dude. I saw your gun. Would have come in handy, don't you think, a little while ago?"

Jake's usually ruddy cheeks were pale above his five o'clock shadow of stubble. The only reaction to her criticism was his twisted half-smile, half-grimace.

"I promised the Brits I wouldn't carry unless it became necessary. Tonight it sure became necessary."

"Ya think?" Meg asked, sarcasm spilling over.

In a brief moment of spite while they were talking with the Garda, she'd felt tempted to reveal that Jake was an American federal agent working with British Intelligence. If it was true those bikers were shooting at *him* — they might've known who he really was—then destroying Jake's cover might endanger his life even more. That she would not be a party to. She didn't want Jake hurt any more than she wanted her grandmother arrested.

She was glad she'd kept quiet. Despite it all, he was a good guy just doing his job. Still, she was in no mood to let him know that.

"And you call yourself a dull guy," Meg spat. "Oh, that's right, that was your cover. Dull banker. Believe me, Jacob Bernstein, after this is over and I've got Grandma back home, safe and sound, I never want to see you again!"

He said nothing. Just let out a long huff and drank his beer. His shoulders slumped and he hunched over the glass. For a second, she almost felt sorry for him.

For a second.

Jake paid the cabbie with euros. Once inside the hotel, still lugging the small cardboard box, he turned to Meg and lowered his voice.

"Come to my room."

She whirled on him, anger rising again. After the shock at the cathedral rectory, the running chase to the library, the police questioning, and then the confrontation in the pub with an indignant Mike McCoy Junior, Jake expected her to sleep with him?

"Don't even think it, pal!"

He stumbled a little, placed a hand on her shoulder for support. His face blanched and he grimaced again. Blinked a lot, too, as if he were struggling to stay awake.

"Not that . . .help . . .need your help. Not a rock, Meg. A bullet. My leg . . .it's bleeding again."

Meg's heart skipped a beat. He looked like he was about to faint. Grabbing him around the waist, she helped him walk to the elevators. A couple from the motorcoach glanced over from their cozy group of four and waved. Their faces showed concern when they saw Jake lurch to the side.

"A little too much Guinness," she explained tightly. They rode up to their floor, Meg still holding onto him as firmly as she could. Jake was listing from side to side, closing his eyes against the waves of pain.

"You have a First-Aid kit?" he choked out.

"A small one. Jake, let me call a doctor."

"No. Too many questions. Get it. Bring it." He opened his room with the card key and she helped him ease down on the bed.

"First let's see how bad it is." Meg unsnapped and unzipped his dark trousers, tugged them off while he lay spread-eagle on his back. The paper towels he'd used to stanch the blood were soaked through, reddened and soggy. His right leg was sodden with blood. Even his sock and white briefs. Her heart thudded and her stomach lurched. God, too much blood. She felt sick, ready to throw up again. She swallowed it down.

"Dammit, Jake, you should've said something!" She dumped the sodden paper towels in the trash can, hurried to the bathroom and pulled hotel towels off their bars. Rushed back to the bed and wound the white bath towel tightly around his right leg, covering the jagged wound. "Hold it tight if you can."

She hoped the pressure would diminish the loss of blood. Then pulled his socks and briefs off and threw them in the bathtub.

"I think the fleshy part got it," he rasped. "Bullet went through, thank God. Didn't hurt much until the pub. Could've been a lot worse . . ." Both legs quivered. Meg stared, frowning. What did that mean?

Jake glanced down at his leg. "Adrenaline . . ." His head

slumped back and he passed out cold. His head lolled to the side. Still wearing his leather jacket and sweater, his arms flung open. He was naked from the waist down. With another damp towel, she wiped the blood off his bare skin, but the wound kept seeping blood. She ran and grabbed another towel to wind tightly around his leg.

She needed to stop the blood. The wound needed stitches. Indecision froze her. She stood there, staring at him.

Like a little boy with tousled dark hair, he lay there looking helpless.

The realization struck her, deep inside, tugged at her. He trusted her with his life. This big, tough FBI dude was lying there, half-naked, as vulnerable as a baby. He trusted her to do the right thing. He said he was crazy about her.

How did she feel about that? Slowly, emotion flooded her. Omigod, she was falling in love with the guy.

Meg frowned. Well, how stupid was that?

"Dammit to hell, Jacob Bernstein! You are nothing but trouble!" Meg grabbed his cardkey and shot out the door, mumbling. "Anything with testicles and tires, always trouble."

In her room, Grandma was asleep, thank God. It would be the devil to try and explain away the evening's events. Meg rummaged through her grandmother's suitcase, found the traveling First-Aid kit, grabbed it, then paused to look around. A bottle of sleeping pills sat on her grandmother's side of their shared nightstand. Also a bottle of painkillers for her grandmother's rheumatoid arthritis.

Meg crept to the table and tapped out four pink painkiller capsules, enough to last Jake through the night and tomorrow. Another small bottle sitting by a glass of water contained Gran's white sleeping pills. Jake wouldn't need the sleeping pills, not after their forced run and the two pints of ale he'd drunk while talking to Mike McCoy Junior. Still, she tapped out two sleeping pills, just in case.

She had a lot to think about. In her jacket pocket was a folded up Quit Claim Deed, written in both the Irish and English languages. She'd promised Young Mike she'd have her grandmother look it over and sign it, giving him full title to the Muckross Stag. What did her grandmother need with half ownership of an Irish pub, anyway? Especially since she really had no legal claim.

There was no doubt in Meg's mind that her grandmother was not Mary McCoy.

Who she really was—Meg was *not* going there now.

The paperback book, one of the historical romances her grandmother loved to read, was resting beside the bottles of pills. There was something sticking out of it, a brochure of some kind. Meg sensed something out of the ordinary. She opened it, perused it quickly. The brochure was in English, French, and German.

The title was *Blood and Honour*, the last word spelled the British way. Obviously a political tract of some kind, it made references to the National Socialist League, the British First Party, and the NPD, whoever they were. She didn't have time to read any more and replaced it inside her grandmother's book.

The Irish man's words harked back. "Could be skinheads. There's a bunch in Dublin . . ."

Skinheads. The woman said something about the Celtic Wolves being white supremacists? Did this brochure "Blood and Honour" have anything to do with those thugs? Why would her grandmother have such a brochure?

Again she couldn't ignore the hard knot in her chest and the sinking, sick feeling in her stomach.

There wasn't time to solve this riddle.

Jake needed help.

CHAPTER TWENTY-FOUR

"Use the butterfly bandages. Don't forget, Neosporin first."

He was conscious. Meg swatted his hand away and growled. "I'm a coach, Jake. I know first aid. Here, take this sleeping pill."

"I don't need—"

"Take it! You want me to help, take it." She assisted him to sit up enough to swallow the tiny white pill with water from the same glass he'd used minutes ago to down the painkiller. Finally he eased back down, surrendering to her ministrations. He was too weak to do anything else and Meg was too stubborn to argue with.

She was a pissed-off woman and he was feeling no pain. Literally. Damn, that drug was strong. And Meg's grandmother took these every day? No wonder the old woman's mind was muddled. No wonder she'd forgotten her cover story. Sixty-five years and God-knew-how-many painkillers and other pharmaceuticals later, Mary Snider—or whoever-the-hell she was—was as confused as the Mad Hatter.

He wondered if Mary Snider would be declared incompetent to stand trial. Drug addiction—no, her best bet for a defense was dementia. Ow. He felt that one. Tried not to wince as Meg poured tincture of iodine into the wound.

"Sonuvabitch." he ground out through clenched jaws.

She then pinched the jagged edges of thigh flesh together, put one part of the butterfly bandage on one side of the wound then the other part on the other side. The two bloody gashes—entrance and exit wounds—needed three butterfly bandages each to close. She stanched a little more blood with a washcloth then cleaned around the areas. Meg was doing a good job.

Jake began to breathe more deeply, now that the worst was over. The painkiller was taking effect, too. Good thing that ricochet bullet didn't hit the bone—or that'd be the end of this assignment, he thought.

"I think we're both jocks at heart. But, Jake, that doesn't mean I can't figure things out. We have a lot in common but a lot that's different too. You say you're crazy about me. I care about you . . .but things are *not* that simple. You know it and I know it."

He knew Meg was talking just to take his mind off the pain. Although she'd lost it at the cathedral, she was holding it together now. His admiration for her leaped a couple of notches.

"I like that about you. You're a smart jock." *I like everything about you.*

"What?" Her angry tone had softened a little.

He rose up on his elbows and glanced around him. His clothes were puddled on the floor next to his jacket, sweater, and undershirt. The rest of it, God knew where. There he was, bare-chested and showing his junk. Didn't give a rat's ass. Meg had seen him naked, had enjoyed his body last night. One night . . .he wondered if there'd be any more.

Maybe that was all he was going to have with her. One night of hot lovemaking, total bliss. From the present frown on her lovely face, he'd been lucky to get that much.

"You're . . ." He was having trouble forming the words. *You're what I've been waiting for all my life.* He plopped back down.

"If it becomes infected, Jake, so help me. I washed it with that iodine solution, but if it gets worse, you're going to the

hospital. Let your MI5 friends take over this fucking assignment of yours."

Whoa, she was royally pissed off. With him, this job, everything. With MI5. Which reminded him. He glanced at his
watch. Time to check in. But with Meg here, he couldn't.

He hadn't seen either of the MI5 surveillance team in the
hotel lobby. Then again, he'd had such tunnel vision from the
pain and weakness, not surprising. At this point, the main objective of MI5 was to keep Mary Snider from bolting and disappearing. Major Temple was tolerating his presence just to
keep the FBI, DOJ, and DOD—not to mention the U.S. Navy
and Pentagon chiefs—off their backs.

That was his fucking job—keep all the agencies satisfied.
Here he was, about to destroy Meg's grandmother's life and
here Meg was, helping him. She was finishing up, her pretty,
blue eyes clouded over with worry, and not just over him, he
suspected. There was something on her mind.

"Thanks, I owe you big time," he muttered. Their eyes met.

"Jake, what's Blood and Honor?"

Taken aback by her non sequitur, Jake was silent for a moment. Then he connected the dots.

"Skinheads. They're a neo-Nazi, white supremacist organization begun in California, of all places. Now spread into
Great Britain, Ireland, Germany."

"Oh." She continued to frown.

"Blood and Honor's banned in Germany but not Britain,"
he went on. "The group's linked to one of the political parties
there, the NPD. National Democratic Party. They preach a
right-wing, fascist ideology that's gaining fans. Probably a
backlash to all the immigration from the Middle East and Af-
rican countries. England's changing and a lot of people don't
like it." He took a breath and let it out. "Basically fascist
scum."

"I see." She covered the butterfly band-aids with a gauzy

strip that she wound tightly around his thigh two times, then pinned the edge to the wrap and looked up. "How do you feel?"

"Okay. Getting fuzzy-headed but hanging in there. Blood and Honor, where did you learn about them?" A second's pause. "What that Irishman said, about skinheads coming down from Dublin?"

"Maybe." She shrugged her pretty shoulders. Jake noted she'd taken the time to shed her jacket in her hotel room. So she'd had time to discover something else.

"Their magazine, Meg would make your blood boil. It's all anti-Semitic, anti-black, anti-nonwhite immigration, anti-homosexuality. They produce videos promoting a revival of Nazism. Ethnic cleansing, keeping the U.S., Europe, and the U.K. white. They use neo-Nazi symbols—the swastika and Sig Runes. But they're clever. They never use the term Nazi. In some places, they call themselves the November 9th Society, or N9S. The date of Kristallnacht in 1936, when Jewish synagogues in Germany were trashed, Jewish men, women, children killed in the street."

He watched Meg take a deep, shuddering breath then slowly shake her head.

"There's a department of FBI's division of Investigation that keeps tabs on domestic terrorists. This group qualifies. They're banned in Germany but not the U.S. or U.K. This bunch's gone underground in Europe. We know who . . .who their leaders are in the U.S. but not elsewhere." His head was fogging up. Piecing his sentences together was becoming more and more difficult. "I know B and H, Meg. This is my area of expertise . . .counter-terrorism. I collect NSA, DOJ, and DOD intercepts, analyze them and write reports. This . . .this, uh, bunch likes to use old WWII Nazis as poster boys for their . . .their recruitment campaigns."

Meg flinched then was silent for a long moment. "I don't

understand, Jake. Something's happening to my grandmother."

He locked eyes with her. His left hand clasped one of hers, the one remaining on his thigh. For Meg's sake, he softened his voice.

"You know she's not Mary McCoy. She has no real connection to this place. Not to Killarney or Ireland. Never had. Give me time so I can find out who she really is. Don't you want to know the truth? Before she lawyers up and puts on a dementia defense?"

He'd been too blunt with her. She pulled her hand away and stood. Her eyes ran over his naked body then surveyed his face. No doubt at all, they still had the hots for each other. If he could, he would have willed her to stay. Meg, however, had her own mind and resolve. She looked away, her face clouded and crinkled with indecision, pain, confusion.

"I'm afraid. Of the truth."

He had no answer to that. Only she knew her own inner strength. Anger returned to her eyes. A moment later, she was gone.

Forcing aside his feelings, Jake focused on the tour's itinerary over the next few days. Tomorrow morning, the Ring of Kerry. He pictured it in his mind. Panoramas of sea, cliffs, mountains, and islands. Lunch somewhere on the Ring then off to the north for a visit to the National Stud Farm near Kildare. Something about a stallion valued at millions of euros and his harem of thoroughbred mares. Arriving in Dublin by evening.

Dublin. Jake was certain Meg would be hustling her grandmother on a plane for Dallas. He had one more day to uncover the truth about Mary Snider and here he was, laid up with a bullet wound.

Dammit to hell.

Meg was closing ranks around Mary Snider, protecting her

grandmother from MI5's inevitable arrest.

He couldn't blame her.

And now it seemed the old woman had a new team of bod-yguards—ruthless ones. Soldiers of the neo-Nazi organiza-tion, Blood and Honour. What a great American export, Jake groused silently—American white supremacy joining forces with British and Irish crackpots. He'd heard about the Celtic Wolves and their recruitment and training camps. What was their motto? *White Pride, Worldwide.* Their emblem a version of the Celtic cross—the Christian cross overlapping a circle.

Like crosshairs on a rifle scope.

Meg had seen something in her grandmother's possessions that bore the Blood and Honour name. He was sure of it. Maybe her grandmother hadn't abandoned all that WWII Nazi propaganda in her past. Maybe deep in Mary Snider's heart, she was still a Nazi. As a young woman, she'd been fully indoctrinated with the vile philosophy of Adolf Hitler's Nationalist Socialist Party. Jake had certainly seen a glimpse of that one morning over breakfast.

Some people changed. Some didn't.

He thought back—1945. Germany defeated. Hitler dead. Mary Snider, saved from exposure and certain execution by her marriage to an American, reinvented herself. Took her wartime cover and made it permanent. But who was she re-ally? Had sixty years in the States changed her? She'd raised two children then rescued two grandchildren and raised them as her own. Had spent at least fifty years with one man, an American who was probably as different from her German lover as a man could be. Avoided the horrors of wartime Ger-many and postwar deprivation.

One lucky Nazi spy.

So what was her real name? Was her family in Germany still alive? Had Horst Eberhard, alias Thomas McCoy, man-aged to survive the war somehow? Or did the cessation of his letters to Mary McCoy mean his death? If he'd survived, where was he now? Was he using another alias?

On this tour so far, Mary Snider was spending a lot of time with the wealthy Le Blancs. Maybe they weren't just cozy, motorcoach pals after all. Sure wouldn't be the first time that wealthy patrons became involved with extremist causes.

Drowsy, the full effects of both the painkiller and sleeping pill finally kicking in, he nonetheless heaved himself up from the bed, went over to the carry-on and pulled out his laptop and the secure cell phone.

His vision began to blur. He rubbed his eyelids. His head felt disembodied, light and floating. The rest of his body weighed a ton.

No use . . . no use trying to do this tonight. He put back the laptop and phone before falling back on the bed, his legs feeling as though they were encased in cement blocks. The heavy cement spread to his head and he closed his eyes. The specter of facing Major Temple's wrath in the morning reared its ugly head. He'd be furious when Jake failed to check in.

Tough shit.

CHAPTER TWENTY-FIVE

He plugged the laptop in and, while waiting, drank thirstily from the bottle of water Meg had brought him the night before. His thigh pulsed with renewed pain, his head felt sluggish. And he was starving. Never did get food at the pub the night before. They'd been too rattled from being shot at.

Six o'clock. Too early for breakfast. He glanced at the pink pills Meg had left on the nightstand, waited before taking another painkiller. He wanted to be as mentally alert as possible when speaking to MI5.

Gotta rehydrate. Fluids. Stop thinking about Meg and what you'd love to do with her to make her forget her anger. Focus. Focus.

He dreamed that in the middle of the night Meg had slipped into his bed and lain next to him. She'd held him loosely, a slim arm gently draped across his midriff. He felt the heat from her body, heard her whisper something to him.

When he awoke that morning, there was no one beside him in his bed. Her scent, however, a mixture of floral and citrus, drifted over to him from her pillow. He sniffed the pillow again. Then his fingers. Her scent was all over him.

She'd spent the night in his bed. Keeping vigil.

He shook his head to clear his thinking and felt his thigh.

Well damn. He braced himself on one elbow. A new gauze bandage was wrapped around his leg. His thigh was swollen but the bleeding had stopped. Black thread ends spiked up through the gauze. What the hell—?

His fingers touched the tough spiky thread, standing up

like black whiskers. Sutures? He unwound the gauze around his thigh and stared. Sure enough. Someone had stitched up his wounds. A yellowish, antiseptic solution smeared over the two sites — the entrance and exit holes. .22 caliber, most likely. A tiny hypodermic puncture was visible in the red, swollen flesh. Penicillin, most likely.

He plopped back on his pillow and smiled.

Meg. She'd gotten a doctor in the middle of the night. Jake slowly swiveled his head. How the fuck did she do that?

An amazing woman.

She cared about him. His smile widened.

Then he scowled.

Major Temple first. Then a sit rep to FBI headquarters. A moment later, Jake was getting an earful.

"Pierce said two bikers fired at you and the granddaughter, for Pete's sake. And then you talked to the Irish cops in McCoy's pub. Good God, Bernstein, could you have done a better job publicizing your mission by taking out a news advertisement in the Dublin Crier?"

Jake puffed out a breath, holding his temper. Two holes in his leg and no sympathy from this Brit.

"We had no choice. We had to cooperate with the locals. I maintained my cover and Meg went along. If I'd had my pistol with me, there would have been a lot more commotion to worry the locals, I guarantee you. So moving on, what's the report on Horst Eberhard? Is that his real name?"

Jake could detect the sound of teeth grinding down on a pipestem. Temple's patience was running out, he could tell.

Hell, so was Mary Snider's.

"Astonishingly enough, it is. Dug around the archives and found records from Passport Control. Horst Eberhard, the youngest son of Count Friedrich Eberhard of Lower Saxony, came into Great Britain on a student visa in 1934, left in 1938. A check of Irish visas showed he moved into Ireland in 1935.

Thus he had four years to perfect his English, three in Ireland to master an Irish dialect and to look for a target. He must've been a valuable asset to the Abwehr if they were footing his bill all that time."

Jake nodded to himself. "A deep cover mole. Wonder how many Irish sympathizers he recruited during that time. He must've met Mary McCoy in Dublin. Found her suitable in looks, anyway. Was probably looking for a girl who resembled the German agent being trained for the assignment. Unlucky Mary McCoy from Killarney matched up. Then he went about seducing her, or maybe just became friendly. Supposedly Mary was a devout Catholic. But hey, she wouldn't be the first to fall in love and forget her strict upbringing."

For a couple of seconds, he thought of what he'd learned about the real Mary McCoy. "No, strike that. I don't think he recruited the real Mary. She was too staunchly anti-German."

"I agree, Bernstein. By early 1940, plans were in place for the German woman to be smuggled in." Temple interrupted his thoughts. "And assume Mary McCoy's identity, especially after the girl's parents had been eliminated. And what better place than on a crowded ferry? Perhaps the only person Mary McCoy knew on that ferry was the female spy, Hummingbird. Her replacement was standing by, probably studying her. Poor girl had no idea she was at the center of an evil, tangled web of deception. A U-boat might've been in the Irish Sea that very night, waiting to see what developed. They must've received a signal that Hummingbird survived and was in place."

"My theory exactly, Major Temple. I think Hummingbird was smuggled in months before so she could adapt herself to the language and culture. She'd have an ear for dialects. A chameleon, she'd blend in well."

They'd arrived at the same conclusion, Jake thought, though from different perspectives. He then brought Temple up to speed from his own experiences in Killarney — the photo of a young Mary that Meg knew was *not* her grandmother. The letter Mary had written to her parish priest *before* the ferry's sinking, bearing the real Mary's signature. No recognition on Mary Snider's part of important landmarks in Mary's hometown. Not the cathedral, the pub, or her family's home. Not the place where her parents drowned . . .or were killed.

"It all seems to fit," said Temple. "The hummingbird pin, Mary Snider's fluent German, her attitudes, her lack of memories of Killarney, her lack of emotional connection, the forged signatures on the typed letters. They all support Old Mike McCoy's conclusion."

Jake concurred. "When Meg saw the graduation photo of Mary McCoy in those cathedral files, she knew then and there her grandmother was an impostor. She took the news very hard."

Temple harrumphed noisily. "Of course it's a tragedy for the young woman and her family, especially Commander Snider. The U.S. Navy won't be pleased with the upcoming scandal but it can't be helped. You know how complete German records were during the war — bloody fortunate for us too. I uncovered something else."

The major drew out the following silence like a melodramatic stage actor. Jake sighed with impatience even as his thoughts raced ahead to the Navy Commander's reaction to the news that his own mother would be tried in a British court for espionage and war crimes. That a former Navy Seal was a party to exposing her would hit the man hard. And the Navy. Jake felt the bile rise up his throat. His chest ached.

"Horst Eberhard had a wife named Clare," continued Major Temple, "They married in 1932 when she was twenty. By 1939, she was a university professor of Languages and taught French and English. Then she disappeared in 1939. Vanished from the face of the earth. Quite gifted, she was a *wunderkind* of sorts. Twenty-seven when she disappeared."

Jake considered the dates. "If Mary Snider's Clare Eberhard, that'd make her about seven years older than Mary McCoy. I always wondered about that, Major. It seemed strange that a twenty-year-old German girl could do that job, assume another young woman's identity and never get caught. Such a feat would take maturity and dedication. And damned good training. A twenty-seven year-old woman, on the other hand . . ."

He thought of Meg, twenty-six, a full-fledged woman, but in some ways girlishly fragile, unable to deal with the truth of her grandmother's life of lies and deception.

"The *Abwehr* had some dunderheads, but not the *Sicherheitsdienst*. When the SS took over the *Abwehr*, they sent out only their most ruthless and clever of spies. We think Horst and his wife, Clare, were both SS spies. In the SS files the Allies discovered in a Berlin bunker, there were fingerprints next to the code name, Hummingbird. A thousand quid those prints match Mary Snider's. Rather, Clare Eberhard's."

There was a long pause as each man weighed the import of those words.

Jake frowned. "And those SS prints were never matched up to Mary McCoy's? That's odd."

"Mary McCoy was hired by letter," Temple said. "Her prints were sent to the War Office via the local constable in Killarney. Who, of course, verified them at the time. There was no need, evidently, to fingerprint her a second time when she arrived in London. A serious mistake, in retrospect."

"A blunder of awesome proportions," Jake remarked drily.

"If Mary Snider *is* Clare Eberhard," the major continued. "And we believe she is, she'd be—what? Eighty-eight or eighty-nine?"

"Yes, that's right, Major. You can see the beauty she

must've been, but her body's falling apart. She's a tough old broad, but she's addicted to painkillers and sleeping pills. God knows what else. She can't hide behind her cover anymore. I've studied her and watched her closely over the past week. I think she's mentally shutting down. The wall of lies is crumbling."

Major Temple snorted loudly—in agreement, Jake supposed, or relief. He wasn't sure. There was certainly no sympathy in his voice.

"Quite a nasty business. After we bring her in, the photograph of a teenaged Mary set next to the War Office's employment photo, her fingerprints, and the signature analysis of those letters are all vital pieces of exculpatory evidence. Your detailed reports, Agent Bernstein, are all admissible evidence and will ensure a rapid indictment. The trial before a magistrate will be months from now, but I'm confident her sentence will be life in prison. For her, that won't be long, unfortunately. Not what she truly deserves, at any rate. This entirely unpleasant business will be over soon and I can proceed to other cases."

Jake had the sudden image of a freight train roaring past him. The investigation was already out of his hands. Twenty-four hours with MI5 interrogators, and Mary Snider would be spilling her guts.

A part of him stung with the pain her admission would cost Meg. A part of him, he had to admit, felt righteous.

Justice would prevail and there would be closure. Of course the McCoys, who lost relatives, and the families who lost loved ones in that ferry explosion, would find little solace. Nor the families of the murdered resistance fighters in Nazi-occupied France. Nor the Jews who could've been saved.

But such were the vagaries of war. Remove all the propaganda and lies and what did you have left? Nothing but human tragedy.

"I want to emphasize this," he stated firmly. "Meg had no inkling about her grandmother's past. Even now, she thinks it's all a mistake."

"We'll take that into consideration, old boy, when we bring her in for questioning." Jake's gut wrenched. He doubled over with pain. Temple's revelation shocked him to his core. His very nerves vibrated with outrage.

"What? You're not serious—"

"Give that letter to Pierce to post to me right away," Temple went on, ignoring his outburst. "Your reports and that letter will be enough to get a warrant. We can pick up both women in Dublin the day after tomorrow. Tomorrow I'll have our office get Irish approval for the arrest warrant for Mary Snider. Her granddaughter's a person of interest as an accessory after the fact, but we don't expect an arrest will be necessary. Protocol is required, unfortunately. The Irish are a bit touchy about us British barging in and assuming jurisdiction where there is none. Our history as adversaries and all that, you realize."

"I can't accept that Major." His whole being hardened into a ball of iron.

"Can't accept what, Agent Bernstein? Would that wrinkle in our plan be the dishy blonde you've been shagging? Is she planning to flee with her grandmother back to Texas? That won't stop us from extraditing them both. We've done it before, as you well know, but our intention is to arrest Mary Snider before she has a chance to run. The granddaughter is just leverage so the old lady will sing . . .like a lark. We hope you haven't tipped the granddaughter off to our intentions."

"Of course not," Jake lied. "Meg hasn't shared her plans with me. I do know it's possible her grandmother has been in touch with either Blood and Honor or the Celtic Wolves, that neo-Nazi organization here in Ireland. I bet those bikers were members of the Celtic Wolves. They're encamped nearby, playing their war games. I believe they were delivering a message, like back off, Jew, or the next bullet will find its target. Meg found something in her grandmother's things, a Blood and Honor brochure. The group's been communicating with her, or possibly with the Le Blancs. Meg shared that information with me. You can bet *that*'ll be in my final report."

The major swore a stream of invectives.

"Who're these people, the Le Blancs?" the major finally asked. "Why wasn't I told before?"

Jake sighed heavily. "Thought they were just tourists, like everybody else on the coach. Now I'm not so sure." He gave Temple what information he'd learned about them.

"I contacted my office," he added. "They don't have anything on these people. No priors, nothing."

"I'll check them out. French Canadians, you say. From Quebec?"

"So they say." *Chew on that, asshole.*

"I'll double the surveillance team," Temple said. "They'll be there by morning. Keep your head down, Bernstein. We need you to testify at the trial."

"Starting tomorrow I'm packing, Major. Tired of being a target." *Sick and tired of you and your games.*

They rang off.

Jake pushed himself up, took a painkiller, drank an entire bottle of water then went to sit at the desk. His head was buzzing a little and his reserve energy was sapped. Every bone and muscle ached. He was drained from yesterday's excitement. From loss of blood.

Mostly the rage inside him drained him. He'd trusted Major Temple to keep Meg out of the indictment. His reports had verified her innocence, her lack of knowledge about her grandmother's true identity. MI5 was disregarding Jake's assessment of Meg's role in helping him crack the case.

Using her as leverage to make her grandmother confess.

His rage made him want to weep. Made him feel sick with helplessness. Then he spied his Navy sweat pants and the matching sweatshirt. His eyes narrowed. So the major had been keeping his cards close to his vest.

Well, he had a trump card hidden as well.

Jake picked up his FBI-issued cell phone.

CHAPTER TWENTY-SIX

M eg excused herself, claiming a trip to the ladies room
was necessary, and left the breakfast table. Her grandmother and the Le Blancs were speaking rapid French, but her
throbbing headache from a sleepless night was preventing
her from absorbing everything they were saying. Something
about photo shoots in Berlin and Hannover. The Le Blancs
were suggesting they leave from Dublin. Her grandmother
had told them Meg wanted to fly them out immediately.

The Le Blancs were now showing a different face to Meg.
They were clearly upset that Meg and her grandmother were
planning to fly home as soon as they reached Dublin.

Something wasn't right. Meg wondered if it had anything
to do with the Blood and Honour brochure she'd spied in her
grandmother's book.

Moments later, she spotted Jake taking his place in the line
at the hostess' podium at the entrance to the dining room. She
had to pass the line on her way to the restroom. When she did,
she called Jake over to a wall where they couldn't be seen
from her grandmother's table.

Jake limped over to her, favoring his wounded leg. All
warm smiles and hungry eyes, he looked handsome and a little more rested in his Navy sweats, over which he wore a
khaki-colored windbreaker. The windbreaker looked rather
loose about the shoulders, but it was snug around the waist
where it was partly zipped up. He'd shaved and washed his
hair, which gleamed with auburn highlights. Recalling how
she'd touched him during the night as she snuggled against

his body, she didn't dare let her eyes rove down to his hips and crotch.

"Thanks for staying last night," he said in a low husky voice. "And for calling the doctor. I was so out of it."

"You were, totally. You didn't even wake up when he stitched you and gave you a shot. I had the night manager call a local doctor. He'd already heard about the bikers. I guess word gets around in a town this size."

"Thanks, Meg. I didn't realize last night how much I needed stitching up. Most of all, I appreciate the warm body all night. And your concern." He then clasped her upper arm and stroked it with his thumb. With hooded eyes, he looked like he wanted to devour her.

"Aw, Meg . . ."

"How does it feel? Your leg, I mean?"

He grinned. "Healing. The other, uh, appendage needs some TLC."

Meg smiled. "Uh-huh. Give yourself a chance to heal, big boy." She socked one of his bulging biceps. Flirting with this irrepressible man was becoming a habit.

"You're the only healing I need," he added.

When he grinned that certain way — like a little boy sharing a naughty secret — her heart somersaulted. A rush of warmth enveloped her, rippled through her body.

"Look." He pulled a card out of his jacket pocket. "My cell number's on this. It's a four-band international phone. Call me wherever you go. I want — I *need* to hear from you. That everything's okay . . .after you and your grandmother . . .uh, leave."

She frowned, remembering why she'd approached him. Meg took the card and stuffed it inside her bra. His eyes lingered on the swell of her breasts and the cleavage showing above her V-neck sweater, she noticed.

"Okay. I'll call *after* we're home. I want you to be able to claim . . .what do they call it? Plausible deniability?"

"Something like that." Another hand came up to caress her other arm. "Meg, I don't want it to end here."

"From what you've told me, it won't. Not with Grandma. They'll still come after her."

"No, I mean with you and me. Right now your grandmother's fate is out of my hands. You and me, there's still a chance."

Her gaze clung to his, unwavering. How could she let this man disappear from her life? His every feature, look, and nuance of voice, even his particular woodsy cologne, was emblazoned upon her heart and mind.

Yet how could she love the man who was helping to destroy her beloved grandmother?

She closed off those tumultuous, warring thoughts and tugged a folded document out of her jeans pocket.

"Here, before I forget. This is the quit claim deed for the pub. Grandma signed it this morning. It was notarized by the hotel manager. It's all legal. Can you make sure Young Mike gets it?"

Jake accepted it, bug-eyed, open-mouthed. "Sure I can. Meg, how on earth did you get your grandmother to sign this?"

After meeting Mike Junior in his pub the night before, and speaking to his more rational, normal self, Meg had understood the man's dilemma. Caught in a legal limbo, as Jake described it, would be maddening enough. On top of the man's other problems, it seemed cruel not to help him. When the man gave her the Quit Claim Deed, all filled out except for her grandmother's signature, what could she do but accept it and promise to get it signed?

"Grandma's not a monster, Jake," she said defensively. "And neither am I. I gave her a short, simple version of the man's problem. She didn't want the pub so she signed off her half of it. Gave it free and clear to the man."

"To the man who's the rightful heir, Meg," Jake reminded gently. "It's good of you to do this. You're a real *mensch*, Meg Larsen."

"What's that? *Mensch*?" She ignored the implication of his first remark. He bent over her and bussed her cheek. A harmless display of affection in public, but she warmed to it. For the hundredth time, she wished circumstances were different for them. As it was, the barrier between them was insurmountable.

"Yiddish. Means a good, righteous person. Which you are."

Her eyes filled with moisture. Her face and neck heated to his approving words. She felt the flush creep up to the crown of her head. However, when his face hovered again, she backed off a step. There was something she had to tell him.

"Jake, the Le Blancs have been speaking to Grandma in French all morning. They've been talking about photographing her in Berlin and Hannover. I'm not sure why they want to do this, but it has something to do with their business. Or some organization they belong to."

He straightened, looking puzzled. "Berlin and Hannover? When?"

"I don't know. Maybe when we get to Dublin. I think they're very upset. Grandma told them we were leaving as soon as we arrive in Dublin. I think it has something to do with this political organization they're pushing on Grandma. I don't know anything more but I thought you should know what they're talking about."

His expression turned stern, scaring her. He bent close to her and lowered his voice. There was strident urgency in his tone.

"Meg, you can't be a party to this. Here's a warning. Take it seriously, Meg. As soon as we arrive tonight, you take her to the airport. Fly home. If there isn't a flight out tonight to the U.S., then fly somewhere in-between. Madrid, Lisbon, Reykjavík . . . Iceland, for God's sake, if you have to. Get her home as fast as you can. Get her away from MI5. And the Le Blancs."

The hair on her back bristled with fear. Jake paused, clearly troubled. She knew he was about to reveal something he wasn't supposed to.

"MI5's coming tomorrow morning to arrest her. Soon as they get their warrants from the Irish ministry. Do you know what that means? They'll take her into custody. You, too. Take you both back to London. They'll use you to get your grand-mother to confess."

Meg gasped. She jerked back her head. The image of her sick grandmother — and herself — in a jail cell . . . .No, that was too horrible to consider. She shut the vision off.

Jake's eyes crinkled, his expression a study of grim sincer-ity. She had no reason to doubt the veracity of his warning. As if to cover her extreme reaction of alarm, Jake lowered his head again and kissed her on the mouth. As if he were a Lo-thario pestering a girl he'd set his sights on. Several tourists in line, two Italian couples, made gestures and noises of en-couragement.

"*Che benissimo!*"

"*Encorra!*"

More distressed than embarrassed, Meg wrenched out of Jake's hands, then turned and walked briskly away.

Oh God.

She didn't look back. Once inside the bathroom stall, she buried her face in her hands. Her stomach roiled with fear, her chest smarted with shooting stabs of anxiety. Tears of des-pair blinded her, but she couldn't weep.

No time to fall apart, she scolded herself.

Her grandmother was tough. She'd be tough, too.

But they're arresting us. MI5. The British government. Even the

FBI.

They're all against us.

This is all Jake's fault.

To gain control, she breathed deeply, in and out of her mouth, and counted to ten until her inner core had calmed enough for her to think. Her thoughts flew out in spurts.

Okay. Dublin. Tonight. Sneak out of the hotel. Without MI5 seeing us. How? I'll find a way. Yes. I can do it. I'll think of a way.

CHAPTER TWENTY-SEVEN

The Ring of Kerry. A cold, foggy day. One that fit her mood.

On the motorcoach, people huddled in their jackets and coats despite the heater having been turned on. The heater wasn't working well and the coach was like a fridge. Meg wore a black beret over her long hair. The hat kept her head warm and the wool scarf around her neck helped too. As long as she was warm, she could keep the panic lying just below the surface of her mind from returning and obliterating her reason.

Jake was sitting near the front while she sat with her grandmother in the back. Every once in a while, he'd turn his head toward the aisle, as though he wanted to look back. As though he were signaling her that he was worried and thinking of her.

Silly of her, Meg realized. FBI Special Agent Jacob Bernstein was concluding his case and about to move on. She'd probably never hear from him again.

Nor did she want to — the bastard.

He was chatting with Hank, the big Canadian, who was sitting across the aisle. From all appearances, Jake's mood matched hers. Despite Hank's jokes, he barely smiled.

Meg looked away. The gloom outside their coach would be the last memory she'd have of Ireland. How foolish she'd been. To think this tour was going to fill her grandmother with fond, childhood memories of her Irish homeland. Instead, it had become a trap.

In spite of everything, though, she knew deep down that

Jake cared what happened to her and her grandmother. Why else would he have risked his very job to warn her to leave tonight?

And when she and her grandmother vanished from the hotel, *he* would be blamed. They would know he'd warned her. He was a friend who was doing her a favor by warning her. Yet all along he'd collected evidence against her grandmother.

Was running away really the right thing to do? Jake seemed to think so. Maybe this investigation was all a case of mistaken identity. They'd discover another Mary McCoy who'd spied for the Germans. Whatever . . .Her grandmother needed legal advice, an American attorney who'd fight extradition, who'd defend her. Maybe Meg needed one too. Desperately.

To distract herself from her morose thoughts, Meg kept her focus on the landscape. The day was turning out to have the usual cold and misty fog that everyone associated with coastal Ireland. As they rode around the Ring of Kerry, a peninsula jutting out into Kenmare and Dingle Bays, all they could see was gray, dense fog. The sea was invisible except for brief patches here and there. Closer to the coach, she could barely see the green, grassy hills. Steep, rocky cliffs plunged down on the other side.

Inland they passed through fern- and bracken-laden forests, half hidden by swirling mists. Since the coastal views were entirely blanketed, their escort, Robert, couldn't stop apologizing for the disappointing, nonexistent vistas.

Meg couldn't care less.

The same thought churned around in her head. She should never have brought her grandmother to this place. Her good intentions were now paving the way to her grandmother's hell. This was all her fault.

It was Jake's fault.

She had to get Gran out of Ireland tonight.

When they stopped for lunch at Ballinskelligs, overlooking St. Finan's Bay, she was relieved to get up and stretch her muscles. An idea struck her, one that involved the Le Blancs.

The fog had lulled her grandmother to sleep but she awoke as the coach lurched to a stop.

"C'mon, Gran, time for lunch. And a bathroom break."

"I don't feel good," her grandmother grumbled. "I don't think I can eat. Let me stay on the coach."

"No, Gran, you need to move around. It's good for you. It's too cold anyway. We're having lunch with Pierre and Madeleine." Most of the passengers, including Jake, had already disembarked. "If you're in pain, you can have another painkiller, but only with your meal. Remember what the doctor said. No more than four per day."

At least bribing her with a painkiller worked most of the time. That was a ploy to get her grandmother to eat. Before Meg's very eyes, Mary Snider was wasting away mentally and physically. Her deterioration made Meg tremble with worry. What would she do without the only mother she'd ever known?

In truth, Meg realized her grandmother was probably sneaking one or two more pain pills a day than the doctor had prescribed. But what could Meg do? At home in Frisco, when she was at work, the elderly woman had part-time nursing care. Even so, the homecare attendant couldn't prevent Mary Snider from medicating herself. It was a matter of will. They'd tried hiding her daily pills—all fourteen of them—but that was impossible. Her grandmother had found all of their hiding places. And in the last analysis Meg found it too demeaning and cruel to continue. Grandma had promised her she wouldn't overindulge. Meg had decided to treat her like the adult she was and trust her.

Robert helped Meg's grandmother down the front steps

and over to the inn entrance. In the parking lot next to the cliffside inn, a black Land Rover pulled up. Then a red compact Audi drove by and parked alongside the winding cliff road. There were pairs of men in each one. Meg wondered which men were the MI5 surveillance team. The Land Rover disgorged four ruddy-faced men in what might pass for hunting or country clothes, tweeds with suede patches and heavy cords.

The Brits.

She glanced in the direction of the red Audi. Neither man had gotten out. Following her grandmother and Robert inside, Meg spied Jake by the window facing south. Beyond the big panoramic windows of the inn, the fog enclosed them in a vast, grayish cocoon. There was nothing to see. Meg realized that Jake was watching the red Audi alongside the road. His eyes flickered over to her for a moment, and he nodded. Then turned back to the Audi.

The skinheads. Of course. The bikers who'd fired at them the night before. Jake had somehow found out who they were. Were they with Blood and Honour, that neo-Nazi group Jake told her about? The one mentioned in that brochure her grandmother had? Who had called them? And why?

A chill ran through her veins.

Her gaze drifted from Jake to the Le Blancs, the French Canadians who were now beckoning her and her grandmother over to their table by the fireplace.

When Meg had asked her grandmother that morning how she'd gotten ahold of that brochure, Mary Snider said she couldn't remember. Upon further pressing, she admitted Madeleine Le Blanc had given it to her. But her grandmother had insisted it was a harmless, political activist group for which the Le Blancs were fundraising. The German branch of this organization wanted all of them to come to a meeting in Berlin, where there would be a photo shoot for a magazine.

When Meg asked why they would want her grandmother in a photo, the elderly woman looked confused and wouldn't reply.

Her poor, befuddled grandmother was being manipulated by this Canadian couple into taking part in some kind of promotion for this activist group.

An uneasy thought assailed her. Had the Le Blancs been in contact with her grandmother *before* the motorcoach tour? Was the tour just a convincing cover for their other hidden right-wing agenda?

Whatever that was.

Still, they might be the only ones who could help her and her grandmother get to the airport in Dublin that night without the MI5 surveillance team stopping them.

Jake couldn't help them. He'd done enough already.

Pierre Le Blanc helped her grandmother take her seat, removed the elderly woman's coat and solicitously draped it over the back of her chair. His wife Madeleine watched it all approvingly, exchanged a look of satisfaction with her husband as if all was coming together as planned. They became aware that Meg was staring at them.

"Is something wrong, dear?" Madeleine asked, a smile fixed on her perfectly made-up face. She smoothed the sides of her upswept auburn-tinted hairdo with lacquered nails, then fondled the sable mink jacket folded over her lap.

So incongruous, this wealthy, educated couple associating with skinheads. Were they really the ones who'd had the two motorcyclists fire at them? But why? Were they trying to warn off her and Jake from digging into Mary McCoy's past?

That didn't make any sense.

Maybe Jake was wrong about that group. Maybe she was wrong about the Le Blancs. Maybe the whole investigation into her grandmother was a huge mistake. They'd find another Mary McCoy who was the real Nazi spy.

"Oh, just a headache I've had all day. Some coffee will help." She ordered coffee to go with her bowl of Irish stew after a waitress took the others' orders. Actually she was too upset and apprehensive to eat anything.

At a barely perceptible cue from his wife, Pierre toasted with their glasses of wine.

"*A la sante de notre mere!*" he said, indicating Meg's grandmother. To the health of our mother. Huh, whatever that meant. Maybe they were just being overly polite. Going along, Meg clicked glasses. "*Sante, grand-mere!*"

Against Meg's advice, her grandmother was drinking wine with her most recent painkiller. The duo would zonk her out, Meg knew, the entire afternoon. Which, considering the day's miserable weather, was probably just as well. Though she'd need her grandmother alert and mobile that night when it came time to slip out of the hotel and head to the airport.

"Gran, we should leave for home tonight. I really don't mind cutting short this tour. It's very important that we leave Dublin tonight."

Three heads turned to each other and a brief, quiet exchange of rapid German ensued. Meg was shocked. Since when did the Le Blancs speak German? That one time at breakfast, when her grandmother and Jake had spoken in German, they pretended to not understand. But why? Three pairs of eyes bore into her, drilling her with suspicion.

Another fusillade of rapid German. Then the diminutive Pierre, normally quiet-spoken, turned to her.

"What has that Jew cop told you?" he asked in French. "What's about to happen?" His voice was harsh and autocratic, the first time he'd spoken to her in such a way. There was fear in the man's brown eyes. In Madeleine's, too.

Shit! She'd stepped in the middle of something, all right. A nest of fascist vipers.

Meg bit her lower lip. She hated to reveal anything to this

couple, but if they could assist her in getting her grandmother to the airport on the sly, she'd have to trust them.

In keeping with Pierre, she lowered her voice and switched to French also.

"British Intelligence is going to arrest Grandma and me. In Dublin. I need to get her on a plane tonight. We need to go home. Uncle John will get her a good lawyer and everything will be fine."

"*Ce n'est pas possible*," said Madeleine. Her chin came up in an all too familiar gesture. For the first time, Meg noticed the faint resemblance to her grandmother. The bone structure, the height, and slimness. No. Her aching mind was playing tricks . . .

With deliberate hauteur, Madeleine Le Blanc took off her tinted glasses. For the most part, Meg had ignored this couple over the past week. Distracted by meeting Jake, their intense attraction, discovering who he really was and the danger her grandmother was in had occupied her every waking moment. Now, for the first time since Meg had met the woman, she observed her eyes. The same hue of dark, sapphire blue as Meg's grandmother. As Meg herself.

"*Pourquoi pas?*" Meg asked. "Why not? Why isn't it possible?"

"Because my mother is coming to Germany with us."

"Y—your mother?"

Meg looked over at her grandmother. Gran nodded and mumbled something in German to which Madeleine replied. Too hurriedly spoken and too idiomatic for Meg to understand.

"What's going on? Is this some kind of sick joke?"

Madeleine sneered and continued speaking in rapid French. "No, darling Meg. The only sick joke is your association with that Jew cop." The woman's hand shot out to grab Meg's wrist. "You've done enough. Thanks to you and what you've told that Jew, your grandmother's in danger. We all are."

Her grandmother's crooked, gloved hand seized her other wrist. Meg looked at her grandmother. There was a glazed-over look about her eyes, a slackness around her mouth.

The damn painkillers were muddying her mind.

"Gran? I didn't help him. I was only looking for the truth."

"It's okay, Meggie dear. You're young and naïve. Too good for the rest of us." Her grandmother let go of her wrist and patted the back of her hand. She held up her glass of wine and sipped. "Ah, not bad for such an out-of-the-way place. What do you think, Pierre?"

Pierre smiled condescendingly and murmured approval at the elderly woman but kept vigilant eyes on Meg. Surreal, Meg thought. Her grandmother had no clue what was going on.

Madeleine, however, did. She kept a firm hold on Meg's wrist until Meg wrested her arm away, darting the woman a look of warning. Her first instinct in the midst of this crowded dining room was to call Jake over for help. As if reading her mind, Madeleine's reaction was smooth, calm, and crackling with disdain.

"Careful now, Meg. You don't want to alarm the British, do you? Then you and Clare will never get away. They're here, of course, watching our every move. So what do you want to do, Meg dear? Sound the alarm, or let us help our dear Clare escape?"

Meg looked at her grandmother. The elderly woman was smiling with encouragement, as if she were urging Meg to try out for the cheering squad at the high school. There was an air of disconnect about her grandmother's demeanor. An air of unreality. Meg sensed that her grandmother didn't fully comprehend what was happening.

Oh God. What do I do now?

"Gran, I don't know why they're calling you Clare. Your name's Mary Snider. We have to leave. We have to go home. To Texas. We're can't go to Germany with the Le Blancs. We have to fly home tonight."

"But I must do this," her grandmother said blandly, her dark blue eyes pinning Meg tenderly. "You've said many times over the years, dear child, that you wanted to see where I was born and grew up. We'll do that now. We'll just do it sooner than Madeleine and I planned."

"Do what, Gran?"

"Go home, dear." Her gloved hand fluttered about her blondish-white curls. "This place is not my home."

"But Texas . . .?"

"Non, Meggie. *Chez moi. Allemagne.*"

My home. Deutschland.

CHAPTER TWENTY-EIGHT

The red Audi hadn't budged from its spot. As prearranged with the MI5 surveillance team, Jake offered himself as bait.

Disregarding the click-clack of lunch dishes being served behind him, he went out the inn entrance. Just beyond the Audi was a lookout site where tourists could park and get out. Guardrails were knee-high. Inquisitive fools, if they had a daring mind, could step beyond the railing to look over the edge of the cliff.

He headed in that direction. Walking by the Audi on the roadside, Jake swung out his camera, hanging by a strap around his neck. Close to the cliff, just a foot beyond the guardrails, was a patch of open air not blocked by the fog. Pretending to be enticed by the limited but dramatic views of the cliff, the crashing surf and rocks below, Jake stepped over the guardrails and aimed his camera.

Two car doors opened then shut. Jake didn't look up. The plan was working. By the entrance, he knew, two MI5 agents were taking position, .45mm pistols at their side. Jake reassured himself by slipping his right hand inside his jacket and thumbing off the safety of his pistol. Nothing would please him more than a confrontation with these two bastards.

His hand returned to the camera. He held it steady for a shot at the waves below. Boots crunched on the gravel lining the road. He heard one of the skinheads snicker and mumble something about smashing Jew heads. The driver carried something in his hands. A Taser gun? They were going to zap him, render him unconscious, then push him over the cliff, Jake concluded. Or die trying.

C'mon, assholes. Let me teach you Jews no longer lie down. Times have changed, you dumbasses.

From his peripheral vision, he saw the two skinheads halt and murmur to each other. One was holding something to his ear. Talking on his cell phone and keeping his voice low. He heard the man's Irish accent.

They abruptly pivoted around and returned to their car. The engine gunned a couple of times, made a U-turn then took off down the road. Going in the direction of where the motorcoach was heading after lunch. North.

Would they meet again later that day?

Jake was betting on it.

He returned to the inn. The blond Pierce and his partner, an older man named Badgely, wore looks of confusion as they approached him.

"What happened there, Bernstein?"

Jake shrugged. He reached inside his jacket and thumbed the safety back on. "They got a call. I think they plan to meet us later down the road."

Eager for action, Pierce's face was crestfallen. "What's the next stop?"

"Kildare. The Irish National Stud farm."

"What time?"

"About four, according to our guide."

"Well, fuckit," swore the older guy, Badgely, "I was hoping we'd get a little piece of 'em out here. The bloody fog's putting me to sleep. And I'm the one driving."

Pierce grinned. "Can't wait to nab these bloody wankers. Could tell by the tattoos on the back of their heads they're Celtic Wolves. Temple says there's a Canadian couple in this coach that's running this fuckin' neo-Nazi show."

"Possibly. Keep an eye on them," urged Jake. "She's the tall, middle-aged woman in the mink jacket, auburn hair. He's short, effeminate, wears a fedora most of the time. They're cooking up something with our target. Don't know what it is."

"What about the informant? The granddaughter?"

"She doesn't know anything," Jake said curtly. "She's just as much in the dark about this couple as we are."

"Can't wait to clap handcuffs on the old bag! You sure her granddaughter isn't trying to obstruct justice?"

"I'm positive," said Jake, not liking the direction of Pierce's comments. "On the contrary, she's been helpful."

Badgely smirked. "Wish Temple would give me an assignment like yours, Bernstein. Wouldn't mind getting some so-called *help* from a pretty young thing."

Pierce guffawed. "Oh yah, sure, you hound-dog. You'd send a dish running in disgust." Badgely smiled good-humoredly and flipped his partner the bird. When they looked over at Jake, their expressions changed.

Pierce sobered quickly. "Sounds like Temple's got everything in place. Soon as the Irish minister gives the nod, in we go." Pierce spat, glanced over at his partner. "Let's go in and tip a pint, Badgely. Nothing else to do while we wait for these tourists to finish up."

Jake noticed they waited five minutes before following him in. The inn's bar area was already full of sightseers, disappointed by the weather but not about to waste the day without their favorite ale. The two new agents sent by Major Temple that morning were sitting at a small table in the dining room, making furtive glances around the room. Their eyes connected briefly with Jake's before he looked over at Meg. Jake wondered if the new guys were picking up any conversation from her table.

The tiny transmitter he'd snagged into Mary Snider's coat days ago was no longer working. Jake suspected the Le Blancs had discovered and removed it. If the new guys had a mike directed their way, Jake couldn't see it. Then he spied something. The feather and ribbon contraption on the hatband of one of the men's hats concealed a small mike, he'd bet. Which reminded him . . .

He fingered the GPS transmitter he'd taken from his bag of tricks that morning. If the Le Blancs were planning on whisking Meg and her grandmother off to Germany, the tiny transponder might be the ticket.

From Meg's tense posture, Jake knew something was wrong. Her grandmother, looking spaced out, was staring vacantly at Meg. As though she didn't have a care in the world. Not so for the Le Blancs, who were communicating intense displeasure.

Madeleine Le Blanc was speaking nonstop to Meg while she held one of Meg's arms in a viselike grip. He knew Meg would never tolerate that kind of manhandling from anyone. A glance to his right. Pierre was just returning from the men's room, a thoughtful expression plastered on his smooth-shaven face. Beads of sweat trickled down his bald pate.

The effete man glanced over at Jake, nodded a greeting, squared his fedora and continued on his way.

Some kind of confrontation was going down, Jake knew. Though he wanted to, for Meg's sake, he couldn't approach their table. The Le Blancs would be spooked and God knew what they'd do. He had to be patient and let things play out. Let the Le Blancs and Mary Snider make the next move.

He'd be watching and waiting.

Hank and the two New Jersey sisters called him over to join them for lunch. Unfortunately their table was situated at the other end of the dining area. The tables near Meg were all taken.

Okay, well, this trap was a bust. Maybe later . . .

CHAPTER TWENTY-NINE

Twenty minutes to go before they'd be boarding the motor-coach. The fog was even soupier now than it had been an hour ago. The coach passengers were finishing lunch and some were already stirring in their seats. God help him, he'd never sat in one place so long in his life as during this tour. Even at his desk at work, he was up and about once every hour. This sedentary coach tour was making his butt itch.

Of course, having Meg close by and unable to touch her made another part of him itch. With his previous undercover assignments, when one of his duties was to schmooze a woman in order to get intel, that was a kind of playacting. Playing the role of womanizing seducer. A ladies man or player.

That was a job. If you had a certain look and background that fit the job, you were expected to do your duty. Typecasting, maybe, but he'd been rewarded with promotions as a result. Grandpa Nate said once, right after Jake had joined the FBI, *You have gifts, Yakov, you use them. Just like anybody else.*

This time, however, he wasn't acting. His mind was crowded with thoughts of her, yearnings to hold her, talk to her, even just to sit next to her and feel her thigh rub against his. She filled his every waking moment. Juggling his emotions and loyalty to Meg with his duty and loyalty to the FBI was . . . Well, he hated to admit it, but it was driving him to distraction.

The FBI might fire him for insubordination if MI5 got wind he'd alerted Meg to their arrest warrant. Major Temple and his team would throw him to the dogs.

And rightly so.

He watched her get up and head for the ladies room.

"Excuse me, I need to walk around," he told Hank and the two sisters. One of the girls offered to join him but he waved her off in what he hoped was a polite dismissal.

Jake went out the entrance after first nodding an okay to the MI5 guys at the bar. Pierce and Badgely were relaxing now that the Audi was gone. Frankly, Jake was too. Maybe he was too relaxed.

It paid to case a building before entering, and that was exactly what Jake had done when the coach passengers had disembarked. A precautionary tactic, he'd skirted the building, noting where the door to the Ballinskelligs Inn was located — the north side of the building, opposite to the restaurant and pub. Outside the Inn's exterior door was a pathway leading to a wooden stairway down the side of the rocky cliff to a little secluded beach below.

Having scouted the inn's office, he knew a door on the far side of the office opened directly into the restaurant's kitchen. A shortcut for the servers on their room service runs. It was through this door that Jake went at the mild objection of the teenage clerk behind the inn's check-in counter.

He took a circuitous path through the kitchen, gesturing to some of the cooks with a thumbs-up and throwing everyone a friendly smile. People responded to smiles like butter on pancakes, probably thought him a half-soused tourist who'd gotten lost.

Another door took him to the alcove where the restrooms hid modestly behind a curtain. He stood there until Meg emerged from the ladies room. Surprised, her pretty mouth gaped open. She looked perplexed as he took her hand and retraced his steps through the kitchen and office.

"How much for a room?" Jake asked the teenage clerk.

"Fifty euros."

"Fine." He threw down a bill and grabbed the key.

"What are you doing?" Meg finally asked, overcoming her shock.

He hushed her with a finger to her lips. He led her up the creaky wooden stairs to a room midway down a dimly lit hallway. Fifty-four bucks for this dump, Jake thought. There should be a law against soaking the tourists.

Inside the tiny room, the double bed beckoned but he ignored it. At least the damn place had picture windows facing the sea which, of course, were useless that day. Must be damn cold at night too. No private bathroom, either, just a sink with thin, cotton towels.

Oh well, they weren't staying long.

"Jacob Bernstein, what are you doing? Are you thinking-" Meg stood there, slightly outraged, her arms akimbo. "We don't have time for that. Not that I'd ever have sex with you again anyway."

He shot her a fulminating glance. "Actually that's not my plan." From his jacket pocket he removed a round electronic device the size of a quarter and a half-inch thick. "It's a little bulky, I know, but it'll transmit within two miles. One of our latest toys. A limited range, but it's all I brought with me."

Squinting, she touched the smooth outer surface. Metallic on one side, plastic on the other.

"What is it? What does it transmit?" she asked, wild-eyed.

That got a small grin out of him. Civilians, he thought. If they only knew what electronic miracles were out there.

"Location, Meg, within a two-mile radius. What you said this morning about photo shoots in Berlin and Hannover got me thinking. Sounds like the Le Blancs are planning a detour for you and your grandmother. Maybe at the end of the tour, maybe sooner. Did you tell them about MI5's plan to arrest your grandmother in Dublin tomorrow?"

She nodded. "Yes, I thought I might need their help in getting away tonight. Without MI5 following us."

"And me? Did you think I'd renege and prevent you from leaving?" He stood stock still, wanting to hear it from her own lips. She didn't trust him—and here he was risking his career for her.

Her deep blue eyes met his and locked together. The tilt of her head conveyed her indignation.

"I trust you to keep your word to me, Jake. You wouldn't have told me they were going to pick us up tomorrow if you didn't want us to get away tonight."

He inhaled deeply and exhaled in relief. The GPS beacon he held in his hand was for her and her grandmother's benefit. By giving it to Meg for safekeeping and concealment, he was officially in collusion with their escape plan.

Another line he'd stepped over.

If MI5 discovered Meg with the transponder, Jake's career was toast for By-the-book Bernstein.

Jake found himself breaking all the rules in the Field Manual. Strangely enough, instead of feeling uneasy and guilty, he felt justified. His bosses wouldn't see it that way, however. Not unless by monitoring their whereabouts he was keeping Commander Snider's mother and niece relatively safe. Keeping his targets safe and available for further investigation trumped premature prosecution. At least it did for his conscience. That's what he'd told his supervisor that morning. Terry agreed but reminded him that MI5 wouldn't. Now they were both sticking their necks out.

"Okay, good. I'm glad you trust me."

"I do, Jake." She glanced at the GPS device in his hand. "I don't trust the Le Blancs. They know we're being followed. Those two guys from the ferry and now two more. They know they're British intelligence. So far they think you're a private detective hired by the British. The Le Blancs are planning something, and they're feeding Grandma a lot of bullshit."

"What do you think they're planning?"

"Some kind of promotional photo shoot for their neo-Nazi group." She frowned up at him. "Beyond that, I'm not sure."

"Photo shoots with your grandmother as the poster girl. A successful, never-caught Nazi spy from World War II."

"My God!" Meg sat down on the bed, astounded.

Ignoring her reaction, he looked for places to conceal the GPS transmitter. His portable receiver with the LED screen was safely pocketed in his carry-on. Since the Le Blancs had most likely searched and found the tiny transmitting mike he'd placed on Mary Snider's coat lapel days before, now they'd be looking for an obvious place.

Meg was staring at the object in his palm as though it was a repulsive tarantula.

"Meg, this GPS beacon will help me track your location in case the Le Blancs take you some place you don't want to go. Or they take away your cell phone and you can't call me." He pulled her up, unbuttoned her jacket, surveyed her clothes.

"But then MI5'll know where we've gone," she protested. She let Jake lift up her sweater then drop it. He gazed down her snug jeans to her sneakers. No place there for the beacon. Her pants were too tight and the beacon too bulky. He stared at her curves for a moment.

"No, this is for my information only. I won't let MI5 see my tracker. I promise you." He scowled. "Okay, Meg, do me a favor. Take off everything. Down to your underwear."

"I don't believe this!" she exclaimed. But she did as he asked, even kicking off her sneakers. Jake examined each article of clothing—the shoes, jeans, sweater, jacket—before gazing up at her beret. She took it off and handed it to him, sitting there in just a black bra and matching bikini panties.

Her beautiful body was a powerful magnet. After realizing the beret's inside hem wouldn't be strong or wide enough to support the transmitter, he tossed the hat on the bed. Then he looked at her, standing there in just her underwear, her eyes brimming with trust . . .and something else.

She was giving him a speculative survey, her eyes resting on the tenting bulge in his crotch, his sweatpants stretching and making room. A small moan of regret escaped her then.

"Wish things were different for us."

"I know. This is a helluva way to court a woman," he conceded apologetically. His eyes roamed over every muscle and curve of her body. He savored all the touching, stroking, fondling of their one night together. Relished the feel of her skin, warm and silky. Her citrusy, flowery scent. He couldn't count the second night with her — he'd been practically comatose.

Cold, dumpy room, scaring her half to death with intel toys . . .God, Bernstein, you sure know how to make a woman love you.

"Since when are you courting me?" She sat back on the bed, leaning back on her hands, her elbows cocked. Still in her underwear, her breasts thrusting half out of her bra.

"Since the first time I saw you." He smiled with irony, admitting to himself he was lost from the first moment he'd set eyes on her.

You lovesick fool
Your career's about to crash and burn.

What Meg did next surprised even him. Suddenly she reached up. Her hands seized his hips and pulled him closer to the bed. Jake began stripping off his clothes with alacrity. Off flew his windbreaker and sweatshirt, followed by a more gingerly unstrapping of his shoulder holster. He laid them on the floor, then untied the waistband of his sweatpants.

He stopped, his hands frozen at his waist. A quickie in this dump? What a memory to leave her . . .

"Jake Bernstein, are you courting me? Yes or no?" she repeated, her voice dripping with sass.

"Doing a half-ass job of it, but yeah." He smiled.

"Well, let me be the judge of that."

Her eyes sparkled with humor as she pulled down his trousers and briefs, exposing his huge erection. She scooted back on the bed and shimmied out of her panties at the same time. She glanced at her watch. "C'mon, cowboy, we have only ten minutes!"

No time for recriminations, he thought.

Screw this dump. Screw this case. Screw my career.

He bent over her in reply, his knees on the creaky bed. The kisses he smothered her in were deep, wet, hot. Her long legs encircled him, her heels digging into the small of his back. She locked her arms around his neck and her legs around his back, encouraging him to ride her. He growled and thrust into her. He pumped hard several times, caught up in the moment, each one deeper than the one before.

No more thinking. Just out-of-this-world rocketing pleasure. He was ready and so was she. When she moaned his name, he thrust one last time. He felt her spasm at the same time of his release.

Damn, so in tune to each other . . .it was uncanny.

"Strange courtship," she murmured. She pulled his head down for another deep kiss.

He smiled down into her beautiful face, so open and relaxed. Her fears had momentarily vanished, and for that he was glad. If making love with Meg Larsen banished all her boogeymen, then he'd be happy to oblige . . .every day of their lives.

"Yeah, damn strange," he affirmed. "No romantic dates, no flowers or champagne — it's been crazy. Surreal."

"With you, surreal is okay. I'd like those romantic dates . . .someday. On the bright side, Jacob Bernstein, you're anything but dull."

He shot her a rueful smile, stood up and handed her a towel. "I'm sorry it has to be like this, but I promise you . . .I'll move heaven and earth to give you those romantic dates."

"Don't know how, with you in Virginia and me in Texas."

"'Least we're in the same country. I promise you I'll make it happen."

"Good. I'm counting on you, big boy," she reminded him, a wry smile animating her flushed face. "Now give me that GPS thing. I'll find a place to hide it. Just make sure no one can track me except you."

"Trust me, Meg." He looked down at the gauze wrapping on his thigh. A little blood had oozed through to the top layer of the dressing. Meg noticed it too.

"You're going to need that looked at again." She frowned as she began to shrug on her panties and sweater.

"Yeah, I know. Dublin," he reassured her. After pulling up his pants, he bent down and kissed her. His way of thanking her for her concern but cutting off further debate. There were more pressing matters at hand.

She shimmied into her jeans and was fully dressed as he was lacing up his sneakers. He placed the transmitter in the palm of her hand. She promptly hid it inside her bra cup, undetectable under her heavy sweater.

"If you end up somewhere in Berlin and Hannover, I want to be able to find you. This couple's ruthless, Meg. Don't think they're not. I think they control a gang of skinheads here in Ireland. Maybe their influence extends to Germany, I don't know. Just be careful. Don't provoke them into violence, okay? Pretend to go along. I'll find you. Use your cell phone whenever you can, but in case MI5 is monitoring mine after you and your grandmother leave, speak in code."

Her expression grew serious once more. He hated to see her worried. Hated the idea that Meg and her grandmother were falling under that couple's control. Hated even more the possibility he might never see her again after today.

"Code? Like what?"

"You said they were talking about photo shoots in Berlin and Hannover. If they take you there . . .for Berlin, tell me your plane had to stop in Boston on the way back to Texas. B for B. If it's Hannover, your plane stopped in . . ."

"Houston. I get it. I'll improvise."

"Good, you're a quick study. MI5 will think you've gone home but they'll expect you to get in touch with me, so my cell phone might be monitored. At least for the first twenty-four hours after you leave. Enough delay for me to get to Germany and the right city."

Meg looked uncertain. "You'll ditch the MI5 agents?"

"You bet. Unless you don't want me to follow you?"

"Of course I want you to follow us. I don't trust those people. You won't believe this, Jake." Meg was preceding him down the inn's narrow wooden stairway. "They've been speaking German to Grandma, calling her Clare. Madeleine's even calling her Mother. And Grandma's so zonked out, she believes them."

Jake tossed the key on the counter as the blushing teenaged boy watched them gather by the kitchen door.

"They're calling her Clare? Then the Le Blancs already know she's Clare Eberhard. Your grandmother must've revealed her true identity to them."

They lingered beside the kitchen door, reluctant to part. Jake's pulse quickened at the melancholy look Meg wore. She shook her head morosely.

"I thought I knew my grandmother. I don't really know her at all, I guess. I think Gran was in touch with the Le Blancs before this tour. I think they met up on purpose."

Her voice sounded on the verge of breaking, so Jake consoled her by stroking her face with the back of his knuckles. He wished like hell he could assure her that his investigation had cleared her grandmother. Just the opposite was true . . . and now the Le Blancs had unwittingly confirmed his and

MI5's theory.

So Mary McCoy Snider was indeed Clare Eberhard.

The SS spy's wife. A Nazi spy herself.

The two most successful Nazi moles in Britain...never caught by the Allies. Horst and Clare Eberhard.

And now...what the hell did it matter?

"Your grandmother's been living her cover story so long it's become her. Or she's become it. Maybe she reinvented herself and became the woman her American husband wanted her to be. Aren't some women like that? They lose their true selves when they link up with a domineering man? In your grandmother's case, staying Mary McCoy Snider was a matter of life and death. With your grandfather gone, she's drifting back to her old self. The Clare Eberhard she used to be."

Meg searched his eyes. "You may be right. Or maybe she's a blend of both."

"You'd never do that, would you? Lose your true self to fit in with a man and his life?"

Her dark blue eyes narrowed. He was testing her and he could tell she knew it.

"Just let a man try. One thing I've learned along the way, Jake, I do my own thing no matter what. No one's going to beat me down and make me into someone I'm not. And that's a fair warning to you too."

"Good. I like that about you."

She smiled wistfully. "That's what all the men say at the beginning."

"I'm different, Meg."

They took a long moment to stare at each other. This could be the last time they saw each other alone in a long while. Or maybe the last time ever. Meg's trust only went so far.

The image of his mother—paint brush in hand, squinting over her latest canvas—flickered to mind. Her strength and independence had sparked more than a few arguments between his parents but his father continued to adore her.

"I like strong women." He broke off. The lump in his throat made it difficult for him to speak.

As if reading his mind, Meg too had watery eyes. They came together and kissed long and hard. Then he stepped back and away.

Finally he cleared his throat. "Go back through the kitchen, Meg. I'll go outside, around the front. I don't want the Le Blancs to know we've seen each other."

Before Meg left, she turned to him. "I like the way we see each other." She grinned.

He chucked her gently under the chin. Her smile vanished, replaced by a frown.

"I think the Le Blancs are crazy."

"Be careful, Meg. Don't provoke them."

She nodded soberly.

The Le Blancs weren't crazy, he thought, but they were fanatics. And fanatics had a way of justifying anything they did.

"Don't let them find that beacon."

They exchanged a long troubled look before she disappeared into the kitchen. A feeling of uneasiness overcame him. He'd had little choice, but he now wondered if he'd done the smart thing by giving Meg that GPS transponder.

What if the Le Blancs found it?

What then?

CHAPTER THIRTY

The sun was low in the sky. Another two hours on the road and they'd take their tour of the thoroughbred stud farm. An hour after that and they'd be in Dublin. Jake still hadn't spoken to Meg, but the apprehensive expression on her face when he looked back a few times spoke volumes.

Once during a bathroom and snack break near the city of Limerick, she'd climbed down and approached their guide, Robert. She held up a map and let him take hold of it with one hand, apparently asking him directions or determining how much farther to Dublin. It didn't take a genius to realize she was arranging a detour to the airport, maybe before they reached their hotel in Dublin.

Jake hadn't considered that possibility. But then the black Land Rover would follow her and her grandmother to the airport and prevent them from leaving. They'd never be able to get off the ground. Surely Meg realized that.

Dammit, Meg, help me out here.

He didn't want MI5 bringing obstruction of justice charges against her too. He was keeping his distance from her so as not to alarm her grandmother and the Le Blancs. But second-guessing their next move was making him frantic with worry.

They already knew Mary Snider's arrest was imminent. The Le Blancs wouldn't want to get caught in the cross-fire. With their political ties to right-wing organizations, even though Blood and Honour was legal in the U.K., they'd still want to avoid a brush with MI5. One would think, anyway.

In line at the rest stop's café, he pretended to brush against

Meg as she waited for her cup of espresso at the counter. She was so wired, her eyes darted about and she kept fidgeting with her purse. The Le Blancs were close by, seemingly holding her on a short leash. Pierce and Badgely were taking turns spotting Mary Snider, who'd remained on the coach. The two new agents lounged around the café, keeping eyes on Meg and the Le Blancs.

"Hey, Meg, how are things?" he asked casually. It would have looked peculiar if he'd ignored her. "Looking forward to seeing the most valuable stallion in Ireland?"

She shrugged, glanced over at the Le Blancs. Then smiled up at him. "Sure. I used to ride horses a lot when I was younger. You can't live in Texas and not be around horses. You?"

Moving over so that his back blocked the Le Blancs' view of Meg, Jake said loudly, "Nope, never been around 'em. Water's more my scene." He mouthed, "What's going on?" He tried to take hold of her hand but she moved out of his reach.

"Robert says you need to pay for the excursion in Dublin," she said loudly, "You know, the Irish dance festival. You should go see him. You're the only one who hasn't paid."

Her espresso arrived and she walked over to the far end of the café to sit with the Le Blancs, her eyes shuttered, her expression closed off.

Sensing Meg was trying to clue him in on something, Jake paid for a coffee to go then sauntered out of the café. Robert was smoking with the driver by the front of the motorcoach. Jake approached, careful to keep his back to possibly prying eyes in the café.

"Meg says you have a bill for me to pay. The Irish dance festival in Dublin."

The man gave Jake an inquisitive look, his eyes settling significantly on the slight bulge on Jake's left side. So Robert Morse knew who he was. Temple must've decided to widen his need-to-know net. Clearly not happy about his mission, their guide passed him the invoice sheet. Underneath he slid a postcard. Jake took both and strolled to the other side of the coach.

The postcard showed the cathedral in Killarney, one of many scenes the old codger, Danny Boy, had been selling that day of their jaunty car ride. He remembered buying a handful of postcards himself. The wiry Irishman had provided such welcomed comic relief. He'd made Meg laugh.

Jake flipped the card over. Five words — *Berlin*. Reichstag. *Hannover. Engesohde Friedhof.*

Berlin and Hannover were both in Germany. Of course he knew the Reichstag. That had been the building's name during the Nazi Third Reich era. Now it was the Parliament Building of present-day reunited Germany, home to the Bundestag. The building had been damaged by the Soviets during World War II but had been restored to its former splendid self.

Good place for a photo shoot.

But Engesohde Friedhof? A cemetery? In Hannover?

Jake looked up at the sky and swore. What the hell were the Le Blancs and the old bat getting Meg into?

The motorcoach veered off M7 and took a country road over low-lying hills and grassy fields. Finally a large sign in white-and-green announced the Irish National Stud Farm. One of three large coaches, their driver parked in front of a huge, wall-high hedge in the lot nearest the road. It was clearly a tourist attraction. Numerous cars and three motorcoaches clogged two main parking lots. Jake watched as the black Land Rover took a place at the other lot, where most of the visitors' cars were parked.

Robert led the entire group to a meeting area, then

introduced the gentleman who'd be leading their tour of the farm. While Jake surveyed the buildings where their group was standing—an information center, gift shop, and re-strooms—Donald McDonald, as he called himself, gave them a brief lay of the land. A middle-aged man with a paunch, Donald was stoop-shouldered, thin, and had such a bad case of rosacea on his face that his cheeks were almost purple. He wore cord trousers and wool plaid shirt, befitting a farm worker. Speaking in a lilting high-tenor Irish voice, he gave them a few facts about the farm before starting out.

Over twelve-hundred acres, the stud farm provided a lot of space for their approximately ten stallions and ninety mares and foals, all thoroughbreds with the highest pedi-greed papers. El Cid, their prize thoroughbred stallion, had won numerous derby trophies and boasted a current value of over six million euros, or about seven million American dol-lars. Thee coach group exclaimed their appreciation in unison.

Jake noted the MI5 men taking their positions. Badgely stayed with Meg and her grandmother, who was holding onto the arm of Madeleine Le Blanc. Meg's eyes met his. She quickly looked away. The perpetual frown pinching her pretty face meant only one thing to Jake. Something was go-ing to happen.

Pierce was sticking close to Jake, at his very elbow. One of the new guys sent by Temple was staying in his car in the far parking lot. Another was lounging by Robert and the coach driver on the left side—open door side—of the motorcoach, sharing a smoke break and pretending to be another coach driver waiting for his group to return.

Jake didn't like this. They were spread out too thinly. But he had no chance to say anything as their tour group took off after Donald down the road. The tourist buildings fell behind them as they passed barns and other outbuildings on their left and came to a large fenced pasture on their right. Mares grazed amid oaks and evergreens, a bucolic scene which normally Jake would have enjoyed.

Not today. The tension squeezing his chest increased when Pierce nudged him.

"The ladies fell behind and went to the gift shop, looks like. Or maybe the restroom."

"Which ladies?"

"The two targets."

"Anyone else?" Jake stopped and gazed down the road they'd just walked.

"The Canadian woman."

About a hundred yards back, Meg and her grandmother, aided by Madeleine Le Blanc, were entering the gift shop. Then he lost sight of them. Another large group of tourists, keeping pace with their own guide just behind them, blocked his view.

He didn't like that development.

Not one damned bit.

Donald urged Jake's group to keep moving so his voice wouldn't have to compete with the other group's guide. As one, they moved by the vast pasture on their right and stopped at a large multi-acre paddock on their left, where newborns cavorted with their mothers. Several nursed contentedly at their mothers' teats. At the vanguard of the group, Donald explained the process of separating the foals from the other possibly hostile and jealous mares. Life on this stud farm had its own share of dangers.

Growing more uneasy, Jake turned to Pierce.

"Maybe you should go back and give Badgely some help. Keep Meg and Mary Snider in sight."

He glanced around and relaxed a little when he spied Pierre Le Blanc in the middle of their motorcoach group. He was walking beside Hank Philemon and the two New Jersey sisters, chatting amiably. Jake's intention was to keep *him* in constant sight. Convinced that Pierre Le Blanc had given instructions to the two skinheads at the cliffside inn, Jake was watching him for any unusual or sudden behavior, such as using his cell phone in the middle of their tour of the farm. The man could be a decoy for the main operation back at the tourist center, but Jake doubted Mary Snider and Madeleine would be taking off without the little man in the fedora. Or without Meg.

"Yeah, you're right. Something's going down."

With that, Pierce broke into a sprint, back toward the visitors' buildings they'd just left. Since the road back to the parking lot and entrance buildings wound around in an arc to their right, Pierce was soon out of Jake's sight.

He reached inside his windbreaker to thumb off the safety on his 9mm semi-automatic pistol, then thought better of it and left the safety on. There were too many civilians milling around, not to mention valuable thoroughbreds in every direction. Temple would have his head on a plate if he provoked an incident or caused the demise of any of Ireland's prizewinning former racehorses. That would be the end of his undercover fieldwork and most certainly the end of his FBI career.

Keeping Terry in the loop was prudent, but nothing his supervisor did would save Jake's sorry ass if he shot and killed one of these thoroughbreds. Hell, one of these animals was worth more than he was.

Like Pierce, though, the hot queasy feeling in his gut was telling him something was wrong.

His guts never lied.

CHAPTER THIRTY-ONE

Five minutes later, Jake's tourist group approached a series of long rectangular paddocks. Inside each spacious paddock, a thoroughbred stallion either paced or trotted, expelling testosterone-fueled energy with each whinny and snuffle. Each stallion tossed his mane and tail like narcissistic opera divos, as if, strangely enough, each magnificent animal knew his worth in their human-controlled world.

The sturdy fence bordering the roadway was six feet high, built to withstand an angry thoroughbred if necessary. Between individual paddocks, the fencing was double-thick — two stretches of six-foot high hardwood fence preventing two high-octane stud stallions from attacking each other.

Donald pointed proudly to one paddock.

"El Cid. This handsome lad has a value of over six million euros. Not that he doesn't work for that claim to fame. He entertains the ladies, he does, eight to nine months of the year. A tedious job, of course, but, poor boy, he's got to do it."

A solid black stallion trotted back and forth along the double-fence side, challenging — in horse-gestures — his neighboring pal, a bay stallion with black mane and tail. Both alpha males halted occasionally to stare each other down, snort and stamp their hooves until one of them grew bored and trotted away down the fence line. More often than not, the other one would follow suit and show off his prowess along that same fence line. They'd stop, stare, toss their mane and hike up their tails, then trot off again. Seconds later they'd repeat the same king-of-the-hill mannerisms.

All posturing and puffing out one's chest. Kind of a horse's way of playing bully in the school yard, Jake thought. For a minute, even he was intrigued by their aggressive, alpha male behavior.

They reminded him of a couple of guys he knew in the military. Probably the way Jake would behave if another guy came near Meg. Yet what could he do with Meg in Texas and him a thousand miles away in Virginia? He'd have to do something about that. If she wanted him, that was. She certainly wanted him a few hours ago. But would she want him around all the time?

Just as germane, what would he sacrifice in order to be with her? He couldn't answer that offhand.

"El Cid spends four months a year here in Ireland while the mares on the farm are in heat," Donald continued expansively. "A couple of years ago we had a few of the Queen's thoroughbred mares here for a visit. I'm here to tell you they left quite satisfied. The next four months, El Cid will travel to the Middle East in his own private jet and entertain the ladies in the desert, prize thoroughbred mares owned by rich sheiks, Arab princes, and oil barons. Then he's back with us for a bit of a rest, poor fellow, before he goes to work again. It's a tough life, wouldn't you say, folks?"

Appreciative chuckles followed. Jake saw Pierre consult his watch. A minute later, he did the same. Five o'clock on the dot, Jake noted.

As the group moved on toward a large, two-story stable building and yard, Jake hung back, allowing the group behind him to flow past him. He sensed he was missing something.

He was a good half-mile away from the parking and entrance area. Pierce hadn't called his cell phone to check in. Neither had the others. At least twenty minutes had passed from the time they'd begun their tour of the farm with

Donald.

To his immediate left ran a smaller roadway, wide enough to service the compact trucks and tractors that seemed to roam around the farm, carrying grain feed for the horses, gardening supplies, and other farm equipment. The road seemed to provide immediate access to the barns and appeared to cut through to a more direct route to the visitors' buildings.

Jake strode toward it. He sensed something and glanced back. Two men had broken away from the second tour group that was passing by and were now following him — different ones from the thugs in the Audi. These were older men. For a second, he wondered how large the Le Blancs' network was.

More Celtic Wolves? Or their German counterparts?

He didn't have time for another thought.

Amping up for a run, he took off, digging under his windbreaker for his gun. He was about to unsnap the holster strap when he had to slow down. There was a guy on a tractor parked in the middle of the darkened breezeway between two barns. Jake braked to a stride to slide around the tractor. If he had to, he'd use the tractor as a shield and pull out his gun. He started to wave the man off his seat, trying to warn him.

"Hey, bud, get down —"

The man's arm flung out, something silver at the end. With a burst of air, two darts shot out and pierced the front of his jacket. Jake was stunned. He cried out as two sharp stabs of pain like daggers punctured his abdomen. He heard a crackling sound and smelled sizzling flesh as a jolt of white-hot electric current arced through his body.

Pain shot through him, paralyzing every muscle. Mercifully, everything went black.

Meg accompanied her grandmother and Madeleine, both of whom claimed an urgency to use the women's room, although she suspected something was amiss.

She used the toilet herself, then stood outside the elderly woman's stall while Madeleine went into hers. Impatient to join their group, she called out to make sure her grandmother was okay and able to fend for herself. When she didn't answer, Meg called out a second time. Madeleine reappeared and looked under the stall door.

"She needs help, Meg, but the door's locked. Go to the gift shop, dear, and get some help. One of the women. Quick."

Without thinking, acting in confusion, Meg stepped outside the restroom. Two men, waiting outside the men's room across the alcove, seized her arms. One wrenched them back while the other held a cloth over her nose and mouth.

A chemical smell pervaded her nostrils, making her gag. The men's strength was overwhelming, but she fought them and tried to cough out the toxic chemical until exhaustion overcame her. Her strength drained out of her. Their arms were like vises constricting her torso. She was terrified that she'd suffocate. Before she could wrest her face free, a dense fog took over her mind. Seconds later, she went limp, then blacked out completely.

Chapter Thirty-Two

Pain. As though someone had punched his abdomen with an ice pick. Throbbing head. Weightless body.

When Jake came to, his mind was dazed and disoriented. His body felt numb. Paralyzed. Alarm didn't set in until his mind cleared. Slowly the memory of what had just happened pieced itself together, like windblown fragments of a leaf coming back together.

The whole puzzle began to crystallize. The chain of events fell into place in his memory. The dark breezeway. Two men chasing him. One guy on the tractor . . . lying in wait.

A clever set-up. Masterminded by the Le Blancs? Carried out by their Blood and Honour minions?

He swore silently. One limb at a time, Jake took inventory. Broken bones? No, thank God. But his entire body now was trembling, shivering from the shock. His abdomen was on fire. A Taser. He'd used one himself at the FBI Academy in Quantico. Depending on the voltage, the size and physical health of the victim, and how many times the perp zapped the Taser, you could be incapacitated temporarily . . . or killed.

He tried to move but couldn't. Pain shot through him, the aftereffects of the electrical current. Fortunately he was a big enough man and in good physical shape—

He heard a familiar sound. A snuffling, wheezing sound. And the smell. A hot, fetid odor fanned his face.

God, no, Not the damned horses,

Jake squinted open his eyes.

Shit.

276

El Cid's flaring nostrils and open mouth, baring two rows of large, yellow teeth, appeared inches from his face. The stallion didn't appear to like the intrusion into his paddock. One hoof kept pawing the ground by Jake's left side. He raised his head a little and realized the horse — all two-thousand pounds of him — was standing directly over him.

If he sat all the way up, his head would hit the horse's chest. El Cid wouldn't like that.

How the hell did he get there?

Oh sure, compliments of those damned thugs.

What better way to get rid of a meddlesome Jew? They must've seen the humor in their method. Let the horse stomp him to death. The authorities would call it an accidental death.

The weight of his S&W Sigma pistol — the thugs hadn't bothered to take it — reminded him of another alternative. For a moment, he was tempted just to shoot the goddamn horse, but something stopped him.

Several somethings. If he shot the stallion, the animal could collapse on top of him, crushing him to death. The Irish government would have his hide, would probably sue the FBI for damages, and that would be the end of his career in law enforcement. Of course, none of this would matter if he were dead.

Hell, what was more important? His life, or a seven million-dollar horse?

Considerations which gave him pause for a second or two. Finally Jake found his voice, rough and gravelly. "Okay, El Cid. Move back so I can get out of here."

The stallion didn't like his voice either. In fact, he reacted with a startle. He reared up on his hind legs. All Jake could see was a massive belly and large, angry male genitalia. His forelegs and hooves hovered overhead. If those came down, he'd be crushed like a watermelon.

Hooves hit the ground, kicking up dirt clods, just above his head.

Jake choked on the dirt. His hands automatically went up to his face.

The stallion lowered his head again and turned it from side to side, eyeing the strange human beneath him with one eye then the other. His dark brown eyes glowered in rage. His lips curled back from his upper teeth. Then he reared up again, this time backing up a little on thick hind legs. El Cid opened his mouth and let out a loud rumbling neigh.

Shit.

A frantic, sidelong look revealed the fence to his left. He wasn't in the middle of the paddock. The thugs had thrown him over the fence, so he'd landed not far from the corner. They just hadn't expected him to wake up in time.

Thank God the bastards had miscalculated something.

Now or never, Bernstein.

In desperation, Jake heaved himself to his side, his arms braced against his torso, and rolled. He kept rolling toward the nearest fence. The stallion's hooves came down on the earth with a terrible thud. They pounded the ground, sending up vibrations. Dirt and rocks flew like rocketing missiles.

No point in trying to stand — he'd never make it.

Jake kept rolling. Two more feet to go to reach the first fence. If he could get to the lane of grass between the two stretches of fencing . . . .

El Cid stomped toward him, whinnied his fury, and reared up again. Thud! One hoof missed Jake's head by inches. A cloud of dirt and debris caused him to choke and spit. One more time he rolled, this time faster.

He skimmed the underside of the lowest fence board and rolled over to his back. El Cid's deadly hooves chewed the ground beside the fence. The horse bellowed, enraged that his intruder should have escaped him. As Jake lay there on his back in the safe, four-foot wide lane between the two fences,

El Cid's neighbor trotted over. Both stallions pranced around angrily then slowly settled down. Their massive heads and long necks loomed over the fence, staring down at the pitifully weak human. Jake prayed that the two stallions couldn't break through those boards.

The bay stallion pushed his massive chest against the first barrier. The boards held. El Cid, eyeing the competition, did the same. Jake thought he heard a crack. The top rail on El Cid's side bent but didn't break.

Jeez, the fence railing was as strong as the walls of Troy. Jake made a silent prayer of thanksgiving. He'd narrowly escaped being stomped to death by a horse that cost more than he'd ever make in a lifetime. An ignominious way to go.

His body ached all over—his lower chest, where the Taser darts had pierced his skin. His shoulders and arms—how they'd dragged him. His leg wound had opened up again, and the pain was fierce.

How much time has passed? Where the hell's Pierce? And the others?

Meg!

Adrenaline pumped through his veins as fear swamped him.

A man's voice, shouting. Then other voices.

Pierce called out, "Bernstein, what the fuck—"

Jake rolled onto his stomach. He inched his way on his elbows up the middle lane to the fence bordering the road. He felt the two holes in his jacket, then the ones in his sweatshirt. Like shallow ice pick holes, the wounds hurt like hell where the darts' needle-prongs had hit their mark. A little higher up and one of the darts might've hit close to his heart. Another bit of luck.

He groaned. Every muscle in his body ached. He stopped for a moment to catch his breath, then clenched his teeth, grateful his head and body were still in one piece. He lumbered shakily to his feet and patted his holster. Gun still there.

His roll to safety hadn't dislodged it.

Well sonuvabitch. The bastards had been so confident he'd be killed by the stallion they hadn't bothered to disarm him. Or maybe they just didn't have the time.

One more row of fence to slip through. He crouched and threaded his way through the fence boards facing the roadway.

Pierce ground to a stop before him, bent over and panting. Badgely and the two new MI5 agents fell in behind him. They were all exclaiming at once. In their rush to speak, their words jumbled together, making no sense. Three of the four bore bruises on their faces. Two had split, bloody lips.

Jake swayed, feeling dizzy. His hands balled into fists as Pierce helped him lean back against the front of the double fence line.

"Guys, for Pete's sake. One at a time."

The blond MI5 agent shook his head in wonder and rage.

"Those fuckin' Irish!"

"Give me the bad news," Jake said. "What happened?"

Pierce let go of his arm and stepped back. He ran a hand through his dark blond hair.

"Not sure, actually. Someone conked me on the head as I turned the corner of the first barn I passed. Just came out of nowhere. Bollocks. Didn't even see the asshole. When I came to, I ran to the gift shop. The ladies were gone, Badgely here was out cold and handcuffed in the men's room."

"You new guys—what happened?" Jake looked at them both, standing behind Pierce and Badgely. Their dapper country clothes were looking rumpled and torn now. As they sputtered out their stories in a noisy cacophony, Pierce held up a hand.

"One of them, Williams here who stayed in the car, got off a few shots but was pinned down behind the Land Rover. The bloke by the motorcoach, Penton"—Pierce clapped a hand on

Penton's meaty shoulder — "Penton got jumped by two thugs. Two others grabbed Robert Morse and the driver. Penton ended up all trussed up with the two men inside the coach. The keys are missing and the ladies' bags are gone. The guide's going bonkers. When I left, Morse was on the phone with Global Adventures. They're threatening a lawsuit. And when we get to Dublin, Temple's going to beat our asses to a bloody pulp."

"Meg . . . her grandmother — gone?"

"Snatched right from under our noses," groused the older Badgely. "Though not for lack of trying. We were bloody well outnumbered. I'd say three to one. Williams, who got off a few rounds, counted at least twelve. Maybe more."

A chorus of agreement ensued.

"They were with that other tourist group." Williams cast Jake an apprizing stare. "Came in separate cars — I counted four. Wore hats, jackets, and cameras to blend in with that coach group. We know they weren't the same two we saw in that red car on the Ring of Kerry. Not the skinheads. A whole different bunch. So what the bloody hell happened to you?"

"I was blindsided by a Taser as I was running between the two big barns. Shocked me out cold. They must've placed me in the stallion's paddock after that last group passed by. Couldn't have been more than five minutes later." Jake brushed the dirt out of his hair, swiped down his jacket and trousers. Felt the wounds on his abdomen. They hurt like hell.

He remembered something.

"The girl and her grandmother? Did they go willingly?" Jake asked Williams, already knowing the answer to one but not the other.

"The grandmother, yeah. The girl, no. One guy carried the girl into one of the cars that took off. Looked unconscious. I had to be careful not to hit her or the old lady so I stopped firing. The old lady was helped by the Canadian woman. She was walking on her own, from what I could see. Four black SUVs in all took off. Looked like rentals. That Canadian couple, too, they left willingly."

Jake leaned over, deflated. Braced his hands on his thighs and took a deep breath. Fought to gain control. The situation was worse than he'd thought. He expected them to take the old lady but was hoping they'd leave Meg. She didn't know anything, nor was she a follower of their fascist extremist crap. She had to be forced, probably drugged.

So why? The reason was clear. They needed her to keep Mary Snider—Clare Eberhard—calm and functioning. The old woman depended on her granddaughter for nearly everything.

Damn. Outnumbered and outmaneuvered. He'd underestimated that bunch. Blood and Honour activists. Or a paramilitary arm of the group.

And he'd underestimated the Le Blancs.

Meg called them crazy. Not crazy. The set-up was perfectly planned and executed. Their assailants weren't just local yahoos, they were well-trained. Amazing that no one was killed.

The GPS beacon he gave Meg to conceal would be found and then he'd never be able to track their location. With certainty now he knew the Le Blancs were taking them to Germany—for propaganda photo shoots. Maybe even meetings with members of their neo-Nazi organization.

To dispose of when no longer useful?

A sudden thought occurred to Jake. "How many airports between here and Dublin? The nearest one—how many kilometers?"

"I've worked this area before," Pierce said, leaping to follow Jake's train of thought. "At least three, all private, with charter jet service. The nearest one's within a ten-minute drive. They have at least forty minutes on us, so they could be anywhere by now. Probably already in the air."

Williams looked over at the others. The three men nodded. Apparently they'd already discussed their next move.

"Look, Agent Bernstein, we could run down all these airports, but we have no authority to halt or cancel any flights, private or public. The Irish staff would thumb their noses at us. Temple won't have the warrants until tomorrow morning. Until then he told us strictly surveillance."

"Yeah and we fucked that up." Jake sighed. "One of you guys, get Temple on the phone."

Pierce looked miserable. "I already did. He's just left London."

Jake hung his head in angry resignation.

"God, this is so jacked!"

The American slang confused Pierce and the others.

"Sorry?"

"Jacked?"

"Never mind," muttered Jake.

Tasered, nearly trampled by a multi-million-dollar horse . . . and he never even un-holstered his gun. Five men on surveillance and they lose their two targets.

What a major fuck-up.

And Meg. What was going to happen to her and her grandmother after they were no longer useful to that fascist organization? He was supposed to protect the two women as well as investigate them.

Jake breathed in deeply. Cleared his head. *Think!*

Five words.

Meg's message. To him only.

Berlin. Reichstag. Hannover. Engesohde Friedhof.

He'd keep his promise to Meg. If he could discover her and her grandmother's whereabouts, he wouldn't betray his promise to her. After all, what was a man if a woman couldn't trust him? He'd promised her.

He'd take his lumps from MI5 and then disappear. With

Temple's permission or not, he was flying to Germany. He'd see this one through to the end.

CHAPTER THIRTY-THREE

M eg inhaled deeply and shaded her eyes. A sunny, warm day in Berlin. Something to enjoy. Or so Madeleine Le Blanc had reminded her just a few minutes ago.

But not with a tall, young weightlifter standing stiffly beside her, guarding her. He called himself Wolfgang, wanted her to call him Wolf. And he wasn't letting her out of his sight. He'd slept near their locked bedroom door last night, stationed himself outside the bathroom when she'd used the facilities in that Berlin flat. He spoke a rough kind of German that Meg couldn't understand but the Le Blancs could. They spoke another kind of German—*hoch Deutsch*—to Meg's grandmother.

The other young weightlifter stood outside their rented limo—at attention, his hands at his waist. The limo driver— another Blood and Honour member, Meg suspected—stayed behind the wheel. All three men had alert eyes and military postures. They didn't say much, and what little they did say was murmured to each other in the same German dialect beyond Meg's comprehension.

Pierre and his wife weren't taking any chances she'd escape or call for help. They'd taken her cell phone and passport while she was unconscious—for the time being she was at their mercy. From the state of her clothes, they'd searched her also.

Fortunately she'd had the foresight in the rest stop bathroom, before they'd arrived at the Stud Farm, to hide Jake's electronic GPS beacon in a place the Le Blancs and their neo-

Nazi musclemen hadn't thought to look. To be on the safe side, Meg had declared to her grandmother that she'd begun her menstrual period and had resorted to sanitary napkins when she couldn't find any Tampax in the rest stop store.

The Le Blancs hadn't dared to search beyond a cursory examination of her clothes. Not with her grandmother present. Not if they wanted her grandmother's cooperation. Mary Snider—or Clare Eberhard, which Meg had finally come to accept as her grandmother's true identity—was held in high esteem by the Le Blancs and their followers. Whatever this organization was—Blood and Honour or something else—the Canadian couple controlled its minions, Irish and German. And they were determined to hail Clare Eberhard as their heroine. A heroine come home sixty years later to bask in glory.

Maybe not glory. There were no parades or medals. Just two crazy neo-Nazis and their followers. Certainly this Wolfgang was one of them.

Meg silently shifted from one foot to the other. She was weary from worry and lack of sleep. She could tell her grandmother was exhausted, too. The rush to leave the thoroughbred farm, the hurried flight in a small chartered jet to Germany, and the overnight stay in a borrowed flat had thrown off the elderly woman's rest schedule. But her grandmother had insisted, when Meg had awakened in the private jet, that she wanted to do this. It was important to her, Meg recognized.

More than important—Meg sensed it was vital.

Not only was her grandmother avoiding arrest by the Brits, but she was in her own way, Meg sensed, paying homage to her true homeland, Germany. Maybe even saying, after all these years, hello and farewell.

Pierre was the self-assigned photographer, posing her grandmother and Madeleine in front of the Parliament Building's entrance steps. The neo-classical building, or Reichstag,

was the center of Berlin and the new reunited German Republic. Once the scene of many Nazi Party rallies and parades, the
Thirties and Forties-era Reichstag had been the heart of Hitler's regime. The passionate believers in that fascist state had
held their largest, most fervent displays of nationalism in
front of this very building.

"Are you German?" Meg asked Wolfgang in her halting
German.

The young hulk, sporting a blond buzz cut, piercing blue
eyes, and a black leather jacket, said nothing. His eyes roved
up and down her body before he turned away. Didn't crack a
smile or a frown.

"I'm learning German," she added, hoping to thaw him
out. If she could learn a little about him, she'd learn more
about the Le Blancs.

This guy was well-trained. All he said was, "*Gut für dich*",
which Meg translated as Good for you. Said with a hint of
sarcasm, she noted.

To which she muttered under her breath, "Well, kiss my
ass."

That comment cracked a smile. "I wish I could," Wolfgang
mumbled in perfect English. He smirked, then grew serious
again and turned back to watching the photo shoot.

Meg scowled and scooted a foot or two away from his side.
Don't provoke them, Jake had warned. She decided he was
right. She was no match for Wolfgang and his two muscular
cronies. Nor the Le Blancs. Having seen their handguns while
on the jet, she knew they were armed and dangerous. The
three hulks as well.

While traveling up the Lindenstrasse from the Potsdamer
Platz, the Le Blancs had discussed the various photoshoots
they'd planned with her grandmother. Berlin was first, then
various locations in Hannover, Clare Eberhard's hometown.
Gradually, in bits and pieces, Meg was learning the truth

about her grandmother's origins.

The Le Blancs had already photographed Meg's grand-mother standing outside Churchill's War Rooms. The scene of Clare's greatest deception, they now crowed, and her greatest triumph.

The horror of everything made Meg's flesh crawl. Made her stomach cramp into knots. Her grandmother had once spied for the Nazis. Caused the deaths of countless Allied pilots and their crews on bombing runs over Germany. Exposed French Resistance fighters and other Allied sympathizers who hid Jewish civilians, resulting in their executions. Meg had read the books and seen the movies. Entire families executed because they dared to hide a Jew or Allied soldier. Her skull shivered with such horrors.

Madeleine had even fastened her grandmother's valuable, jeweled hummingbird pin on the elderly woman's coat lapel, which the Le Blancs wanted displayed in the photos. Fortunately, in English, so that Meg could understand, Madeleine had explained its significance. The pin represented her grand-mother's code name during the war and all that she had accomplished for the Third Reich as one of their most successful spies. It was a gift from the Gestapo's *unter fuhrer*. Meg wondered how Madeleine would know such a thing unless her grandmother, Clare Eberhard, had told her and Pierre.

Not for the first time, Meg wondered who the Le Blancs really were. And how had they found her grandmother?

"You recall the glorious parades from the Potsdamer to the Reichstag, *Mutter*," said Madeleine. The woman was now using the term *Mother* to address her grandmother. "You were there when *der Fuhrer* gave his stirring speech at the mass rally in 1933, when the National Socialist Party came to power. Your father was a high-ranking official of the Party who then became an Under Minister of Culture. You were there. Do you remember how proud you and your mother were? How proud Horst Eberhard was? The count's son, who'd married into a family of great political influence. And, to show his devotion to his new wife's family, he became an SS officer and then a spy. You were so proud of him."

Her grandmother's eyes glowed with a sheen of long-faded memories and emotions, now made vivid by these prompted recollections. Madeleine was stirring up in the elderly woman the passion of her past fanaticism.

"Oh yes. I was there, though just a teenager. I was nineteen, I think. I had just married Horst. We were so excited, so much in love, so happy for our country. We were looking forward to serving the Third Reich and making it victorious. Any way we could. No sacrifice was too big."

In the limo, Clare had turned to Meg and in English recalled that time when all seemed possible in pre-war Deutschland. The Third Reich was the answer to all their prayers. Adolf Hitler was their messiah. Meg realized her grandmother, in this unusually lucid period, was trying to help her understand what life was like then and why she'd joined the SS intelligence service.

"By then the Abwehr was under suspicion. Admiral Canaris could no longer be trusted and der Fuhrer wanted another intelligence service that he could trust. Horst said only the SS was loyal to our Third Reich. He knew my gift with languages. Horst had the same linguistic abilities. We used to teach languages at the university. We both spoke English like natives. French, too. It seemed natural that we would aid the German cause by going to Britain and spying there."

Meg had remained silent, letting her grandmother take her hand. Her own was limp, clasped inside the gloved, grotesquely twisted hand of the elderly woman. Too choked up to speak, Meg could only stare at their two hands and wipe away her tears. The bond they'd shared all these years, though now frayed, still tied one generation to the other. With a shudder of emotion, Meg listened to her grandmother's explanation.

"And then, just twelve years later, April, 1945, the Soviet flag was raised over the ruined Reichstag building. Ruined by Allied bombs. All of Berlin. All of Germany . . .ruined."

"Yes, a terrible outcome," exclaimed Madeleine.

"Hannover, too," cried her grandmother. "Though I tried to warn them. I discovered from Captain Ferguson one night that the RAF was going to bomb Hannover early the next morning. My home. My family. I broke protocol and radioed to warn them to evacuate the city. Later I learned there hadn't been time to evacuate everyone. That was payback, you see, for the London blitz. For Coventry and all the other English cities bombed by the Germans. I wanted to save my city. I wanted to save everyone but I couldn't. When it mattered so much, I failed."

Meg watched fearfully as her grandmother's voice rose in shrill hysteria, her eyes growing large with the pain of remembrance. The elderly woman's breathing grew shallow. She began to pant and perspire.

"Madeleine, can't you stop this?" Meg urged the woman. "Grandma's getting all worked up! It's not good for her heart. The stress—"

Madeleine shut her off with a raised finger. A glance to the husky, young man at Meg's side was an implied threat. If Meg behaved, she'd be allowed to come along on their photo shoots. If she didn't, Wolfgang would keep her at the flat, shackled . . .or forced to undergo another body search. The lascivious way Wolf looked at her occasionally, and the way he'd fondled her through her bra and snug jeans during the first search was message enough. What he did with her at the flat did not concern the Le Blancs. That was their implied threat.

"Meg, be quiet and learn something. Your grandmother

represents for all of us in the movement the history of our great past. The grand potential of the Third Reich."

The potential for disaster, Meg thought, one that many reasonable-minded Germans had foreseen. Unfortunately Hitler and his black-shirts and brown-shirts were clever and diabolical at eliminating dissenters from their midst.

"Yes, those early days were a wonderful time, so full of promise," her grandmother affirmed shakily. "But then the war . . ." The old woman frowned and clenched her hands together, her mouth trembling.

Now, standing in front of the old Reichstag, it was Pierre's turn to bolster the old woman's flagging enthusiasm. He posed Clare and Madeleine at the bottom of the steps before he set the timer on the camera resting on its tripod.

"The National Socialists could have won the war, Frau Snider, had the U.S. not gotten involved," he said in French. "All of Europe surrendered to the Third Reich like falling dominoes. Great Britain would have fallen, too, thanks to our brilliant scientists and the V-1 and V-2 rockets."

He turned off his grim expression and smiled triumphantly. Then he strode over to stand on the other side of her grandmother.

"Dear lady, you gave advance warnings of enemy bombings, exposed enemies all over Europe, helped the Heinkel bombers find their targets in London and elsewhere. At great risk to your own life. You are truly to be commended and admired. Our magazine spread of you will do just that. Hail you for the heroine that you are. The praise is long overdue."

It was apparent to Meg that Pierre knew his World War II history. And now his propaganda story and photos of Clare Eberhard would be used to recruit new young fascists. Like Wolfgang. Her grandmother wasn't thinking clearly, for those same stories would also seal her fate.

Not that the Le Blancs cared.

Meg sighed and took a long, impartial look at her grandmother. Praying for insight, Meg wondered if this was the true Mary Snider. Who really was this Clare Eberhard? A ruthless, Nazi fanatic who killed and spied for her country? Or a lovesick woman led astray by her fanatical father and husband? As Clare's story unfolded, Meg began to see a more complete picture of the woman she'd loved all of her life. Just as Jake had told her once.

Finally the entire truth was emerging.

Did her grandmother ever love John Snider, the American pilot who thought he was marrying an Irish woman who'd spent the war years working for the Allies? Meg frowned. Poor Grandpa Snider. What would he have done if he'd known the truth?

What would Uncle Jack do when he discovered the truth about his own mother? Would that destroy his Navy career?

Did Meg's own mother know the truth? Was that why she was so screwed up? Why she was estranged from her elderly mother?

"Clare, the work you and Horst did was vital, as your story and these photos will attest. You will rally and inspire an entire new generation of followers. Like our grandson there and his friends. Imagine, Clare Eberhard. The only German deep-cover spy never caught by Allied intelligence. What an amazing story!"

A remote clicked away in his hand as one exposure after another was shot. By Meg's side, Wolfgang was making a video of the entire photo shoot with a handheld video camera. Minutes passed. Pierre changed their poses several times, as did the young man his stance.

Meg squeezed her grandmother's shoulder. "The other mole, the Black Widow. Wasn't that Catherine Collier? Didn't she ultimately fail?"

Her grandmother's gaze drifted from Meg's face to a

faraway place in the distance. Clare Eberhard stopped smiling.

Pierre and Wolfgang stopped filming.

"Yes. I discovered that she was a double-cross agent. The British had turned her and made her spy for them. Horst gave her a traitor's death before he left England."

Understanding, Meg's hand flew up to her mouth, stifling a gasp. Madeleine ignored her and patted Clare's shoulder.

"No doubt a fitting bullet to the head." She shifted to French as she glanced about her. Other tourists had stopped nearby to take photos.

The elderly woman shuddered. "My only regret is that Horst did not survive the war. When they took him out of Ireland and England and sent him to Italy, to gather information about the Allied invasion down there . . .oh God, I knew it would end badly."

Madeleine adjusted her pose. "We've read several accounts of what happened to him. No one was certain."

"The Americans caught him, but he convinced them he was a British soldier who'd lost his unit. I learned later from an Army friend of John Snider that a Messerschmitt pilot separated from his squadron and came low and machine-gunned him down. The Wehrmacht was withdrawing from Italy but trying to protect their southernmost line, the Gustav line. Such a godless world, that Germans mistook my poor Horst for an Allied soldier . . .they gunned him down like a dog."

"A terrible end for such a patriot." Madeleine shook her head. Madeleine, Pierre, and Wolfgang bowed their heads in a moment of silence, their fists over their hearts. Her grandmother also bowed her head.

Meg watched their tribute to Horst Eberhard. She was amazed to observe the contradiction before her. Her grandmother's behavior, too, was a contradiction.

At times she seemed lucid, her total recall appearing

remarkable when speaking about the distant past. But when brought back to the present, she appeared disoriented and confused, as if her mind was now fixated on the war and nothing else.

Without warning, her grandmother dissolved into sobs. Meg, having never seen her grandmother cry before, started to go to her, but Wolfgang pulled her back. His big hand cramped her arm like a vise. Meg longed to kick him in the balls. Instead she recovered her composure, buried her fury, and watched helplessly as the Le Blancs fed her grandmother's habit. '

"I'm sorry. I need another painkiller." Clare sobbed.

Against Meg's protest, the Canadian woman had taken over her grandmother's carry-on bag with all the medications. In control of the drugs, Madeleine whipped the bottle of painkillers out of her pocket. With a hurried look at Pierre she gave the old woman a pill, washed down by one of the cold beers they'd carried with them from the limo's fridge.

"Madeleine, please," Meg objected. "She shouldn't have another one, not until tonight. Certainly not with beer. Her doctor warned against overdosing."

An ominous look from the Le Blancs and a painful arm-squeeze from Wolfgang discouraged her from saying more. She recalled Jake's warning. For her own and her grandmother's sake, Meg shut up.

Madeleine was quick to calm the elderly woman down.

"Ah, but *Mutter*, *Vater* didn't survive, but I did. Thank heavens dear *Grossmutter* sent me away to Zurich. Your youngest sisters and I were saved by your mother's wisdom. She disobeyed her husband and sent us to safety."

"My sisters? Dietlind and Stefanie? Will I see them in Hannover?" Clare's sobs subsided. She looked hopefully at Madeleine.

"Of course, dear *Mutter*," Madeleine assured the old

woman, patting her arm consolingly. "As I wrote to you, Pierre and I were able to locate them. The task was difficult, but finding you and my aunts became the sole reason for my existence."

Her grandmother had a German-born daughter? This Madeleine was actually the daughter of Horst and Clare Eberhard? Was that why her grandmother was so easily manipulated by this couple? Gran believed that Madeleine was her long-lost daughter?

Meg noted the quick, guileful look exchanged between Madeleine and Pierre Le Blanc. The smug 'expression on Pierre's face was slowly replaced by a speculative one when he glanced over at Meg. Then he returned to his camera to adjust another setting.

Meg's heart sank. In that instant, as the Le Blancs exchanged looks, Meg's question was answered. Madeleine was *not* her grandmother's long-lost daughter. Sure, she probably fit the physical type. She was the right age. It was feasible that Clare's young daughter could have been sent to Switzerland during the war. But her grandmother would have received word long before now that her daughter had survived.

Her eyes brimming with tears, Meg caved and let them stream down her face. The Le Blancs' claim was simply a ruse to get Clare to cooperate, Meg was certain. Clearly they were exploiting her in a cruel and devious way. What would that do to her grandmother's health when she ultimately discovered the truth about them?

Madeleine led the elderly woman slowly up the entrance steps to a spot beside one of the massive columns. Pierre and Wolfgang followed, with Meg strong-armed along. She felt the GPS beacon abrading her crotch as the man forced her to walk closely beside him. Not the most sanitary place to hide the transmitter Jake had given her. She hoped the damned thing was working.

Tucked inside a sanitary napkin that Meg was wearing inside her panties, the GPS was transmitting their location. Meg prayed it was, anyway. Madeleine had searched her suitcase, had found nothing out of the ordinary except a box of sanitary napkins, which she'd noticed Meg buying in the rest stop store. The simple explanation Meg had given her seemed to suffice. It wasn't comfortable, but it was concealed. Good thing she'd put it in when she had, for the goons had taken her totally by surprise at the stud farm. Unconscious afterward for a while, Meg was certain the beacon would have been found had she not hidden it well.

The transmitter was beckoning Jake. if he was within range, that is.

Please, Jake, get here soon.

Meg hugged her arms as a cool breeze fluttered through nearby plane trees. Despite a smidgen of hope, Meg was pessimistic about the beacon working. Her mind shivered with fear. What if Jake told MI5 where they were going and British intelligence discovered them first? Her grandmother would be arrested and thrown into jail. Maybe she would be, too.

Maybe that was the least of her worries.

Maybe she and her grandmother would be safer with the Brits. After Madeleine and Pierre were finished with her grandmother, then what would happen to them?

The Le Blancs were lying. Meg sensed it. They said she and her grandmother could fly home from Hannover, with a stopover in Frankfurt.

She shot her grandmother a baleful, warning glance but the old woman ignored her. Clare Eberhard was lost again in a fantasy, reliving the past with the aid of the duplicitous Madeleine and Pierre Le Blanc.

Meg wiped the tears from her cheeks. Her Gran was one tough woman, no matter who she really was. Or what she'd done. Her blood ran in Meg's. She'd be tough, too.

And hope and pray that Jake would keep his promise.

CHAPTER THIRTY-FOUR

Jake shot Pierce a fulminating look. Nervous about flying and their assignment, the Brit had talked his ear off during the entire hour-and-a-half flight. Even the tetanus injection and antibiotics the doctor in Dublin had given Jake, and two of Meg's painkiller pills, hadn't been enough to tune out the voluble Pierce. Still, the leg wound was no longer bleeding and the swelling had gone down. Meg would be happy about that. The puncture marks on his chest from the Taser gun had been swabbed and disinfected also. They were sore, but there was no permanent damage done.

The thing that hurt the most was his pride.

And his fear over Meg's and her grandmother's safety.

He and Pierce had just landed at Templehof Flughafen, Berlin's airport, after having endured two excruciating hours of debriefing with Major Temple and the Irish deputy Minister of the Interior in Dublin. When a roomful of irate Irish government officials were finally satisfied that all had been done by the MI5 agents and the lone FBI investigator to keep the passengers on the Global Adventures motorcoach safe — and their precious multi-million-euro stallions free from harm — Temple had given Jake and Pierce the go-ahead to pursue and arrest the kidnappers, the Le Blancs, the suspected Nazi spy Clare Eberhard, and her granddaughter Meg Larsen.

According to Major Temple, the Le Blancs were using aliases and the stolen passports of a French-Canadian couple in their sixties. He had no clue what their true identities were but an Interpol databank was running their passport photos.

298

He expected to hear back from Interpol's headquarters in Lyon, France within twenty-four hours or less. By then, Jake had concurred with the major, the couple could be long gone. They'd use Clare Eberhard for their own propaganda purposes then ditch the elderly woman and her granddaughter. How they ditched the two women had all of them worried. Even Major Temple.

Temple had a lot of his reputation at stake in seeing Mary Snider brought to trial. A part of him could sympathize with that need to see justice done.

Jake had informed the MI5 agents about Meg's earlier tip, that the Le Blancs were planning photo shoots with her grandmother in Berlin. And that they'd begun speaking a dialect of German with each other that Meg couldn't understand—and, she suspected, neither could her grandmother. Temple had suggested either an Austrian dialect or Schweitzer Deutsch, and Jake had concurred.

He'd omitted mentioning their going to Hannover, however. That way, Meg's information would confirm her cooperation with the investigation and possibly prevent MI5 from charging her with obstruction. Yet the Intel Jake had omitted still give him some leeway.

He and Pierce had forty-eight hours only. Then Temple was notifying Interpol and sending out border alerts and APBs. After that a huge dragnet would close in on all four—the kidnappers and their captives.

Jake had no intention of escorting Pierce, the assigned MI5 agent, all the way to Hannover, or even around Berlin. If Temple eventually figured out the Le Blancs' plan to film Clare Eberhard at what Jake suspected was her family's gravesite in Hannover, then more power to him. That would be done without Jake's help, as he intended to get to them first—to give Meg and her grandmother their last chance to fly back to the States and get legal help.

He intended to keep his promise to Meg.

And to hell with the consequences.

Pierce had no idea about the GPS beacon, nor Jake's tracking device, hidden inside the locked compartment of his aluminum suitcase. As soon as Jake could, he'd take it out and start using it.

Also unknown to Major Temple and his MI5 team was Jake's encrypted phone calls back to FBI Headquarters and one emergency call to a certain Navy commander stationed in San Diego.

Jake and Pierce checked in to their hotel, the Marriott der Berliner on the Lindenstrasse, after two AM. They eschewed the porters and carried the bags up to their shared room. Two double beds faced them. Pierce practically dove onto his with a loud groan of fatigue.

Exhausted, but mentally churning with his plan, Jake poured himself and Pierce some Schnapps from a bottle in their minibar. Fifteen minutes later, Pierce's snoring could be heard from the bathroom, even while Jake was showering. The man sounded like a freight train.

Jake dressed rapidly, slung the carry-on over his shoulder ,and grabbed the handle of the aluminum suitcase. He looked back at the sound sleeper.

"Sorry, old chap," said Jake, borrowing some Brit-speak. "Gotta do this myself."

Downstairs, he grabbed a cab, which left him off at a car rental agency on the other side of the city. Using cash from an ATM machine halfway between the hotel and the rental agency, he paid for the car, a fast, eight-cylinder Mercedes sedan. He used one of the two FBI-issued false passports and drivers licenses he'd brought with him to register for the rental. If he wasn't too late, the Le Blancs and their captives would still be in the city. They would have arrived by sunset, so they had at least six hours' lead time on Jake and Pierce.

With that in mind, Jake drove to a two-star hotel on Bismark Strasse, near the Lietzensee Bridge. He showed the clerk the false passport, paid for the room with euros, and checked in. In his small, utilitarian room, he plopped down on the double bed. His feet hung over the end and the mattress was hard and lumpy. Well too bad, he thought. They'd never look for him in this dive, a place he'd known from his earlier, more frugal travels to Germany.

He'd given a wakeup call of six AM. Less than four hours' sleep — not ideal — but he could manage. His eyelids heavy, he was suddenly drowsy from the day's physical workouts and the painkiller he'd taken on the jet. His leg no longer throbbed but the rest of his body felt almost numb and heavy with fatigue. Unfortunately, so did his mind.

He needed to sleep.

The memory of his and Meg's sexual fling in that dumpy cliffside inn perversely filled his head. He could feel her arms and legs around him, enclosing him in her warm, loving embrace. That was the thing about Meg. It wasn't just about the physical attraction or the sex. Though, baby, that was great. She was hot, sexy, playful . . . There was more. Meg was giving more of herself, and he felt it. She cared for him . . .

That possibility flooded him with a kind of joy.

He awoke with a start some nine hours later. He'd slept through the wake-up call. Sunlight filtered through the flimsy drapes. He rubbed his eyes and stared at his watch, then let go a stream of curses.

Damn. Still dressed in the clothes from last night, Jake jumped up, hurried to the bathroom and washed his face. With quick, deliberate moves, he retrieved and prepared the tracking device, then carried it down past the small hotel lobby and to the locked rental car in the hotel's parking lot. He'd stored the aluminum suitcase in the trunk the night before but had retrieved his shoulder holster, pistol, and FBI badge.

Once settled inside the rented Mercedes, he set the tracker, a hard-plastic box with an antenna, on the spacious dashboard and hooked it into the car's cigarette lighter. He spread a laminated map of Berlin that he'd purchased in the airport on the passenger seat.

He studied the map.

His hotel wasn't located in the center of the city, but Jake figured he could start there and work his way into the center. One eye on the tracker's LED screen, with its programmed Berlin-street map, he'd drive to the center near the Tiergarten and Potsdamer Platz then slowly circle around in a kind of spiral, gradually moving outward. Of special interest was the area near the Brandenburger Tor, or Brandenburg Gate, the Ebertstrasse, and Unter den Linden, the main thoroughfare.

Of course the building containing the German Bundestag near the Spree River. Meg had indicated the old Reichstag would be the scene of a possible photo shoot. That was where the Nazis held most of their victory celebrations, the building's balconies draped with red flags emblazoned with black Swastikas.

If he couldn't pick up anything there, he'd have to widen his circle and that would waste time.

He didn't have much of that. It was nearly noon in Berlin.

Forty-eight hours...now minus twelve... Thirty-six hours to find Meg and her grandmother.

Before MI5 arrested them.

Or before something worse happened.

Chapter Thirty-Five

M eg could barely eat more than a few bites. The schnitzel and potatoes on her plate swimming in gravy made her feel sick. They were having lunch — *mittagessen* — in a restaurant in the heart of Hannover's Alt Stadt district. Her stomach clenched so tightly she knew she'd be sick if she forced herself.

Not so Madeleine and Pierre and Wolf. They ate with gusto and toasted each other and Clare Eberhard with one glass of beer after another. Her grandmother, whom Meg was not allowed to sit next to during their entire stay so far in Germany, was still mesmerized by Madeleine. Sitting across from Meg, the elderly woman hung on Madeleine Le Blanc's every look and word. She kept calling her Hannah. As Meg had just learned, Hannah was Clare's little girl, placed in the care of her grandmother when Clare left her homeland to become a spy in England.

The pieces of the puzzle that were Clare Eberhard's life gradually fit together, much to Meg's amazement. How such a woman could leave her young child for a life of espionage in an enemy country during wartime was beyond Meg's comprehension.

But Clare Eberhard was a fascist fanatic. Or used to be.

From what Meg had heard about the war from her grandmother's reminiscences of that era, Meg could glimpse the larger picture. The fanatical fervor encouraged by Clare's father, a high-ranking official in the National Socialist Party. Her husband's — Horst Eberhard's — training in military intelligence. Clare's and her husband's linguistic abilities. The extreme national pride of the German people at that time. The jobs and prosperity created by the Nazis' military buildup. The grand hopes for a thousand-year Third Reich. The honor of sacrificing oneself for one's fatherland.

Meg was beginning to understand.

All the ingredients were there for the terrible choices her grandmother had made. Would Meg ever be willing to do the same for her homeland? She wondered about this as the Le Blancs, Wolf, and her grandmother conversed conspiratorially over dinner in a rapid German that Meg couldn't understand.

She withdrew into herself and her reflections. Americans were usually skeptical about their government, and rightly so. Hadn't their forefathers written into the Constitution rules of law and balance of power to protect people from the tyranny of government leaders? That was the beauty of the Constitution.

What the WWII-era German people had failed to do was prevent the tyranny of one man and his followers from subverting those rules of law. The turning point was when the Reichstag, loaded with like-minded Nazis, allowed Chancellor Hitler to develop a cult of personality. They passed into law a prohibition against speaking out against *der Fuhrer*. The penalty was death. That much Meg had learned in school and from books about the war. And those who tried to stop Hitler and his Nazi minions were silenced quickly. Dissent was never given the chance to grow.

They believed for too long the lies of a tyrant.

"And so we're going to meet my sisters at the cemetery?" her grandmother asked, a quiver in her weak voice, close again to tears.

Meg's eyes stung with unshed tears, herself, and her throat ached. Her grandmother's mental health was quickly declining before her very eyes, and the Le Blancs refused to call a physician. Just as callously, they were building up the elderly woman's hopes and spirits. Meg worried what would happen when the truth hit her grandmother.

Meg didn't believe for one minute that Clare Eberhard's sisters were still alive. If they were, they would have been in touch long before now. Nevertheless her grandmother's mental state had deteriorated so much that she believed such outrageous lies.

Madeleine nodded while sipping her beer. Pierre called for the check and signaled to Wolf to escort Meg outside. Apparently they wanted to speak more confidentially with Clare Eberhard. Meg tried to warn her grandmother with her eyes but Wolf yanked her up and out of the restaurant before she could communicate her feelings.

The muscled young bodybuilder took Meg's upper arm as they walked along the sidewalk. Evidently Wolf had been to Hannover before. He pointed to a Gothic-style red-brick building.

"The Alt Stadt district is very nice, don't you think?" he asked her in heavily accented English, to which she nodded. "That is the thirteenth-century old Town Hall. It was destroyed during the war by American bombs. The city rebuilt it in the fifties."

Ever mindful of Jake's advice to stay calm and not provoke them to violence, Meg glanced around. The city was indeed beautiful, filled with neo-Gothic and half-timbered buildings, hallmarks of this area of Lower Saxony. Strangely enough, she was getting a history lesson on Germany along with being terrorized by her captors. This was part of her grandmother's life, so Meg was willing to learn what had made Clare Eberhard who she was. Whether she could ever understand was another question.

Meg refrained from mentioning London, Coventry, and

the other British cities bombed nightly by the German Luftwaffe—the Blitzkrieg strikes—which terrorized Brits for over a year.

For a second she was tempted to kick him in the balls and set off running. Jake's warning sprang to mind for the hundredth time and she repressed the urge.

"You saw the old Market Church," Wolf went on, switching to simplified German. "Destroyed by the Americans in June 1943. The heaviest air raid on Hannover was by the British in October the same year. Within forty minutes, over four hundred planes dropped thousands of mines and bombs. Almost seven thousand civilians were killed. Hundreds of thousands lost their homes. For what? There was nothing here in Hannover of military value."

Meg understood most of what he said although some of the numbers escaped her. Her thoughts turned to the cemetery they were about to visit. Standing stiffly beside her, his hand squeezing her arm, Wolf appeared uneasy. She had a sinking feeling something bad was going to happen.

"What are we going to see at this cemetery? This Engesohde Friedhof?" she asked him.

"Your grandmother's family burial vault." He frowned and looked away.

"I don't think that's good for my grandmother's health," she said, but he ignored her. He had his orders and, like a fanatically loyal goon, was carrying them out. "She'll be devastated when she learns the Le Blancs have been lying to her about her family."

Wolf just looked away and growled out a warning in German. He steered her into the rear of the black limo waiting at the curb. The two hulks in front glanced back, muttered something in that same German Meg couldn't understand. Wolf laughed and looked at her with a lascivious glint in his eyes. Angry at whatever they were saying about her, she crossed her arms over her chest and stared out of the window.

Let them laugh. I'm still wearing that beacon.

Five minutes later, the black limo, with the Le Blancs and her grandmother aboard, drove past a manmade lake that Madeleine called the *Maschsee*. She pointed out the new Town Hall, the *Neue Rathaus*, on the other side of the lake. It was a huge splendid Neo-Gothic stone building with a massive copper dome in the center. Its location across the lake lent it a certain grandeur.

So she wasn't Irish, after all. She was German-American, Meg reflected. She wasn't sure how she felt about that. Her Grandpa Snider was German-American, too, but his identity was American-based. Her Gran — Mary, Clare, whatever her name — was German. Whatever that meant. All she knew was that the post-war Germans she'd met while traveling were more like Americans she knew than practically anyone else. Practical, hardworking, proud of their country.

Both Meg and her grandmother stared in admiration at the Neo-Gothic *Rathaus*. Tears trickled down Clare's drawn, crepey cheeks. Her gloved hand shook as she pointed to the majestic building. Pity tugged at Meg's heart. Gran was so overcome with emotion that she was speechless.

"Grandma, your hometown is beautiful. I wish you had told me the truth. We could've come here instead of Ireland. I wouldn't have told the police. Or anyone. I would have kept your secret." She would have too.

Clare's dark blue eyes settled slowly on Meg, widening a little, as if she were just now becoming aware of her presence in the limo's large seating area.

"Meggie." Her grandmother smiled weakly. "I couldn't come back. I knew I was wanted. My friends in the Party warned me. So I stayed Mary McCoy, even after your grandfather died. My son wanted it that way. He was afraid for me."

Meg's jaw dropped. "Uncle John knew?" A moment of shock passed. "Did my mother know, too?"

"Who?" Clare asked. Confusion knitted her thin, white brows. "Your mother? I'm your mother, child. You know me, Hannah dear."

Again her grandmother's mind seemed to be wavering between the distant past and the present, blending the two at times. More than once, her grandmother had called Meg by the name of the child she'd lost during the war—Hannah. But Meg had thought her grandmother was referring to Meg's mother, Hannah Snider, the wayward, estranged daughter who was now with husband number five.

As far as Meg knew, her mother showed up once a year at Christmastime, then disappeared with the latest in a string of husbands or boyfriends. Meg could barely speak to her, even at their annual reunion. Now she began to suspect that Clare's American daughter—Meg's own mother—also knew of her mother's true identity. Was this the possible reason for their estrangement?

Other times her grandmother referred to Madeleine as Hannah, the German daughter she had with Horst Eberhard. At any rate, her grandmother's slackening hold on reality made Meg anxious. The doctor said that slurred speech and mental confusion might be signs of ministrokes.

Apparently swamped with bewilderment, her grandmother sputtered into a frowning silence. Madeleine regained control of the situation by pointing out other landmarks, most of which Clare could barely recognize. The city had changed so much when it was rebuilt, according to the Le Blancs.

Which made Meg curious. And bold.

"You're not really Canadian, are you?" she brazenly asked the woman and Pierre. "Le Blanc isn't your real name, is it?"

The couple exchanged a shrewd smile.

"Who we are and where we live are none of your concern,"

Pierre said. "We work for a movement that will one day reach global proportions. We are grooming leaders in every corner of the world. Including your country, Meg. That is all you need to know."

Meg's eyes smarted. The pressure of repressed tears brought pangs of a headache. Recalling Jake's words, she thought it wise to stop probing, to let the FBI and MI5 or whoever hunt these people down. All she wanted was to get her grandmother home. It had been Meg's idea to come on this trip, and therefore it was her responsibility to get them home safely.

Again the beacon abraded her sensitive flesh as she squirmed in her seat, reminding her that Jake might help her accomplish just that. Yet he hadn't located them in Berlin. Fear crept down her spine. Maybe he didn't care enough. Maybe he'd just given up and flown back to the States. Maybe MI5 had arrested him for breaking his cover and for warning her and her grandmother. Something broke inside her. Tears spilled over and streaked down her cheeks.

Jake, find us. Please don't let me down.

Madeleine lifted her chin imperiously. "Ah, here we are. Pierre, remember your tripod. I want you in this photo too."

They'd stopped at a turnout along the curb. An ivy-covered wall bore a sign in block letters: *Engesohde Friedhof* and other German words Meg didn't recognize. Certainly not the main access into the cemetery. She noticed a small, gated entrance along this segment of the wall, probably for pedestrians.

Meg recognized the name and the German word *friedhof*. Her heart began to pound. This was one of the places she'd written on that postcard she'd left for Jake. He'd know they were coming here. Hope fluttered in her chest.

"Wait here," Pierre ordered the driver and the other hulking man in front in a German Meg could understand. She listened closely. "Wolfgang, just you come along. Too many of us will attract attention. We won't be too long. After this, we must leave quietly and quickly."

Wolf had never left her sight in the past twenty-four hours, ever since they'd arrived in Berlin. She wasn't surprised that he would join them, but the rest of Pierre's message? Wolf's eyes met hers. Realization dawned on her. This was going to be a fast stop.

Their last stop?

They'd take their photos, then leave? Then where to? What would the Le Blancs do with Meg and her ailing grandmother?

Surely they could see her grandmother needed medical assistance. Her speech had become slurred, her balance rickety, her delusions more pronounced. Her tough, stoical grandmother was one moment weepy and the next withdrawn and sullen. As though she were having an emotional breakdown right in front of them.

If Meg had her cell phone, she'd be calling an ambulance.

What would happen to her grandmother if they didn't get her medical attention? And soon?

Dammit, if only she knew Madeleine's and Pierre's diabolical plan.

But they weren't sharing . . . at least not with Meg.

CHAPTER THIRTY-SIX

Jake stood behind the tall cypress tree whose long thick branches and foliage concealed him from the graveled walkway facing Clare Eberhard's family vault. He'd observed the restaurant in the Old Town district into which they'd dined earlier, had watched the blond bully manhandle Meg when they'd stepped outside. Hidden from their view, he'd been tempted to barge in and pummel the guy. Biding his time, though, Jake followed the GPS tracker. Taking a few shortcuts, he'd arrived at the cemetery before them. He'd set up surveillance near the vault, having learned from Major Temple in Dublin that Clare's maiden name was Meyerhoff, her hometown, Hannover.

Fortunately Jake's GPS tracker had picked up the beacon's signal as he was driving in the vicinity of Berlin's Brandenburg Gate the day before. After that he'd followed the black limo to a private residence in a southern suburb of Berlin. Parked at a block's distance, and keeping the two-story building under surveillance, Jake had watched at least two dozen men and women enter what appeared to be a private dwelling. Obviously a meeting was taking place. Three hours later people emerged and drove away. The driver of the limo and another man left also. Inside remained the Le Blancs, the blond muscle, and Meg and her grandmother. Probably *guests* of the dwelling's owners.

Stakeout was not Jake's favorite field assignment, but he'd bought enough food and drinks to hold him during the evening and late into the night. Urinating into a jar was not his favorite kind of relief, either, but he couldn't risk losing his targets by driving away and finding a public restroom. Peeing on the bushes along the street was also not an option. Too much traffic. And he couldn't risk being taken in by the local *Polizei*.

The next morning he'd kept a steady pace with the limo on the Autobahn, following at a four-car distance as he'd been trained. The three-hour journey from Berlin to Hannover was tiring so he'd pulled into an Autobahn rest stop for espresso. Stopping was dicey, but he'd eventually caught up, following the beacon's signal and putting pedal to the metal in his smooth-riding Mercedes sedan.

Good girl, Meg. She'd hidden the damned thing well.

Now it had come to this. The other destination Meg had marked on the postcard. Engesohde Friedhof. The cemetery where Clare Eberhard's family rested in peace.

The cemetery was huge, rows of mature trees, graveled walkways, and statuary lining the various partitions. At the main entrance there was, in typical German fashion, a large organizational map with an alphabetical listing. It didn't take long to find the Meyerhoff family vault. He also noted its proximity to a small parking area by the walk-in gate and assumed the elderly Clare would not be able to walk much farther than the approximate thirty or forty yards from curb to vault.

Of course, they could have found her a wheelchair at the main entrance, but the pea gravel walkways would prevent its use. No, Jake was fairly confident that the Le Blancs and their group would enter from the street side. That would work for his other plan too.

The sky had turned overcast, dark rainclouds billowing in from the north. He'd bought an overly large umbrella for concealment. Not knowing what to expect, he was banking on having just that one muscled goon to take down. Pierre wasn't much of a threat, but he didn't want to alert the Le Blancs too much in advance. They'd be carrying weapons.

As a precaution, Jake carried the loaded pistol in the outside pocket of his trench coat. Safety off and at the ready. He had his four-band international cell phone handy to make his next call.

God, he hoped he wouldn't have to use his gun. That always complicated things with the locals. Jake didn't want trouble from the German Republic, since only MI5 had authorized his covert work, not German intelligence. But he'd do what he had to if push came to shove. Easier to ask for forgiveness afterward than permission beforehand.

Waiting, he took in deep, calming breaths. And thought of Meg and her grandmother. Above all, he had to keep them safe.

Dark clouds had whipped up a cold breeze, chilling Meg. She buttoned her pea coat, made sure her grandmother's coat was buttoned up to her chin. As she helped her grandmother walk along the graveled path the Le Blancs told them to take, Meg noticed Clare's hummingbird pin on her coat lapel. She hadn't taken it off since they arrived in Germany. Madeleine called it Clare Eberhard's Iron Cross—what the Wehrmacht used to give their fighting patriots, the ones who'd sacrificed for their country and who'd displayed valor on the battlefield.

Pierre led the way past looming trees whose arching branches formed a bower over their heads. Meg noticed neoclassical statues, burial vaults, and gravestones of all sizes. Obviously the Le Blancs had been here before, probably scoping out the precise spot. They knew exactly where to go. Which was why they'd parked in the pullout along the curb.

As Pierre pointed to a large vault to their left, Madeleine pulled something out of her purse and deposited it into her grandmother's coat pocket. Something about the woman's expression alerted Meg.

"What was that?" Meg asked. Her grandmother faltered, lost her balance, and nearly fell. Both the Le Blanc woman and Meg seized her in time and lifted her. "Gran, are you all right? Shall we sit and rest?"

Her grandmother shook her head.

"*Mutter* dear," Madeleine said in German. "It's not far. You'll see your sisters soon. They were told to meet us there. At your family vault."

"What did you give my grandmother?" Meg asked again with clenched teeth, ignoring Wolfgang, who wasn't far behind her.

"Not your business!" barked Madeleine.

"How dare you!" she countered. "My grandmother *is* my business. You don't care about her. You and Pierre, you're using her and lying to her!"

"Shut her up!" Pierre screeched to Wolf.

The young hulk grabbed her arm, pulled her to a stop and slapped her across the face. Her head jolted back and her ears rang for a moment. The pain was minor, however, and stung only a little, but the attack triggered her pent-up fury.

Meg let go of her grandmother. She lashed out and kicked the man's shins. Wolf swung his arm back to hit her again. Her grandmother cried out and thrust out her arms to protect Meg. Losing her balance, she toppled against Madeleine. Both went down on the graveled walkway. All three women cried out.

Meg's rage gave vent. She sprang up and flew at Pierre. Her fists pounded him about the head. The side of the tripod hit her shoulder, knocked her down again. When she looked up, Pierre stood over her, the tripod raised as a weapon. Wolf was bearing down on her with a raised fist.

Meg cradled her head in her arms in self-defense, curled

into a ball, and cried for help.

"Stop!" Madeleine shouted in German. The two men halted.

Meg raised her head and looked up. Madeleine was pointing a small gun at her. Meg recognized it. A twenty-two caliber pistol.

She looked from the woman to her grandmother, who was dumbstruck with shock. Then to Pierre, who was threatening to wield the tripod like a club. Outnumbered, Meg held up her hands.

"Cooperate, Meg," threatened Madeleine in English. "Or it'll go bad for both you and your grandmother. We'll take these photos and afterward leave you both in peace."

Meg clambered to her feet, her hands still raised in the air. Interesting choice of words, she worried, especially inside a cemetery. Were the Le Blancs going to shoot her and her grandmother? Leave them by the gravesite to die?

"What do you mean? Leave us in peace?" Meg glanced to each of the three captors. Their faces revealed nothing.

Around the curve in the walkway, a tall man approached. His upper body was hidden by a large, black umbrella. Her vision was blurred with tears but his walk seemed familiar.

Her eyes stopped stinging as hope arose in her chest like a bubble of happiness.

"I'm warning you," repeated Madeleine. "Now put your hands down, for God's sake. You'll draw attention. You don't want any innocent bystanders hurt, do you?" She came closer and dug the pistol into Meg's ribs. "Now help your grandmother. It's just a few meters more."

Meg trudged alongside her grandmother, her arm propping the sick, elderly woman around the waist. The family vault came into view behind a large hedge. The structure shared the private corner with nothing else except a tall cypress tree. The marble burial chamber was huge and rose at least ten feet above the stone plinth it rested on. A small garden of ivy and ferns stood behind a low railing of wrought iron.

Although tense and shaking violently, her grandmother appeared to be in a kind of daze. The Le Blancs were forgotten as Clare stared at the white-marbled burial vault.

"Grandma, is this it? Your family crypt? It says Meyerhoff. Was that your maiden name?"

A stone bas-relief of a large family crest above a list of names bore an eagle in flight on one side and what looked like swords and blossoms on the other. The Meyerhoffs must have been a prominent family, Meg concluded.

Clare squinted her eyes behind her glasses and studied the marble face. "Yes, Meggie, that's our family crest. Please, read to me the German."

Behind her, she could hear Madeleine and Pierre with their cameras. Wolf was hanging back in the middle of the walkway. Meg ignored them. She was engrossed in seeing firsthand the remnants of her grandmother's German family.

"It says *Geliebt, nie vergessen.*" She understood that much German.

Loved but not forgotten. At the bottom of a list of names.

Madeleine was clicking away with her camera in one hand, the gun in the other. Pierre was setting up his tripod, screwing on his movie camera. Wolf was watching the man approach them, then his attention was also drawn away. Pierre was asking him for help.

Tears streamed down her grandmother's cheeks. Meg choked up herself. "It's beautiful, Gran . . .the crest, the vault . . ."

Suddenly the names above the sentimental saying registered. Everyone in the Meyerhoff family who'd lived during the war were buried there in that vault. *Gesterben,* Meg read. Died. Her eyes locked on the date. October, 1943.

The Allied bombing of Hannover.

Clare's parents, Fritz and Helga Meyerhoff. Her sisters, Dietlind and Stephanie. Their husbands. Clare's brother, Helmut.

Clare's little daughter, Hannah.

"Oh my God," Meg cried, her hand flying to her mouth.

Beside her, her grandmother gasped as she, too, read the names.

"No-o-o!" One long, shrill cry of agony escaped her grandmother's open mouth. Then the elderly woman collapsed.

Meg fell to her knees beside the unconscious woman. She lifted her grandmother's head and cradled her in her lap. What she feared would happen had.

"Help her, please. Call the medics!" Meg begged the Le Blancs. She looked up and her heart leaped into her throat.

A fragment of her mind heard the sirens in the near distance. They were close. Obliterating all that noise was the scene right before her.

His umbrella closed, Jake's leg shot out and swung around to connect with Wolf's abdomen. The blond hulk's head jerked back as Jake's left fist coldcocked the man's jaw. Wolf's legs crumpled and he went down with barely a cry. The commotion—swift and deadly accurate, drew Pierre's and Madeleine's attention. Both pivoted around, but not fast enough.

With one hand, Jake swung down the shaft of his closed umbrella to strike Madeleine's arm. His motion sent the pistol hurtling to the gravel. Another hard swing to the woman's head, and her knees buckled. Dazed, she fell to her hands and knees on the gravel. A moment later Jake lifted his outsized semiautomatic pistol to Pierre's head. The little man froze. He raised both hands, his camera spilling to the ground in front of him. Beyond them, Wolf lay flat on his back, arms outstretched.

"Pick up the pistol, Meg."

Speechless with surprise, she scrambled to pick it up, stuffed it in her jacket pocket then returned to her grandmother.

"C'mon, Pierre," Jake snarled. "Give me an excuse to put a bullet in you. Nothing would please me more."

Pierre shook his head like a frightened terrier. "Careful now, Jake. We're just taking photos, no law against that."

"Oh yeah? What about assault and kidnapping for starters? You wanna bet that Interpol has a rap sheet on you two? Listen Pierre,-or-whatever-the-hell-your-name-is, take her" — indicating Madeleine, who was having difficulty rising from the gravel — "and get the fuck out of here."

Pierre was shocked. "You're letting us go?"

"Listen you neo-Nazi dirtbag, I have my own agenda. Interpol and MI5 have theirs. Before you take off — and take your punk-ass thug with you — leave Meg's and Clare's suitcases by the curb. If you don't, I've got your limo's license plate. I'll report the theft of their bags to the local *polizei*. That'll lead to a host of other charges. Do you understand me?"

Pierre helped Madeleine to her feet. The woman shot hateful glances at Jake and Meg, then a disdainful one at the elderly woman lying helpless on the ground. As if the old woman's hysterical collapse had ruined their plans — whatever they were.

"Jake, she has our passports," cried Meg, pointing at Madeleine. "And my cell phone. In her purse, I think."

He swung up his left arm and aimed the umbrella like a sword at Madeleine's head.

"Give your purse to Meg. Easy now. I've never shot a woman before, but you can be my first. My first Nazi too. I can almost hear Grandpa Nate cheering me on."

Madeleine, muttering oaths, tossed her purse on the ground at Meg's feet. Quickly Meg perused the contents. She gathered her grandmother's and her American passports and her cell phone. Nothing else looked relevant. She tossed the bag scornfully back at Madeleine's feet. Something else nagged at Meg.

"I know why you wanted to exploit my grandmother, but how did you find her? How did you get her involved again in all this Nazi crap?"

Madeleine sneered while Pierre tugged harshly on her arm and mumbled something under his breath. Not such a bad-ass anymore, he appeared anxious to leave. With one foot, he nudged a stunned Wolf to a sitting position. Jake moved around to point his pistol at all three.

"We found her easily enough after an old Irishman came around to one of our meetings asking questions. I wrote to her until I could establish her true identity. Your grandmother was quite a find. Quite a feather in our cap."

"You couldn't leave her alone," accused Meg. "You made her dig up her Nazi past and made her believe again."

Madeleine drew herself up and shot Meg and Jake imperious looks of contempt. "We didn't make her do anything. She's never left the movement. We don't call ourselves Nazis anymore, but we're powerful and growing in numbers. Every year we grow stronger."

"Yeah, yeah, one day you'll rule the world. Enough of your fascist bullshit," growled an angry Jake. "Get out of here before I change my mind. Those sirens you hear — I called them. Medics are on their way. The *polizei* right behind them."

Jake turned and watched the three Neo-Nazis retreat down the walkway toward the small gate along the street. They were cursing in Schweizer-Deutsch the entire way, Pierre shoving before him the furious Wolf. Maintaining control, Jake never let his eyes swerve from the couple and their young thug as he sidled up to Meg.

A klaxon sounded the arrival of an ambulance just outside

the gate. Screeching tires and pulsing strobe lights beyond the high wall sent the threesome hurrying out of the gate. Their behavior convinced Jake that the couple was wanted by the German police and Interpol.

Her grandmother continued to lie motionless on her side.

Meg felt as though she'd been holding her breath for minutes. She inhaled deeply then let out a long, shuddering breath. Her mind cleared a little more.

Meg's fingers touched her grandmother's neck. Her pulse was thready. Panic and pity churned together, made her woozy.

"She's barely breathing. They've got her carry-on, Jake, with all her meds. In the black limo."

His eyes glued to the gate, he dropped the umbrella.

"I'll go meet the medics and check on your bags."

He sprinted to the gate then motioned back to her. A minute later he was back, nodding at Meg and carrying both carry-on bags. Their suitcases leaned against the wall by the gate. To her amazement, the Le Blancs had complied with Jake's bidding. His pistol was no longer in sight as he snapped open his cell phone.

Fast on Jake's heels strode the uniformed medics in white shirts and black trousers. They barraged Meg with questions in German, which Jake translated. Her mind and emotions in a turmoil, she caught the basic message. Her grandmother's heartbeat was weak and she wasn't responding. They were giving her oxygen and taking her to the nearest hospital. Would she take the woman's purse and other valuables with her, and would she and her friend follow in their own car?

Another siren sounded nearby then faded. For a moment, while the medics attended to her grandmother, Meg watched, aware with half her mind that Jake's back was turned. She had no idea whom he'd called but she hoped it wasn't MI5, alerting them to their whereabouts. A moment later, Jake snapped shut his cell phone then gave his full attention to translating for her. Sick with worry, Meg's head swam and she listed to the side. Jake caught her around the shoulders. Leaning her head into his body, she let loose with another stream of hot tears. The emergency team placed her grandmother on a gurney and pushed her down the walkway to the gate.

"Meg, the *polizei* have put out a bulletin on the black limo. I identified myself and told them about the kidnapping. You'll have to verify that and possibly press charges if they're caught. They don't know about your grandmother, so let's keep mum about that. Okay?"

Meg understood and nodded. She let Jake support her with a strong arm, welcomed because her knees felt rubbery.

"I called your uncle, Commander Snider, yesterday from Dublin. Just called him again. Told him you both were safe but your grandmother's very ill. He's in transit to Germany. Left this morning."

Uncle John—who possibly knew the true identity of her grandmother—was coming. Thank God. She'd felt overwhelmed by everything that had transpired this past week. Slowly her heart rate returned to normal and she calmed down. Relief flooded her and new tears leaked out of the sides of her eyes. She felt foolish but couldn't will them to stop.

Thanks to Jake, they were safe. For the moment, anyway.

When her weeping subsided in his rental car, following the white and red ambulance, Meg stared at him. He wore a two-day old stubble on his face. He looked haggard and depleted.

"You tracked us? Does MI5 know where we are?"

"All the way from Berlin. Good luck they never saw me." He glanced over and shot her a reassuring smile. "No, I ditched the Brits and came alone."

"Are you in trouble, Jake? For helping us?"

"With MI5, maybe. Not the FBI. I squared it with my supervisor, A.D.D. Thompson. Your uncle, Admiral Snider, contacted DOJ and DOD. He did most of the work for us to smooth things over. I convinced the FBI to give me the approval to track you on my own. It wasn't exactly by the book, but we felt justified in spinning it our way. I'm usually by-the-book—" He glanced over at Meg. "Well, not this time. I made an exception in your case."

"Did my exception almost get you fired?"

"Almost. But so far I haven't messed up too badly." He smiled. "Don't think MI5'll be asking for any more favors in the near future. And they won't be reciprocating anytime soon, either. Here's the deal, Meg. You and your uncle will have to get your grandmother back to the States as soon as possible. Before Interpol and MI5 come swooping in." He frowned, turning the wheel as the ambulance took an abrupt left into a hospital driveway. "Speaking of tracking, where did you hide that GPS beacon?"

She grimaced. "You don't want to know."

He swerved into the nearest parking stall and stopped.

"No, I really need to know. Professional curiosity."

She told him.

Jake stifled a laugh with a cough. "You should join the Bureau. You're a natural."

She seized his hand in a rush of appreciation and brought it to her lips, kissed his big knuckles, then let his hand go.

"You didn't let me down," she breathed. Joy flooded her chest and warmed her. Tears threatened again but she managed to keep them in check.

"I promised you, Meg." He threw her a quick smile before opening his door. "I keep my promises."

Some men don't let you down.

Men like Jacob Bernstein.

CHAPTER THIRTY-SEVEN

"The truth is, Agent Bernstein, I didn't know what to believe. She told me about Clare Eberhard and the Nazi spy, Hummingbird, two years ago, when she started getting phone calls from this Madeleine Le Blanc. But I thought it was just her old age talking. You know, mild dementia playing tricks on her mind. Maybe the story coming from an old movie she saw. I ignored it because I couldn't believe it was possible."

Commander John Snider shook his head in sorrow. "All this time she was living a lie. Covering up her past. Living in fear that she'd be discovered." His eyes swimming, the Navy admiral cleared his throat in obvious embarrassment.

Jake made a curt nod. He wondered whether Meg's Uncle John was revealing all he knew. In his opinion, he didn't need to know and he didn't care. What happened now was out of his hands. The FBI would be in touch with MI5 as soon as Mary Snider, alias Clare Eberhard, returned to the U.S. No doubt I.C.E. and the State Department would get involved. And there would be another investigation, possibly hearings. Possible deportation and criminal charges brought by the Federal Republic of Germany's War Crimes unit of the *Deutsch Bundesriegerung*.

He'd enabled Commander Snider to get legal counsel for his mother, and that was all that mattered. One Navy man to another, Jake had extended the man and his family a courtesy based on a timeless code. A code of honor which superseded all other codes, as far as Jake was concerned. He owed Meg and her uncle that much.

If Mary McCoy Snider—or Clare Eberhard Snider—was eventually brought to trial for war crimes, that wasn't up to him or the FBI. Another organization would determine the woman's fate.

"I'm just glad you contacted me," Admiral Snider continued, "let me know how my mother and Meg had been abducted, how you were tracking them. I'm afraid in MI5's hands, there would have been a media circus. Like vultures, the tabloids would have dined on this scandal for months. There's a possibility I would have lost my command. Maybe more. The Navy—well, you can imagine the fallout."

"I'm happy I could help," Jake said. He meant it.

Assistant Deputy Director Thompson, Jake's boss, had approved his contacting the decorated Navy commander days earlier, when it was certain that the Brits were closing in. With the Pentagon brass's approval, the case was now classified, and they'd kept Commander Snider's reputation and career intact.

The Brits, MI5's Major Temple included, didn't like things one damn bit. But, for the present, they were being kept at bay. For a while. The major had learned more and had called Jake with the news. The Le Blancs had eluded the German police but Interpol agents were hustling to pick up their tracks. Disappointed that Jake had let them go, the man had telegraphed his anger via the phone line. When the circumstances were explained, the Brit had calmed down, but Jake could hear him take out his frustration on his pipe stem.

The Le Blancs, one of the couple's many aliases, hadn't been on any of Interpol's criminal databases. However their photos matched those of a wealthy German Swiss couple by the name of Brommer. Red-flagged by Interpol, the Brommers held elegant fundraisers in a number of European locales for various extreme right-wing causes. They had a post-office box number in Zurich, but their residence was unknown.

Whenever they surfaced, either agency would pounce. Still, Jake had to admit to himself, something about this case was missing.

Retribution? Well, there was no doubt in his mind that Clare Eberhard had suffered greatly. Both mentally and physically. She'd lost her entire German family. But technically she'd escaped the legal justice she deserved.

Redemption? Who was he to judge that? In raising an American patriot, Commander John Snider, and guiding both Meg and her brother, Jack, to be law-abiding citizens and caring individuals, Jake supposed Clare had redeemed herself in a way.

But did that make up for all the deaths she and her husband, Horst Eberhard, had caused? A higher power would be the judge of that, he concluded philosophically.

"Let me buy you a cup of coffee," Admiral Snider proposed. "And you can tell me about your Navy Seal days."

The commander lifted his Navy officer's cap and placed it on his head. The man was shorter than Jake by a few inches but carried his slim build with full military bearing. Dark hair flecked with gray, he appeared to resemble his American father more than his German-born mother. Yet he had the symmetrical features and pleasant smile that made Clare and Meg such pretty women.

Jake nodded, suppressing the urge to give a Navy salute. He was about to fall in beside the man when a tall, stocky nurse appeared at the doorway of Clare's hospital room.

"Please, come and sit with Frau Snider," she urged Jake in German. "Only you, Herr Bernstein. For the moment, she wants to see only you."

Jake threw a puzzled look back at Admiral Snider, shrugged his shoulders, implicitly asking for the man's permission.

"Go ahead, Jake, if I may call you that. I'll get some coffee and bring some back to Meg. She must be exhausted. She hasn't left my mother's side since yesterday."

They all were exhausted, Jake realized. He and Meg had been at Clare's bedside, rotating in and out, maintaining a vigil for over twenty hours. While the nurses fed the old woman intravenously, monitored her vital signs and explained the effects of a series of mini strokes, they'd waited for Meg's uncle to fly in from San Diego. Jake had gone to meet him at the airport that morning. Meg's brother was flying in later that day from San Francisco. At long last, Jake was looking forward to taking a backseat to this family crisis.

When he entered the hospital room, Meg looked up. She was sitting in the same chair as she had been two hours ago — beside the bed, holding her grandmother's hand, stroking it silently.

Such devotion. He loved her all the more for it. When Meg loved, it was deeply and to her very core. He was sure of that.

That quality in her bode well for him . . .he hoped.

Her deep blue eyes turned from sorrow to warm approval. She communicated with them in a way she hadn't before. Jake felt her love and gratitude emanating from them, and the naked emotion humbled him. At least she didn't blame him for what had happened. For that he was relieved.

Meg arose and came over to him. Her arms encircled his waist and she buried her face in his chest. She was exhausted to the point of dropping. He held her for a moment, happy to give her solace and comfort, aware that her grandmother was watching them. He kissed her hair then her temple.

Tearing his eyes away from Meg, he glanced over at Clare. She was fingering the hummingbird pin with her one good hand. Her other hand lay lifeless, paralyzed along with the entire left side of her body. One side of her face dragged down, marring the last of her attractive looks. As if one side of a wax image of her face had melted.

Despite his own deep feelings of indignation at the spy he knew as Clare Eberhard, Jake felt sorry for the woman, Mary Snider, who'd raised Meg. The young woman he'd hopelessly fallen heads over heels in love with.

Meg took his hand and moved them over to the door, out of earshot of the elderly patient.

"Grandma wants to talk to you, Jake. She wants you to bring a recorder later tonight. She wants to give you her story." Meg fished something out of her pants pocket and passed it to him. He took the tiny, cellophane-wrapped packet and enclosed it in his fist. "That horrible woman slipped it in Grandma's coat pocket," she whispered into Jake's ear. "It's a capsule of some kind. Poison, I think."

She moved out of his arms, darting him a tremulous, encouraging smile.

"I need a break right now. You talk to her, okay?"

"Sure." He glanced at the little packet in his hand. The FBI lab would analyze it when he returned to Headquarters but he'd bet a month's paycheck that Meg was right.

He held Meg back for a moment longer.

"Does your grandmother know I'm a federal agent?"

Meg leaned into him and whispered into his ear.

"I told her you're an FBI agent, you're my boyfriend, *and* you're courting me. Would that be an accurate statement, Agent Bernstein?"

He suppressed a surprised laugh with his fist. Still smiling, he slipped a small white box into Meg's hand.

"You bet," he said. When she opened it, her eyes widened. "Bernstein is also the German word for amber. It literally means warm stone."

She took out the gold chain with the yellow-colored amber pendant attached and hooked it around her neck.

"This isn't your way of saying goodbye, is it?"

"Hell no," he said, taken aback that she'd regard the gift in that way. "No way."

He was thinking in terms of Clare's recovery and possible war crimes trial. He'd be called to testify against the old woman, which naturally would stir up Meg's resentment. There were still many hurdles for him and Meg to jump over before they could have a normal relationship. He wasn't counting on anything going smoothly. "This is . . .uh, in case we don't see each other for awhile."

"I see. Thank you, Jake. I love it."

A shadow passed over her face a second before she kissed him lightly on the lips. Then she left the room.

Jake returned to the elderly woman in bed, confusion creasing his forehead. Had he said something wrong? Meg hadn't sounded entirely pleased, although it was apparent she liked the gift. Maybe he should've given her a definite time frame of their meeting again. But the hospital environment, and the situation with Meg's grandmother, discouraged him from committing to anything more.

He gazed down at the stroke victim. One eye was half closed and drooped but the other followed him like he was in her gun-sight.

"A recorder, Frau Snider? Tonight?"

Clare nodded. She moved the side of her mouth that wasn't paralyzed and dribbling with saliva. He bent down close to her face to listen. Her voice was scratchy but incredibly strong.

"My confession. My story, Agent Bernstein. I want you to record it," the elderly woman muttered in German. "On one condition."

Jake raised his eyes again to the old woman's ravaged face. He nodded then lowered his ear to her mouth.

"Meg mustn't hear it. Ever. It's a terrible story — war is terrible."

"Why me, Frau Snider? Why now?"

"Because my Meggie trusts you." One side of her mouth curled up into a grotesque, defiant sneer. "Because I will never go to trial."

At ten o'clock that evening, Jake turned off the miniature digital recorder. The size of a small matchbox, the recorder had an extra sensitive microphone and could carry up to eight hours of sound. Clare's confession had taken only two. All in German. Exactly the way she remembered it.

When he got up to leave, he saw a sheen of defiance in the old woman's eyes. She'd told her story and remained proud of the role she'd played in the war. As she weakly muttered at the end of her confession, they'd all sacrificed for a dream.

"The dream wasn't rotten . . ." Clare rasped. "Only the men who betrayed it."

He said nothing. *No, the dream was rotten.*

A rotten dream of lies, Jake wanted to add. Lies that nearly destroyed all of Europe. That duped and killed a million young men. That produced the Holocaust. Six million Jewish men, women, and children snuffed out in the most horrible ways.

He said nothing. What was the point?

Trying to reason with a fanatic was futile.

Something Clare said toward the end of her confession haunted him. The words were whispered without a shred of malice, uttered in a tone of tired resignation.

"You're a Jew. You know what dreams become. Desert sand."

He looked down at her shriveled, gnarled hand clutching the blanket and wondered whether he should touch her. She didn't want his pity. Nor his forgiveness. Which he never could give, anyway. He could never understand how she could've become a part of such evil.

The mangled hand turned over, palm upward, crooked fingers splayed.

Without thinking, Jake laid his hand upon hers. Lightly. One flawed human touching another.

"Frau Snider, I'm in love with Meg."

For a second, one of her eyes flared. Then one side of her mouth curved down to match the drooping side. She was beckoning with one crooked finger. He bent down again.

"*Liebe.*" Love. "Nothing else matters . . .nothing."

She closed her good hand into a slack fist and turned her head away. Jake withdrew his hand and left her bedside.

Early the next morning, the nurses found Clare Eberhard Snider dead, the hummingbird pin clutched in her hand. As one of the German nurses told Jake on the phone, sometime during the night she'd taken an overdose of sleeping pills, which she'd hoarded and hidden, evidently, in a secret compartment underneath the jeweled hummingbird pin. They were amazed at how she'd accomplished it, for only one hand and arm were capable of moving.

Jake heard the news at the hotel but wasn't surprised. High ranking Nazis had considered committing suicide an act of honor when facing arrest or capture. Like the Roman legionnaires of Imperial Rome—only the Nazis preferred cyanide pills or bullets from their Lugers. He just wondered how long Clare had been planning to do that. And testifying to the elderly woman's occasional clarity of mind, she'd even made a backup plan—the hummingbird pin and its deadly contents.

Clare had warned him. She would never go to trial. Even then, she'd already made her fateful decision.

Meg and her family would be upset, though, and that pained him. According to the nurse who'd called him, the family members had just been informed and they were

rushing back to the hospital. Clare must have timed her suicide when she knew her family would be back at their hotel
for the night.

A part of him yearned to console Meg. For most of her life
her grandmother had mothered her, loved her, treated her
well. She'd be devastated by the turn of events. Maybe she'd
link Jake's private taping to her grandmother's despair.
Maybe she'd even think Jake had driven her grandmother to
taking her life. Had spurred her on to that fateful decision.

It wasn't a lack of courage that made him decide not to return to the hospital. This was a time for only family to come
together to grieve. It would be hypocritical of him to join the
small group of mourners. Instead he sent cards of condo-
lences to Meg's and Admiral Snider's hotel rooms and hoped
they would understand. Then Jake left for Hannover's
Langenhagen Airport.

The only work left for him to do for his final FBI report in
this case was to translate Clare's confession and send audio
and transcribed copies to MI5. Lady Sarah's diary was apparently in the possession of the Le Blancs, or Brommers. If the
couple was located and the diary found, then MI5 would finally have their proof that Lady Sarah, grandmother to the
young woman engaged to marry the English prince, third in
line to the crown of England, was once a Nazi spy. And traitor
to her country.

Until then, all MI5 would have was Clare's deathbed testimony. And the buried wireless, if it was still there under sixty
years of dirt and rocks. Jake wondered what the Brits would
do with such evidence. Would they make it public or keep it
hidden, just as the Pentagon and DOJ would keep classified
Admiral Snider's relationship to another Nazi spy?

He wondered if Major Temple would feel cheated of a public trial. No doubt.

In a way, Jake did too.

For Meg's sake, and Admiral Snider's though, he was glad. Some lies were best buried.

ABOUT THE AUTHOR

A retired high school English teacher, Donna loves to read, write, travel, and play golf with her husband, Joe.

Made in the USA
Las Vegas, NV
12 March 2024

87056867R00187